DAMAGED

LIBRARY SYSTEM RESET
BOOK TWO

KATIE HANNA

Book Cover by Illustration by Marko Horvatin
Typography by Inorai
1st edition 2024

For Lola
For being relentlessly enthusiastic and supportive, not to mention a great friend.

1

CALM WATERS

Now that the Library was partially stabilized, it meant it no longer shook like a wet dog when it needed Quinn to do something. Not that her vertigo went away entirely, just that it wasn't induced by the Library throwing her around and sucking her into its own little pocket dimension.

Over the last weeks, Quinn had met more species than she'd read about in genre fiction, learned that talking furniture was an actual one of those species, and discovered that magic was real.

Not only that, but she'd gained two elven teachers in Milaro and Malakai, or friends, or something. But she also had an owl companion, Aradie, who was all the purple, green, and blue shades of midnight. Not to mention a talking, morphing-into-anything-he-wanted-to Library manifestation. Although Lynx was currently having a bit of a memory crisis.

All in all, as far as a magical Library went, this one was holding up pretty well.

Except for the whole sending her to world where time worked differently which made her deadline tick down even faster. And then there was the retrieving very important books from the chaos infested world of Dabilian where everything had been turned to igneous rock.

But apart from those things . . . everything was pretty great.

Quinn stretched, feeling nicely rested after the last few days. She pulled on a pair of comfortable pants—like those leggings with pockets that looked like slacks she'd always admired. Business casual on the outside, soft and stretchy on their deceptive little comfort side. She chose a soft white button-down blouse and a loose bow that was sort of like a tie around her neck came next.

She could have sworn she'd seen librarian uniforms outfits like this. To be fair, she was trying to appear a little more professional but thought she'd probably revert to yoga pants and sweatshirts soon enough.

Either way, she was all about ease of movement and comfort. Next, she grabbed a little badge and popped it on the left side of her chest. It simply read *Quinn*. It was much easier than introducing herself as a librarian; she liked just being a big part of the whole.

Finally, she pulled her black-brown hair up into a high messy bun, where two curls immediately came loose and attempted to annoy her face. She sighed. It seemed not even magic could fix her hair.

It had been a lovely few days since they returned from the Dabilian home world. She could almost forget that she'd been practically bitten in half by a mimic—an actual monster chest trying to eat her. She shook her head at the memory. Aradie hooted and landed on her shoulder. Luckily, all of her clothing now had a leather pad in the precise spot the owl liked to sit. At least she'd avoid her shoulder getting shredded.

Aradie hooted again and cast some images at Quinn.

"Yeah, yeah, I get it. I'm taking a while this morning. Today's the big day." Nothing was going to dampen her mood this morning, not even a sometimes judge-y night owl. Who, it seemed, didn't always like to use mindspeech. Images were so much harder to interpret.

Aradie craned her neck around and looked at Quinn, her black iridescent feathers sparkling in the bright morning light that shone through the windows. Windows that Quinn couldn't see out of because of how high up they were. She still had no clue where in the universe they actually were.

"What? It is a big day!" she said, raising an eyebrow at the bird. "The books should be ready; we should be able to use them today."

The owl nodded, and Quinn smoothed down the uniform she'd chosen for the day, ready to face everyone downstairs. Even if she was running a bit behind late for the unwrapping of the three books they'd saved from the Dabilian home world. She made her way down the stairs into the wonderful Library she'd been sucked into.

The Library over the last few days had become a lot livelier. It seemed word was spreading that it being open was not a hoax and that the Library was, in fact, actually open. She descended the stairs very quickly, now quite certain of her footing as she ran down the spiral staircase, only to be greeted by Dottie at the bottom.

"You're late, Quinn," the little bench said, her tone obviously disapproving. "We really have to make sure the books are fixed."

A pang of guilt hit the Librarian. "I know, I apologize."

"Did you sleep in deliberately? Did you oversleep? Did you overdo it last night? Have you been eating?" The bench's words practically tumbled over one another.

"I have *not* eaten yet. I didn't stay up too late, but I do think I worked a little bit too hard yesterday." Quinn attempted to answer all of the questions.

"That's all? You overslept?" Those words gave a distinct hint of disapproval.

And Dottie's disapproval had a way of worming in under your skin.

Quinn decided she should try a new tactic but didn't get very far. "You're not in the best mood today, Dottie."

"Of course I'm not." The bench gestured around with one of her front legs. "Look at the Library. It's very busy!"

And Quinn really took it in this time. Even though she'd got a glimpse of it as she walked down the stairs, there was actually a line at the check-in counter. Jim and Bob, the Aracnio brothers, didn't seem to be dealing with it as well as she'd like.

Malakai and Milaro were nowhere to be seen. Although in his defense, Milaro had been gone a few days. She guessed he probably had kingly business back in his empire to take care of. Why he hung around the Library so much, she still wasn't quite sure, apart from the fact that he seemed to be the Library and Lynx's long-standing friend.

And Malakai had needed a couple of days to recover from his wound.

"Dottie, shouldn't you be overseeing the Aracnio brothers?"

"Well, I was just coming to check on you," she said hurriedly and trotted off back to the check-in desk.

Quinn frowned. "That's odd." She shrugged, knowing Dottie would step in and at least help. She glanced around, unable to see Lynx yet. He didn't appear to be there.

"Did you call for me?" He popped up right next to her.

Quinn was quite proud that she didn't let out a yelp at his sudden appearance. "You've got to stop doing that. I was *not* directing my thoughts at you."

"You weren't directing your thoughts at me, but you weren't concealing your thoughts from the Library, which means I could hear them." He paused, giving her a rather disappointed look. "Really, Quinn, it's been a few days now, you should have got a hold of this."

She glowered at him. "Seriously, I've had a lot to get a handle on."

He grimaced. "True, true . . ."

"And I almost got eaten by a chest, by a mimic chest." She finished off the barb.

"Oh, you're exaggerating." Lynx waved it away. "Malakai said you barely got a scratch."

"I didn't get a scratch. I just very almost got a lot of scratches, and my head bitten off." She scowled at him.

"Quinn, don't catastrophize your encounter with the Mishimi-naghakufrepil!"

She scowled at him. "I'll catastrophize any encounter where an apparent table turns into a chest that wants to eat my head. And it was a mimic."

Lynx shrugged and changed the subject. "Have you had breakfast yet?"

"No."

"I believe Cook made you cinnamon donuts." It was like Lynx knew how much that would take her attention.

Quinn grinned at him. "Well, that's worth stopping this conversation." She walked toward the kitchen, smelling the cinnamon in the air, glancing over at her office before she made it there. The Library was definitely coming along. She could feel more liveliness in every aspect around her. The Library was adapting to receiving more books, receiving more patrons. All of their ambient magic leaked into it. Every little bit counted.

At least now there was an actual Librarian to man the helm.

Quinn had long since decided she liked being the Librarian.

***

COOK DID, in fact, have an entire platter of cinnamon donuts, and Quinn was not the only one eating them. He glanced up as she walked in.

"Hello," Cook said. "You are late this morning, Librarian."

Quinn grimaced that even Cook, the kitchen golem, noticed she was late. It was probably a bad thing. Everyone had access to the interface; they could all tell the time. She didn't even really have an excuse herself.

"It's not like I get paid," she muttered under her breath.

Lynx nudged her with a very corporeal elbow. "What do you mean you don't get paid? Of course you get paid."

"What, you're paying me in Earth dollars?" She raised an eyebrow at him.

"No, I'm paying you in Library currency." He scoffed.

Quinn blinked. "There's a Library currency?"

"Yes, it's sort of a universal currency," Lynx answered after a few seconds of contemplating her question.

"And where is this money?" She crossed her arms and shot him a glare.

He caught onto her look and finally seemed a little apologetic. "Well, you have a Library account."

She pinched the bridge of her nose between her fingers and counted to five before looking at Lynx again. "We're gonna have a long talk soon about this whole need-to-know basis, plus your weird desire to keep stuff from me, before I figure out a way to throttle you."

Lynx took an involuntary step back. "All of this should have been in the information that we transferred you via the chip."

Quinn closed her eyes for a moment, filtering through information, and found it. Sort of. The whole transfer was sketchy as hell anyway. "Oh," she said. "Oh, okay, I mostly know. It's just like online banking was back home. I'll be able to access it now . . ." And she was flabbergasted at the fact that the little screen that popped up in front of her had what looked like a very substantial balance of . . . "Is that universal Library currency, ULC?"

"Yes, precisely." Lynx sounded a little offended.

"I'm sorry, I guess I haven't accessed all the notes properly?" Which felt odd for her since the other magic was accessed far more easily. There were what felt like roadblocks through all of her information.

"We've had nothing but trouble with me trying to transfer you the initial information for the Library." Lynx let out a long-suffering sigh. "Once we get the infection of my systems sorted, I'll make sure to look further into this. You should probably just take a night and try to go through everything manually in your brain."

With that, Lynx blinked out of the room.

Quinn cringed. She knew he was in a bad mood.

"Sometimes, Librarian, you can be somewhat abrasive," Cook said, handed her a donut, and walked back to cooking.

Quinn stared after the cook. Cook was probably right. She could be abrasive. She didn't always realize it. She'd have to give the Library manifestation a good apology. As it was, she bit into her donut, glanced around the room and noticed that not only were some assistants sitting at one of the tables, but there were also several patrons at another.

She shrugged and walked out of the kitchen toward the check-in desk. "Do patrons just eat with us now, then?"

Dottie didn't show any other sign of noticing her presence other than to answer her. "Yes. We've always fed our patrons. We have food for everybody. That's the Library. If people need food, if people need shelter, if people need magic, if people need knowledge, they come to the Library. That's what we are."

Quinn decided that Earth really needed a magical Library of its own. She moved farther into the check-in desk and cleared her throat. "Hey, Lynx, I'm sorry. I shouldn't have snapped at you. I'll do better."

He actually flashed her a smile. "I understand it, you know. Perhaps now more than I would have five hundred years ago. This must be overwhelming. Lots of information. Way too much on your plate. I get it. You've done well so far."

"Thank you," Quinn said, preening a little. "We have a bit of time before the final book's done, right?"

He nodded. "It's almost done. The others are ready. Are you sure you don't want to open the others now, Quinn?"

She shook her head adamantly. "In a bit. We went to retrieve all four of them together. We should open them all together."

Next to her, Jim, the Aracnio, spoke to a patron who was returning four very dusty and damaged-looking books. There was a chittering sound behind every word the patron spoke. They looked beetle-like but about as big as a Great Dane. And they were explaining something to the assistant.

"These were my mother's books. They were kept in her burrow. She has been dead for a hundred years. We did not realize until we heard the return alert that we had Library books. We apologize for their condition."

"That's okay," said Jim. "Fines are waived for now."

Quinn didn't understand what the creature in front of her was, even though the Library told her it was a Bectiwode. But the sigh of relief was palpable and understandable in any language. She smiled and nudged Lynx. "It was a good idea to not inflict fines on people yet."

"For now," he said, his tone serious. "In, what, just a little over three weeks, we're going to inflict as many fines as we want."

"You sound positively overjoyed by that fact," Quinn pointed out.

"I like giving people fines. Frankly, every predecessor of yours loved giving people fines, too," Lynx explained.

Quinn grinned. "Maybe I'll let the power go to my head."

Lynx laughed in response, just in perfect timing for Milaro to walk up to the counter and clear his throat. "You two seem to be having way too much fun," he said.

Quinn rolled her eyes. He reached into his dimensional storage and pulled out three very heavy-looking bags in quick succession, placing them on the counter with a thud.

"These," he said, "hold two hundred seventy thousand malachite shards. I have more and I have access to gaining even more. Because I know the Library needs to up its current store levels. This is a small contribution."

Quinn smiled. But Lynx . . .

Lynx looked oddly perturbed.

Quinn nudged him. "Are you okay?"

Lynx shook his head and his reptilian eyes flashed briefly through a plethora of purple shades. "I . . . I . . ." He looked up at her again, confused.

"Is that one of your missing things?" she prodded gently.

He nodded.

"Okay." She wished she could figure out the connection for him. That lost look in his eyes was unbelievably sad. "Malachite's triggering a missing thing?"

He shrugged and looked at her helplessly. "I know it opens the doors, but it feels like there should be something else. Something that I'm not thinking of and not remembering." He looked so down. Quinn just wanted to hug him, but she didn't really think that Lynx was the hugging sort of person.

"Hey, it's okay." She kept her tone even and as soothing as she could manage. "We're going to get this all figured out. Harish and Siliqua are right on top of it."

"I know," he said, but he didn't sound convinced. He began pulling the satchels they put the chaos books in out of the isolation drawer.

"Is that wise to do right now?" Milaro asked.

"The isolation drawer made sure they got the most out of their regeneration." Lynx placed the last bag on the desk. "They'll be absolutely fine."

Milaro raised an eyebrow very surreptitiously in Quinn's direction. She left Lynx to his satchel sorting and walked over to the side entrance to the check-in desk.

"What's up?" She was positioned very close to Jim and Bob as they dealt with the Library's returns.

"Is Lynx okay?" Milaro asked.

"He's just got some real blackouts now. He's not . . ." She hesitated. Was it really her place? Then again, the future of magic in the universe was something they all had concerns about. "At least he can identify these blank spaces, and that he can't remember things or think of things or . . ."

"This isn't good," Milaro said. "This whole cleansing process appears to be taking Harish and Siliqua a lot longer than I anticipated. It's going much slower than I expected."

"Is there anything we can do to speed it up?" Quinn asked.

"Maybe." Milaro looked like a light bulb had gone off for him. "I'll see. Where's Malakai?"

Quinn shook her head. "I haven't seen him today."

Milaro narrowed his eyes. "You were late today, weren't you?"

"What is with everybody knowing I'm late today? I won't do it again. I'm sorry I took a longer shower." Except they were right. She had big responsibilities, but she really just wanted to sleep in. She was quite certain after they unpacked the books, it would be non-stop again. These last almost four days had been such a nice breather. "Look, I'm just trying to weather the calm before the storm. Once we open those books, we're—"

Milaro nodded. "I get it. And I'm really just teasing you, Quinn. You're doing okay."

"I thought so." She waved the thoughts away. There were more important things than her feeling a bit tired. "Anyway, I don't know where Malakai is. What'll we do about, you know . . ."

"You just have to keep an eye on him," Milaro said, his voice still low. "Then I'll talk to Harish and Siliqua and—"

Lynx cut whatever else he was going to say off. "Come here. It's time."

There was so much excitement in Lynx's voice, and he couldn't stop the big grin on his face as Quinn and Milaro moved over to where he stood.

"You open them," he said to Quinn. His excitement must have been contagious because Quinn felt positively giddy. Now they could finally really work at fixing the damned filtration system. If there was one thing she couldn't wait for, it was getting to see the Library in its full and powerful glory.

One by one, Quinn opened the satchels.

She pulled out all four books, very slowly and carefully. Almost reverently, even. They weren't slimy to touch anymore. They were just beautiful.

Laws of Chaos: Upside Down,
Condition: Excellent
Chaos Theory: Myth and Legend
Condition: Good
Reality Combined: Chaos Fever Dream
Condition: Good

But when she placed *Mastering Your Reality Through Chaos* down on the check-in desk, it was like the stitching had disintegrated and the whole thing fell apart.

2

PAGES

Quinn looked down at both of her hands. A few of the pages still scattered in her hands although the binding lay on the table. She couldn't think of anything to say. The book had literally just fallen apart in her hands. Misha suddenly appeared at her side, peering down at the book. A look of consternation was on their otherwise usually impassive face.

"Hmm," Misha said. "I did not expect this."

"Unexpected, all right," Lynx said, a hint of shock in his voice.

"Aradie, got get Narilin," Quinn finally said. The bird didn't even hoot; it just took off like an arrow and shot toward the book hospital.

"I've never seen that happen to a book before," Milaro said, his voice trailing off. Quinn had to admit, neither had she. Definitely not a magically stitched book.

"Well," Malakai said, leaning against the counter as if he'd materialized out of nowhere, "you haven't been stuck in a chaotic realm for a few hundred years, have you?"

Milaro shot his grandson a very withering look.

Footsteps echoed throughout the hall and Quinn turned to watch the beautiful Salosier book doctor running toward them. She never thought that she'd see Narilin running ever. That was a first, perhaps even a last.

Aradie flew out in front of the book doctor, guiding her to the desk.

Quinn heard Narilin draw in a breath, a shocked gasp, and even the leaves down the back of her head rustled in their own type of shock.

"What happened here?" Narilin said. "How?" There was genuine distress in her voice. She trembled as she reached out to touch the pages and her voice shook when she continued speaking. "The pages themselves are still quite sturdy. It's as if the binding dissolved. I think I might be able to restore this. Is this one of the books on chaos filtration?" she asked.

Quinn turned to Lynx, leaving the floor to him.

"Yes, it is."

"Then I will move it up my list and work on it immediately. I will make haste with this repair," Narilin said. "I'm sorry."

The latter was no longer directed at the people surrounding her. She was speaking to the book as she carefully gathered all of the pages together and the binding, placing them reverently in her hands and lifted them gently. Just before she stepped out of the check-in desk area, she turned back.

"We will speak of maintaining books in their proper habitat once I have managed to fix this one," she said, a serious glint in her eyes. She turned her back and walked sedately, as was her usual custom, back to the book infirmary.

Quinn blinked as Aradie settled back on her shoulder.

"Well, I'm glad we have a book doctor," Quinn said, still reeling a bit from the shock of the book falling apart in her hands. She glanced at Lynx. "Can we just get started without that one?"

He raised an eyebrow at her. "I told you that you could get started with just three of them. We didn't have to wait for the fourth to bake."

"There's no need to snap at me because one of them fell apart," Quinn said. "I wasn't the one keeping it in a chaotic freaking chest that snapped at me and tried to eat my heart out."

Lynx actually laughed. "Yeah, yeah, you're right. I apologize." They were going to spend days just apologizing to each other at some point, Quinn could already tell.

"Okay, so which one should we start with?" Quinn asked.

Lynx shrugged, "Before you consider that, you have to know something about this information. You need to understand that these books aren't like the ones you've already absorbed. And they require both a slower rate of absorption, as well as reading. You'll be able to read faster because of who and what you are, and because of, you know, magic, but you will have to read and absorb the knowledge. It'll take you a couple of days."

"A couple of days?" Quinn shrugged. "But I can eat and sleep in that time, right?"

Milaro chuckled. "Of course you can. Right, Lynx?"

Lynx visibly gulped. "Well, yes, of course you can eat and sleep." He looked like he'd been reminded yet again that she was an organic creature, and thus needed that whole sustenance and rest thing.

She chuckled. "It's okay, Lynx, I get it."

He sighed. "I am not up to my usual standard, but I'll get there."

"So do I just go pull up a beanbag and sit down and memorize these books?" Quinn asked, "You're not going to give me a lecture about them or something?"

Lynx shook his head. "No, this is something I can't help you with."

"You or the Library as a whole?"

Lynx chuckled. "The Library won't vacate your head while you read anything. If you need assistance, I guess I'll always be there in some form or another."

Quinn gave Lynx a long, hard look. "Fine, I'm holding you to that. And I'm going to go and find a corner of the Library to sit down and be inspired by these other three books." She picked up all three of them and tucked them under her arms, regretting it almost immediately as she realized just how heavy the three of them combined were.

Oh well, she thought, *I'm committed now.* Plus, she felt stronger since she'd begun training with Malakai. Without another word, she exited the check-in desk and made her way through the Library to one of the back corners where a big, cushy couch sat. It was the sort of couch she'd have thought suited Earth better, as long as it sat in front of an eighty-inch television. It was soft, fluffy, huge, and the perfect place to lie down and lose herself in some books.

Once she'd settled down, letting her back sink into the massive cushions, she pulled the first book onto her lap. "No time like the present to read *Laws of Chaos: Upside Down.*" She opened the book, placing her hands each on either side, closed her eyes, and willed it to teach her everything it could. Little bits of information flitted past, fragments, flowed through to her.

Languages, history, images, both violent and not. She frowned. None of it made sense. Even when she closed her eyes again and opened the first page, going back, she realized that while she could read the words, the content didn't stick the way it usually did when she just devoured a text.

She thought about it and decided to try a different approach. Maybe there was supposed to be a specific order to these things.

"Okay, how about *Chaos Theory: Myth and Legend*? Sounds like it could be the first one," she muttered under her breath, suddenly aware that Lynx had never answered her question about which order to read them in.

You could have asked me, the Library said.

"Well, I . . ." Quinn knew the Library was right. "Fine, what order should I be reading these books in?"

Chaos Theory: Myth and Legend. Reality Combined: Chaos Fever Dream. Laws of Chaos: Upside Down. And then Mastering Your Reality Through Chaos. The Library practically sighed out the words.

"Oh, well at least the broken book won't get in my way of reading these three." Quinn was only mildly irritated. It wasn't like she'd lost a lot of time or anything.

No, it's not, the Library said. And there was a pause, one that hinted the Library wasn't done speaking yet.

Quinn waited as patiently as she was able, which wasn't very much at all. "Oh, come on, finish that thought," she said to it.

It's nothing important. Just that it's very fortunate that book was the one broken. The rest of it is nigh-indestructible. We'll have to work on the stitching properties. Can't have that happen to us again.

"Oh no, you mean you didn't prepare for mimic stomach acid corrosion?" Quinn quipped.

While the Library didn't respond, Quinn could practically sense it rolling its eyes. So she tried again. "You mean it's an uncanny coincidence?"

Yes, the Library said, with what sounded like a long-suffering mental sigh. *Far too much lately has been coincidence, Quinn. I am really starting to dislike this.*

Quinn wasn't sure whether she should be worried that the Library was unimpressed by the amount of coincidences that had happened lately. But it really did seem worried. As much as a universal magical Library in its own little pocket dimension could worry.

Quinn shook her head to clear those thoughts. Coincidence or not, she still needed to learn and understand the role of chaos when it came to magic. She pulled *Chaos Theory: Myth and Legend* onto her lap, opened it, and placed her hands over either side to absorb the knowledge that she could.

This time, images began to make sense.

It unfolded gradually in her mind like it was playing an infomercial.

Chaotic power was the first thing to exist in the universe. It bounced around, flitting from one sector to the next, creating bubbles, planets and worlds, meteors and suns, moons and comets. The universe didn't exist without chaos, and chaos had nothing to feed on without the universe. A perfect symmetry of creation and energy . . . until it wasn't.

She opened her eyes and began to read. Chaotic power fueled everything. It was the basis for all creation, breathing life into everything it touched. Only doing so cost power, and the more it created, the faster that power dwindled.

It needed to replenish itself. Either it consume everything it created, or else consume itself. And in the interest of self-preservation that wasn't even a real choice.

Very little in the universe would choose to consume itself.

Primordial beings attempted to intervene, but the energy of creations didn't like that.

Quinn gasped as more images assaulted her mind.

A world broken and bleeding with lava and ruin. It reminded her of the Dabilia's homeworld, now just a cracked formation of igneous rock. Other worlds split by glaciers running through to the core, iced over by ruined atmospheres . . .

Chaotic energy allowed to run rampant—ruined worlds. Chaos became dangerous to everyone and everything around it. That didn't negate the fact that chaos essence was necessary for the universe's creation and survival.

But the concentrated and undiluted form in which it first traversed the universe, was a destructive power, unimaginable when it wasn't centered on the purpose of creation.

Several ancient species banded together to find a solution.

Quinn frowned as she read further through the book. It was vague about these species. It didn't use names; there were no pictures, and no comparisons she could extrapolate from. She made a mental note to look up what these primordial species were. She'd met the Dabilians in their stone forms, but they obviously weren't the only primordial species.

The book hinted at big creatures, small creatures, magical beings who were made of the elements, not to mention chaotic elements themselves.

The ones who came together to keep primordial chaos under control.

To tame the magic.

With that small revelation, Quinn moved on. Even as she opened the next book, she already felt a surge of difference running through her.

She glanced up at the windows, high above. Faint pale purple mist surrounded them. Even as she looked down, she could see it all throughout the Library when she looked now. Was that magic?

It's not magic. It's the remnants of chaos that help keep the Library in operation.

Quinn did a double take. *Say what?*

When you pull on the tamed chaotic energies, you are using magic. That same power is what fuels the Library, and what the Library distributes to everyone out there.

The Library's tone was gentle. For just a second, Quinn could almost feel what type of entity the Library was. And then it was gone. Just out of reach.

Not now. There's too much to do.

Quinn wasn't sure, but she could have sworn the Library sighed.

More food for her thoughts.

She moved on to *Reality Combined: Chaos Fever Dream.*

The history was written in a rather omnipotent style. It was difficult for her to get her head around, almost as if it was trying to play out in her mind and show her images and pictures of what had actually been before. Now, she had an inherent knowledge, a feeling of the destructive capacity that chaos yielded, of why it couldn't just be allowed to run rampant.

All she really wanted to do was absorb the books and instantly understand them like she had with the beginner tomes so far. This was tedious.

Aradie nipped her ear and glared at her. Quinn glared right back and then sighed. "You're right," she muttered, and forced herself to focus again. It was necessary.

Chaos could create beautiful and amazing things, but when it wasn't outputting that much power, it still *needed* that much power. This meant it drained it from everything it had created. It would lead to a cycle of creation and destruction that just ate the entire universe, consumed it whole. This book, however, told of councils, meetings, trial and error, and the ways they fought to keep chaos from going unchecked and ripping the world it created apart; from undoing everything it had done.

She shivered, suddenly cold.

It is a lot to take in, Quinn. You don't need to do it all at once, the Library told her gently, in that second reminding her of the grandmother who always told her that it was her choice how much or how little she did.

Quinn decided that if she'd been chosen for this, she needed to do a lot. So she continued reading.

There was so much more information. The wiping out of complete species and planets, worlds she'd never heard of and would never get to visit. So much more destruction, with a little bit more creation on the side, before the council finally got chaos under control. Even though it really was a misnomer.

Chaos was never under control.

It was simply regulated so that it didn't begin to turn on the entire universe and rip it apart.

The Library was to be the solution, and thus the ability to filter chaotic power was established.

The filters were placed under the core room.

Quinn sat up straight at that.

Underneath the core room? She hadn't even seen a way down to a below the core room.

She looked around, still alone and glad for it. Her neck had a crick in it and the light coming in from up above had dimmed, making the Library lighting activate.

Quinn wondered how long she'd been at this. She glanced at the time on her HUD and reeled. She'd been at this for almost half the day. Her stomach chose then to grumble, and Quinn decided that it would be a good idea to eat first before she continued.

But she wasn't about to let these books out of her sight, ever.

Hopping up, she pulled all three books to her. But as she did so, the book she'd just been reading fell open at a page a little farther on from where she'd been.

Quinn squinted at a highlighted line at the very bottom of a page. It was written into the filigree work around the edges of each of the pages. The words were scribbled in rushed handwriting that was barely legible. It was so different from all the other notations she'd seen that it really caught her attention.

Replacement Ashiron X982 faulty. Third reminder failed.

Maybe the sabotage went back a lot longer than they'd ever imagined.

3

MEETING PLACES

QUINN SNAPPED THE BOOK CLOSED AND HOISTED IT INTO HER ARMS
with the others, a look of determination stealing over her face. *Hey,
Library, explain "replacement Ashiron X982 faulty, third reminder failed"
to me.*

The Library was silent, even as Quinn made her way down the hall
toward the dining room. The Library still said nothing. *Are you there?
Is this thing on?* Quinn asked, growing slightly uneasy at the complete
lack of response.

Calibrating, the Library responded.

That's odd, Quinn thought, finally reaching the dining room. More
time had passed than she'd realized. There didn't seem to be many
patrons in here. There were only three sitting at the very far end of
the patron table their heads down as they ate and held a discussion.
That was fine by her.

She glanced around the rest of the dining hall. Now that she had a
moment to observe the area, it seemed suspiciously more spacious
than the kitchen area she'd been in those first few days. At least
Milaro and Malakai were there. The elves appeared to be having a
disagreement if their expressions were anything to go by. Malakai
looked up as she approached, but she froze in her steps when the

Library finally answered her question.

Ashiron X982 is one of the filtration pillars.

Well, I gathered that, Quinn shot back at it.

It's faulty.

Quinn took in a deep breath to calm her nerves, using some of the techniques from her mind tomes. *I also gathered that. Why would a book that hasn't been touched for hundreds of years have that written in it?*

The Library paused again, this time Quinn could almost hear it trying to track its train of thought.

Suddenly, Lynx appeared right beside Quinn, his eyes flickering like they usually did when he was researching things, which would go hand in hand with the fact that the Library was also trying to dig up information right now.

"Wait, shouldn't the Library just know this stuff?" she said to him. All of these glitches were getting worrisome. She was starting to feel very grateful that she'd managed to avoid being glitched herself when she was pulled over.

Then again, the information transfer never took properly. It'd been rampant glitches since she got there.

"Stand by," Lynx said. "I can't access those specific records either."

"Aren't you . . . ?" Quinn let it drop. She knew Lynx was the Library. Maybe the Library wasn't always Lynx. Maybe Lynx wasn't always . . . she gave up. She wasn't going to follow that train of thought down the mystical rabbit hole that it was.

There's an error.

There's an error.

The Library as a system wasn't only using single words like it used to. Yet another interesting fact.

"Well, I know," Quinn said. "That's why we're having so much difficulty with this. You can't give me a straight answer." The next thing she knew, Misha was standing right in front of her as well.

"That's something I can explain," Misha said. "The filtration system requires repair. There are numerous supplies we require before we can address the issue."

"I know that, Misha." Quinn kept her tone even, but her stomach rumbled as if reminding her why they were there in the first place. "Look, I need food first."

Cook silently handed her what looked suspiciously like a sub sandwich. It also smelled and looked suspiciously like a meatball sub, absolutely delicious. She wouldn't put it past Cook to have somehow orchestrated getting another of her favorite things.

"Okay, let's go into my office so we don't disturb other people or worry them." She added the last under her breath. With food in her hand and guaranteed a meal, it was easy to say the latter in a soft voice so it wouldn't carry to the few patrons that sat at the edge. She waved at them; they eyed her and hesitantly waved back.

Milaro and his grandson pushed themselves away from their table and joined Lynx, Misha, and Quinn on their way to her office. She raised an eyebrow at them.

"I didn't invite you." She said it in a half-jesting way. She wasn't completely serious, because having their company was usually better than not. Milaro seemed quite adept at being able to explain things Lynx couldn't. Maybe it was the human element, the organic element, or just the fact that he hadn't been stuck alone for the last five hundred years.

Although in the grand scheme of eternity, she didn't see how five hundred years was more than a blink of an eye, but that was another rabbit hole for later.

And Malakai just put her at ease most of the time. Well, most of the time when he wasn't infuriating her.

Milaro flashed her a grin in that grandfatherly way. "Well, we're coming with you, whether you like it or not."

"Figures," Quinn said, but she cracked a smile and led them toward her office. It was just as comfortable and well-outfitted as it had been the first time. Only Misha had added a few lounge chairs and a couple of couches to its contents.

Quinn eyed the supervisory golem. "Did you anticipate we'd be having this meeting?"

Misha shook their head. "I did anticipate that you would be having meetings in general. Though not this one in particular. There will be many people who wish to see you, and it is not always the best for you to discuss things in public areas where anyone might overhear."

Quinn understood exactly what Misha was saying between the lines. What Misha meant was that there were people who didn't want the Library to function, and thus any spies were easily kept at bay if the core of the Library staff carried on their conversations in private.

Logic all the way.

She expected the Library to flash information up in front of them once she called the meeting to order, but instead, it was Misha who spoke. Lynx stood next to Quinn, his eyes flashing through myriad colors and frequencies that she couldn't comprehend.

On a whim, she stood up and balanced her paperweight on his head. At least she'd know when he moved again.

"We are unable to get a read on the filters," Misha said without elaborating, and stood there, watching Quinn expectantly like the Librarian should know how to take command of this.

"Can you explain the filtration system to me?" Quinn asked patiently, her hand stroking the leather bindings of the books she'd placed on her desk. "I've been through these books and nothing is telling me anything."

"How many of them have you read?" Misha asked.

"Well, almost two of them, sort of. I didn't completely read the first, and I'm a chunk of the way through the second. The absorption of these takes time." She paused for a moment, realizing that she instinctively knew which pages she needed to read after absorbing what she could of them. "So far it's been a lot more about how the chaotic magic works and its history and why we need to filter it, without necessarily going into detail about the filtration system."

Misha let out an exasperated sigh. "Very well, I will rectify that." She snapped her fingers. Nothing happened, and Quinn got the distinct impression that Misha had sent Tim and Tom on a discovery mission of some sort to find a specific book. It was the only thing that made sense, especially given the way Misha was extremely irritated right now.

Still, the golem pulled themself up to their full height and began to speak. "There are ten filter pillars in the filtration chamber."

"Chamber? How big is it?" Quinn asked.

"It runs the entire underneath of the main Library. It is vast and never-ending. You will see it soon," Misha said, as if that explained everything.

Quinn frowned at that. The Library was extensive and had branches that weren't even open yet.

"There are ten pillars. They contain the filtration units. They are Ashiron, Byron, Cylion, Dekleron, Esheron, Farinon, Ganyon, Hylaron, Ishiron, and Jarion."

Quinn raised an eyebrow. "I guess you did it alphabetically."

Misha harumphed, was the best way to put it. "The Library uses logic. Most of the time," Misha said, qualifying the statement at the last moment.

"Okay, so the pillars have names?" Quinn prodded, trying to get the information train going again. That meant Ashiron, being one of the pillars, was out of commission. Which only left nine.

Misha's pearly eyes flashed once before she continued. "The pillars keep the lake from stagnating. They allow for every skerrick of mana to pass through the filters. At least two of them must be operational at all times. Two is the bare minimum in times of power shortages, or emergency that still enables the system to keep chaotic power from devouring everything around it. However, only using two was never intended for more than a couple of decades. It is always best for all ten to run constantly when the Library is at full power."

"Except," Quinn interrupted, "let me guess, we don't currently have the power to run more than two."

Lynx finally snapped out of it. He cleared his throat. "We barely even have the power to run two. We haven't had the power to run more than two for five hundred years. That's what slowly leached the power down to critical."

"But don't you get ambient mana from the mana and chaos in there? Or at least the clean mana you output from it?" This whole chaos system was trying to confuse her.

"Not with the amount of chaotic energy running rampant in the upper chamber," Lynx said like it should make complete sense to her.

"Okay, so what do we need to do to repair them? To get the maximum output back up?"

"First of all, we need books returned," Lynx began, stating the bleeding obvious.

"We're getting books returned," Quinn snapped. "Next."

Lynx paused. "Yes, we are getting books returned. And it's a little faster than I anticipated, which is a good thing. Dekleron and Ganyon are the only pillars functioning currently."

Lynx finally moved his head enough for the paperweight to fall off. It passed through his foot when it hit the floor. He flashed Quinn a glare, and she whistled innocently, looking away. When she looked back, she thought she might have seen a very small flash of a smile make the corner of his mouth twitch.

"We are currently unable to connect to the following," Lynx said, his voice slightly more robotic than usual. "We cannot connect to Ashiron, Byron, Cylion, Esheron, Farinon, Hylaron, Ishiron, and Jarion."

"So basically, we can't activate the other eight, even though we have a little extra power, because the connection is gone?" Quinn asked.

"I do not think it is severed," Misha said, her mouth contorting in a slight frown. "But I cannot detect them, Lynx cannot detect them, and the Library cannot detect them. Ganyon is outputting way less power than it should. Which means we don't have the power to reboot the others anyway."

Lynx smiled at the golem. "Precisely. We have to recalibrate them."

"And just how do we do that?" Quinn asked.

"Well." Milaro glanced around. "You'll eventually need to visit the Filtration Lake."

"Okay, why can't we do that now?"

"You'll require protective gear," Milaro said. "Such as protective outerwear, protective masks, food . . . all that good stuff."

"Don't we have all of that?" Quinn asked.

"Quinn, slow down," Malakai said. "You can't get ahead of yourself like this. You need to make sure that you know what you're diving into, quite literally in this case."

Quinn blinked at him, not quite understanding. "Are you telling me it's not just like figurative mana?" But even as she spoke, she realized mana had a sort of essence about it, a visual quality. At least it did the more she learned about magic.

"Precisely. It's chaotic magic, chaotic mana, chaos force, whatever you want to call it. But it's pretty sludgy and liquid-y and you're gonna have to wade through some shit," Malakai said, crossing his arms.

"Oh," Quinn said, not particularly liking his comparison there. She knew he was exaggerating. It couldn't be literal shit, but sludge also didn't appeal to her. *Okay, then, I've got this.* "Then why can't I just go and have a look so that I understand what I'm going to get into?"

Lynx finally blinked and fully focused on her after being silent for the last several minutes. "You haven't finished absorbing the books. You need to at least finish the third one and the two that you've already started so that you understand how to work with chaotic energy. The next book should teach you that."

"Okay," Quinn said, sort of reluctantly, although now that Malakai had described what the lake was like, she paused and turned back to the elf. "You haven't seen it, have you?"

He shrugged. "Nope, just heard stories."

"And who did you hear stories from?"

He gestured over his shoulder to his grandfather. Milaro flashed her a big, goofy grin. "Guilty as charged. I've been around for a while."

She scowled at him. "Come on, Milaro, why don't you just tell me?"

"Because you weren't here fifteen years ago when I started telling him about Library stories." The twinkle in Milaro's eye just wouldn't quit.

Quinn cringed. "Sorry, that was a bit self-righteous, wasn't it?"

"Yes, yes, it was, but this is also a lot to take in." He gave her one of his gentle smiles that let he know she hadn't offended him.

Quinn nodded. "Yeah, I think we've established that now. It's definitely a lot." She sighed and ran a hand through her ponytail. Fatigue was harassing her today. "Moving on . . ."

Milaro and Lynx exchanged looks. "You're going to require resistance gear that is hardier than that which you went to the Dabilian homeworld with."

Misha nodded. "I will have the leathers adapted. I will need several days for this. Perhaps three, maybe. If I can send my gathering golems to get the correct supplies."

Milaro patted Misha on the shoulder briefly. "Let me know. I'll give the Library whatever stores I can spare."

"Appreciated, King." Misha nodded curtly. "We also need supplies for the filtration system. We are almost done gathering enough to replace a full filtration pillar."

"Do they have multiple sections?" Quinn asked, surprised.

"They have hundreds of sections, Quinn," Lynx answered. "Don't worry, by the time you can do this, you'll be equipped with the magic you require."

"Okay," Quinn said. She didn't like the sound of it. It seemed like it might be a lot of work. But there'd been a lot of that lately. It sounded dangerous, and yet perhaps a little exciting

Milaro positioned himself in front of her, his expression serious for once. "Just so you know, it's the most dangerous place in the Library. Only those with express permission and some natural resilience can go. You, Lynx, maybe my grandson, Eric . . . some of the golems. If they're given the correct permissions to move through that part of the Library."

Quinn blanched slightly, but nodded. "Okay, we've got this. So that's a no to me going down right now, right?"

"Yes, it's a no."

Then she perked up as a thought hit her. "Do you think Narilin will have that book ready before I go down?"

"I would hope she has it ready, but it could take several days or more time to repair that. I'm unsure if we have the correct binding materials on hand," Lynx said. "It's a very valuable book, and I would prefer her to take her time with it."

Quinn stared at Lynx for several seconds and decided to go with blunt. "Look, everything's dangerous. We have no time for anything. But you can't keep me wrapped in cotton wool, because I am the Librarian, and I'm the only one who can do some of this stuff. So let me."

Lynx took a step back. Even Milaro blushed slightly.

The manifestation sounded sheepish when he spoke. "That's a fair assessment."

"I apologize for treating you with kid gloves," the older elf said. "We'll help you dive head first into as many dangerous situations as you can handle."

Quinn blinked at him. Somehow, she wasn't sure she'd come out the winner in that altercation.

4

DISCOVERIES

Instead of standing in her office and letting irritation build up, she decided to head to the book infirmary to see how Narilin's repair progress was going. After all, she needed that book as soon as possible. Maybe she could help with something.

Aradie flew ahead of her, obviously excited for the visit. It was then that it struck Quinn; the reason for Aradie's excitement was that all of the other night owls were there.

As she walked through the arched doors, Quinn stopped and looked at them. The doors were beautiful, carved from wood similar to the koa wood of a guitar she'd had as a child. The timber was stunning, but she didn't recall the doors looking like this the last time she'd been here. She blinked again, but the doors remained the same. Intricate carvings adorned the surfaces, even though they were open and pushed back. There were images of books being sewn, being written, flying to shelves, magically appearing. It was quite fascinating.

"What brings you here, Librarian?" Narilin spoke in her beautiful soft tone.

"I wanted to see how the repairs on *Mastering Your Reality Through Chaos* were progressing," Quinn replied.

Narilin's eyes narrowed almost imperceptibly. She took a deep breath, the leaves that were her hair shook ever so gently. Just for a moment, Quinn got the feeling that the book doctor was quite upset with her.

"The book is getting better," Narilin said, each word softly punctuated as if carefully chosen.

Quinn nodded slowly and approached the massive bench that held all of the items required to create and service the books. She pushed some brightness into her tone, trying to alleviate the tension. "Well, that's great."

"You realize it has not even been half a day since it fell apart?" Narilin asked, in a way that was much more direct than her usual way of speaking.

Quinn nodded. "Yes, I just wanted to take a look."

Narilin let out a long sigh. She seemed extremely put out by the visit, which made Quinn's senses tingle. Why on earth would the book doctor be upset that the Librarian, who had the run of the Library, had come to visit her? Quinn filed that away to think on later, as this behavior was decidedly odd.

It certainly hadn't been present the first time Quinn came to the infirmary.

"Anyway," Quinn said, noticing Aradie sitting up on the perch where she had been when Quinn originally visited the room. There were several other night owls on that branch. Quinn narrowed her eyes as she watched them. They greeted Aradie and seemed genuinely happy that she was there. Quinn made a mental note to remind her bird to visit her friends more often.

Birds of a feather and all that.

"As you can see, the restoration of the book is in progress," Narilin said, opening her hands and their long delicate fingers wide as she gestured in front of her. "Is there anything else I can help you with?"

Quinn decided that she didn't like Narilin's tone of voice. It reminded her of the tone her sometimes foster siblings had used. Not the ones she still thought about on occasion either. The nastier ones.

It was one thing to try not to make waves, and keep her head down because she needed as stable an environment as possible. But here,

Quinn was in charge. And Narilin's new attitude was sending all sorts of alarm signals through Quinn's mind.

"Well, I think I'll have a look around anyway," Quinn said, dragging her finger along the edge of the desk and lifting it up as if she was checking for dust. She could practically feel Narilin glaring daggers at her, which spurred her on even more. This was the first time she'd experienced any outward sort of hostility since arriving in the Library.

Dottie's little outburst when she sat on her didn't count.

Narilin had obviously been very upset about the damaged book. Perhaps this was a remnant of that.

Quinn reached out to touch one of the pieces, glad to see that the pages themselves weren't what was damaged. That was at least a saving grace. With her other hand, she touched the binding Narilin was painstakingly working on. Words popped up in front of her face:

Book Restoration: Level One

Quinn blinked at the words. *What was that?* she thought at the Library.

Book Restoration: Level One.

Thanking whatever fortuitous event led to her being able to think faster, Quinn double checked that she'd read what she thought she'd read. *Are you telling me I can put the books back together?*

What sort of a librarian of a magical Library would you be if you couldn't put the books together? the Library retorted.

If the Library Core had been in front of her, she would have glared at it. She wanted to ask it why it hadn't thought to tell her that before. But she didn't. Instead, she nudged the prompt a little to expand on what it meant.

Book Restoration: Level One.

Abilities: Magically bind books together. The binding at this level is limited specifically to beginner books. Must use a cotton thread. Next levels include silk thread and higher level tomes.

Quinn clucked her tongue in exasperation. That meant she couldn't repair this book. Yet. But there were other books she could repair, and there were definitely other books she could make copies of and create.

What else can I do? she asked the Library.

It's about time you asked, it sounded smug. *But perhaps that is something for a more private setting.*

Quinn realized the Library was right, especially since Narilin's current mood appeared to be contentious at best. Quinn looked around again. "I would like to assist you in repairing some of these books."

Narilin raised an eyebrow and appeared slightly surprised. Quinn wasn't entirely certain how she knew that the Salosier had raised her eyebrow, but she was aware of it. The tree-like face often held more expression than Quinn ever thought possible. This one was filled with disdain.

"I am not entirely certain, Librarian, that you will be able to bind a book together. I have magic for that." Yep. Right there. Voice dripping with condescension.

If one book falling apart outside of her control did this, Quinn didn't want any more damaged books coming in under her watch.

"I can do it," Quinn said, her voice came out flatter than she wanted, even though was trying to keep up the illusion of not being completely and utterly exasperated with the Salosier.

This time, Narilin looked slightly taken aback.

"It's a Librarian ability," Quinn clarified, trying her best to keep her temper under control. Those mental exercises were helping, because the normal Quinn would have lost it and walked out a long time ago.

"Then I will have Carty bring you a selection of beginner tomes that require a magical touch," Narilin said her tone less disagreeable. Quinn really hoped that was a hint of relief in the book doctor's tone.

"Come on, Aradie," Quinn called, as she nodded once in farewell at Narilin.

They headed out toward her office. Quinn couldn't help thinking that would be the best place to sit down and go through all of these Librarian skills. As long as the others had cleared out by now.

She'd been under the impression that her skills were all obtained through books, not just because she had connected to the Library and become the Librarian. It felt very late in the game, over two weeks into her stay here, to be learning that she could simply access Librarian abilities because that's who she was.

It seems the chip we gave you to consume also didn't take. At least not completely. The beginning abilities should have been automatically flagged for you with it.

Do you have any idea why the transfer didn't take? Or that the chip didn't work? Quinn was starting to feel desperate. Missing that information, and Lynx and the Library glitching was making what would usually have been a smooth transfer, much more nightmare-like.

Why on . . . no, why in the *universe* did what normally worked not work on her?

After a decently long pause she got her response. *No. It's part of what we're looking into.*

That did little to assuage Quinn's worry.

She was so deep in thought that she almost tripped over Dottie on her way to her office. "I am so sorry, Dottie," Quinn said as her shin collided with the bench's sharp corner, even as Dottie turned away to avoid tripping the Librarian completely.

"It's quite all right," Dottie said, even though there was a shrill part to her voice that told Quinn it was anything but all right or okay.

"I'm really sorry. I wasn't watching where I was going," Quinn mumbled.

"That is painfully obvious." Dottie let out a small sigh and then a short laugh before she continued talking. "Painful for you, that is! Anyway, might I accompany you and help you with whatever you're doing?"

"Have you finished your supervisory shift?" Quinn asked, stopping briefly outside of her office and looking down at her little bench friend.

"I have. Malakai has currently taken over the supervisory position at the check-in desk and I find myself at odds with what to do now."

"Great. Can you go get Cook to make me a snack and come join me in my office?" It felt like Dottie flashed her a withering look, but she trotted off toward the dining hall.

Quinn pushed through her office door while Aradie flew to the back of her office chair to perch there instead of Quinn's shoulder. She'd gotten used to the bird's constant weight, and it was noticeable when Aradie was gone.

Despite having so much to do, Quinn felt like she was in a lull. But one of those that made you think nothing was going to go wrong, when in fact, it was gearing up to do just that.

Still, Quinn nestled herself into the seat and was surprised a couple of seconds later by Carty entering the room with about thirty books on it. She looked at them and frowned. It made her sad that so many books needed repairs. They were indeed tattered and they were all beginner books.

At least that was perfect for what she wanted. "Thanks." She said to Carty as he magicked them onto the floor.

"Always, Librarian," he said as he left the room.

She watched where he'd left from, contemplating the existence of a talking cart. Then again, there was also a talking bench. Not much surprised her anymore. She glanced over the books and nodded to herself. "Should be a good start. Maybe it will even push me through to level two?" she muttered to herself.

There was a snicker that resounded in her ears and Quinn looked around, trying to figure out where it came from. That's when she realized it was an internal snicker from the Library.

"What's so amusing?" she asked.

It's not like a game. You won't get experience points. It's more of a 'the better you get at something, you qualify to gain higher-level skills.' Thus you level up.

"Okay," Quinn said. "That tracks. But you realize that's sort of the essence of experience right?"

The Library said nothing. Quinn was fairly sure it was sulking.

Just as Quinn was about to begin repairing the books, Dottie trotted back in with what looked like a grilled ham and cheese sandwich and a glass of something that resembled milk but smelled like cinnamon. Quinn could get behind both of those culinary choices.

"Well, no time like the present," she said, double checking for the small smooth stone that helped her and the Core's connectivity. "I might mutter to myself a bit, Dottie. I need to communicate with the core and figure out a few Librarian things. Is that okay?"

"Perfectly okay. I will be here in case you need me and to keep you company."

"Thanks for the food, Dottie." Quinn said, giving the bench a fond pet. "For everything, really."

There was a hesitance before Dottie replied. "You are very welcome. Despite our initial encounter, I am glad that you are here."

"Me too," Quinn said, and turned her focus inward.

Quinn positioned herself comfortably, munching on the toasted ham and cheese sandwich. "Okay, show me some of my skills."

Narrow parameters, please, the Library requested.

"Show me my book restoration skills."

Book Restoration: Level One includes: page creation, prose copying, duplication, cleansing, thread levels, and leather softening.

That's a lot of skills. Do all of those skills have to be utilized to level up book restoration? Quinn munched away, her mind racing. It was easier to think faster if she didn't take the time to say the words out loud.

Accumulation of skills in this area will raise your overall book restoration level.

Good to know. Can you show me a list of other skills? she prodded the Library further.

Golem Creation: Level Two.

Book Creation: Level One.

Book Returns: Level Two.

Book Finds—Returns: Level One.

Quinn mulled those over. *Okay, so I have access to the golem creator, and I know that, and I've created multiple ones. I don't need that expanded. Expand on book creation.*

Bookworm spawning

Silverfish formation

Night owl design
Quill designation
Book creation
So I actually create books? That's fantastic. Book creation definition, please, Quinn asked.
Book creation is what is required to create new books on specific affinities and/or create books that are required to form a new affinity.
There was just so much to cover. "Okay, what about returns?"
Book returns
Book recall
Bulk returns
Bulk recall.
Your bulk recall is now at level two. We do not advise you to use this skill on a frequent basis.
Quinn had to suppress a laugh at that one. People probably didn't appreciate constant reminders that the Library wanted its books back. She began on the second half of her sandwich and asked for the Library to show her the fines.
Fines: Level One
Minor fines
Standard fines
Moral fines
Punishing fines
Major fines
Intermittent fines
Bannable fines
Excessive fines
Quinn couldn't help the grin that spread from ear to ear. She was really going to enjoy this whole fining process after the study days were up, when she could finally leverage them.
"So these are all my abilities as the Librarian?"
There is more. There are specialized areas. Species history is accessible with more research and more power than we currently have available. The Library is still critical.
"Okay, can you show me a listing of everything so I can make sure

I don't have other questions?" Quinn popped the last bite in her mouth and took a swig of the cinnamon milk stuff. It was divine.

The Library brought up everything she'd just asked plus a couple of things at the end. Research, power levels. The Library was still in critical power. Quinn didn't like it, but at least it was halfway through now. They'd get there. They had to get there.

But then there was something else. It was fainter as if she couldn't access it. *What's that?*

What's what? the Library responded.

The greyed-out piece down there.

What greyed-out piece down where?

Down at the very bottom, there's research. Power information. Then there's the greyed-out bit. Quinn squinted. *Does that say "Classified Research"? Why is it locked?*

If the Library had been personified at that point in time, it would have blinked at her. *Error. Cannot access.*

"Unlock the Classified Research file," Quinn said out loud. Nothing happened. *How can it be locked from us? Is it really locked from you or are you just trying to have a human sense of humor?*

There was a pause and the Library finally spoke. *No. I can't access that. That information is currently beyond my reach.*

5

DISCUSSION

Myriad responses ran through Quinn's head, but she settled on perhaps the most disturbing. *Are these files a part of your computer-system-brain-thing?*

Yes, the Library said and paused. *They're integral.*

Then why can't you access them? Quinn asked, pushing down on any potential panic she could feel rising up. Surely there was a logical way to deal with the fact that the Library couldn't access specific portions of its brain . . . memory banks . . . whatever.

She was just having problems figuring out what that way was.

There was another long hesitation before the Library responded this time. *I don't know.*

"Okay," Quinn said and looked up as the lighting in her office flickered ever so slightly. She sat up as the floor began to rumble beneath her feet. It was nothing like the vertigo spell she'd had when she was pulled from Earth to the Library. Not that sort of tremoring, more like a very subtle shaking.

Are you okay? Quinn asked.

The Library let out what was almost an audible sigh and the trembling stopped. *I attempted to access the locked information from a different angle,* the Library said. *Obviously, I wasn't successful.*

So basically you should be able to access every single thing in your mind, for want of a better word.

Technically, the Library said. *Technically all information is accessible because it's all contained within me. However, there are patches right now that are blacked out. They are memories or deposits of information both Lynx and I are unable to access right now.*

Quinn leaned forward and accessed the console she built into her desk. It was similar to the one at the check-in desk but this seemed like a little sister version of it. *Does this have everything the check-in desk has?* she asked.

It only lacks the ability to return books.

"Okay, makes sense. That way I avoid the temptation to let people access it from my office." Quinn blinked as she realized she hadn't directed that thought internally as she had been doing.

"Is everything okay?" Dottie asked, trotting closer.

Quinn had forgotten the bench was in her office with her. She almost jumped out of her chair when she heard Dottie speak. "Everything will be fine," Quinn said, in her most upbeat voice.

"You realize you sound about as convincing as three-day-old tuna, right?" The tone of Dottie's voice sounded like the bench would have raised an eyebrow if she had one.

Quinn laughed and then crinkled her nose at the idea of three-day-old tuna. "That's gross."

"Yes, and your response to me was an outright lie." Dottie was pouting.

Quinn felt a tad guilty. They were all in this together after all. "Seriously. As far as I know, everything is going to be okay, I just didn't tell you how long that was going to take. Mainly, because I have no idea myself."

"Semantics," the bench said, but she sounded slightly mollified.

Quinn heard footsteps coming toward them rapidly, running in fact, and she wasn't surprised when Lynx popped into view directly in front of her, with Milaro and Malakai opening the door shortly thereafter.

"What can I do for you, Three Musketeers?" she asked.

They all frowned at her, not understanding her reference in the least. Uncultured swine everywhere. Who didn't know the Three Musketeers? She noticed that Lynx was flickering in and out right then, just like the lights had not too long ago. His eyes were doing that rapid eyelid movement thing again, which meant he wasn't going to hear a word that she said. It took far too much effort to stand up and balance something on his head to see how long it would take him to come around, but she did contemplate it.

"He began flickering when the lights did, and then he went into that shutdown mode where he does that," Malakai gestured with his hands, and paused, his brow furrowing. "Not sure how he ported into here while in that state."

Quinn wasn't sure how that happened either. But then again, he was an extension of the Library.

"Are you okay? I felt the tremors." Malakai's tone shifted to one of concern.

She nodded. "I'm fine."

"The Library seems to be having quite a few glitches," Milaro said, watching her without a hint of a smile. Usually, he was all about levity. Right now, not so much.

"Yeah, glitches," Quinn answered. That was just it. The Library seemed to be having a lot more than just a few glitches. Things were starting to compound and snowball and do whatever things did when they gained momentum before finally exploding.

It's not that dire, the Library bit out at her.

Okay, she thought, trying to keep her tone neutral in her mind.

There was a knock at the door. Quinn looked up to see Siliqua and Harish standing there expectantly.

"Come in," Quinn said, not liking the odds of getting to repair any books, figuring out the Library situation on her own, or reading through the next book on chaotic magic. Still, the Library's current state was obviously very important. Without it, the universe would practically implode. "What do you have for me?"

"Um, I have something we need to ask Lynx." Siliqua wouldn't meet Quinn's eyes.

Quinn shrugged and pointed at where Lynx was still very obviously out of it. "He's not with us."

Those purple eyes flickered once more, and Lynx shook himself. "I'm back."

"Were you trying to find . . ." she asked him but he cut her off.

"I was trying to access that file. I can't access the information."

"Well, at least that's both of you," Quinn said, still unsure why Lynx would be able to access it when the Library couldn't but she'd figure that out one day. She turned to the wood elf. "Anyway, what's the question?"

But before Siliqua could answer, Lynx butted in first. "I need to know, does the access to a locked section of my memory have anything to do with the rest of the corruption you're cleaning out of the system?"

Siliqua hesitated. "That's difficult to say. Without looking into it with specific detail, it could be both yes or no, or even both."

"What do you mean it both is and isn't?" Quinn said, trying not to let her temper get the best of her. She hated it when people were ambiguous. Milaro, at least, made it seem funny. Siliqua, right now, was making it sound as if she was keeping something from all of them.

"We need to research more. I don't know the Library systems intimately yet. No one knows the Library systems that well except for the Library, its manifestation, and the Librarian." Siliqua let the silence following the statement punctuate if for her. "I can't just give guesses based on conjecture."

Quinn pondered the statement. "I guess that makes sense. I just . . ."

"However, as far as I can tell the disruption is from the same time period as the others, but not precisely the same method. That is why it is both a yes and a no." Siliqua seemed to have calmed down now.

"Thanks." Quinn let out a sigh.

"I realize it's worrisome but we'll figure it out," Milaro said in his grandfatherly tone, then turned to his friend. "Lynx, resetting has revealed a lot of complex problems I don't recall from your days before the closure. I realize you weren't expecting the problems. How can we help?"

Lynx shrugged, in an oddly human way. "I wasn't expecting anything. I assumed, apparently wrongly, that in rebooting we would essentially reset the systems and allow ourselves a breather while we gathered more power, slowly gaining access to all of the files, all of the abilities, and everything that we needed to get the Library fully functional again. These complications didn't occur to me. I don't even know where to start."

"No precedence?" Milaro asked, and he looked like he was trying to be extremely careful with his next words. His brow was furrowed, and he touched his chin with his thumb. "Weren't there ways you could have functioned for at least a while longer without a Librarian."

Lynx's eyes blinked, his double eyelids rapidly moving back and forth. "We've never been without a Librarian before, is that what you mean?"

"I mean, couldn't you have recalled the books and had them at least returned, thus giving the Library some more power to tide it over?" Milaro was pressing the issue, and Quinn didn't understand why. Hadn't they already established that wouldn't have worked?

Lynx raised an eyebrow. "That's not how it works, and you know that. If the Librarian isn't linked to the core, the Library . . . loses some of its primary functions. That includes both returning and borrowing books. Usually, that wouldn't be a problem, because the next Librarian is ushered in decades before the current Librarian retires. Sometimes some assistants already have Librarian abilities because of their matching affinities. But in this case, as we frantically searched and lost more and more of them until there was no one, with ultimately no Librarian connected to the core. The Library's functions shut down."

"Isn't that a bit of a faulty design?" Quinn asked. Lynx shot her a withering look.

"No. It's meant to be a failsafe. It is meant to keep the Library in check. As you see, I am fully capable of making my own decisions, thinking for myself, and executing any type of plan I wish to. Or, at least, that used to be the case." He scowled and then shook his head like he was clearing out cobwebs before speaking again. "Anyway, the Librarian's presence means that the Library must operate within the confines of magical filtration that are set out to keep magic in balance. If only one side had access to the filtration system, then, maybe over time, they could stagnate and become less than ideal. However two entities required for the Library to function was considered a failsafe."

"So all you could do was keep the filters running and hope you could find a Librarian?" Milaro muttered the words, obviously deep in thought himself.

Quinn wanted to learn how to read minds.

"We've been over this before." Lynx was using his grumpy tone.

Quinn spoke up. "We haven't been over this before. We've been over everything else. We've skirted around the edges of this before. But you've never actually told us that the Library and Librarian require each other to function on the optimal level."

"Well, consider yourselves told," he said. Lynx shook his head, like he was trying to clear water out of his ear. "I shut down because I had to maintain what little power I had. We did not foresee any problem with being able to reboot the systems back into functionality. Granted. We didn't expect it to take almost five centuries."

Lynx wasn't acting entirely himself. She could tell, and she hadn't known him as long as they had.

Quinn could tell from the look on Milaro, Siliqua, and Harish's faces that they were thinking the exact same thing. She wondered if they were all thinking what they were thinking was what she was thinking. It all seemed very convenient. The files, unable to be accessed, memories that neither the Library nor Lynx could see, all of this pointed toward somebody very close to it deliberately sabotaging the Library. And if what Lynx was saying was correct, then that couldn't have been anyone other than Korradine, Dottie, or perhaps Milaro. It appeared those people were the only ones with such integral access.

Milaro only came into consideration because he seemed to know more than she'd have thought he should as an outsider. And Dottie existed here constantly. While still suspect . . .

Quinn's thoughts gravitated toward Korradine. Perhaps because she wasn't there, but also because of *how* she wasn't.

It didn't mean the others were in the clear yet, but . . .

Quinn doubted any of this had been put in place by Korradine's predecessor, because Korradine, as far as Lynx had mentioned, was the Librarian for thousands, maybe even tens of thousands of years. She didn't say any of it out loud, but she knew she wasn't the only one thinking it, and she made sure to lock those thoughts away from the Library, even if she was fairly certain that the Library entity was thinking about it itself.

Milaro spoke up. "Well, if you come up with anything, you know where to find me. I am required back in my home world. I will take my leave of you for a couple of days."

Quinn raised an eyebrow at him. While she knew he'd have to go home and, like, rule his subjects, it seemed suspiciously convenient. "You really have been spending a lot of time here."

He smiled ruefully. "I know. The Library has always held a certain level of fascination for me, I guess you'd say. Plus, I've always liked Lynx's company."

Lynx shot him an unreadable look.

"What? It's true," Milaro said, raising his hands in the air as if he was doing so in self-defense. He then lowered his voice and spoke to Quinn in a conspiratorial tone. "Just keep an eye on him."

"Not like I'm going anywhere," Quinn said.

Milaro chuckled. "You know you could quite literally go anywhere, right?"

She grinned. "Oh, I know. I keep it in the back of my mind all the time."

Milaro gave her a quizzical look before nodding once and walking out of the room. Siliqua's gaze flickered nervously between Quinn and the manifestation. "We'll attempt to delve deeper into this."

Quinn nodded slowly and was going to ask a question about the previous Librarian, about potential saboteurs, and about trying to understand what she definitely didn't understand right now.

"It's okay, Quinn," Siliqua said, patting her hand ever so briefly. "We'll get to the bottom of this." And with that she turned to leave.

Harish followed her out silently, and Quinn couldn't help but wonder if they were going to find out what this all was, perhaps a little bit too late to help any of them.

She turned to speak to Lynx only to see him blink out of her vision without a word.

Quinn tried to prod the Library for an explanation but got no response whatsoever.

Either it was busy conversing with Lynx, comparing notes, diving into files, or it was busy with Siliqua and Harish. Perhaps the Library was just sulking.

And they were all just leaving Quinn to stew on all the new information all by herself.

Quinn let out a long, suffering sigh, and moved out of her chair as Aradie launched herself off the back to come with her. Plopping herself down in front of the pile of books that Carty had left, she surveyed the amount of work in front of her. Aradie let out a long, mournful hoot.

"You should go visit your friends," Quinn said, scritching the bird behind her neck.

Aradie leveled herself to look Quinn in the eyes and added another soft hoot as if she was asking if Quinn was sure. The owl's whole non-verbal communication was kind of peaceful and welcome sometimes.

"Yeah. Off you go."

Aradie took off and out the door. Quinn watched her for a moment and turned back to the books, the conversation about the missing files still digesting in the back of her mind. There was something she couldn't quite put her finger on. She may as well practice repairing books. She needed the distraction.

Quinn picked up the first book, closed her eyes as she rubbed at the spine, felt the cover, and realized the stitching was loose and some of the pages had been ripped. She opened her eyes and looked at it, opened it up, and kept her hands on the back side of the book so she was touching the binding. It felt serene and relaxing.

Right then, with all the other worries about the Library, this was exactly what she needed. She breathed in and breathed out, accessed her skills, and activated book restoration.

Book Restoration. Activating.

A breeze came out of nowhere and felt like it was suffusing her body and the book in front of her. The pages rippled ever so gently and she could practically see the damaged ones knitting themselves back together. The spine solidified as the stitches returned to their old glory. And finally, the book felt whole again.

She grinned. "That was cool," she said out loud.

"Certainly was," Dottie said. "I haven't seen anybody do that in five hundred years."

Quinn smiled back at the bench.

Malakai, who she'd totally forgotten was still in the room, spoke up. "That was actually really cool. I've never seen that done before."

Quinn grinned, trying to push back the worry she felt. "Thirty books should help me get my skills somewhat under control. As long as I have thread, paper and glue, and my ability, I can fix these books. And then, once I get better at it—I'm gonna fix the whole damn Library."

6

CONNECTIONS

BOOK RESTORATION: LEVEL TWO

Quinn blinked at the words in front of her as she placed the last repaired book on top of the pile. They looked good, even if she did say so herself. She'd taken broken, bent books and made them whole again. It truly made her feel like a Librarian, taking care of them, even if it was with magic.

Even if she couldn't leverage any fines for another few weeks, this was still Librarian work.

"You look oddly proud of yourself," Malakai said, from where he still lounged on her couch.

Quinn shot him a grin. "I learn something new about myself every day."

"About yourself or about your position as Librarian?" He grinned right back.

"Both," Quinn said, decidedly decisive for once. She glanced at her energy levels.

628/792

Huh. It seemed this hadn't been solely an energy-focused task. She checked her mana:

412/650

She realized that accessing her skills and utilizing what amounted to a spell meant that she used more mana than energy. Oh, it was all so complex. Why couldn't it all just be mana? Why couldn't it all just be energy?

"You look like you're complaining in your head," Malakai observed.

"What?" Quinn asked.

"Your facial expression was doing that wiggly thing." He held up his fingers and wiggled them at her as if that explained what he was trying to say.

"I did not make a wiggly face," she said, crossing her arms defensively.

He shrugged. "Actually, you do."

Quinn shook her head emphatically. "Where's Dottie? She'll back me up."

"Dottie is doing your shift at the check-in desk, because you were repairing books."

"Oh," Quinn said. "I should probably go and replace her."

Malakai held up his hand to stop her from bothering to stand up. "No need. You have other duties, after all. You've been at this for a few hours."

"It took me that long? It was only thirty books. I have a skill for it." Quinn realized she actually felt quite stiff as she got up from the floor.

He shook his head. "We'll just have to spread ourselves a little thinner while everything gets reestablished."

"Maybe." Quinn knew he was right, even if she didn't like it.

He took that as a sign to continue. "How about we grab something to eat, and maybe you should get a good night's sleep so you're not late tomorrow morning—because we really need to continue training."

Quinn sighed. He had a point. She was starving again. Using any type of mana or magical energy did make her sort of ravenous. She grabbed the chaotic filtration books before answering. "Fine. Let's go grab some food." She summoned Carty to her, who loaded the repaired books up and disappeared from the room in a few seconds flat. "Oh, well, I hope he knows where to take them."

"Of course he does. He's a part of the Library," Malakai said.

"You know, you can be very condescending."

Malakai blinked. "I'm aware," he answered without a hint of shame and then headed toward the kitchen.

Quinn, decided that she didn't necessarily want to chat while she was eating. She needed to think. She needed to understand where things were coming from. And the best way for her to do that was to head down to the core.

"You know what, Malakai? I have stuff to do. I'm just going to grab a to-go." She glanced at Cook, who very silently placed a box filled with salad on one side and what looked like a gourmet sandwich on the other side. It was like he'd read her mind. She grinned at him. "Thank you, Cook."

"You appear to be busy, Librarian. I understand that you do not always have time to grace the dining hall."

"Yeah," Quinn said, a little worried that Cook might be completely and utterly correct. Just when she thought she could relax, she realized she was always busy. "Sorry, Mal. I've got to duck." She didn't wait for Malakai to answer or for him to be angry at her shortening of his name. She caught him shrugging slightly as he moved away to eat, but steeled her resolve.

Instead of following him, she grabbed her lunchbox and dashed toward the stairs that led to the core.

Taking a deep breath at the top of them, she began the three-story spiral climb down, taking each step two at a time, gripping for dear life with her left hand to the railing.

Finally, she stepped onto the spongy floor below.

The beautiful blue-and-green glow suffused everything again. It gave the appearance of leaves in that sort of triangular overlapping way they appeared when sunlight filtered down through them.

There were only occasional patches of red and orange that flashed in almost a hypnotic pattern. She listened carefully as she took each step, wondering if it would tell her what was underneath them. She was dying to see the filtration room. But she didn't feel ready yet, especially because everyone seemed focused on protective measures. She clutched the books to her chest, knowing that this was probably the best place for her to come.

The best place for answers.

Hopefully.

Finally, she reached the trunk of the core and looked at it, really examined it for the first time. Not just a glance, not just assuming that she knew what it was. The stone-like wood still had beautiful bark markings. The closer she inspected it, she realized that while very tree-like with its branches and its leaves of electrical circuitry lights that illuminated the entire cavern, there was something dynamic about it.

She settled herself down on the floor, nestling into the roots, with her back against the trunk, and picked up her sandwich.

Quinn, the Library said to her, even as Quinn's back made contact with the trunk. *What brings you directly to visit me?*

"I have a few questions," Quinn said, taking a bite, "and I feel like this way you can't avoid answering them."

There was a rumbling behind Quinn's back that felt oddly like the purr of a cat. *That is a very astute observation.*

Why is it easier for me to talk to you when we have contact here? Quinn asked.

For a few seconds, there was complete silence from the Library. Whether that silence was outside or inside Quinn's head like it always felt when she was this close to the core, she couldn't tell. She glanced up into what would have been boughs of a tree if the core was actually a tree. She watched where all the branches intersected, separated, and diverged with their intricate overlapping leaf-like appearance.

Finally, when she'd almost given up on hearing and answer from the Library, its voice resonated through her. *This trunk, this core, is a direct line to me.*

Quinn perked up at that. "What do you mean 'a direct line' to you? Aren't you the core? Aren't you this trunk?"

Again. Just a fraction of hesitance before the answer. *I am, but I am also more than that.*

Quinn squinted skeptically "That sounds like an extremely evasive way to say that the Library is just a small part of you."

It was the first time she truly heard the Library laugh. The sound resonated through her, chilled her bones for a moment, but not in a dangerous way, more in an uplifting and light way. The sound tinkled through the entire room like somebody was making music with glasses filled with water. It was freeing and airy. All of the different, what she'd previously assumed were electronic lights, that made up the leaves, flickered in time with the sound.

You are entirely correct.

"And that's all you're going to tell me," Quinn stated. "You're not going to explain or be like, 'Congrats, you figured it out.'?"

Well, you haven't figured it out yet. You've just come to a logical conclusion given the evidence presented to you.

"You sound an awful lot like my mother used to."

This time the Library sighed. It was a much more melancholic sound than the laugh, and it still affected Quinn right through to the core, her own core.

"It's uncanny the way you do that," she said to the Library. "You're most definitely not a machine."

I seem to remember Lynx and myself having told you that I am not one of these computers you are used to from Earth. I am galactic. Universal, in fact. The Library chuckled and the sensation tickled the soles of Quinn's feet. *I have transcended the necessity to be slotted into any singular conformity. I am what I am, Quinn. But that is beside the point. You have questions.*

"Of course I have questions," Quinn scoffed, and then decided to pull no punches. "What *is* wrong with you?"

The sigh echoed throughout the room, rebounding off the distant walls and the high ceiling. *I do not know. I was careless. I have been . . . There are parts of me that are broken, which you know.*

"Was it Korradine?" Quinn asked, knowing and yet not wanting to know the definitive truth.

Another pause.

I believe that to be a possibility. Although my memory about those times is very . . . sketchy, I think is the word you would use. I cannot recollect events, or instances. There are literal gaps in my mind. I don't know what was done during them. I don't know why or, even more importantly, how they were removed. It isn't enough to completely halt my functions, but I have to admit to being out of my depth in this case.

"Okay," Quinn said, "then it's time we figured that out. It's time you stop tiptoeing around everything and just tell me some stuff. Either you're going to trust me or not, but I've been here almost three weeks. This is getting ridiculous."

You have a point. There was a long pause again while the leaves above flickered rapidly. *I believe you probably won't get overwhelmed anymore at this stage. You have an extraordinary affinity for the magic of the universe. You are in many ways much like I was when I was first born.*

Quinn blinked. "You were born? You're like a creature?"

The Library chuckled. *Nice catch. I am more than that. I am the Library.*

"And we're back to that again. If you can't be honest with me, then I'm not going to help you," Quinn said. "We need to work as a team. I can't help you if I don't know what I'm doing. I think I need your help to absorb this book and to finish reading these other books. And we have to get to the bottom of this sooner than later, or I can't fix that filtration system."

Very well. What would you have me do?

Quinn wasn't entirely sure she could trust the Library to be this contrite . . . but she hoped it wasn't about to back out.

For the next little while, Quinn opened the last book and began absorbing what she could from it. Somehow it seemed easier, smoother here with the core. Then, she turned to read the rest. It was so soothing, leaning against the core's trunk, feeling the ebb and flow of power all around her. The Library was in the distance, just in the back of every single thought she had.

It was there as if she was monitoring everything on a live frequency, like she was watching social media livestream, just on a more vast and intricate scale. Quinn decided this had become her new happy place.

I'm glad of your company, the Library said.

"Are you really? You can't lie to me here. And you can't skirt around the answers here either." Quinn wasn't in the mood to be placated.

I'm aware.

"Hey," Quinn asked suddenly, "The manifestation, what is Lynx? Isn't he . . . real?"

Lynx is an extension of myself. He was the eighty-third version of a manifestation that I created. The others were not quite right; they did not last long. But when Lynx appeared, he was perfect. I have to admit, I think I would be lost without him. The Library fell silent.

Quinn mulled that over in her mind. "Well, couldn't magic just bring him to life and then you would have a real partner?"

Magic can bring everything to life, all sorts of things to life, even things that shouldn't be brought back to life. But then I would require another manifestation with the same level of connection that we require. I do not wish to replace Lynx. He is, in my very vast mind that currently has a few holes, irreplaceable.

"Okay, just curious," Quinn said. She turned back to her book and read more. The filtration system was complex, almost convoluted as if there was a little too much complexity woven into the way it functioned, yet it brought in chaotic magic and filtered it out to be distributed in a loose form from the books. They didn't just bring magic in and out of the Library. All of the magic contained within it was key in filtering to its utmost capacity.

Quinn had a lightbulb moment. "So while the Library was closed . . ."

Exactly, the Library said, *We have an oversaturation of chaos currently in the filtration chamber. And because the filters are wearing down, we may encounter an overload. Several worlds have already . . . Well, the Dabilian homeworld was not the only casualty. Several star systems, several planets have already experienced chaotic backlash.*

Quinn frowned. "Okay, so . . ."

A notification flashed up:

Chaos Filtration - Approaching Expert Level 1

Missing Component: Mastering Your Reality Through Chaos

"What does that mean?" she said to the Library, hoping it would be more forthcoming.

It just means that you have obtained the knowledge you needed to from these three books. You just need to get the one that Narilin is currently repairing. You require more skills for the filtration system.

"Like what?" Quinn asked, suddenly overwhelmingly tired. "I mean, I thought I just needed to read these books, put on protective stuff, climb all the way down and figure out how it worked. What else do I need?"

The filtration chamber is dangerous to most organic creatures. So there are several precautions we must take before we send you down there. Acclimation is of vital importance. You will require these two books: Breathing Through Chaos *and* Fighting Chaos Saturation. *You will need to absorb those books and let them digest, I guess, would be the appropriate way to refer to that.*

The Library paused and Quinn felt a brief flush of warmth cascade down her entire body. Like the Library was scanning her.

That's odd, it said.

"What's odd?" Quinn said, hugging herself to ward off the sudden chill that popped up after the warmth left her.

You are.

Quinn rolled her eyes. "Elaborate."

There's something in your frequency, I haven't noticed until now, though I confess I never looked after the initial scan. We haven't spent this much time together yet . . .

"Is it bad?" Quinn asked.

No, it's just unexpected. We did pull you from a star system that has no access to magic whatsoever. The ley lines don't reach there; the chaotic magic doesn't flow there. Not since its creation. But you, you are an outlier. You have all of the affinities. I don't even know if you'll need these chaos books, the Library finally said.

"What do you mean?" Quinn asked, a little startled—and maybe a little scared.

From every scan I've run since you walked in here today, you are not as susceptible to chaos as I'd assumed you would be.

Quinn hesitated before pushing for an answer. "What do you mean I'm not susceptible to chaos?"

Exactly that. It means that chaos isn't going to affect you nearly the same way as anybody else I've ever come across.

7

SUSCEPTIBLE

The words rang through Quinn's mind.

A lot of things ran through Quinn's mind.

However, at the forefront of her thoughts, she couldn't shake one persistent idea.

"Haven't you scanned me before? Seems hugely remiss not to have," she mused.

The Library's voice managed to sound quite offended when it replied, *Of course we scanned you. I'll have to talk to Milaro about this turn of events. We had to scan for you to find you and locate you with pinpoint accuracy to pull you through to our little dimensional pocket. So yes, we scanned you.*

"Well, why are you surprised by my chaotic resistance, I guess?" Quinn said, trying the phrase out on her tongue and realizing she liked it.

We don't scan people for chaotic resistance. Chaotic energy levels is a definite scan. But resistance is not a standard one. We pull everyone through a doorway to us directly. They bypass any type of chaotic magic that's evident in space by traversing through to our dimension.

"Don't you think, with the rampant run of chaos, that anything related to chaos should be a regular scan?"

There's an alarm that gets set off if anybody enters the Library who has high chaotic magic content in them. There was a pause as if the Library needed to figure out how to phrase something better. *Think radioactive contamination back on Earth.*

Quinn mulled that over, but it still didn't sit right. "Doesn't it stand to reason that anyone with higher tolerance or with a saturation of, I guess, chaotic radiation, that they could potentially be a conspirator?" Quinn asked very carefully because the Library seemed quite put out, and Quinn couldn't tell if it was with her or perhaps with itself.

Library protocols already notify us if somebody tarnishes the area around them in the Library. We immediately isolate them. But this could be potentially added protection. Given our current situation, that is.

"You sound awfully hesitant," Quinn said.

I'm hesitant because I don't understand why this isn't something I'd already implemented. It feels like I would have done this already, and yet it is not in place.

"Could that be one of those gaps that you're missing?" Quinn asked.

The Library laughed, another tinkle of bells chiming but in a discordant way. *It very well could be, and it very likely is.*

"Are you getting worse?" Quinn asked.

The leaves jostled ever so gently, their circuit-like lighting somehow melancholy.

There are simply more holes than expected. After almost five hundred years of emergency power mode, there were bound to be some glitches. I just didn't anticipate it being to this extent. We'll patch them up. Siliqua and Harish appear to be getting close to a solution. But the Library didn't sound overly confident about that.

"Is it possible to scan for entrants and see if there's anyone with the same signature that Kajaro had?" Quinn asked, softly.

No, I did not scan Kajaro's signature. Or at least, there's no record of his scan. If the Library had a face, Quinn was certain it'd be frowning.

Quinn felt slightly deflated, but then again, this world had magic—

wasn't anything possible? "Is it something you can do through memory?"

No, the Library said. *That is not something we can do through memory. We can sift through memories. There might be a tell evident in some of his mannerisms if you are willing to let Milaro help you analyze those. But we can't scan a memory.*

Quinn nodded. "I need more mind magic training anyway. Sounds like a plan."

If we can get some more security measures in place, it'll be easier too. Can't be too careful now we are technically open.

Quinn perked up at the last. "Do you think there's the chance that one of the assistants is or even was, I don't know, a spy?"

The Library hesitated. *I wouldn't discount the possibility.*

"Doesn't it make sense for whoever is doing whatever has been done to take advantage of the fact that we aren't up and running at full capacity? That we don't have full power, that our scans aren't as encompassing as usual, to insert somebody into the midst of our operation? Or at the very least, send patrons to scout us out?" Quinn worked through her scattered thoughts as logically as possible.

The Library answered thoughtfully. *It doesn't matter if they don't have the Librarian's signature because they don't need it just to be an assistant or just to return a book.*

Quinn shivered. "Do you think I'm in danger?" she asked suddenly.

Yes, the Library responded immediately, *and with you in danger, we're all in danger. So just be careful who you trust, Quinn.*

Not precisely the answer or reassurance she was looking for, so Quinn took that to heart and gave it some serious thought. She'd have thought that the Library would already have screening processes in place for those people who entered it. It made her uncomfortable that they couldn't immediately identify potential saboteurs. There was a lack of security measures here, but why? And so she spoke up.

"Why hasn't this just been a normal safety protocol to scan every single person who walks into the Library?"

Privacy. We're not here to police the people, Quinn. We don't control who borrows the books in any other form than to require that they return by a certain date or be fined. Or we will retrieve the books by force, as you have already performed. Bans are rarely levied, and then only in cases of repeat offenses.

The Library's knowledge is available to everyone, no matter their heritage, no matter their species, and no matter their intentions. To possibly withhold the magic from people who might have nefarious thoughts is a level of assumption, control, and gatekeeping that the Library is not supposed, nor inclined, to exert. Thus, invading people's privacy by doing too detailed a scan is tantamount to exerting a type of control we aren't supposed to.

"That makes more sense than I thought it would," Quinn muttered to herself, still not only confused but also slightly concerned by the fact that they didn't police who got the knowledge and magic. She guessed that was the point of a universal Library of knowledge.

Its only purpose was to distribute the knowledge, not to control how it was used.

Some part of her couldn't help the thought that maybe the Library was partially responsible for loads of destruction. But the Library didn't do the actions. It simply provided the knowledge, and the person or being who absorbed that knowledge would then use it incorrectly. She guessed it was the same as just learning chemistry at school. Not everybody went and made explosive devices.

Satisfied with the explanation, she did have another question. "But shouldn't you, like, understand why I have this? Chaotic resistance, or whatever you're saying I have?"

The Library laughed, again. *Probably for the same reason that you have every single affinity currently available to be absorbed or learned. I have some theories, but I need to cement the ideas first. You're a little bit of an enigma, Quinn. Technically, you shouldn't exist.*

"But I do," she said, trying her best not to pout at the Library's answer.

Yes, you do. I'm not omnipresent. I'm not a god. I'm simply a being who puts knowledge first.

Quinn didn't want to question that, because the Library was letting lots of little tidbits flow out for her today. She was going to figure out exactly what the Library was, one of these days. And then she'd slam that card down the table and go, "Ha!" But that was for later.

"Okay, I get it. You're just a Library. The universe works in mysterious ways," she said, wiggling her fingers like she had jazz hands, in an imitation of Milaro.

Precisely, the Library retorted, with a somewhat smug tone. Quinn decided now was as good a time as any to change the subject. She had a lot of food for thought, and a lot of chaos research to perform on her own.

"Okay, so I have a bit of a list," Quinn said. "Repair the filtration system, which involves getting the last book from Narilin, which I will go up and do in a minute. Have Harish and Siliqua calibrate your system to find the corrupted and missing files. Double-check our book return status and see where we are power-regeneration-wise." She tapped her chin in thought.

How about I help you by creating a list that will allow you to mark it off?

"You're going to give me like a quest again, aren't you?" Quinn asked suspicious now.

Yes, I am. I think that sounds like a fantastic idea, the Library said, smug again.

"Ugh, fine." And right before her eyes, the list popped up.

Repair the filtration system.

Calibrate and find the corrupted and missing files.

Book return status, including all of the branches.

New assistants required.

Replenish building and operational supplies.

Train in defensive applications.

Train in offensive applications.

Train in mind magic applications.

Quinn let out a deep sigh. "What's this? We need more assistants? We've only had the ones we have for a week."

And you've had a couple of thousand books returned. You need more assistance. There's too much to do in the Library to only have two people and an occasional supervisor running the desk. Now that people know that they can't borrow, the Library is getting a lot more internal traffic. Or at least it's starting to.

Quinn pondered that. "Good point. I'll go and talk to Misha."

Excellent. Is there anything further you require today, Quinn?

"You wouldn't be keeping anything else from me, would you?" Quinn asked, suddenly sure that the answer was going to be a lie anyway.

Not really, the Library said and then amended the phrase. *Not intentionally right now. I will be able to tell you how much I'm keeping from you when I recover my own memories.*

Quinn narrowed her eyes. "You're making light of that, aren't you?"

Yes. Just stick with Lynx. He has access to the same information. He will react to anything that jolts a memory the same way I would. Try to keep him close unless you need to leave the Library. I have several diagnostic things that I need to run.

"Diagnostic computer-like?" Quinn probed.

Seriously, not a machine.

"So like a brain diagnostic?" Quinn pushed even farther.

I'm not going to tell you yet. You'll probably figure things out before I do. I sort of hope you do.

Quinn was starting to hope so too. "All righty, then." She finished the last bite of her sandwich, packed up her food, leaned against the trunk, and patted it. "I like spending time with you. It's calm down here. I can think better, clearer." She wondered if the Library could smile. She felt like it was.

I appreciate your company as well, Quinn. Now shoo. I have people to speak to and diagnostics to run.

Quinn trudged up the stairs. There was no other word for it. Her energy was sadly lacking. So much that she checked her energy levels.

200/762

Odd, and she didn't understand why, she hadn't used any of it . . .

She left that thought open and waited for the Library to answer it.

I may have borrowed some of your energy while you were sitting here. Since you were sitting down, you weren't exactly using it.

"Next time, tell me or ask. That's considered polite."

Understood. I'm unavailable for the next while now.

And suddenly there was a haze where she usually perceived the Library. It was disconcerting and uncomfortable now that she noticed the absence.

Quinn knew that the Library had been using her energy. It was just part and parcel of being the Librarian, but it still felt weird for it to suddenly be gone. She stopped and surveyed the Library, surprised at the underlying murmur of conversation that whispered through it.

She glanced over at the check-in desk and saw Jim and Bob, the aracnio brothers, as well as Eric behind it. They all seemed a little harried. Farther into the Library, she could see Geneva, Finn, and Danio, all bustling in between different Library patrons of which there seemed to be dozens.

Geneva fluttered like the fae she was, her golden hues sparkling in the lighting. Finn scampered; there was no other word for it. The Ilgonomur was diminutive but no less fast at their job. And Danio managed to clop silently on his centaur hooves. He was probably using magic to make that happen.

The first several seating areas, as far back as Quinn could see from where she stood at the stairs, were overrun with people. There were cups of tea, all sorts of beings flipping through books, heads bent over the same book, discussing things, pointing at portions of the texts.

It was amazing to witness, and reminded Quinn of study sessions at the library back at her university. Except it was all on a much grander scale with a plethora of different species that on Earth would never even have thought to exist.

She smiled. This was so much better than just pursuing library science as a major.

"What are you grinning about?" Malakai asked suddenly at her elbow.

She blinked at him. "Where did you come from? Do you have a homing beacon on me or something."

"Nope. I'm practicing my stealth," he said, waggling his eyebrows.

She raised her own in silent skepticism.

"No, seriously, Quinn, I am practicing my stealth. Gotta keep practicing or I'll lose the ability to sneak like a . . . ninja, I believe it is."

Quinn smiled. "Do you not have ninjas here?"

"Well, several different worlds have ninjas or an equivalent. Mine does not. But that's why we have a Library, to research and discover new things." His grin echoed how she felt. Proud to be here in this vast depository of knowledge.

Even if it was a little run down, broken, and malfunctioning right now.

Misha, she thought in her head, and suddenly the golem was there. "We need more assistants, and we need more golems, is that correct?"

Misha nodded. "I would suggest another half dozen assistants. At least." They paused, their moon like eyes rippling for a moment before they continued. "And we require two more shelving golems. Tim and Tom can technically keep up. Though we are golems, we do still have energy requirements. It is better to let us rest and recuperate what energy we have expended during the day. Our intake is reaching too high a capacity for Tim and Tom to keep up and not damage themselves."

Quinn gasped. "Damage themselves? Oh no. Definitely, let's make two more shelving golems. Do you need more storage golems?"

"I need another gatherer. We are falling behind in some of the regular maintenance."

"Do we have enough materials for a gatherer?"

"Once the shelving units are assembled, we will have enough for two gatherers, but that would leave us short to create any other type of golem." Misha sounded hesitant.

"Then make two. That gives us more potential to gather the building and operational supplies that we need." Quinn accessed her HUD to authorize it and in the meantime adjusted the settings so that Misha had a little bit more autonomy over the golem creation and maintenance modules. She had a distinct feeling that if she didn't, with the golems increasing in number, it'd become a huge time sink Quinn couldn't afford.

"Excellent. Thank you, Librarian."

"Is that too much?" Quinn asked, suddenly uncertain of her decision.

Misha fixed her with a glare. "Do not second-guess yourself, Librarian. I asked for one and two is better than one. More efficient in the long run, as are the new permissions you granted."

"Okay, then." She watched Misha nod once and walk toward Tim and Tom.

"Hmm." Words flashed across the screen.

Golem gatherer creation initiated.

Countdown timer: 6 hours and 51 minutes.

Shelving golem creation initiated.

Countdown: 6 hours and 23 minutes.

That's a lot longer than it was the first time we made them, she thought toward Lynx even though she had no idea where he might be.

Preserving power.

I get it. "Hey, Lynx." She turned to the manifestation who suddenly stood quietly on her left.

He raised an eyebrow. "Already ahead of you. Sent out another 'Library seeking assistants' alert."

"Excellent," Quinn said.

All of a sudden, Aradie swooped out toward her, landing firmly on her shoulder harness.

Quinn scritched the back of the bird's neck as it preened into her touch. Glancing at Malakai and then at Lynx, she spoke. "I would love for you to accompany me to the book infirmary so I can finally read that book."

Quinn had a list to work on, and she was going to finish it as soon as possible.

8

HEADS UP

THE BOOK INFIRMARY NEVER FAILED TO AMAZE QUINN. EVEN THOUGH the books had tattered pages, cracked spines, and broken stitching, the environment still held a sense of wonderment that made it easier for Quinn to relax.

Narilin stood directly behind the massive repair desk. She looked up as they walked in, and Quinn thought her eyes widened in shock. Faster than she'd ever seen the Salosier move, Narilin came around the other side and fell into what appeared to be a curtsy or a bow of some sort.

"Librarian, welcome to the book infirmary," Narilin greeted them, her tone far more submissive than any she'd previously used.

"I've been here before, Narilin," Quinn said, a little unsettled by the sudden deferment and very polite speech. Considering the way they'd left things last time, she'd been quite positive that Narilin blamed her for every single book that had ever been broken anywhere, ever, and hated her guts.

"I would like to apologize for my outburst when last we met," Narilin said, and Quinn couldn't detect even a hint of deceit in those words.

"Oh," Quinn said, "well, that's absolutely fine. I get it was an emotional time, considering an important book was hurt."

Narilin drew in a very deep breath and let it out shakily. "Thank you. I get very emotionally invested in the books I tend to. They live and they breathe. They are magic, they are alive, and that is why we learn from them. When I see them so badly damaged that the pages have literally fallen out of them, it incenses me, and I become quite other than my usual self."

"That's okay, nothing to forgive. Let's just try not to do that again," Quinn said. Still, her mind raced over everything they'd been through when they had their standoff. It seemed like such a one-eighty. But how well she got along with Narilin was neither here nor there right now. She needed to get the last book and get into that filtration room.

"Is it ready?" Quinn asked.

"Yes," Narilin said. "I halted work on all the other books and simply made this a priority, as I was aware that you needed it as soon as possible."

"Thank you," Quinn said, genuinely meaning it. She held out her hands and Narilin reverently took the book and placed it in them. "Please take good care of it. The stitching is all renewed. I cleaned and oiled the outside of it and the pages have been reinforced to the best of my ability."

It certainly felt like a well-loved book in Quinn's hands. "What level book restoration do you have?" Quinn asked suddenly.

Narilin blinked at her. "I am at level nine."

"Wow," Quinn said, "that's so cool."

After a second's hesitation, Narilin spoke again. "It is also an ability you have, correct?"

Quinn nodded.

"Excellent, if you require any pointers or any advice I would be very glad to assist you, Librarian." Narilin inclined her head.

Quinn took the olive branch. "I got done with the ones you sent me last time. If I get some spare time I'll come in and help you fix some simple beginner books."

"That would be nice."

Aradie, through the entire conversation, stood ever so quietly, trembling on Quinn's shoulder. She glanced at the bird, whose eyes were fixated on Narilin.

What's up? she thought at the bird, giving it a shot.

In response she got a series of images from her last encounter with the Salosier. It seemed that Aradie didn't appreciate Narilin's attitude. But perhaps there was more to it than that. Quinn slotted that into the back of her mind as future food for thought. Narilin was an enigma. And right now, Quinn wasn't entirely sure if that was a good thing.

"We have to be off. Thank you so much for this." Quinn smiled, and waved with the book.

"Excellent, Librarian." Narilin's smile held a hint of relief.

As they exited the infirmary, Quinn decided a full night's sleep was in order. After grabbing some food in the kitchen, she bade farewell to both Lynx and Malakai and headed up to her room. She was extremely tired. Probably not helped by the Library's penchant for borrowing power all willy-nilly. Perhaps it came with the territory of learning, of absorbing so much knowledge that her brain had to work overtime.

It wasn't a normal physical fatigue. It was more mental and emotional. She was okay. She could deal with it. As long as she got some decent rest.

Aradie flew to the head of her bed, and Quinn sat upright to start with and absorbed what she could of the book. For hours, she read through *Mastering Your Reality Through Chaos*.

The information within was vast and encompassing. The ability of chaos to create, both bring to life and destroy, to create havoc, but also beauty at the same time. Chaos was tricky and insidious. She'd have to be on guard against it. It could get into every crevice of your mind and play tricks unless you built up vast mental protections.

That was probably part of how Kajaro got into her mind in the first place. It send shivers down her spine at the recollection.

Quinn made a note to herself that, in the morning, she would seek out Milaro and make sure they continued their training.

When she was finally done with the book, she knew it was late.

She'd probably be late again down to the Library in the morning. As long as she could sleep tonight, it'd be fine.

Adulting was definitely not her favorite job.

She was asleep before her head fully hit the pillow.

Chaos is insidious, and it will find a way into your mind if you aren't careful.

That specific phrase from the book echoed through her mind. She opened her eyes, confused at first at the unfamiliar surroundings. Her thoughts finally came together and she realized it wasn't a dream—at least, not in the usual way. Here, where the stone halls and corridors and arched doorways stretched out before her, was precisely like the terrain she had encountered Kajaro in last time.

She was back in her head.

Quinn did her best to calm her breathing. She could feel Aradie outside of the of this visage, outside of the dream. But the bird wasn't panicked this time. She was there, letting Quinn know with her presence that she was calm. Which meant there was something different about things this time.

Logically, Quinn could tell this wasn't the same dream, but it did stem from the same source. She checked her mind as best she could. The ball was still imprisoned, the orb pulsing within the box where they'd caged it. She knew it was there, every day, and she only hoped Milaro would help her destroy it soon, because this sort of dream wasn't something she wanted to return to.

She attempted to close her eyes, calm her breathing, and send herself back into slumber away from this place. But that wasn't to be. She sighed and decided to walk the halls instead. She checked her shielding and went over everything she'd learned from Milaro. All of the exercises, all of the warding, all of the protection. She wasn't going to let Kajaro win, not this time.

Not ever.

The hall spread on. There were no corridors leading off it at first, not like last time. There were other subtle differences too. The whispers she could hear weren't immediately directed at her. And the stone reminded her more of some of the ruins she'd visited in Europe before her parents had passed. Old castles—decorative. They even seemed faded, like her memories of the time.

Quinn crept along, quietly, wondering if perhaps she'd been pulled here not only outside of her control, but also outside of Kajaro's. This didn't seem as intentional as the last one. It wasn't as nightmarish. And so far, there also hadn't been attacks and manipulation directed at her.

Yet.

That difference allowed her to get a grip on where she was and what she might need to do while she was here.

She crept as silently as possible along the wall and took the left corridor when it appeared. That was the way of the whispers and sibilant words she couldn't quite make out. She moved slowly, closer and closer until she heard, without a shadow of a doubt, Kajaro's voice.

"Soon," it said. "We will have control soon."

"What makes you think that?" A feminine voice spoke. It was distorted slightly and could have been one of the other Serpensiril who had been in Quinn's previous dream, but she couldn't see them. She could only hear them, and definitely didn't recognize the voice. So it was all supposition, assumptions.

She poked her head very slightly around the corner, grateful for the shadows that reached this portion of the hall. She had to suppress a gasp when she saw Kajaro. He looked pale. If a snake's head *could* look pale. Far pastier than he had been, anyway. He sat at a table. His robe draped over him so loosely, it made her realize he'd also lost body mass. Was this her mind? Had she perhaps visited his?

The idea hit her, and she realized that this was somewhere in between. It wasn't his intrusive spell that dove into her brain. No, this was her watching him without him knowing . . . Kajaro was not in control here. How she'd been drawn into this space, she had no idea, but she was going to leach it for every drop of information she could.

The female spoke again. "You are too weak now. That was a risky plan. You almost died."

"I did die," Kajaro replied in a raspy voice. "It was on purpose. I'm only lucky they didn't think to take my body with them. It was a hard fight. Their inexperience in battle played in my favor."

"I'm aware. But you're pushing your luck, Kajaro. There are elements of chaos that will eat away at you, too." His accomplice practically spat the words at him.

"I am fully aware of this," Kajaro responded. "Still, they did take the ring."

"But they haven't inserted any of the books yet. You said it would work." She sounded angry again.

"Of course I said it will work. They're not that astute." Kajaro sounded smug.

"Are you sure? Because you couldn't taint the book you had to return. It was impervious."

Quinn perked up at that comment. Taint the books? It was a good thing she hadn't tried to scan them into the system. It was even better that she set them aside and made sure that the goop on them didn't touch anything important. Quinn tried to steady her breathing as anger crept up on her.

"It's all a matter of time. We do have our people there. They are watching. The Library will unravel. It's only a matter of time," Kajaro said. "And then chaos will reign supreme."

"I hope you know what you're . . ." The female began again, but Kajaro cut her off.

"Wait," Kajaro said, his head suddenly whipping around to look in the shadows directly at where Quinn was. She pulled back, but she was sure he'd already seen her.

"It seems," he said, "we have an unwelcome guest."

"How? This is—"

"Shh . . . They don't need to know that. All they need to know is that we know they're there, and they're not ever waking up again."

Kajaro was up and moving before Quinn could blink.

She felt a flutter of panic emerge in her stomach, yet at the same time, an odd peace along with it. She could tell Aradie was sending that sensation to her from outside of her mind, but it was welcome, steadying, and helped her think clearly.

Quinn stood up and raced back the way she'd come, readying herself. She grabbed onto every single thing that she had learned from Milaro. Every single thing about strengthening her defenses. She knew they were still low level, so she built a second wall behind them, pouring in all the mental strength she could muster.

Mental Fortitude: Level Two

What the hell? she thought, but dismissed the notification immediately. There was no time right then. Reinforcing her shields even more, she pulsed mana into them. Very slowly, she could sense Kajaro and his companion slithering toward her. A clear, almost water-looking missile made its way toward her, and she deflected it, absorbing some of it to reflect it back at him, just like she'd done when practicing with Milaro and Malakai. A gasp of surprise emerged from the Serpensiril.

And right then, Milaro popped into view, directly next to her.

"What? I thought . . . How are you here?" His arrival momentarily interrupted her flow as she sputtered at his appearance.

He shrugged. "I set up an alert, just in case something happened. We're not letting anybody ambush you, Quinn."

She couldn't describe the sense of relief she felt at his presence, that momentary flash of safety, of not being alone. He was so much stronger than she was.

For now, anyway.

"Okay, just do what you've been doing. I'll work on disabling however you got roped into here." He scrunched his brow with concentration and flashed her a smile.

"Thank you," she said, short of breath from all the exertion maintaining the mental shield in a defensive formation took.

After several seconds, he spoke again. "It's all set up. I'll extract us. Just defend while I prepare the gateway."

So that's what Quinn did. She intercepted anything Kajaro and his companion threw at her. Each impact felt like a bowling ball landing on some part of her body. It hurt her head. It hurt her stomach. She felt like she was going to vomit after the fourth rebound return. Sweat poured down her brow and back. Breath came to her in gasps.

Still, she persisted. It helped that the rage on Kajaro's face fueled her petty side.

And suddenly, everything snapped.

It was like glass shattering over her as the image fractured and disappeared.

She sat up in her own bed, with Milaro and Lynx watching her, their expressions filled with nothing but concern.

"Are you okay?"

"Yeah. I think." Too many thoughts rushed into each other as she tried to answer them, honing down to one singular question in her mind. "How is he still alive?"

"Kajaro is still alive?" Lynx asked. But he didn't sound surprised.

"Yes," Milaro spoke up. "He's currently regenerating."

"Not surprised," Lynx said. "I thought the retrieval of the book, after he refused to return it, went too smoothly. Not to mention that his body was gone when we went to try and retrieve it."

"I didn't know that," Quinn gasped out, still regaining her breath.

Lynx shrugged. "Wasn't overly important at the time."

Quinn still felt slightly winded. "So it doesn't, like, just disappear after a few minutes like it does in a video game?"

Quinn knew Lynx wanted to tell her that this wasn't a video game. But he was very polite and did no such thing. All he did was raise an eyebrow and change the subject. "Tell us what happened."

Quinn gave them a very quick rundown.

"There are so many ways he could have gone about this," Lynx mused.

Milaro nodded his agreement. "He could have used a false death spell. I mean, it's extremely high level, but so is he. He could have used a potion. There are so many concoctions for such an effect. Although you do have to be adept or you'll die painfully for real."

"Frankly, he's also a reptilian and you did use ice in your attacks." Lynx sighed. "He could have slowed his heartbeat down enough to trick the ring. Although I'm not positive about that one."

"He wanted us to take that storage ring. He wanted us to scan the books into the system and infect it further," Quinn said softly, as the mental tiredness began to kick in.

"'Infect it further' means he knows the system's infected." Lynx practically growled the words out.

"Which brings me to another point," Quinn said. "There are definitely spies in the Library, but I have no idea who. Aradie didn't find them."

Aradie hooted. She sounded insulted. But also maybe a little ashamed.

"But you know . . . it'll be okay," Quinn said, suddenly feeling oddly positive. "We know now. That he's alive, I mean. He didn't expect us to know that this was going to happen. They expected to take us by surprise, but we know. And we can prepare. And we can be more vigilant."

"True," Lynx said. And he seemed to perk up, the tension in his shoulders lessening a little. He smiled. "Yeah, nothing better than being prepared. Let's see if we can figure out a way to welcome our little spies."

Quinn grinned. And Milaro clapped his hands together. "I think we're going to get along famously."

"We already do," Quinn said.

"No, I mean, we'll get along famously with that plan." The king gave her a wink.

She laughed, actually feeling lighter despite the heaviness of the dream.

Lynx smiled at her, his eyes fully focused on her for what seemed to be the first time in ages. "Well, Quinn, I'm going to let you digest that book and get some rest. I hear organic beings like to sleep sometimes."

She laughed and he continued. "Get in some mental training with Milaro and figure out how the hell you got into Kajaro's mind. And we need you to tackle the filtration system first."

"Got it, boss," she said to Lynx. In a way, the Library and Lynx were sort of her employers. He flashed her a smile.

Despite the gravity of the entire night's events, Quinn actually felt like they were making progress.

9

CHANGE OF PLANS

THE REST OF QUINN'S DREAMS WERE UNEVENTFUL.

When she woke the next morning, she stumbled through the waking up process, feeling slightly groggy, and pulled on some random clothes.

As she opened the door, Misha suddenly stood next to her.

"Librarian, we convened while you slept and made some necessary decisions," Misha said.

Quinn raised an eyebrow, suppressing a yawn. She wasn't even completely awake yet to the extent that Misha was sort of blurry. "What decisions?"

"Milaro insists that you prioritize your knowledge absorption and training. I am sure you also agree this is the right course of action," Misha explained.

Quinn blinked, mainly because there was still sleep in her eyes, but also because this sounded like they were slowing down for some reason. She could get on board with that considering she'd barely had a breather for the last few weeks. "Okay."

Misha continued once Quinn spoke. "Dottie will take over your supervisory shifts, and we will manage without you for anything that isn't huge."

A short while later, Misha ushered Quinn into her office, where books were stacked chest-high on her desk. Quinn groaned and turned to the supervisory golem. "You want me to absorb all of these books?"

Misha shook their head. "No. These are merely some of the returns we cannot yet file away. A new drawer is currently being prepared for them as we speak but for now, we need a place to put them. Milaro will . . ."

"I'm here," the elf king said, appearing in a whirlwind of robes. "Today is a busy day for all of us. You need to build, break down, and rebuild your mental defenses until you level your skill up, and, or can do it in your sleep."

"Okay," Quinn said, well aware that she seemed to be agreeing to a lot of things this morning before she'd even fully woken up. But they all seemed to be making sense.

"In the meantime, you need to focus on mind multitasking. I want you to absorb these three books." He pulled three books out from behind the piles and set them on the desk.

A sliver of overwhelm wormed its way into her thoughts. Quinn sighed. "Sure, sir." She added a mock salute.

Milaro raised an eyebrow this time, a slight smirk on his face. "Sir?"

She was being sassy to a millennia-old elf. Maybe not the wisest choice. "You're acting like a teacher. I guess I need a teacher. I'm just —" But she was cut off as Lynx walked in with Aradie flying directly behind him.

The bird swooped down with a small pouch which she dropped into Quinn's hands. It held what looked like an apple and a small breakfast sandwich.

Quinn grinned. "Looks like you read my mind," she said to the bird and scritched her neck.

"Milaro, you need to go speak with Harish and Siliqua. I'll stay with Quinn," Lynx spoke up.

Quinn looked at the manifestation. He appeared to be fine. There was no flickering, and she couldn't see through him, which was more comforting than she'd realized it would be. He seemed very much like the Lynx she'd first met.

Except in human form.

"What can I do for you, Lynx?" she asked as Milaro waved and took off.

"I thought I'd keep you company." He smiled at her, but there was some hesitance behind the expression.

"But there's more to it than that, isn't there?" she pushed.

Lynx grinned. "And I wanted to let you know that the broadcast for assistants that we just sent out went not only to the same planets and worlds that we originally did, but also to a dozen more that we're certain of our standing with. I'm hopeful of the response broadening our assistant intake. Narilin has requested that we allow some of her brethren to come and assist with the Library as well."

Quinn wasn't sure what she thought of that, considering the recent encounters she'd had with the Salosier. But if there was one thing for sure, the beautiful, willowy tree lady definitely loved the books in the Library more than almost anything. Quinn could at least sense that much sincerity from her.

"Fine," she said, "but we have to interview them all, and I'm not doing interviews until after I fix the damn filtration system."

"Perfect." Lynx inclined his head. "I have set interviews for a week's time."

"Oh, good," Quinn said. "That just means I need to refine the skills I have and learn some new stuff. Replace the filters and keep my strength up." Quinn reached for the serene spot in her mind that she'd learned from some of those original mind books.

She breathed in, calm now, and leaned toward Lynx. "I've got this. Just let me go through these books, okay?"

Lynx flashed her a smile. "Thank you, Quinn, for adapting so well, despite everything."

"Yeah, what else am I gonna do? Stuck in a fantasy world and all I got was a magical Library." She winked at him. "It's okay. I didn't really have much back home anyway."

"That's pretty convenient for us," he said.

"It is, isn't it? I'm okay here. You don't need to hang around while I absorb. There's plenty else to do." She didn't want to monopolize Lynx's time, regardless of whether or not the Library wanted her to keep him close.

"Very well," he said, and then added almost as an afterthought, "Just call out if you need me and I'll be here straight away."

Quinn waited until Lynx left the room before letting herself drop into her desk chair. Despite the fact that absorbing books made it extremely fast to learn everything, Quinn felt like she didn't always process the information properly.

When she read from a book, she absorbed the knowledge slowly, or at least that's what the case had been back on Earth. But here, it was like she absorbed all of the knowledge at once and gradually everything came to her. Like one of those sponge animals that expanded when wet.

Perhaps she could combine the two methods. Absorbing the book, and then skim-read through the pieces that didn't immediately make sense. That way she could find the pieces of information that she was having difficulty processing. That made sense.

There was just something cozy and soothing about curling up with a big book and reading through it. She sighed and pulled the first book that Milaro had tugged forward to her.

Levels of Mental Fortitude Broken Down.

Energy Required: 289

Quinn cringed. She was going to need some of those energy balls. She pulled open the drawer next to her and took the four she had remaining out. Her current level was 812 of 812, which meant the Library wasn't currently leaching off her energy levels, at least.

Hopefully, the Library could keep that at bay while she learned these books.

Just as she was about to absorb the first book, the new shelving golems, Tank and Tide, came in with Carty. They moved to her desk and bowed ever so slightly. Tank, sincerely, looked like a completely normal red clay golem. He was big and burly and had only marginally defined his body a little more when he was given his name.

But Tide had this wispy type of clay hair that really seemed like clay seaweed. Tide gave off a general feeling of the soothing senses Quinn always associated with the ocean. They'd spoken to her more than any of the others, internally and with aura, not with words of course. Quinn got the distinct impression, as Tide picked up a pile of books, that he was actually smiling.

"Thank you," she called after them as they left.

Quinn absorbed the book. *Levels of Mental Fortitude Broken Down* was very technical, with descriptions of differing levels of mental control. It didn't tell her how to do them; it just explained to her what they were. She understood why Milaro had given her this book to read, but at the same time, she felt like her time might have been better spent on other books.

She needed to push through and practice enough to level her mental barriers up so that she could protect her own mind. Once they got there, from what she understood of this book, she and Milaro working together should be able to cast out the orb they'd imprisoned inside her mind.

Emphasis on should.

Quinn wiped her brow even though she wasn't sweating and took a bite out of one of the balls. Chewing away, she pulled the next book into her lap.

Recognizing Mental Manipulation and its Effects.

Energy required: 312

"Boy," she said out loud, trying not to cringe at the energy cost, "this one should be good."

That seemed like a lot of energy required. Flipping open the book, she saw an inscription on the inside. Donated by Milaro, King of the Areiltháhnish. She guessed that was the official name for high elves. Maybe she should have called up his information a bit sooner. Still, "elf" was much easier to say.

She wondered if the book contained magical knowledge passed down through his lineage.

This book explained to her how someone like Kajaro managed to get a mental hook into her. He had unsettled her while they were battling. To be fair, she'd feared for her life the moment he'd cackled from the other side of the lake. Using that fear and that insecurity, he'd inserted his insidious thread to build an entire world inside her mind.

But to do so effectively, it needed to be orchestrated. That was insane foreplanning.

Just on the off chance the Library got another Librarian? Seemed very sus.

She *tsk*ed as she put the book back down, gobbling up another one of her energy balls. She was still losing energy, but at least these were keeping it at bay. She cracked her neck from side to side and sat there, thinking through what she'd just learned from this book while eating the apple that Aradie had brought for her. Building and rebuilding her walls constantly while she processed all the information.

There were so many ways to get into somebody's head. It was frightening, and this information was available to anybody who had a mental magic affinity, from what she understood.

She flipped the book closed and looked at the tiny barcode on the spine. It had, if she counted correctly, seventeen different color variations. Which, as far as she knew, depicted what affinities could absorb each book. Not to mention that anybody could read the book.

Although that didn't mean that they could execute what was in the book. Without having the affinity, it was just words and theory.

Was the Library too lax in its controls? Perhaps. But it wasn't a policing unit. Her own morals constantly warred with this juxtaposition of ideals. Maybe that very fact was one of the checks and balances of the whole system. She sighed, tearing down her mental walls and rebuilding them once more.

Suddenly a message flashed up in front of her.

Mental Barrier: Level 2

Finally. Maybe Milaro would be able to teach her a more secure way to keep her mind under control once he got back here. Maybe she'd even be done with these books by then. She pulled the next book toward her.

Dream Walking Through Mental Fortitude

"Could have used that last night," she muttered to herself. Although, to be fair, that was probably why he'd picked it for her. She got ready to absorb yet another book.

Energy Required: 298

"Okay," she said, "here goes nothing."

This book wasn't donated by anybody. At least, it didn't have an inscription. She opened it, splayed her hands on the pages, took a deep breath, and closed her eyes.

This time it felt like there was wind rushing out of the pages to fluff her hair. It was a good thing she kept it in a ponytail. Dream Traversing. It was so much more complex than she'd thought it would be. How had she managed to walk into his?

Did that mean that the orb inside her was leaking enough of Kajaro's essence to enable her to latch onto it and enter his dreams? She frowned. That couldn't be right. Surely that needed to be a more deliberate action.

Quinn ran everything through her mind again, all the information she had just gleaned, everything about how she needed to level up her mental fortitude skill to protect herself from people like Kajaro, who could worm their way in through negative thoughts.

This put a whole different spin on so much. She took a deep breath, trying to analyze everything that happened over the last few weeks. There were inconsistencies in her mind. Not just because the Library was malfunctioning, or that she'd been sent out to retrieve books from someone who wasn't going to give them back.

She'd believed Kajaro to be dead. This thought weighed on her mind for weeks. Even though technically Malakai had been the one to land the killing blow, Quinn couldn't help but feel guilt, as she'd contributed to his apparent death.

And all of it over a book.

Granted, they weren't just any books.

And now she found out Kajaro wasn't dead, which meant he had orchestrated this entire thing, and possibly everything that led to it. This thought stayed with her while she continued to build and rebuild her defenses.

She checked the other drawers and pulled out a writing pad and a quill. "Aradie, is this a magic quill?" she asked.

Aradie hooted a negative into her ear.

"Good to know." The last thing she wanted to do was create a tome of some sort about what she was thinking, but writing things down always helped. So, Quinn wrote herself a timeline as she knew it so far.

- *Lynx speaks to Librarian about retirement and goes into reset mode.*
- *Librarian decides to retire once he is out.*
- *Activates retirement.*
- *Suddenly all Librarian candidates disappear and there are none to be found.*
- *Over the next 50 years, the search becomes more frantic until the Librarian's retirement timer runs out and she dies, leaving the Library without a Librarian.*

"Hmm, that's very convenient," Quinn said, mulling things over by talking to herself. Part of her had to wonder if Korradine was even dead. After the whole fiasco with Kajaro, she wasn't about to take anything at face value.

"I wonder what happened while Lynx was technically offline. If the Librarian didn't think directly at the Library, then the Library wouldn't have known what was running through the Librarian's head, because by this stage, Korradine had had hundreds of years to perfect her own mental techniques. But why would a Librarian think this way? How could she want the Library not to be the Library anymore? That's what I don't understand." She tapped the end of the quill against the desk, but being a feather, it was far less satisfying than the tapping of a pen.

"Hoot," Aradie said, as if she could understand every word Quinn was saying. Which she probably could, being a magic bird and all.

"Do you understand?" Quinn turned to the bird.

Images flashed in front of Quinn's mind of Korradine. When she was younger than Lynx's depiction those couple of weeks ago. It was like a quick-aging video that showed so much detail around the former Librarian and how Lynx and her interacted. The Library in full swing. The Library full of people.

And the Library returns desk piled high with books.

But wait . . . was that Kajaro in an image?

"Is that Kajaro?" Quinn asked.

"Hoot," Aradie said, as if it was obvious.

"Is that Kajaro borrowing the book he didn't want to return?" Quinn drummed her fingers on the table. "Can you show me that again? And pause it, don't keep it going."

Aradie showed her the image again. It was definitely *DeKarlyle's Thesis of Spatial Distortion*. He spoke with Korradine for a good couple of minutes before taking the book and leaving the Library.

"Well, that's not suspicious at all," Quinn muttered.

Suddenly, the pieces clicked ever so slightly. Not that she hadn't considered this before, but these images were proof. "Did you not show this to Lynx? Lynx doesn't remember?"

Aradie flashed more images into Quinn's mind, apparently not in a speaking mood at that moment.

"Okay. Okay," Quinn said, getting the message. "You did, but that was back then and he doesn't recall it now."

She couldn't tell if anything had been done to the filtration system. Obviously, Aradie hadn't followed them to the filtration or core rooms. But this was important information. Korradine was the one who loaned DeKarlyle's book to Kajaro.

Quinn needed more information, more records that came from places other than the Library archives. But it was a good step.

The more urgent concern at this moment was the filtration system. Quinn was pretty sure it had been sabotaged as well. The note in the book, the failing output of the two filtration pillars even as she absorbed the books. It all added up.

She needed Milaro to come back. It had been a few hours, and she knew he was busy, but she had so many questions. And Lynx, with the holes in his memory, was in no state to answer them.

Too many things didn't line up. Glitches that she needed to be explained. She just wasn't sure how to contact the elf king.

She stepped out of her office and walked towards the front desk where Malakai was stood conversing with Dottie about something. There weren't many people at the check-in desk. It made her a little sad. The only two were being served by the aracnio brothers.

"Malakai, can you mentally fetch your grandfather, please?"

He sighed and a brief blank look passed over his face before he answered. "Done."

"Thank you. I'll be in my office," she said, heading back to work on her mental multitasking while she waited.

She didn't miss Malakai's raised eyebrow, but there were some things she needed to confirm before she shared the rest of her findings with anyone. At least right now, she felt like things weren't stagnant.

She was actually beginning to make some progress.

10

DIGGING DEEPER

Milaro's knock at Quinn's door pulled her out of myriad thoughts as she was leafing through one of the *Mental Manipulation* chapters.

"Thank you for coming," she said.

He walked into the room. "Malakai seemed to think it was urgent." He sounded concerned as he placed a hand on the desk.

"It is, sort of. At least, I think it is." Quinn calmed herself, clearing her mind of clutter and focusing intently on what she'd been thinking about. "I leveled up my mental barrier, and I need you to teach me the next level. Also, I had a thought, what can we do to provide mental defenses for those around us who don't have one of the seventeen affinities that can use these books?"

Milaro took a step back to get a better look at her, his expression thoughtful. "Well done on the level-up. It's good to see you're thinking ahead."

"I think I have to now." She frowned as she realized just how true those words were.

"But that doesn't seem to be enough to pull me back from my kingdom with urgency?" Milaro asked softly.

Quinn sighed. "I just realized how much work went into setting up this entire Library sabotage, probably for centuries under all your noses, without the Library being any wiser simply because the Librarian could successfully separate her thoughts from those of the Library."

Milaro tapped his chin with his forefinger in thought. "Okay. I do have some exercises I'll give you to help you with your next level of Mental Barrier. But first, what started the deep thinking on sabotage?"

Quinn raised an eyebrow. "You mean apart from that whole 'the Library still can't even function properly because of it' and 'oh, they might be out to kill me' parts?"

Milaro winced. "Yeah. Apart from that."

She shrugged. "Aradie showed me some visions—that's how she communicates with me when she doesn't feel like speaking or emoting. Her hoots are easy to interpret for the most part, but sometimes she has a lot more to say and she plays me images from her memory. One of those included Kajaro checking out *DeKarlyle's Thesis of Spatial Distortion*. He spoke at length to Korradine while checking it out, which in and of itself isn't necessarily suspicious, but from what I could tell, it was during the time that Lynx was offline resetting himself. Which makes it a lot more interesting. And if Korradine had locked her thoughts off, the Library would have no way of knowing what they discussed."

Quinn waited for Milaro to digest what she'd said.

He certainly took his time. Finally, he spoke again. "There were no other Librarians or assistants around them?"

"None that I could see."

"That's very interesting." He mulled that over. "And I'm assuming the Library itself has convenient blanks then?"

Quinn's eyes grew wide. "I'm not sure, but I know Lynx memory has gaps around then and that their memory blanks mostly line up."

"I'll see if there's any other ways we can retrieve the information. Any other night owls perhaps . . ." Milaro sighed. "I was overjoyed when I realized the Library was back . . . but now, it's gotten so complicated."

"True," Quinn said. He definitely wasn't wrong. They just had to find a bright side. "But we have a lot to keep us busy at least. Including having filters to change, right?"

"Yes, we do, Quinn. We're waiting on the filtration chamber suits to be ready so that you all can go down there and tackle it."

"Suits? Plural?" she asked.

"Oh, yes." Milaro's eyes took on that mischievous twinkle. "Malakai will be accompanying you."

She cocked her head to one side and crossed her arms. "So you've decided Malakai's accompanying me?"

"Malakai is probably"—Milaro paused, as if he was considering how to phrase the rest of what he wanted to say—"shall we say, the best equipped to assist you."

"How do you mean he's best equipped to assist me? Lynx is coming with me already. He literally can't get hurt down there." She watched for Milaro's response very closely.

"Of course Lynx is coming with you, and he can manifest solidly and assist you that way. But just in case there's something down there that we haven't counted on yet, I would feel safer if you would take Malakai with you." Milaro was pulling the grandfatherly card again.

Quinn still wasn't convinced. "But isn't it dangerous for, like, everybody to go down there?"

Milaro hesitated before answering. "Malakai has some species advantages, shall we say."

Quinn narrowed her eyes. Milaro held up his hands. "Just like we're taking precautions for you even though you'd likely be fine. Malakai has direct species lineage advantages when it comes to chaotic energies."

Quinn mulled that over. She wasn't exactly sure how to take that. Granted, she'd never poked into his personal life despite all the juicy hints some of his comments left. Some of those offhand comments on the Dabilian homeworld and in the Library had really piqued her interest, but general species information shouldn't be off-limits.

"You're not going to tell me why, are you?" she asked.

"Well, you did read the species books. You could always go and find more of those." Milaro tossed her a wink this time.

Quinn scowled. "You could just help make it easier, Milaro."

Milaro leaned a little closer and spoke very softly. "Yes, but his is not my story to tell, Quinn."

She sighed because he was right. A sliver of guilt wound its way around her. "Fine," she said. "Just give me the exercises. Show me how to do whatever the next step is so no one can ever plant a bomb in my mind again."

"The next step is to weave a protection field."

"Weave? Like knitting?" she asked.

"No, like weaving, like in and out over pillars that you set up so that there's no gap." He made weird wavy motions with his hands that were only more confusing.

"And what visual do I use for that?"

"Use whatever you can imagine would make it safer and sturdier."

"Okay," Quinn said. "Way to leave it wide open."

Milaro laughed. "What works better for me might not work for you. Bricks are the easiest one for the first level because at some stage everyone has played with building blocks.

"Ah," she said, seeing it now. "That tracks."

"Excellent," the elf king said. "Now if there's nothing else, I really do have to be going. I won't be gone too long, I promise."

Quinn looked up into Milaro's earnest face and felt actually safe. He really was dependable and grandfatherly. "Thanks for coming."

"No problem. Just make sure you practice properly."

"I will," she said.

Quinn truly meant it when she promised Milaro that she'd practice.

She was absolutely committed to practicing as much as she could. To making sure she wasn't ever left as vulnerable again.

True to her word, she managed to erect a wonderful barrier of posts around her original barrier, as she didn't think it prudent to leave herself defenseless while learning a new technique. Then, she began closing them in like a fence.

However, she found herself disliking the wooden panels. Instead, she began to weave cloth, opting for a type of leather. Yet she couldn't understand how it wouldn't have holes. Perhaps the posts needed to be closer together, or maybe it needed to be stitched afterward. It was far more complex than building with bricks. Regardless, she set her mind to work on it while contemplating other matters.

She thought about all the chaotic magic resistance items they needed. Even if she was technically not really susceptible to it, she didn't want to take any chances. They required pills and food to up their resistance, and the same leather armor they'd worn when they visited the Dabilian homeworld. There was so much to consider.

Why was it okay for Malakai to come along? Surely, it was dangerous for him too, especially where chaos magic threatened to leak into the Library and the filtration system struggled to maintain any type of barrier. Why would someone as caring as Milaro send his grandson into danger? That meant he wasn't in any real danger. If it was lineage and species-dependent, then perhaps the Darigháhnish were a chaos elf species?

Frustrated, she smacked her hands down on the table. "Concentrate, Quinn," she muttered to herself. Aradie burrowed into the side of her head as if offering consolation. She still needed to figure it out, but if it was lineage-related, then . . .

"Wait," she said out loud. Massaging her temples, she ran through the thoughts in her head, the sudden barrage of information that she needed to reason through. She couldn't just dive into something irrationally. She had to sort it methodically, especially when the fate of the universe might hang in the balance.

If Malakai's ability to accompany her was lineage and species-related, then did that mean Quinn's affinities were perhaps lineage and species-related? No. Wait. That didn't make sense. It couldn't be human-related. No other human on Earth had abilities like hers, ruling out the species. But did it rule everything out?

"Misha," she called, directing the thought toward the golem. As expected, the supervisory golem landed right in front of her, softly, with no noise but the slight whoosh of wind that brushed Quinn's hair back from her face.

"You called, Librarian?" Misha gave her a very slight bow. Quinn grinned at the golem. Misha had to be one of her favorite people so far, always diligent, always ready to help, and usually ready with an answer. Which was refreshing, considering so many of the people around her insisted on beating around the bush.

"Misha, I need you to do something for me."

"Yes, if it is within my power, I will do it."

Quinn sucked in a breath and asked before she lost her nerve. "I discreetly need information on the Darigháhnish elves."

"Oh, they are not called elves here, just the Darigháhnish. Elves are not one of the species of the universe," Misha corrected her.

"Okay, then I need as much information on the Darigháhnish as a species as I can get." Quinn still thought of them as elves, but that was her problem. She'd try to make sure she didn't say it out loud anymore.

"Why do you not just ask Malakai?" Misha asked, cocking their head to one side. "Would that not be the appropriate thing to do?"

"No, I don't want to know Malakai's specific story. That would be prying. If he ever wants to tell me, I'll be ready to listen. But until that time, I won't pry." Quinn was adamant about that. She paused for a few more moments.

"Very well." Misha inclined their head in understanding.

Quinn continued. "What I do need to know is what makes the Darigháhnish so special when it comes to chaotic magic. There wasn't much in the book Malakai gave me a while ago, just a very basic rundown saying Darigháhnish keep to themselves and it's best to stay away from them. What I need to know for me to tackle and understand this filtration assignment is why it isn't dangerous for somebody of the Darigháhnish people to come with me down there."

Misha contemplated her, those pearl-like eyes shining. "That makes perfect sense. I will get you the tomes that are applicable from the history section."

Quinn started. "We have a history section? Is the history itself magic?"

Misha glanced at her. "Have you sincerely not looked at the catalog?"

"Well, I glanced through the catalog, but I didn't exactly have a lot of time to process it."

Misha let out what sounded like a sigh with a bit of a whistle to it. A golem sigh. "Of course there is magic based in history. There is magic based in everything." Sometimes, Misha could sound condescending.

Quinn decided to let it slide. "Anyway, I need the information discreetly. Just on the species, whatever, but not on his specific lineage. Oh, and do you think it would be possible to pull my personal history?"

Misha turned back toward Quinn. "I do not understand, Librarian. Your history, do you not know your own history?"

"I do, but my parents died when I was young. I don't remember everything about them. And I thought, if perhaps Malakai's lineage allows him to be around the chaotic energy, then maybe that's what gives me my affinities and my chaotic advantage as well."

Misha watched Quinn for a few moments before inclining their head. "I do believe it will be possible to retrieve your information, but you will have to give me time to figure out the proper way to do this. It may require more power than we currently have, more resources than we can spare, or just more time than I can currently allocate."

Quinn nodded. "That's fine. I just . . . it was just something I thought of when I realized that, because of Malakai's heritage, he was going to be able to accompany me down there with less danger to him than it would be if I took, say, Geneva or Finn."

"Yes, you should also think about taking Eric," Misha said. "His ability to fly could be useful."

"Good point." Quinn nodded. "He doesn't necessarily need the protective gear, does he?"

"No, he does not, Librarian." Misha's mouth lifted ever so slightly in what passed for their golem smile. "The preparations have almost all been made—just waiting on the suit reinforcements now. I will take my leave and get you the information you have requested as soon as I am able."

Quinn watched as Misha disappeared—there one second, gone the next—and pondered her next step. She knew she had to continue learning how to weave the barrier. She also knew that she had to practice the mental acuity exercises Milaro had so kindly given her. But she couldn't shake the feeling that everyone had a lineage and maybe something in hers would explain why she had been on Earth when maybe she should have been in this part of the universe instead.

"That's just silly." But the thought stayed with her. Quinn sighed and stood up, stretching. She hadn't named the storage golems yet, the gatherers, because she hadn't seen them. Tank and Tide were just the new shelving golems. Although she liked the T trend. Tank, Tide, Tim, and Tom was probably going to get really confusing if she continued to stick with T, considering they were probably going to need up to a couple of dozen of them in the end.

She paused at the threshold of her office, glancing back. It was tidier now that the golems had retrieved some of the books that were on her desk. Aradie flew to her shoulder and she walked out into the Library. There was a general murmur as she did so, not directed at her, but just underlying everything now.

There were maybe a dozen people in the Library from what she could feel that weren't directly related to being staff. She could sense where everybody was. Nobody was somewhere they shouldn't be.

Although Lynx was in the kitchen.

She was pretty sure he didn't eat. But if she knew him, he was arranging for the provisions that they needed.

Quinn decided to make her way over to the kitchen there and paused just before she entered when she heard voices inside.

"Are you sure she does not require these anymore?" she heard Cook asking.

"Probably not," Lynx said. "There's been some anomalous activity around our Librarian. We need to figure out why."

Quinn couldn't agree more. She stepped into the kitchen and grinned at Lynx, crossing her arms. "Do tell me what more we need to figure out about me?"

But instead of catching him completely unawares, as she had

thought she did, he grinned at her. "You realize I knew you were there, right?"

She laughed. Of course he did. She knew where everybody was. Why wouldn't he? He was a part of the Library, after all.

"No, it's just your chaotic magic affinity is unique. And there are perhaps some other ways we can enhance your unique physiology to, well, better filter the system." He smiled at her as if in apology for talking about her.

Quinn perked up. "You mean I might be able to help the Library in other ways than just wading through chaotic sludge?"

"Isn't that logical?" Lynx asked.

Quinn nodded. "Yeah. Yeah, I suppose it is."

11

WAITING

QUINN WASN'T THE MOST PATIENT PERSON IN THE WORLD, OR, AS IT turned out, the universe. Lynx's idea to have her figure things out meant training her magical affinities to the point of exhaustion.

After another couple of days spent practicing her skills, rebuilding and reconstructing her newly learned mental barrier, working at the check-in desk, and refining her understanding of all the details in the four chaotic magic books. She felt like she was back at university, studying.

She found herself sitting in her office, wondering why the armor wasn't ready for them to head down to the filtration chamber yet. They barely left a scratch on them after returning from the Dabilian homeworld. She didn't understand why it was taking so long for the chaos-resistant armor to be completed, at least for this task.

She sighed and ran her hand through her ponytail, tugging it down, twirling it in her fingers, until she realized that she was exercising an extremely old bad habit. Aradie hooted in her ear.

"Yeah, I know you're concerned. So am I. I really . . ."

But the owl hooted again.

"Oh, you're concerned about me," Quinn said. "No, I'm fine. I'm just impatient. Like, really exasperated."

Aradie leaned far away enough that Quinn could get a good look at her, and she swore the owl was giving her an extremely level side-eye.

"Look, I don't get it, okay?" Quinn threw her hands up. "We gave them the armor back in tip-top condition, all things considered. Fine, mine had a hole from a stab wound, but I'm sure magic can mend that. I just want to get this done. We have so much to do that the Library needs more power to be able to do."

They really did. Looking at the list of things they needed to accomplish, was enough to make her head spin. Aradie let out a very low hoot this time.

"You want me to find something else to occupy my time instead of complaining about how much time it's taking?" Quinn rolled her eyes. "Thank you so much for your wisdom."

Aradie lifted off her shoulder and went to perch on the back of the couch, shooting her a wounded look.

"I'm sorry. I'm testy."

You certainly are, the Library piped up.

"Well, well, well," Quinn said. "It's nice to see you. What, for the first time in the last three days?"

Don't blame me. I've been helping get your armor fixed, the thing that you're extremely irate about now.

"Thanks," Quinn said. "I thought you were working on memory-related stuff."

That too. I'm able to multitask

"So does that mean I can go get the armor?"

Not yet. Do something more constructive with your time.

Quinn twirled in her chair, realizing the Library wasn't going to give her anything else. "Fine," she said out loud and reached forward to access the console from her desk and pulled up some of the statistics from the Library.

Library Re-Open Duration: 239 hours

Quinn blinked. So almost a full ten days. She frowned, at the time. The standard twenty-four hours per day being relevant here in the Library always got to her. But maybe there were reasons Earth ended up going with that format after all. That was a whole other can of worms she had no time to deal with right now.

She scrolled down a little bit further, waving at the display with her hand. It functioned similarly to a tablet. If a tablet ran off hand gestures.

"3,782 books returned." She frowned. That didn't seem like so many. That meant there were still 14,960 books remaining. She cringed. It felt like they'd barely made progress. But, she guessed, maybe some people still didn't believe the Library was open. It wasn't like the mana presence in the universe had changed yet.

If she'd understood it correctly, that wasn't going to happen until they could open more filtration pillars.

She went through the rest of the information. 341 of those 3,782 books couldn't be checked in, because Siliqua and Harish had not yet completed their task. That was another thing to add to Quinn's ever-growing list. She needed to talk to them. It was a bit worrisome that after ten days of the Library being open, they still weren't able to just return every book.

Harish and Siliqua seemed to think they'd be able to resolve the issue fairly quickly. Although given their lifespans, ten days was probably the blink of an eye.

Quinn sighed. They had drawers out in the check-in desk, lined with the same substance as the satchels that they used for the chaos books retrieved from the Dabilian homeworld. It performed the same function. Even though these weren't drenched in chaos sludge, it was to prevent any potential leakage into the system of any foreign matter.

Just in case.

Couldn't be too careful while rebuilding a broken universal Library.

Making sure the books didn't exacerbate anything by being in the vicinity of the system was a solid precaution, but it was still irritating that she couldn't return those books to their appropriate areas yet.

So technically, only 3,441 had been actually returned.

Quinn frowned at the number. Considering they'd been open ten days, that was a decent return rate. Not too shabby for a Library people weren't sure had really returned. "Well, let's just have a look, let's break that down. What about the branches? How close are we to opening the branches?" she asked the system directly.

1,428 books are relegated to the General Magic Library. Of these, some 850 are intermediate or higher level volumes.

Quinn frowned at the numbers. "Okay . . . that leaves 2013 books that are split up between the requirements for the other branches."

Would you like to list these branches out?

Yes or No?

Quinn motioned toward the Yes answer, and a listing appeared directly before her eyes.

Requirements for Library Branch openings. Defined by relevant book count only.

Horticulture: 283/720

Bardic/Musical: 209/897

Culinary Arts: 229/282

Crafting: 312/730

Alchemical/Medicinal: 111/384

Combat: 472/837

Academy: 397/785

Total: 1804 Books/Tomes/Codex

Quinn sat back and stared at the statistics in front of her. She'd never really liked statistics as a subject. It really wasn't her thing, but she had to admit it looked impressive, especially that culinary arts only needed another fifty-three books. If they got it under fifty, she felt that would call for a refined list they could then specifically target for retrieval.

Cook would probably love to have that branch open first. After all the wonderful cinnamon donuts he'd made her, she had to admit to having a very, very soft spot for Cook. Not to mention it looked like that branch in particular would be the easiest to open.

"Well, that's the Library portion taken care of." She flicked through stuff again, back and forth, double-checking the amounts. Another three books had been returned since she started looking, but they all belonged in the general magic area.

It was obvious that the amount of books being returned had slowed considerably in the last few days. Still, it wasn't a bad outcome. Three hundred and seventy-odd books a day, that was pretty good on average, but that average would be going down shortly. With almost fifteen thousand books left, they couldn't afford for it to slow down yet. She sighed. "Yet another thing we'll address after I go down to the filtration chamber."

Aradie sat on the edge of her desk now, casting Quinn furtive glances.

At some stage during Quinn's statistical analysis of the Library returns, the bird had moved closer again.

"Come on, sit back on my shoulder. I wasn't angry at you, remember? You were angry at me." A little warbled hoot came out as if Aradie was saying, *Well, can you blame me?* Which, really, Quinn couldn't.

"Personal statistics page." Quinn made sure to be specific in the command so she didn't pull up age-old statistics from the Library itself. Sometimes knowing how old the Library was made everything that was happening feel overwhelming, whether or not she used her newly acquired mental abilities to even herself out.

When she pulled up her statistics, Quinn raised an eyebrow at them. "

Name: Quinn
Age: Irrelevant
Heritage: Earth, Sector 12942
Species: Librarian
Energy Capacity: 912/912
Mana Levels: 1085/1085
Alignment: 101%
*Affinities: 1722**
Tome Knowledge: 8
Affinity Level: 9
Determination: Rising
**As far as the Library can determine*

Quinn frowned at the human portion of her species being missing now. That seemed oddly timed.

She took a deep breath, didn't let it get to her, and moved on. Or at least she tried to. Maybe the system was glitching because the Library had been doing a lot of glitching. She just didn't have time to pursue anything else right now except for the bloody filtration system.

"Focus, Quinn. Focus." She slapped her cheeks lightly and moved on.

She crossed her arms and muttered at the asterisked portion of the readout. "As far as the Library can determine, what does that mean? Is that because I will continue to have all affinities even as they become available and expand? Is the Library just completely about to break down?"

I'm not completely about to break down. Stop thinking so loudly.

"Sorry." Quinn wished she already had the mental conversation directing to a state of it being muscle memory.

As I mentioned, you're unique. We'll all figure it out after we have a chance to discuss things once we have more power and the filtration system is out of danger.

"I know. This is just frustrating." But the Library didn't seem to have anything else to add to that. Quinn sighed and decided to check another thing.

She checked the Library energy levels.

Library Energy Levels:

Critical Energy Levels: 6,882 of 10,000

That was, like, two energy units per book that were actually returned to the system. That was oddly specific, and somehow she wasn't entirely sure that's how it worked. That would mean it didn't count the books they couldn't yet input because of their categories. However it tallied the power gain, they were at least getting close to the next level.

Suddenly, Misha popped into view right in front of her desk. "Quinn, the garments are almost ready. Could you come, please, and bring whomever you are taking on this journey with you, please?"

Quinn didn't have to be asked twice, even if she'd almost jumped out of her chair in fright when the supervisory golem appeared.

As Misha popped back out of vision, Quinn walked out into the Library, gathered Malakai, Lynx, and Eric as well, and herded them toward the storage room.

Pushing all thoughts of the statistics she'd just been over and of her own personal stats page aside, Quinn focused on the storage workshop.

Eflin and Hale were hammering out the last of something on one of the workbenches. Quinn would not have chosen the names Eflin and Hale, but she thought it prudent to let Misha name some of the golems.

It took some convincing and explaining that Misha was sort of their direct family. The golem had practically side-eyed Quinn, but eventually relented.

Quinn wasn't certain she'd do that again. Eflin and Hale, however, appeared to like their names for the most part. They had little quirks about them, ways they nodded, especially a sweet and shy way for Eflin. Eflin was probably Quinn's favorite supply golem.

She turned to Misha, gesturing toward the work bench. "I thought you said they were almost done."

"Oh, they are. They are just ironing out the last one for Malakai," Misha replied, with no inflection at all.

"Fantastic. What do we do? Why has it taken so long?" Quinn asked, finally.

Aradie nudged her with her wing, and Quinn glared at the owl for a moment. "Look, explain to me what the big deal was about getting the armor adapted. We didn't ruin it last time and since then we've found out I might even be okay down there."

"You most certainly returned them mostly unblemished." Misha beckoned Quinn over to the bench and pointed at the armor. "We had to make adjustments. You see, this is a different version of the material. It is a rubberized version that repels the water with wax as well. Sludge will not penetrate it to touch your skin in any way. In theory, anyway."

Quinn raised an eyebrow in question. "I thought you said I was impervious. Am I not? Isn't chaos not supposed affect me much?"

"That's what the scan said," Lynx butted in. "But I'm still not sure what submerging you in an entire lake of chaotic sludge is going to do for your complexion."

Quinn cringed. "Okay, noted. I take that under advisement. So basically you had to build completely new suits."

Misha nodded. "Precisely."

"Why didn't you just tell me that instead of making me wait, assuming that you were just prolonging the inevitable for whatever reason?" Quinn managed to escape pouting, but only barely.

"And why," Misha asked, staring straight at her with those rather disconcerting moon-like eyes, "would we make you wait, Quinn?"

Quinn shrugged, realizing that she'd taken some of her itty-bitty hang-ups from Earth and brought them over here with her. "You probably wouldn't," she said carefully.

"Perfect," Misha said, and then gestured back to the garments that the golems had finished up. "What do you think?"

"These are like"—Quinn laughed—"footie pajamas that are diving suits." She was delighted. They were similar to the stuff professional divers wore.

"Footie pajamas?" Misha asked, like she was tasting the word. Then she smiled that straight lined smile and continued without waiting for an answer. "They have an interior-exterior zip that will allow you to waterproof the area so no liquid gets through at all, should you fall in."

"Should I fall in? Or need to wade into it, you're saying?" Quinn asked nervously.

"Well, you shouldn't fall off the filtration device, but we do have to think of all eventualities," Misha stated.

"The thing is, Quinn," Lynx piped up, "we're not sure what your chaotic wavelength means. It could mean that if you touch it, nothing happens. It could mean that if you touch it, it magically heals you. It could also mean that if you have too much prolonged contact with it it'll take over and subvert your mind, turning you into an evil villain. And no one wants that."

"How do you know that hasn't happened already?" Quinn pulled her best evil grin.

Lynx blinked. Twice. "Not the time for jokes, but . . . that wasn't bad."

"Fine," Quinn said, "I don't really want to be an evil mastermind. Much."

"Excellent. So listen." He flashed that very cat-like smile at her. "You need to wear this at all times, just in case you need to get into the mana lake. We'll show you when we get down there. Just try not to make actual direct contact with the chaotic sludge, any part of it, until we can actually get you to a point where we can run some tests and figure out just how big an impact everything has on you."

Quinn let out a nervous laugh. "Hey, I'm good. I don't want to volunteer myself as tribute to fall into a vat of sludge."

Malakai actually laughed. "Good, because I don't really want to dive in and get you back out."

"You're going to be fine anyway, Malakai." Lynx dismissed the comment with a wave of his hand. "It's just an extra precaution for you because of your unique genetic makeup,"

"Look at us." Quinn sighed at him, rolling her eyes as she continued speaking. "All unique and special and stuff. And Eric, does he need a suit?"

"I do not require to hide from chaos," Eric said. "I process chaos very differently. And I will protect you where I can."

"You can't really fly me out of places, right?"

"I'm not that strong." He raised both eyebrows as he looked her over.

"You know, on Earth, I would have taken offense to that. I would have assumed you were body shaming me." Quinn let the statement fall nice and flat.

Eric actually had the good grace to blush. "I do apologize. That was not my intention."

"Good." Quinn clapped her hands together, noticing that she really was hungry. "I need to grab a quick lunch, but otherwise, do we have everything?

"We have the same breathing food and repellent food. And just in case, we also have the same injury balm. Our kits are made up." Malakai handed her a crossover bag.

"We can head down once you've eaten," Lynx said, like he was proud of remembering some of them had to eat. "You'll just have to access the console first to give them both temporary access."

"Do you want to wait until tomorrow and feel more rested?" Misha asked.

"You know what? I'm feeling great energy-level-wise." Quinn patted her stomach. "How about you guys?" She looked at Lynx, Malakai, and Eric.

They all nodded.

Quinn took a deep breath. "I think we should just go down now before I have complete and utter second thoughts."

And so, looking like they were about to go and dive into the ocean sans oxygen tanks, with little pouches that were liquid proof holding all their supplies, Quinn, Lynx, Malakai, and Eric headed off to eat before going to swim in chaotic sludge.

12

BENEATH THE CORE

Malakai gasped softly as his feet touched the soft and spongy floor of the core level and looked like he was about to speak. Lynx beat him to it. "We go this way."

Quinn raised an eyebrow at Lynx when he began to turn away from the center of the room. "What way?"

"This way, trust me." And the three of them followed Lynx to the left. Quinn was sure they were going to walk into the wall, but instead, they walked past a section of it into what looked like a very dimly lit, tightly spaced corridor.

Sure, her claustrophobia wasn't going to overreact to this at all.

Fantastic.

"What's this?" she asked, trying to distract herself from the space that felt like it was shrinking in on her.

"It's a service tunnel," Lynx said very slowly, as if he wasn't entirely certain how to explain it. "People . . . other than you, should never get close to the core. Frankly, even this is pushing it, but I don't believe this is something just you and I can correct. Using the tunnel, we circumvent the entire core cavern and we don't risk anybody else being, shall we say, contaminated by that energy."

"Contaminated by the Library's energy?" Quinn asked, not entirely sure what to make of that.

"Why do you think the Librarians are required to have very specific affinities, Quinn?" Lynx said softly. "If they don't have those, the Library's core will destroy them. There's no way to link to the Library fully, as you do, unless you have the affinities that allow you to do so."

"Oh," Quinn said, feeling a little sad to know that no one else could lend the core company like she enjoyed doing, "I just thought it was a magic thing."

"It sort of is. It's also a neural network compatibility thing and for a lot of people even trying to connect to the core or trying to be directly near the core would result in mostly fried brains." There was a lingering sadness in Lynx's tone. Like he'd seen precisely that happen.

"Ew," Quinn said at the visual.

"At least there'd be something for zombies to eat," Eric said, his tone flat.

Quinn couldn't help the laugh that escaped her. Maybe it was nervous laughter because she couldn't help but wonder what might have gone wrong if she hadn't truly been compatible. But it was also partially because Eric wasn't from Earth, which meant zombies must really exist.

It made her wonder just who had visited earth in the past to have so many different creatures of mythologies and stories actually exist. But now wasn't the time for this train of thought!

Right now, she had to concentrate on the filtration system. It didn't seem like something they could afford to screw up.

"Well, I learn something new every day," Quinn said.

"Me too," Malakai said, walking against the outer wall, and furtively glancing over his shoulder. "Are you sure this is far enough away from the core that I'm not going to have my brains melted?"

Lynx tossed him an evil smirk. "Maybe. But you are a DaríghÁh-nish, so how would I know?"

"That's a low blow," Malakai said. But even his lips were tugging up, he was fighting a smile too.

Quinn grinned to herself as they continued to walk the long circular corridor. Lynx wasn't kidding when he said that this was taking them the long way around the massive cavern.

Finally, after a little bit of small talk and several more minutes, they came to an opening. They stood on a landing. On one side were stairs that led down.

Quinn leaned over the railing and peeked. "Wow, that has to be, what, sixty-odd stairs and a landing? And wait, there's more after that."

Lynx nodded. "Yes. It's two levels of steps, so about a hundred twenty steps for every level, or story of the Library. The landings are there to let you rest up, especially if you're climbing up them."

"What's that?" Quinn pointed to the metal doors several meters down from the stairway entrance.

"That is the elevator and right now I wouldn't trust it not to stop and leave us in the middle of the rock." Lynx sounded very matter-of-fact about the whole thing.

"Oh," Quinn said. Aradie chose that moment to alight off her shoulder and glide down the stairs. Quinn glared after the owl, wishing she could do the same.

"But," Lynx continued, "if we get the filtration system up and running like we need to, that shouldn't be a problem anymore and we'll be able to take it back up."

Quinn felt a wave of relief rush through her. "I like that. Walking down stairs is a lot easier than walking back up them."

"Yes, especially since right now there are eight landing levels, so you're looking at about nine hundred sixty steps," Lynx said.

"Seriously?" Malakai groaned. "That many?"

"Hey, think of it as a leg day," Lynx said, grinning.

Malakai scowled at him. "You can just teleport down there and cheat," he said, at the same time that Quinn spoke.

"I've never been a gym person," she muttered under her breath.

Malakai laughed. "Yeah, that shows in your training. Trust me."

"There's no need to be mean about it," Quinn said, but she felt a little more lighthearted than she had a few minutes ago. Malakai was right though. "Why don't you just blip to the bottom, Lynx?"

"Same reason Eric isn't just going to descend vertically."

"I'm not?" Eric shrugged at Lynx's flat look. "I guess I'll grace you with my company."

They all groaned and began the trudge downstairs.

"Um," Quinn said, after they'd passed the first landing. She didn't like the way all she could hear was the touch of their feet on the steps. It was a very dull sound considering the surface of the steps was similar to the floor in the core room. "Tell me, shouldn't we have brought repair supplies with us?"

"Of course we should have," Lynx said, "and did. Malakai and Eric both have them in their storage."

Quinn wondered why she had completely and utterly forgotten about the existence of storage. "My mind has apparently become a sieve," she said.

Another two landings passed and Quinn was starting to sweat despite going downstairs instead of up them. She wanted to say *Are we there yet?* but she very obviously knew they were not.

Malakai nudged her with his elbow. "You feel up to this?"

She flashed him a smile. "Yes, I actually do."

"Good," he said. "So stop sighing every ten steps,"

She grimaced. "Am I really doing that?"

"Yes."

"Okay," she said, and started running over her mental exercises as they took the rest of the stairs to keep her mind occupied.

The whole rest of the way down, while she demolished and rebuilt her new mental barrier tighter and tighter, she couldn't help but wonder just what it was like down below. She had thoughts about it, of course, but she knew that nothing was going to hold up to whatever it was.

When they finally reached the bottom, it didn't immediately open out into the cavern. Instead, they found themselves in a small ante chamber, and Lynx stopped them all.

"Okay, pop one of your resistance balls," Lynx instructed.

Quinn had to stop herself from snickering like a twelve-year-old boy. Lynx flashed her a stern look, and she barely managed to choke down the laughter.

"We're about to walk in. I guess we're going to see if the suits can withstand the amount of chaotic energy that is theoretically bouncing around down here at the moment," Lynx continued.

"Why can't we feel it here? Aren't we super close?" Quinn asked.

"Yes, but there is a magical barrier in place that basically keeps the fumes from entering the Library," Lynx explained.

"Oh, good to know," Quinn thought. At least there was a barrier, so if she totally botched the entire operation, maybe they could at least evacuate the Library?

Malakai nudged her again. "You realize that you show almost every thought and emotion on your face, right?"

Quinn could feel herself blush, especially since he'd mentioned something similar before. "Well, I didn't realize it was that bad, but I do now."

"Don't be so hard on yourself. You're not going to screw it up. It was screwed up long before you got here," Malakai attempted to reassure her.

Quinn barked a laugh out in surprise. "That actually makes me feel better, thanks."

"Are we up for this?" Lynx said.

Eric crossed his arms, hovering in the air. "We've been up for this all day," he said. "I wish you other beings would just hurry up. I could have been down here hours ago."

"We can't all fly yet, Eric," Lynx retorted.

"That's quite obvious," he said. But there was still a grin on his face as they proceeded forward.

Quinn had to stop herself from being distracted by the *yet* in Lynx's reply and directed her attention to the fact that Eric had apparently walked through a solid wall, as had Lynx in corporeal form. She could feel the barrier as they walked through it and fervently hoped she wouldn't get stuck in the middle of a wall.

"'Watch out for that tree,' my ass. 'Watch out for that bloody stone wall,'" she muttered to herself.

And then most of the thoughts in her head simply stopped. Right in front of them was a chamber, a cavern, so huge and encompassing that Quinn couldn't even comprehend it's sheer size for a moment. It spread so far out in front of them that she could barely see the other side.

At even intervals, all throughout this massive underground body of liquid were round pillars that rose all the way up to the ceiling. Eight of them were dark. Their sides, not the same stone as the rest of the ceiling or walls, had a strange blackness to them. They looked sort of like those old computers in movies that had pieces you could slot in and out of them. But these were dormant; there were no flashing lights. There was nothing.

However, over to the right and relatively close, stood one massive pillar. It was lit up beautifully, with blues and greens interspersed, going through dark blue, through many different greens, to a brilliant and pure light blue. Quinn knew from her readings that the chaotic elements had to go through filtration stages. It made sense that different colors would represent those different steps.

Around the base of that pillar, the black sludge was thin. It was easy to catch glimpses of the mana as it lapped at the base in a circumference of brilliant blue. The liquid moved. At first, she thought the black covering was solid, and perhaps cracked in places, but she realized that it was sludge. Thick, probably about two feet thick, the whole way around, except for right next to the fully functioning filter.

Beneath the sludge, now and again, as the liquid moved, she could see a beautiful, brilliant blue shining through.

Magic and Mana—practically sparkling.

Lynx sighed. "It's shrunk. I should have known."

Quinn blinked. "You mean it's supposed to be bigger than this."

Lynx shrugged uncomfortably. "Usually, when it's fully operational and thriving, you can't even see its end."

Quinn mulled that over and looked around at the massive cavern. She found it difficult to believe it could get bigger.

And then, she finally focused on the tenth column, at the very far back left. It wasn't doing as well as its front-right cousin. Those little filter patches were more yellow, orange, and red, and in some places even black, than they were blue. There were only a few functional strips from what Quinn could tell from so far away. But the rest were very obviously, and brightly, malfunctioning.

Because the sludge around that pillar, even though it was so far away, she could tell it was almost as thick as the sludge right near her foot.

She turned to Lynx. "You've got to be kidding me. That's the one I have to repair?" She pointed to the malfunctioning pillar.

He refused to make eye contact as he nodded. "Yeah, the one on the very far end."

"You have *got* to be kidding me," she repeated.

Lynx still refused to meet Quinn's gaze.

"I'm waiting," she said. "Why did you run that one down? Shouldn't they have been changed long before it got this bad?"

He sighed. "Look, we ran on minimal power to avoid stopping filtration altogether. Over the decades, we would swap which filters were active. Booting a third one up as we powered the second one down, briefly allowing them to overlap. At some stage during the closure, all of them have been active. It's just that several months ago, this one started having difficulty, which meant that we couldn't swap it out for another because we lacked the power to do so since it wasn't operating at optimal levels. Not to mention the others disappearing from our view through the system around the same time. That's when I started reaching even further with the search for a new Librarian. I was desperate."

Quinn cringed. She was only just now truly grasping *how* desperate they must have been when they found her. "Well, why can't we activate it now?"

"Because we're pretty much running on one filter and the amount of power required to fully reignite one of the other filters is a lot more than when you're just transferring operation. We can't afford to transfer from a malfunctioning filter right now. It'll be different once we hit the next power level, but we're still a ways away from that."

"And we can't wait that long to change it. I get it." She thought it through for a second. "So now you need to tell me how the hell am I supposed to reach that filter? The sludge isn't solid. Don't tell me to walk on water."

"That's the interesting part of this. Usually, we would use one of those." He pointed off to the corner where there was something that almost looked like a paddleboard.

"And let me guess, you can't paddleboard through sludge." She groaned at the thought of trying to paddle that thing through something as thick as sludge.

"Precisely." Lynx answered.

"So what do you suggest we do?"

"We are going to have to use a roundabout way to get there."

"Just spill it, Lynx." Quinn almost snapped but managed to leave it at clipped.

"Stop beating around the bush," Eric said. "Don't expect me to fly her. I can't do that."

Malakai, in the meantime, had withdrawn one of his swords. He was polishing at a spot on it.

It was a sword Quinn hadn't seen before. It glinted black, sort of like Aradie's feathers did. Iridescent colors shone through it in a way that reminded her of tempered steel.

"We're going to have to cut through it for want of a better word," Lynx said.

Quinn grinned at the fact that he'd picked that phrase up from her. There was no way he'd ever said that before she came along. "You don't mean me, right?"

"No, you can't cut through it. That's why Malakai is here." Lynx gestured to their non-flying party member.

Quinn turned to the elf prince. He shrugged. "It's a, shall we say, hereditary ability." He didn't sound excited by it at all. He cracked his shoulders back. "Let's hope it works," he said, and took a few steps back.

He glanced at all three of them, waiting. Then rolled his eyes and spoke again. "Step back further. You're not going to want to get hit by the aftermath of this."

Quinn shivered. She suddenly felt like this was a very bad idea.

"Okay," she said, watching him. "Be careful," she called out.

Malakai flashed her a grin and took a deep breath. He wound his arm back, holding the sword in a backward grip. He executed an intricate series of turns. Halfway through, the blade began to glow with an eerie, green-black light. Then he swept forward, going in low and dragging his right knee behind him as he lunged and executed a low, reverberating slice. A whooshing of wind accompanied the action.

And then it hit the sludge.

A backlash of wind knocked the rest of them on their. But when Quinn looked back to where the sword strike had hit, about six feet by four feet, was clear blue mana.

13

THE LAKE

The way Malakai's sword cut a neat area of sludge away, while the remnants of the breeze it left behind whisked the sludge to pile on top of more of that crap a short distance away, was a fascinating sight to behold. It was also very time consuming.

Quinn ran through her mental exercises while he continued to clear away for them. The air down here was thicker, not as filtered as she was used to. No real pun intended there. But there was definitely something less than pleasant about it. The sludge gave off a dimly sulfuric scent. Not the most delightful.

She glanced over at Lynx, who was supervising while Eric dragged something into view.

"What is that?" she asked.

"It's the skiff," Eric snapped.

"The skiff?" she asked, crossing her arms and casting a glance back at the paddle board he'd indicated earlier.

"Yes, skiff," Lynx inserted, while Eric tugged it over and got it ready to put into the clear path of mana water. "We're not all going to fit onto that paddleboard."

Quinn realized that the skiff was a very flat, large piece of material, wood-like in appearance. Although it didn't look like any wood that she'd seen before. It was about eight feet wide and about twelve feet long if she had to guess, and at the edges there was about a six-inch lip that should keep any mana liquid from breaking over the side. If mana lakes had waves, that is.

"That doesn't look very big."

"Well, it's the larger of the choices." Lynx shrugged.

"Can't we just magic one into existence?" she asked.

Lynx spread his arms out, but it was Eric who answered. "Have you looked around here? I don't think we'd need to be doing this if you could just magic down here without the excess chaos trying to rip you apart."

While no one spoke, and Malakai continued his sword work, Quinn realized this chamber was alive with noise. There was a constant sludgy lapping at the shore where they stood, but there was also an underlying sound that she couldn't quite place. It sounded like a pump, maybe? "What is that noise?"

"That's the pump," Lynx answered, not truly paying attention to her. "It maintains the pipes that flush the residue out of the lake. Partially it's infected mana. So, you know, build-up."

"Is it supposed to sound like that?" she asked.

Lynx shook his head. "Nope. But once we get this done, it'll be a whole lot better."

"If you say so." Quinn frowned and looked at the wide skiff with its two long paddles. "Why doesn't it have a motor?" she asked.

Lynx raised an eyebrow at her. "What good would a motor do in that liquid? Don't you think it would churn everything back together?"

"But don't the filters separate it?" This was getting confusing.

"The filters suck the water through from underneath and cleanse it of chaotic energy and redistribute it to the universe. Generally, there aren't more than sludge flecks on the surface of the lake. If there are leftovers after filtration, usually the creatures in the lake will take care of them," Lynx explained calmly.

As if to punctuate his words, there was a dull pop in the middle of the lake, followed by a sucking sound as some sort of eel-like creature jumped like a dolphin. Quinn balked at that. "There are creatures in the lake?"

"They're mana-dense creatures. They're not interested in anything but the mana and the sludge."

"And they're also capable of helping rid the lake of sludge?" Quinn blinked furiously at so much new information.

Lynx nodded. "Without their help, we would have been completely overrun and there would never have been a Library to summon you with."

"Good to know." Quinn didn't feel very good about it at all.

Finally, Malakai cleared a very large portion of the sludge away, revealing the beautiful sky blue mana underneath. While the sludge slowly seeped from where it had been piled, it would take a good fifteen to twenty minutes to begin refilling the path he'd cleared. He sheathed his sword and glanced over, some of his usually meticulously tied hair hanging in his face. "So we all get on the skiff and paddle out?"

"Not quite yet," Lynx said, motioning to Quinn. "You need to come over here, and place your hand on the front of the skiff."

Quinn glanced down and it looked like a series of runes, very similar those in Lynx's hair.

"Place your hand on them."

And she did. Suddenly a screen popped up in front of her.

Linking to Librarian

Calibrating . . .

Calibrating . . .

Thought directions accepted.

Direct thoughts appropriately.

Quinn raised an eyebrow. "So what, now it's going to let me direct it?"

"Yes, we only need the paddles for course correction," Lynx said. "The sludge isn't exactly cooperative."

"Good to know," Eric said, crossing his arms as he hovered in the air again. "There was no way I was going to be able to paddle."

Quinn got into the skiff with Malakai's help and glanced at him. He seemed to be sweating slightly and looked a little pale.

"You should probably eat one of these energy balls," she said and gave it to him.

He flashed her a weak smile and did exactly as she'd suggested.

"We'll have to move slowly," he said. "I'll need to clear the way from the bow of the skiff so that we have the ability to cut through the sludge a little easier. But since my movements need to be smaller so we don't capsize, it won't be quite as effective."

"Okay," she said, glancing up toward the malfunctioning pillar. It had to be at least four football fields away. That was, what, just over a quarter of a mile? This place was massive.

"The distance is deceptive, Quinn," Lynx said. "That is a lot more than a quarter of a mile."

"Why does it seem so close, then?" she asked, strengthening her mental barriers again since she'd obviously inadvertently let that thought escape.

"It's all a matter of the layers in this place. It's about a mile away. Think of one of your earthen neighborhood blocks."

Quinn looked all around the lake. "Those pillars are all about, what, half a mile apart, then?" she recalibrated how she perceived the entire area.

"Approximately," Lynx said.

Sometimes Quinn wondered if he didn't explain things fully because sometimes the answers were a little too convoluted. She could live with those instances.

Quinn fell silent, directing the skiff toward the pillar, Ganyon. All the while, she maintained her mental barrier exercises, though she doubted she could make them any stronger. She wanted to figure out how to make mental cement, so that nothing could ever get through.

She glanced out over the massive lake, pondering its mechanics. She needed diagrams to understand this whole filtration cycle thing. "So . . . which one of these is Ashiron?"

"Ah." Lynx's eyes darkened and a scowl passed over his face quickly. "Directly opposite Ganyon, on the other side of the lake."

Quinn peered over, squinting. But it was dark and devoid of any movement. The sludge pile-up around the base appeared to be heftier than anywhere else. It writhed and moved as if of its own accord. Quinn shuddered. "We'll deal with that one once we've sorted the repairs, right?"

Lynx nodded as his scowl crept back into place.

Every now and then, she thought she saw a bulge in the sludge that covered the top of the mana.

"It's okay," Lynx said, leaning in. "That's just one of our little amphibian friends."

"Are you just going to leave it that vague, or are you going to tell me what they're like?" She paused before adding, "I mean, I saw the eel-like one dolphin jumping but . . ."

"Other than that one, they're unlike anything you have on your homeworld. So yes, for now, I'll keep it vague, because that's not why we're here." This time he hesitated before continuing. "When the lake is clear again, we can come watch its inhabitants."

Quinn grinned. She liked that idea.

Malakai performed a miniature version of the sweep he had done to clear their initial path. The skiff rocked fiercely, and Quinn almost toppled over the side as it swayed from side to side.

"Sorry about that," Malakai said. "I'll aim for less impact next time."

Quinn nodded as the skiff continued to move slowly forward and adjusted her stance wider to hopefully compensate for anymore rocking. The runes on the craft glowed, propelling it ever so slightly. She watched Lynx direct the skiff with occasional corrections through one of the paddles. The sound of the pumps in the background reassured her that everything was as it should be . . . comparatively, anyway.

She turned back to look at where they'd come from. About five hundred feet separated them from the edge, and she noticed that the sludge had already begun closing back over their path.

"That doesn't look good," she said.

Lynx shrugged. "Sludge is gonna sludge."

She glared at him. "Where did you get that saying from?"

He shrugged. "I just thought it appropriate."

She rolled her eyes, but couldn't help grinning. "Thanks, Lynx. It feels a little dire down here."

He shook his head. "It's no more dire than anything else that we've had to take care of since you got here."

"Oh, so you mean it's pretty much necessary to avoid the end of the universe?"

"Precisely," Lynx said. "Everything happens for a reason, Quinn. We just haven't figured this one out yet."

Quinn fell silent after that rather prophetic take on their current circumstances. She decided to take in the first pillar they passed. It wasn't right next to them, but it was gigantic up close. It rose all the way up to the ceiling, seven or eight stories above them, even if just going by the stairs they'd come down. She looked all the way up, craning her neck.

"That's ridiculous. Does it really reach the ceiling of the cavern?"

"Yeah, of course it does. It takes it all up through the pillars in the Library to distribute the mana." Lynx gave her a look that said she should have already figured that out.

"Oh. Interesting," Quinn said. "But the filters don't go all the way up, do they?"

"Nope, they do not. So you won't be quite that high." He smiled at her encouragingly.

"Great, I've never been very good with heights. Five stories versus eight, that should be no problem." Quinn couldn't keep the sarcasm from her voice.

"We're not leaving you to do it alone, Quinn. We've got safety gear."

"I know," she said, but right now she was feeling decidedly grumbly. "Why do I have to come and do this? You'd think the Librarian could delegate a little more."

"Right now, you have to do it because you are the only one properly hooked into the system. Everything that gets changed down here requires Librarian approval. And the only reason we could keep swapping between filters for so long was because the Library was in emergency mode. That alone enables certain criteria to be overruled and run solely by me. So right now, you are required to do this. But going forward, the Library should have enough power that it won't need to use your energy and your corporeal form, shall we say, to do it."

Quinn clenched her fists in an effort to stop them shaking. "It's just . . . it's a lot all at once." She hated how often she heard herself saying that.

"There's nothing we can do about it." Lynx's voice was soft, and reassuring. With perhaps a hint of pity. "We're almost there, Quinn. Just a little bit more and things will get easier."

And that's when Quinn noticed the strange, bloody reddish-black fog that rose up off the sludge the farther out in the lake they got.

"What is that?" she asked, popping another one of the chaos resistance balls into her mouth for good measure, even though there was still a good thirty minutes left on the other one.

"Oh," Lynx said, glancing at it, "that would be chaos miasma, I guess you could call it. It's not usually here when the filters are up and working properly, but like I said, we have an excess of chaotic energy down here and well, that's one of the side effects."

"So the fish or sea creatures or whatever they are, they don't absorb that?" She was still eyeing it warily.

"No. No, they do not. That is part of what needs to be filtered." He tapped her armor. "And it's why you wear these"—he pointed to the resistance outfits—"and consume the resistance balls. Just to be on the safe side."

Every few minutes, the skiff shook and they all braced as Malakai continued to clear the way ahead of them. Quinn eyed the miasma with a very apprehensive feeling growing in her stomach. She was beginning to have an attack of the nerves. "So how will we do this?

"Eric will fly up with the filters next to you while we strap you and Malakai into the harnesses that you'll be able to scale the pillars with." Lynx said very matter-of-factly.

"Are you kidding me?" she said. "I have to scale that?"

"How else did you think you'd replace the filters?" Lynx actually sounded shocked.

"Really? Have you done it yourself, Lynx?" Quinn glared at him.

"No, but I've been there while it's been done. Sometimes we have to resort to manual means of accomplishing goals. So let's just get the Library power stockpile filled up, and then you're not going to have to do this much."

Being angry with Lynx for the state of things wasn't productive and it really wasn't fair either, but that didn't mean that she wasn't pissed off that she had to do all of this stuff when she hadn't even applied for the position like the assistants had. "Fine. So, Eric will fly the supplies up and I will replace the filters. What's Malakai going to be doing up there?"

"Making sure you don't get hurt." Another comment by Lynx that sounded as if he thought she should already know these answers.

Quinn calmed her breathing, and her mind, and finally spoke again. "And what's he supposed to make sure I don't get hurt by?"

Lynx pointed above them.

She glanced up and realized that something was flying around up near the cavern ceiling. They'd looked like dots at first, but now she saw they were moving. "What are those?" she asked.

"While Aradie may be able to take care of some of those, as she has been doing since she flew down the steps ahead of us, Malakai will make sure none of them get you in the air."

"You mean they might dive-bomb me?"

"Or worse," Lynx said. "Those are chaotic miasma drones. Like I said, it's not a frequent occurrence. It's just gotten really bad down here."

Quinn used the calming exercises again. They were drawing closer and closer to the Ganyon pillar. And it rose up above her. They were almost there. Just as the skiff began to pull across the Ganyon filtration pillar, Quinn got a message pop-up:

Mental Barrier: Level Three.

And that was when something bumped into the skiff from underneath. Quinn stumbled to the side, barely catching herself on the pole support, only to turn around and see Malakai in the midst of completely overbalancing. He had been, she thought, about to take one of his strikes to clear the rest of the way. His arms flailed, including his sword arm, and she had to duck under it as she reached forward, grabbing onto the pole next to her and managed to catch his hand. The strain pulled at her until he righted himself.

"Thanks, Quinn." He seemed a bit shocked. "That was entirely too embarrassing."

Quinn turned around to Lynx and said, "I thought these amphibian creatures were supposed to be friendly."

"Well, they are, they're just a little eager to meet you, maybe." He winked at her.

The skiff practically grated into place next to stone steps that went down into the sludge. Lynx tied them off with a rope, and then helped them all onto the stairs. The base of the colossal column was much larger than Quinn had expected. It must have been a good forty feet square.

As her foot hit the main landing of the pillar, a pop-up flashed in front of her.

Welcome Librarian, to Pillar Ganyon
Connection Status: Infected; Replacement Urgent
Treatment: Required
Effect: Dangerous
Do you wish to synchronize?
Yes or *No*

14

____

PILLARS

QUINN BLINKED AT THE WORDS IN FRONT OF HER. "LYNX?"

"What?" he said as he finished tying off the skiff.

"What does this mean? It's trying to link with me." Quinn pushed down on the confusion. Since she was already linked with the Library, she assumed it was with everything inside of it . . . or a part of it.

"Well, of course it's trying. It's part of the Library. You should . . ." He glanced and reassessed as he realized what was in front of her. "That explains everything. Infected; replacement urgent." He sighed. "Okay, well, I mean, do you want to save the pillar or not?"

"Of course I do." Quinn indicated that, yes, she wanted to synchronize, activating the process. She was not, however, prepared for the sheer amount of information that spread throughout her head. Some of it felt as if she was watching the pillar corrode from the amount of miasma and chaotic energy that began to stockpile in the cavern. The time in the vision sped up, showing her the not-so-gradual decay of the filtration system. At the end of the visions, another pop-up appeared.

Do you wish to hook into the harness system?
Yes or No?

She glanced over at Lynx again. "So the harness system is a part of the pillar and you're not just going to hoist me up, climbing wall style?"

"Of course it's a part of the system. It's an entire machinery mechanism integrated into the pillars themselves." He scoffed.

"Why didn't you tell me that?" she asked.

"You didn't ask? I assumed that you would assume the harness was attached." He shrugged.

Quinn took a deep breath, mental fortitude for the win. She left the prompt and minimized that section of her vision. She glanced up at the top of the pillar.

Up close, it was even more daunting than it had been as they approached. Then she focused on the massive filters right in front of her. They were shoved in, in sections four wide, with about a foot between each section. Each filter was about two feet high and maybe half a foot wide and they went all around the circular exterior. "Okay, so these filters are massive."

Lynx's brows furrowed and he looked slightly confused. "Did you expect them to be small, given the size of the pillars?"

"Not really," Quinn said, "but looking at them from a distance, they seemed smaller than this. How am I supposed to balance with these?"

"Once we have enough of the components that we need, we'll make filtration golems, and after repairing this pillar, you'll be able to delegate maintenance to them. Right now, we do not currently have the correct supplies to create said golems, nor do we have enough power to activate other functions." Lynx shook his head. "This needs to be done the old-fashioned way. And you're not just going up in a harness, you'll be on a platform. It's not as dangerous as you're picturing."

"Old-fashioned." Quinn let out a sigh. "So there'll be a trio of us up there. Malakai, Eric, and I?"

Lynx nodded "Malakai has the ability to kill the pests flying up there, and Eric has a weight-reduction satchel that is lined with its own chaos-destroying system so he can dispose of the contaminated ones in midair with you."

"Good to know," Quinn said, as she turned that idea over in her mind. "Okay, I guess I do want to use the harness system." She indicated *yes* on her interface and immediately heard a whirring and some clicks and bangs as something shifted into place. She didn't look up.

Instead, she noticed that her HUD flashed more information across.

Current filters available: 1,782.

Current replacements required: 1,291

"That sounds like a lot of work," Quinn muttered under her breath.

Malakai nudged her. "Of course it's going to be a lot of work. What hasn't been a lot of work since you got here?"

Quinn laughed. "You make a fine point, my elven friend."

"Stop calling me that," he said, with a long-suffering groan.

She winked at him.

Just then, what looked oddly like one of those window-cleaning devices from high-rises in cities like New York and Chicago reached the bottom level. It appeared to be anchored into the pillar directly on tracks that ran between the different filter sections.

"This is it," Quinn said. It was about four feet wide and about ten feet long, slightly curved to match around the massive pillar. "It's a good thing you've got wings," she said to Eric.

She opened the little gate and stepped into it. There were harnesses and belts. She put one of the latter around her waist and her thighs, tightening each strap, and then clipped what looked like harness wires into place in two of the heavy-duty fasteners. She couldn't quite reach the third one at the back.

Malakai stepped in and relieved her of the hook, clipping it firmly into place. "There you go."

She grimaced. "Thanks for that. I don't want to plummet to my death."

He flashed her a smile. "Well, how do you want to do this? You want us to start down here and work our way up, or start up high and work our way down?"

Quinn gazed back up at the top again and felt queasy at even the thought of being there. "I think I'll feel more comfortable if we start up higher and work toward the ground. Like it's a reward to be back on solid footing."

"Sounds like a plan," Malakai said, as he too snapped himself into a harness. He didn't appear to need any help fastening his clips.

The next thing she knew, Lynx was also in the movable platform with them, but he perched in the middle and, of course, added no weight to it, so he didn't even make it budge. The upside of being incorporeal on command.

"Okay, then," he said. "Up we go, Quinn."

She tapped on the edge a couple of times. It was there in her mind, just like the skiff had been. She thought directly at it, asking it to move up to the top so they could begin replacements in an efficient manner. The movable platform jolted ever so slightly once before moving quite smoothly and far too fast for Quinn's liking up to the highest filters.

The journey up, while speedy, was also somewhat soothing once she got used to it. It felt like an amusement park ride. She just hoped it didn't suddenly plummet and lose its brakes on the way down. Or even just randomly come uncoupled plummeting her and Malakai to their deaths.

Aradie swooped over, tossing a couple of visions at Quinn.

"Oh," Quinn said, as one of them flashed through her mind. The creatures up here that Aradie was chasing looked oddly like massive flies, except they had about eight multifaceted eyes and as many wings. From what she could tell, they buzzed around each of the pillars like a swarm of angry bees. She shuddered, hoping that the bird and Malakai could keep them away from her.

The movable platform came to rest about five stories up and Quinn refused to look down. Instead, she focused on what was directly in front of her.

Begin replacing filters in section 39B.

Yes or No?

"Yes," Quinn said.

There was a clicking and the sounds of what to her resembled a hydraulic system releasing itself. Four of the filters jutted out ever so slightly and Quinn picked the first one out, her gloved hands not making contact with what looked to be extremely dirty filters. Goop dripped down what was left of the internal material. Eric held a massive bag out to her. So big, that it dwarfed his actual size. She inserted the waste filter and it disappeared.

"Don't these have to be replaced all the time?" she asked as she began to pull out a new one from her own satchel.

Lynx shrugged. "Not really. The pillars are usually self-cleaning. Purified mana is an excellent cleaning agent. Full replacement doesn't usually need to happen for hundreds, sometimes thousands of years on each pillar even if they're all being utilized at the same time."

The answer made Quinn thoughtful, even as she eyed the massive flies starting to move closer to their pillar.

There were definitely way too many coincidences in this whole conspiracy against the Library thing.

Malakai cut one of the flies in half, and it fell over the moving platform past Quinn's face. A sliver of blood landed on the platform itself. Quinn waited a moment, realized that the blood at least wasn't acidic, and felt slightly safer. She finally placed the filter she'd been holding into its relevant slot. It clicked in, but it was obvious the filters wouldn't be moved back into place by the mechanism until all four were done.

Three more and as she pushed the third one in, clicking it into place, the hydraulic sealed itself again, but they remained in a deep blue pulsating light instead of flicking through the many colors she'd seen from one of the others.

"Interesting color," she said.

"It's recalibrating." Lynx offered by way of explanation.

There appeared to be about twenty filters reachable from each platform stopping point that needed replacing, with four stopping points around each level. And about twenty-three or so vertical rows that she'd need to get through. Several sections had control panels inserted in them instead of filter slots. It was going to take a lot to replace all of these. Still, Quinn went on to the next and the next section. Then they were moved around to the stopping point with the movable platform. She got into a rhythm, pulling filters out, disposing of them, replacing, pulling out, disposing, replacing . . .

It fell into a monotonous, if satisfying, cadence.

Quinn sighed as her shoulders began to ache ever so slightly from different actions than she was used to. At least she had a solution for it.

Taliar's Regeneration: Activated

That should help with the soreness at least.

The one other thing that she did notice in the back of her mind was the miasma drones. They seemed to constantly inch closer to where they were working on the pillar. She needed to concentrate only on the filters and the system and getting it back up and running. But their constant presence unnerved her.

The air on the nape of her neck felt like it was electrified. It felt like she had tens of thousands of eyes focused on just her, like they knew she was the one who was making these possible. "So tell me, Lynx, what's it with these blow flies?"

"Well, they're actually miasma drones."

Quinn raised an eyebrow.

"Miasma drones. That's their name." He sounded slightly defensive.

While she'd gathered that from the previous description, she hadn't realized Lynx had a thing for not giving creatures nicknames. She scanned the creatures with the Library.

Miasma Drones

*Levels: 85**

**level denotes age and not power in creatures such as the drones.*

"These things don't die in like a week or something?" Quinn said, disbelieving.

"No, they tend to hang around and just get bigger and bigger and bigger the more they feed off the miasma. So let's get those filters changed," Lynx said, his fake enthusiasm really hitting a nerve with Quinn.

"You have a lot of creatures that gorge themselves on power residue in this place," she muttered under her breath, not expecting an answer.

There was too much work to be done anyway. The whole process began to get sort of obnoxious. She'd lost count of how many filters she'd actually replaced. On the bright side, however, they had moved about nine levels down.

"We're getting through this," she said.

"Yes, but you're starting to look pale," Malakai said, and pulled out a bag of food from his own storage ring. "Here, Cook made us lunch, dinner, and breakfast."

"Oh, great." It was only upon seeing the food that she realized just how famished she was. Her stomach even punctuated the sensation with an audible growl. "I guess we're going to be here a while."

She bit into the delicious sandwich after taking a moment to cleanse her hands and munched away happily. This wasn't really so bad. A short break gave her a welcome new perspective. It was monotonous and annoying, but they were making visible progress. At least Malakai, Lynx, and Eric weren't bad company either.

Craning her neck she looked back up at where they'd come from and noticed that many of the rows were now oscillating between the same beautiful color spectrums that the functioning pillar did. It just took each row a while to calibrate.

Glancing down, she wished for a second that she hadn't, but she could have sworn the chaotic sludge was already becoming thinner around the base.

She popped the last of her food into her mouth and glared at the flies she could see. Their buzzing never stopped crescendoing.

"Come on, we better just keep going," she said. The sooner they got done with this, the faster she'd get away from those damned drones.

Quinn set about getting back into the rhythm of ripping out and replacing the old filters. Some of the ones she was coming across now were so black that any filtration particles from within the actual filter had dissolved into a black, goopy mess.

She managed to spread out a plastic sheet Malakai handed her from his inventory to catch most of it, filtering it into the bag that Eric was holding. This last section was particularly nasty, and she had a feeling that going forward, much of what lay beneath them would be the same. The miasma had really screwed up this particular pillar.

She was lucky she didn't really have a queasy stomach or this would have been a lot more difficult to navigate.

Quinn was so focused on her current rhythm of ripping out the used filters and replacing them with new ones that she lost track of her surroundings. The dedicated pattern with which she removed, destroyed, and replaced the filters held all of her focus.

"Quinn?" Malakai's voice held a tremor in it.

"What?" she said, still almost robotically ripping out the next bad filter and replacing it with a new one. She refused to let anything interrupt her rhythm.

"You might want to . . ." He was speaking very softly, extremely calmly, and oddly slowly for Malakai.

"Spit it out," she said just as softly, because some part of her brain recognized the fact that maybe there was currently a necessity to speak that way. An image flashed through her mind courtesy of Aradie, and Quinn's hand stopped mid-insertion.

"Oh . . ." she breathed out.

There were a lot of things that Quinn was never fond of as a human on Earth. One of those things was summertime with flies that hung around everywhere. One of her foster homes in her early teens had been on a farm, and flies were everywhere that summer. It was one of her least favorite memories. So the image Aradie showed her reignited portions of a past she'd prefer to forget about.

For just a split second, her mind panicked, and that was when some of her mental training took over. Yes, she could understand that from the memory she had, being panicked was a definite option to choose, but that was just it. She didn't *have* to choose that option. She knew what flies were like, and *Mental Fortitude and Time Dilation* had taught her one very specific thing: she could think so much faster and so much longer than outward appearances suggested.

She'd been sucked through into another world and thrown into a magical Library that defied her definition of what she would have thought a Library would be in a magical world. It had so many problems, worse than computer programming, worse than glitching systems, and yet it had somehow became home. She'd be damned if she was going to let a bunch of overgrown horseflies interfere with that.

Calculating their distance in what seemed like an eternity but in reality was only a couple of seconds, Quinn dug deep into the knowledge she'd gained over the last few weeks. There was so much of it, but she dismissed all irrelevant information inside of a split second.

Not All Just Hot Air: That Which Doesn't Float Sinks had been a magnificent book. She hadn't given it nearly enough credit for being what it was.

Coming back into herself, she looked over her right shoulder beyond Eric.

"Move," she said, barely waiting for him to comply before she flung out her right arm. She faced her palm toward the incoming swarm of drones.

"Gravitas."

She spoke the one word and it echoed through her skull, no, through the entire filtration chamber like the deep intonation of a bell clang. The sound resonated around her, channeling out toward the drones that numbered perhaps a hundred.

Then a surge of wind hit and encased every single one of those incoming miasma drones.

For a split second, they seemed to hover in the air right next to Quinn, only about ten feet away from her, and then almost as one, they plummeted, gathering speed as they covered more air into the miasmic sludge below. A loud, sucking sound floated back up to where they were on the platform, and then there was actual silence.

Quinn breathed out, blissful in the absence of buzzing. The rest of the drones appeared to have taken the hint. She brushed her hands against each other and pushed the filter she'd been replacing back into the pillar, thus activating the hydraulics again.

Nobody else moved, nobody spoke. Finally, she looked over at Malakai. "What?"

"That was so cool," he said, a massive grin on his face.

"Yeah." She had to agree with him. "It was, wasn't it?"

15

RESET ACCOMPLISHED

Quinn couldn't quite get out of her head how amazing that release of power had been. It surged through her body, out of her hand in a rush of strength and certainty. It left all her senses tingling, wanting to use more of that power. Not necessarily to inflict gravity on head-sized flies, but in general, to have access to it, and to be able to accomplish tasks with power she could never have imagined as a child.

Still, there was a lot more left to do, and now at least she had an agenda for what she would be doing with any spare time she had. Stronger wasn't even an excuse anymore. It was a cold, hard fact.

Then a thought occurred to her. "Don't the miasma drones feed off the sludge?" she asked, turning to Lynx, who was still gaping at her. "Close your jaw, Lynx. Answer the question."

He blinked himself out of his mild case of shock and answered. "No, they don't feed off the sludge. They feed off the miasma that rises from it. They kind of plummeted through that. I'm pretty sure the eels and the rest of the sludge are taking care of them."

"Really?" Quinn said, somewhat disappointed. Although she didn't like the idea of them flying back up to the platform newly empowered or something. "It would have been much more satisfying to drop them onto a solid floor. I'll have to remember that for next time."

"Next time?" Lynx asked, raising an eyebrow. "Are you planning to come down here and drop a lot of miasma drones onto solid surfaces just for the fun of it?"

Quinn laughed. "Of course I'm not *planning* on doing that. I just mean when I need to use this ability again."

"Yeah," Lynx looked at her with a different light in his eyes. Quinn thought it might even be slightly calculating.

She cleared her throat and looked back at the row of filters she was working on. "Okay, well, we're almost done with this row and we can move on again."

Even while she took out, disposed of, and replaced the old with fresh filters again, Quinn couldn't help but feel a sense of pride in what she'd accomplished. It was just one spell or ability or whatever it was, but it worked. Heck, it worked so well on a problem that even had Malakai worried initially.

What's more, she'd simply known somewhere deep down exactly what she needed to do because the book had told her.

Maybe absorbing the books wasn't the only way to learn the magic within. Maybe it took time to stew over the knowledge it imparted. Perhaps she needed to allow the books to direct her when her knowledge became a necessity.

Either way, she was going to figure it all out . . . when time permitted.

The platform moved around to the next filter slots and they started yet another row. It was monotonous enough that she could run over everything she'd just done in her head, analyze her movements, and recall how much energy or mana it had taken her to perform that action. It was a lot less than she had thought.

Energy consumption: 40

Mana consumption: 80

Surely that had been a lot more than eighty mana. At least, it felt like it.

The whole incident meant that now Aradie was able to stay closer to the platform. It seemed that the rest of the not-so-little miasma drones decided staying away from the people working on the pillar was probably a better idea than plummeting to their deaths below. Maybe they even operated off a hive mind. That way they'd be able to, well, communicate with each other like they were apparently doing.

Now that piqued Quinn's interest too.

The work carried on and on. Her shoulders ached, and she used her healing capabilities again. Her stomach rumbled, and they paused and ate food again.

So many hours passed that she lost count.

Finally, *finally*, she replaced the very last one. And they hopped out of the moving platform onto the solidity of the filtration pillar. Her hips felt stiff despite the intermittent healing she'd performed. There must have been some constant movement on the platform they used because when Quinn's feet hit the actual ground she felt like she was still swaying ever so slightly.

Sort of like when you get off an airplane or boat and feel like you're still moving.

"My neck is killing me," she said.

Malakai gave her a sympathetic smile. "We were up there for seventeen hours. I'm surprised you're still cohesive."

"Really?" Quinn said. "I don't feel tired."

"You healed yourself like four times while we were up there," Malakai said. "That'll rejuvenate all of your muscles and your energy levels. Of course you don't feel drained. But that doesn't replace sleep, it just makes you feel better about it. It's not the best way to deal with the fatigue."

"Whatever, Dad," she said.

Malakai laughed. "Don't call me that again. Funny but *way* too weird."

She thought it over and realized it really was. She was way too old to be using that as an insult. "Sorry. I might be a lot more tired than I think."

"It's all good." He gave her a brief pat on the shoulder and moved down to the skiff area.

"Quinn, over here," Lynx called. She walked over and stood in front of one of the control panels that were interspersed throughout the entire pillar. "This is the main panel you'll need to activate the pillar to reset itself completely. Right now it's still operating on reserve power, which is why there's barely been a change in the density of the sludge."

She brought up the HUD.

Ganyon Pillar Filtration Capacity: Rectified.

Filtration Capacity: 100%

Initialize Reboot?

Yes or No?

Quinn shrugged. "I guess that's a 'Yes, we want to reboot the filtration system of Ganyon.'"

There was a shuddering as everything powered down. For a split second, Quinn wondered if she'd done the right thing. What if it couldn't boot back up? What if they then only had one filtration pillar? What if they couldn't boot up one of the other filters?

After what seemed like a very long moment, it shuddered once more, and all of the lights began to shine. One after another they lit up in a cascade effect all the way up the entire pillar until it was completely lit up with those beautiful blue lights.

She watched in awe, marveling at the lights. "I guess we did it."

"Almost," Lynx said. "Now reset it."

Quinn blinked at him. "What do you mean? Doesn't it do the same thing?"

"No, rebooting meant a complete recalibration and rebooting of the entire system from its base up. Cleansed the interior and its complete and utter functional systems. Resetting means that you need to reset the filter pattern." The manifestation explained it like it should have been prior knowledge.

"Oh, sure," she said, and asked it to do that too. It was probably more information she was supposed to get on transfer. At some stage, that excuse was going to get very old.

When they'd first arrived at the pillar, there was an ever so slight vibration beneath her feet. Quinn attributed it to the fact that they were on a body of moving liquid, which would naturally lend some vibrations to everything.

However, as the reset took place, she could feel the power within the pillar start to well up, power that far exceeded her own abilities. Quinn realized that those initial vibrations had been whatever mechanism, magic, or power that made the filtration system work.

A soft, low thrumming began underneath her feet. It was almost like one of those bed massagers set on low that went through her entire body. The tightness in her shoulders eased ever so slightly, as did the crick in her neck.

"Wow," Quinn said. "That's some powerful stuff."

"Yes," Lynx said. "Some of the majesty is returning to the Library." His tone held a hint of wonder.

Quinn couldn't blame him. She wasn't sure if it was just her mind playing tricks on her, but he seemed less pale, less see-through even without tapping into power from the Library. The lights in the filtration panels began to flicker through greens, to blues, to deep blues, occasional blacks, and all around them, the water began to churn ever so subtly, pulling the black sludge remnants of the chaotic magic down and presumably into the filter.

Filter Restoration: Level Two.

Filtration Chamber Navigation: Level Two.

Librarian, will you navigate the controls?

Yes or No?

Quinn blinked at the notifications in front of her. Then turned to Lynx "What does this all mean?"

"Well, it should be hooking up to you now because it's operational again, you know, minimally, but the filtration chamber is now operating at its bare minimum instead of below it." Lynx shrugged like he was only speaking common sense.

He looked so relieved that Quinn wondered how much time the Library really had left in it before it finally managed to find and fetch her. From everything she'd seen, they had been downplaying the severity of its status.

She looked at the prompt and thought, *What the hell . . .*

She clicked yes.

A feeling like a warm flush of heated air suffused her entire body. It took away all fatigue and any lingering pains, so much more than the tremors had when they raced through her body. This took her to the next level. Her mind felt clearer than it had in weeks.

Pillar synchronization with Main Library Core Reestablished.

Additional Filter Pillar Activation Possible in 47 hours, 35 minutes, and 26 seconds.

This can be done remotely. Ashiron pillar is malfunctioning. Do not enable Ashiron pillar. Caution advised.

"Can I make it so that Asheron pillar cannot be reactivated without my prior authorization?" she asked the control panel.

Ashiron pillar restricted. No one other than the Librarian may reactivate Ashiron pillar. Lock in place.

"Well, that should give us time to figure out whatever was up with that note in my book," Quinn muttered to herself. She frowned and then realized that everybody was staring at her.

"Don't mind us," Eric said. "Just have a nice little conversation with yourself."

"You know I'm not speaking to myself," Quinn said. "The pillar is talking to me."

Lynx raised an eyebrow. "The pillar is talking to you?"

"The interface is talking with me. The whole core system, whatever. But this pillar in particular is the one that started it." She realized she sounded a little childish.

Lynx cleared his throat, his entirely incorporeal throat. "Well, we should really get back to shore."

"Should we, though?" Quinn said.

"Yes, we should," Malakai chimed in.

Eric glanced at them all. "Well, I'm done here. You don't need me to get back, right? I'm off." And he literally took off, zooming across the lake.

"Would be nice to be able to fly," Quinn mused.

"You'll get there soon enough," Lynx said.

"Fly?" Quinn turned to him in surprise.

"Well, yes, you can already hover to get out of the way of things. So flying is just, you know, the next three or four logical steps." Lynx shrugged and flickered, reappearing on the skiff where he called out up to her. "There's books on it, you know."

Quinn sometimes wasn't sure if the manifestation was pulling her leg or not. But in this case, she was going to choose to believe him and use that as something to aim toward.

"Well, let's get going, then," she said. "I think—I think we all need sleep."

Malakai chuckled. "You definitely need sleep. Your words sound tired."

"Well, maybe I am a bit tired. I did just spent five minutes communicating with a pillar." She looked out over the entire lake, at all the darkened pillars. "So which one's Ashiron again?"

Lynx pointed in the direction. It was all the way back on the very far side. "That's Ashiron."

"Okay. I can see . . ." She pondered that for a moment. It would be the most difficult one to get to by the looks of things. So it wasn't a bad thing that they weren't going to reactivate it anytime soon. Now she just needed to figure out exactly what was wrong with it before she did anything about it.

"Come on, my lady," Malakai called out. "Your chariot awaits."

She glanced down and realized that the sludge wasn't up to the bow of the skiff anymore. The filtration system was already clearing a direct line around the pillar.

"Wow," she said. "That works really fast."

Lynx raised an eyebrow. "That's nothing. You don't even understand. The bare minimum should have kept this pretty much at bay. The fact that it got infected is what worked against us. Otherwise, this lake would have been fine."

Quinn ran that over in her mind. Something didn't feel right about the whole scenario. "Do you think it was possible for someone to sabotage the pillar directly?"

"No. Not this. Who could it have been? If anybody who isn't authorized by the Librarian personally to come down here comes down here, an alarm sounds. Nobody can get here without prior permission. Even Eric couldn't have come down here before you allowed him access."

"Oh," she said and she realized her head was starting to pound. "Okay then, Malakai, let's just make our way back."

There was so much that Quinn still needed to do and needed to think about. But first, she required some sleep. Besides, she still had two days before they could even activate the next filter.

And she planned to spend all of that time getting stronger.

16

INTO HER OWN

Sleep was an understatement, Quinn thought when she woke.

When she returned to her room, she realized her energy was running precipitously low, beneath two hundred, which began to tread into dangerous territory. She barely remembered to remove her shoes and protective gear before collapsing into bed. She didn't wake up until the next day.

She'd been out for almost twenty-four hours.

The sleep rejuvenated her body, but she could also feel something new. Since having unleashed that power down in the filtration chamber, Quinn realized she'd barely scraped the surface.

She was the Librarian, and with that came a certain innate measure of power.

While she'd fully understood that absorbing the book knowledge was a part of her position, until now, she hadn't completely comprehended just what that might entail. The power she'd exuded sent all sorts of possibilities cascading through her head.

If she played her cards right, if she really applied herself to learning and training, couldn't she legitimately defend the Library? Wasn't she in charge here? Shouldn't she be delegating more to leave time to train?

Suddenly, something popped up in front of her.

Priority Listing - Librarian: Quinn.

Prioritize:

Strength

Library Fine Definition

Pillar Activation

Task Delegation

Library Returns

Energy Amplification.

Once these are complete, the list will continue.

Quinn raised an eyebrow. The Library appeared to be getting to some of her thoughts no matter how dense Quinn made her mental barrier. She was getting a lot of lists from the Library lately, or perhaps it would be more fun to call them quests. She shook her head. They felt a lot more annoying than that.

Nope, lists it was. She was better at ticking off lists. Very good at it, in fact.

Quinn needed to increase her strength, and what better way to do that than to improve on the skills she already had?

And that was how she found herself in the training room with several books she'd gathered.

She sat down on one of the training mats and spread the books out in front of her. "Okay, Aradie," she said to the owl, who was perched on one of the training dummies, "let's see if I can do this mental fortitude training myself considering I can't always rely on Milaro to tear himself away from the world he governs to come and give me lessons. He must have hundreds of thousands, if not millions of people under his command. I can't keep taking his time."

Aradie hooted in a way that almost sounded like a consoling coo. Still, Quinn smiled at her. "Okay, so *Mental Fortitude: Hanalo's Guide to Barrier Mastery.*" She frowned. "I thought these were supposed to be clever titles to entice you to want to read them?"

Aradie threw an image at her that denoted a beginner and an advanced person. "Oh, this is an intermediate book, so you're telling me that once a student is already interested in the subject matter, you're sort of already hooked, so the titles no longer matter as much."

Another two hoots from Aradie, which could have meant anything from "Why yes, Quinn, you're correct" to "Oh my god, humans are so silly." Quinn wasn't sure, but she preferred to think that it was the former.

She spent several hours analyzing her barrier, making sure that the strands she wove were the tightest they could possibly be. There were hints in the book. It described the construction of the barrier by telling her to act as if she was knitting with sticky fabric so that the strands actually stuck together when they were done. Once she was finished with the entire wall, all she had to do was solidify it. That word alone practically acted like an elastic band, and everything became taut between the posts as she had erected it. It wasn't as solid as she wanted, but she guessed she had to get better at it before she'd hit that threshold.

Not bad, not bad, she thought, *but my work isn't done because this needs to be a reflex and not take me ten minutes to build.*

And so, she ripped it down and began over and over again, playing it in the background of her mind, sorting her thoughts, and turning half of her attention to the next book, *Hot Air: Not All Talk.* At least that title made her laugh.

However, it didn't go into the detail she'd hoped it would. The original book she got her knowledge of the gravitas ability had been *Not All Just Hot Air: That Which Doesn't Float Sinks.* But the thing about that book was that it explained the way air worked in relation to gravity. The explanation was only in the book to show how air and gravity were related.

However, gravity was an offshoot of wind and air, not to mention marginally related to earth, so perhaps her having affinities for everything enabled her to understand the mere mention of it. Still, it was very confusing. Shouldn't she only have the abilities given to her by the books?

The Library inserted its own commentary, *No, that's not quite how it works. You should have access to any affinity your mind has the capacity for.*

As you possess all the affinities, so should you inadvertently be able to interpret and understand information, even if it's not precisely from a tome related to it. As long as there is enough information for you to process into comprehension, it should suffice.

"That sounds very confusing," Quinn said.

It's not really confusing if you think about it.

"I am thinking about it, and it's very . . ." Quinn scrunched her eyebrows, trying to see the answer she knew was just out of reach. "Oh! So I have a predisposed ability to understand the subject matter of all of the affinities."

Isn't that what I just said? the Library asked, sounding slightly irritated.

"That's technically what you said; it just took me a moment to understand it." Quinn pouted.

The Library sounded like it sighed.

"It's good to have you back," Quinn said. "You've been really quiet lately."

I had several functions that I had to reassess and realign. I think we might be getting close to a solution on the infected sections Siliqua and Harish have been working on.

"Seriously?" Quinn said. "That's awesome."

Yes, but right now you're busy. I'm sorry I interrupted.

"No, no, no, thank you for interrupting. I really . . . I was struggling a bit with understanding."

You're okay, Quinn. Just keep going.

It was difficult not to dwell on what the Library said, but it was right. Quinn had far too much to do. The book, *Hot Air: Not All Talk,* while not exactly what she had been looking for, was still very important. Its title suggested that hot air was capable of much more than people assumed.

From volcanoes and volcanic eruptions to speaking in controlled and influential ways, there were so many different applications of air. She couldn't imagine having to read through every single one of these books without being able to absorb the knowledge to process it.

Although, she had to admit, if she'd discovered the magical Library without having been the Librarian, she would have devoured everything any way she could have.

In the background, she still divided her attention and constantly tore down and rebuilt her mental barriers. Even though she hadn't dreamt of the snaky lizard man the last time she went to sleep, it didn't mean she wouldn't get pulled into that strange dream dimension again.

The next time, maybe she wouldn't be the one in control. She had to be prepared for that. To understand how to turn the tables on somebody who'd been doing this for millennia, she needed a deeper understanding. That's why she'd sought out *Dreamscaping: Not Unlike Landscaping.*

"Somebody really needs to come up with better titles than these," she muttered. She'd liked the funnier titles; they'd been a nice distraction.

Aradie swooped from where she was sitting and came to rest on Quinn's shoulder, tugging at her hair with her beak.

"What?" Quinn said. "You want me to be careful with this one?"

The bird nodded, keeping its solemn gaze very firmly focused on Quinn.

Quinn reached up and scritched Aradie's neck. "I promise, I'll be careful with all of this."

The book went on to differentiate between being in one's own head in a dream state, or being pulled into somebody else's space. If she was pulled into someone else's space, unless her mental barrier protection was at a high enough level, they'd have the ability to turn the dream into an actionable space.

This meant that what happened in the dream could actually affect her corporeal body. Quinn shuddered. She didn't like the sound of that. She was determined that she would not become a victim to it. She began focusing more of her attention and energy on tearing down and rebuilding those walls.

Dreamscaping: Not Unlike Landscaping, went into great detail about how to create her own world. It explained why the first experience had affected her so badly. But what it didn't explain was how they planted that sphere in her mind in the first place.

Of course she knew the basics. She was aware he'd taken a hold of her fear and used that to slide his trap in. But that didn't explain how he did it.

The sphere that was still trapped inside her mind. She needed to know how much energy leaked out of the prison they'd locked it in. Quinn paused, reinforcing the box, yet again. She wasn't about to let Kajaro win in the end.

Also, what if it could break out of that prison without her realizing it? What if it had already seeped into her very subconscious inadvertently? Plus, she couldn't help but wonder if it was a Serpensiril-specific skill to plant traps in people's minds, or if it was something she'd be able to do too once she understood enough.

Basically, she was left with more questions.

It wasn't something she wanted to ask Milaro and it wasn't something she necessarily wanted to tell the Library, which is why she had her thoughts locked down as tightly as she possibly could.

Quinn pushed the book aside with some reluctance. There was no more for her to expand on within its pages. She'd need to dive deeper into Dreamscaping . . .

Gravity Works: Plummeting as a Means of Attack, Refined was the next one. This book, which she had never seen before and had only just absorbed, was the one where she *should* have gotten that gravitas ability from. Because it was uniquely primed with gravity attack spells. Nothing in the previous book mentioned anything to do with coating everything in a gravity-dense shield so that it couldn't move and thus allowing it to plummet to the ground.

Or, as Quinn liked to put it, letting gravity do its thing.

And yet it was something she'd known instinctually, which meant some of the wording in the previous book must have unlocked that logical conclusion for her.

She massaged her temples as a massive headache threatened to waylay her. Still, this was the fourth book she'd absorbed. Maybe she was being a little bit too greedy with the knowledge. Her energy was sitting on low. It was only at 321.

But she'd been lower before and not got this hammering headache. Maybe she was just overdoing it. She popped an energy ball into her mouth to give herself a boost and then paused. She really had been eating those like there was no tomorrow.

Aradie held out a claw. "You want some too?" Quinn said. The bird shook the claw. "Okay."

Quinn broke off a little bit of another energy ball and popped it in outstretched claw. The bird ate it and fluffed her feathers as if she'd had the best meal in ages. Quinn guessed it was made out of some sort of seeds and jerky type stuff, so it was probably okay for birds, right?

Quinn stood up and brushed herself off. "Well, no time like the present to start training what I've learned."

There were a few hours left before she would have to reactivate the next pillar, and she made use of every single minute of that time. She crafted energy balls of air, infused them with gravity, and watched them drop, smashing to the ground beneath. The first time she managed to make an indent in the ground, she asked the Library to please reinforce the area.

However, instead of reinforcing it, Tim and Tom suddenly showed up with a strange liquid that they poured onto the floor. They waved and left the room immediately thereafter. Quinn blinked at the liquid spreading all over the floor, the main area in the training room.

Once it reached the edges, it solidified.

The Library spoke. *It should now be like the floor is down with my core. Soft, yet not. And it will absorb more of an impact.*

"Thanks," Quinn said. "But . . . can't you just create things out of thin air? Why didn't you just . . ." She wiggled her fingers.

Some things are still better quality if the time is taken.

Quinn didn't want to argue that an instant liquid solution didn't really seem like taking time, but thought better of it. Maybe the liquid itself took time to procure. "Thanks again. I should have thought of protecting the floor earlier."

There's no need for thanks, they replied.

Quinn wondered what was wrong with the Library. It sounded a little annoyed. Not that it felt like the Library was directing that annoyance toward her, but still.

Quinn resumed her training. Turning air into a substance that could be weighted was more difficult now that she had to focus her thoughts on it. That one moment she'd had in the filtration chamber, that crystal clarity she'd had that all she needed to do was force the miasma drones down with gravity. She wanted her power to work like that again, and she wasn't entirely sure if she'd be able to recreate it as precisely.

"Can you do training simulations?" she asked the Library.

What do you mean simulations?

"Well, like where you give me a scenario and I use my abilities to defeat it." Quinn had watched hundreds of hours of science fiction shows that had similar things.

Like this? And suddenly there was a swarm of about fifty miasma drones.

Quinn grinned. "Exactly like that." She flung her hand out, allowing the wind to buffet out as she yelled, "Gravitas!" For a split second, all of the drones halted. Then all of them plummeted to the ground and dissipated. Their little projection bodies, or holographic forms or whatever, faded to nothing.

Is that what you were looking for? the Library asked.

"Yeah, that's perfect." Quinn hoped this would help her reflexes, and to figure out ways to navigate her abilities in a constructive and efficient manner.

I'll figure out a way for you to access it without directly having to speak to me. You'll have to give me some . . .

But loud footsteps running down the hall toward her cut the Library off.

"What's that?" Quinn said, turning to see Malakai rush into the room as he burst through the doors.

"You've got to come, Quinn. Harish and Siliqua have figured it out."

Quinn didn't need to be told twice. She took off after the elf prince, Aradie swooping to join them.

17

SOLUTIONS

Harish and Siliqua stood at the Library check-in desk, speaking with Milaro, who'd obviously returned to the Library. His long robes and hair complemented each other well as always, sweeping like the wizard robes that Quinn always imagined elves to wear.

He was really the only one of them who behaved like he was out of a typical fantasy world. For the most part, anyway—he seemed a bit too jolly sometimes. She also often wondered how he found time to be at the Library so much when he was the ruler of his own domain. But she guessed that was a him problem.

Quinn was extremely excited to hear what Milaro's friends had to tell her.

"Well, what is it? What do you mean you've solved it?" she asked, looking around expectantly.

"We think we've figured out how this infection spread so undetected," Harish explained. "As opposed to just being aware that it was sneakily done when checking the books in. It appears that a membrane or filament, as you will, was able to enter the system undetected through the actual scanning process, going directly to the area of that book's expertise. That wouldn't have been too bad with only a few books, but over time and thousands of books, it built up and began to leak over into other sections."

"This was deeply thought out, then," Quinn said. "It sounds like it was planned for a long time."

Lynx looked like he'd eaten something rotten from the way he scrunched up his face.

Harish nodded. "It didn't take place over just a few years. Not even solely during Lynx's hibernation. This was hundreds, if not thousands of years in the making."

Milaro frowned. "That doesn't even sound possible."

"But it is." Siliqua cleared her throat. "You see, if you trace the pattern left behind by the—shall we call it an infection?—it's similar to the rings on tree trunks. You can tell approximately when this alien substance began to enter the system."

Lynx shook his head, the tone of his voice was flat when he spoke. "I don't even understand how I wasn't aware of this."

"To be fair," Quinn said, "none of us are sure what you *were* aware of, and that's not your fault. This was a master plan of some sort."

"I know you think that makes me feel better," Lynx said, "but it really doesn't. It just means I was complacent in my duties and I failed the Library system in its entirety."

You did not fail. The Library's voice rang out to all those near the check-in desk. *Not everything is always black and white.*

Quinn cringed. "Exactly what the Library said. Sometimes, despite our best efforts, things don't always go as planned."

"She has a point," Siliqua piped up.

Lynx stood a little straighter, but didn't say anything.

Quinn glanced around the desk. She saw Siliqua, Harish, Milaro, even Malakai was lounging about, leaning against the desk, looking out toward the Library as if he wasn't listening to every single word they were speaking.

Eric and Geneva were in charge of check-ins right now, but nobody was at the check-in desk to return a book at that precise point in time, so they too were listening, and doing nothing to hide that fact. Dottie was the only one not there that Quinn was surprised by.

"Okay," Quinn said. "What exactly is our status on being able to reopen borrowing?"

"Well," Siliqua said, "we're now working on a way with Lynx and the Library to get the chaos filtration as a part of the check-in process so that that sort of filament can never leak into the system again. We still haven't completely cleansed the entire Library, but we're almost there. We only have a few more subjects to do."

"Wait, what do you mean?" Quinn held up a hand to stop Siliqua from speaking. "Like, you want to scan each book with something as they come in?"

"Yes," Siliqua said, "perhaps with a wand or a magical skill we develop. Or have the console do it as it registers the book."

"What about an ultraviolet light? Wouldn't that work?" Quinn asked, remembering Earth and some of the neat little cell phone cleansing devices they'd had around the world.

Everybody looked at her. There were like seven sets of eyes focused directly on her. She suddenly felt like maybe she'd spoken out of turn.

She rushed to explain herself. "Well, back on Earth we used ultraviolet light devices with like a high frequency or something. I'm not a science person, but I'm sure you could magic an ultraviolet wave of light, right? I mean, I learned that book the first time. You know, that: *Bright Light Starters*? Wouldn't something a little bit more advanced than that have the sort of ability that we're looking for to just, you know, rip any of that chaos energy away?"

Everybody was still looking at her and by now Quinn felt extremely self-conscious.

"You know," Milaro said slowly as if he was still running over the idea in his mind, "that's an excellent idea, Quinn."

"You don't have to sound so surprised. I'm not unintelligent. I'm just not used to magic." She felt oddly insulted.

Milaro, at least, had the grace to blush. "I apologize if that's how it came across," he said. "I just wasn't expecting that sort of magical solution to come from you."

"You know, Earth might not have magic, but we made our own

form of magic with technology. There's a lot of stuff that you could do with this around the Library to make things work a lot more efficiently and in a much faster way." She did her best not to sound too pouty.

"Really." Lynx crossed his arms. "You think you can make the Library work better than it currently does?"

Quinn gestured vaguely at the entire Library. "You know, I think I could at least make some improvements considering the amount of crap we've had to clean up since I got here. So yes, Lynx, I could. But right now is not the time. There are still more pressing things we need to accomplish and fix before I share my many ideas."

"I like that," Lynx said. He smiled. "Maybe pulling somebody from a magicless world to ours will reap benefits in the long run."

"Maybe, but we'll never know if we don't refocus on what we were talking about and get the Library back to where it needs to be," Quinn said gently.

"Ah, sorry. Carry on," Lynx said.

"Very well," Siliqua said. She seemed only mildly irritated by the interruption. "We're developing a process where books cannot be placed back into the collection without passing the scan before re-entering the system. It's just not a viable choice for us to spend three days per book cleansing them as you did for the ones you retrieved from the Dabilian homeworld. Instead, we will separate the books out so we can cleanse them all together. I would suggest that we develop this ultraviolet light for future instances while we work on clearing out what has already been damaged."

"The more I think it over, the more I think this can be done," Milaro said. "I'm sure if I combine *The Sunlight Creates the Shadows* with *Hidden Light that Sees More*, we might be able to come up with a cleansing light."

He muttered to himself for several seconds, and then his face lit up. "That's brilliant, Quinn."

She held up her hands in a stop action. "Look, I'm glad you think I'm clever, but I'm only suggesting something I've seen done back on Earth. I didn't develop the idea in any way."

"Still, it's good that you thought of this application." Milaro seemed determined to compliment her.

"Thanks," she said and turned back to Harish and Siliqua, "Anyway, are you saying that once we have this up and running, we'll be able to accept books back as they are, and we'll be fine again?"

"Technically, yes. But we need to develop a system-wide warning that will detect anything amiss with the books should anything go wrong. That way steps can be taken to rectify the situation immediately before we reintroduce a potential problem book to the collection," Harish said.

"Well, that sounds like a plan," Quinn said.

"Hold on," Lynx spoke up. "You said almost all of the infected areas have been cleansed, and we can start accepting books back, right? So which ones have been cleansed?"

"Oh," Siliqua said. "Fire magic, air magic, and related and combined affinities have been cleansed. The horticulture, specifically in-ground growth, is also rectified. The regenerative culinary arts have also been cleared, which is very important, because I believe that you've run out of some of those specific herbs and ingredients. Cook will be enthused."

Harish took over, smoothly, with barely any transition. "However, we have to let you know that we're still working on the hand-to-hand combat section, and the fire, air, and electricity masteries in combat, as well as advanced protective spells. We're not floundering, it's just that it's taken a lot of effort to get these ones done."

"Is there any reason they're taking longer to get done?" Quinn asked.

"Well, yes," Harish said. "These are extremely complex areas, and because they are so complicated, the way the filament or slime has managed to weave its way throughout that particular database of magic is just as complex. There are certain elements we need to employ to remove them, and we have not quite managed that yet."

"Well, that makes sense, I guess," Quinn said, still amazed how they'd managed to find all of this. Then again, this was part of their specialty. "So do we have an estimated time this is will take us at all?"

"Well, I would think"—Siliqua paused as she thought it over—"probably another two to three days, and then the Library will be fully functional. Hopefully, in that time, the Library and Lynx, and perhaps Milaro, can come up with some sort of immediate fix for when books are returned."

Quinn couldn't believe it. The Library was going to be fully functional shortly, or at least, insofar as returning books was concerned. "Another couple of . . . wait, two to three days, right?" She turned to Lynx. "Isn't that about when our applicants are going to start arriving for the next load of interviews?"

"Yes," he said. "In fact, about two and a half days."

"Oh, this is great timing. Are we ready for them?" she asked, suddenly worried about having a whole slew of new interviewees.

"We're about as ready as we're going to be. Readier than we were with the first bunch, because the filtration system is working."

"True," Quinn said. "About that, how can you be so sure that we got the filtration system to work properly again?"

"Haven't you been checking the levels, Quinn?" Lynx asked.

"Oh." She looked down at her HUD. There, the beautiful blue line at the bottom was creeping up to that ten-thousand mark. "So it doesn't only get refilled by book returns?"

"No. Now the filtration system isn't causing us to directly lose mana, our power is gradually increasing. There's like less than a thousand to go." Even though she was super excited by it, there were 998 left to go. They were sitting at 9,002 of 10,000 units.

It was really difficult for Quinn to contain her excitement. For the first time since arriving, it felt like things were actually starting to work out. As if maybe, just maybe, fixing the Library wasn't going to be impossible.

"Can't you feel it? Can't you feel that the Library is getting stronger?" Lynx asked, sounding decidedly tougher himself.

Quinn closed her eyes and let herself sense the ambiance around her, the thickness of the air, the way the wood beneath her feet had a very subtle thrum to it as if it was real and alive and breathing. Maybe it was, with all of the knowledge held within it, but then she remembered it was probably also because the massive pillars scattered throughout the Library helped distribute the mana back into the universe.

"Yeah," she said, "I think I can feel it."

Lynx simply glowed, ever so slightly, his runes twisting in his hair as if they were doing a happy dance.

"That's fantastic timing for all of us, isn't it?" said Quinn. "Is there anything I need to do to get ready for this round of interviews?" she asked Lynx.

"Not really. Just quiz them again like you did last time. I think everyone from this batch has worked out well."

"Darn right, we have," Eric said as he finished checking in a couple of the newly cleansed books.

Finally. Having to keep the books separate was a strain. Geneva laughed, but she was a little flushed, so Quinn knew she'd liked the compliment.

"So we'll have Dottie, myself, Mil . . . oh, sorry, Malakai interviewing them?" Quinn asked.

"Well, and me," Lynx said. "I will interview this time too."

"What about me?" Milaro said. "You almost said my name. That must mean that you want me to interview them too."

"Don't you, like, have a kingdom to run?" Quinn asked.

"Yes, I, 'like, have a kingdom to run,'" Milaro answered, "but I'm extremely good at delegating and I'm perfectly capable of splitting my awareness. Which you would know if you'd been practicing the exercises I gave you. It is an extremely useful skill."

"It really is," Quinn said. "I'm practicing it right now. Did you know that I taught myself the third level of mental barrier all by myself because you were off running your kingdom?"

"Wait. Am I supposed to feel bad for not being here, or proud of you for your accomplishments? What reaction am I supposed to be giving you?" Milaro asked.

"I'm still technically a young adult, so anything you do is going to be wrong." Quinn gave him a wink.

Milaro laughed, that hearty sound that echoed through the entire library. "Ah, Quinn, it's good to have you here."

"I'll agree with that. Anyway, we'll conduct the interviews, and you should make sure you don't need to be at home more than you think you do," Quinn said.

"I shall consider myself chastised. But if I don't have anything urgent to attend to, I will be here. As it is, I will assist Harish and Siliqua in finishing this last stage of their plan. The more I think about it, the more I believe I can figure out a way to integrate this ultraviolet into a simple scan for returned books!" Milaro sounded positively ecstatic.

"Well, that's ideal, isn't it," Quinn said. She was scrolling through some of the information in the HUD in front of her on the console. "Oh, wow, did you guys realize? With these books that Geneva and Eric are currently returning, we now have almost all of the culinary branch ones?"

"Yes," Geneva said as she put in the last one. "I'm done with them now."

"That's 267 of 282 books!" Quinn felt like something was finally making progress. "We only need another fifteen books to open the culinary branch."

"Which is great." Lynx grimaced slightly. "Only fifteen books. But I do believe we're still slightly behind when it comes to the herbs and ingredients."

"We're still sitting at 192 of 287 of those. And if the horticulture section has been cleansed, which they said it is, that means Farrow and Cook can concentrate on the remaining ninety-five items. Although, 287 ingredients? Isn't that like nothing?" Quinn paused, confused.

Lynx chuckled. "No, that's 287 herbs and more with magical properties. Specific things that have to be in the possession of the Library before it can open that branch. Those are not the only ingredients the branch will use."

"Oh," Quinn said, feeling a little silly for having assumed that. "Anyway, doesn't that mean we can open the new branch soon?"

"It does," Lynx answered. "Once we've got the energy levels up."

As if on cue, an alarm sounded. More like one of those alarms you set to remind yourself to do things, but it still made Quinn jump about a foot in the air. "What is that?"

Filtration process functioning at 100%

New pillar activation permissible within these parameters.

Filtration Chamber Energy Levels: Low

Suggestion: 3rd Pillar Activation

Do you wish to activate a third filtration pillar?

Yes or No?

Quinn looked up and grinned. "Guys, I think the Library is well on its way to recovery."

And then she chose: *Yes.*

1 8

EVERYTHING

Usually, when Quinn chose "yes" in response to a prompt, things happened immediately. This time, when she chose "yes," the system prompted her further.

Which pillar do you wish to activate?

Ashiron, *Byron, Cylion,* <u>*Dekleron*</u>, *Esheron, Farinon,* <u>*Ganyon*</u>, *Hylaron, Ishiron, Jarion?*

Quinn frowned at the question. Dekleron, and Ganyon were greyed out. Ashiron was actually in bold red, which she assumed was because they'd instructed the system to seal that one for the time being. At least until they could figure out what the cryptic message in that book actually meant.

If they could ever unlock that bloody file.

But Quinn didn't quite have the visual of where the pillars were positioned. She'd seen them from such a low vantage point that picturing them in a top-down sense didn't quite compute.

"Show me a diagram of the pillars," she said, hoping for the best. Lo and behold, one popped up. She studied the distribution of the pillars. Ganyon and Dekleron were diagonal from one another. The other corners contained Ashiron and Jarion. "Lynx, don't you think activating Jarion gives us the most even spread we can get right now?"

"Sort of. Ashiron would make it balance completely once we need four, though, and I don't know that we'll have that pillar repaired yet." He sounded hesitant. "It's on an entirely differently level of complex."

Quinn frowned, studying the diagram again. "Byron is a little off, but it would still work if it comes to that and we still can't activate Ashiron."

"Okay. That would probably do." Lynx was obviously observing the layout from his own vantage point. "Yeah, okay, Jarion. That's probably our best bet for the third."

From his tone, Quinn thought he might actually be happy that she asked his opinion. His confidence was somewhat shaken since he'd been forced into the core. She indicated Jarion to the system.

Activate Pillar: Jarion

Yes or No?

"Yes," she said.

Flushing Filters.

System Activation Process: 24 hours

Another pillar will be available in 168 hours or 7 days should the power requirements be met.

Quinn felt something shift deep beneath her feet, ever so subtly. She knew the filter wasn't active yet. And she didn't quite understand what flushing it out meant. But since she hadn't had to change the filters, it was probably a magical process that allowed them to be cleansed as long as they weren't infected to the point of falling apart. At least, that's what she guessed.

"You'd be right," Lynx said, confirming her idea.

"I left those thoughts wide open." She grinned at him. "So that means we've got the filtration chamber back on track, right?"

Lynx smiled back. "Yeah, the filtration chamber is currently operational. The more it can filter, the more filters we'll be able to activate, and the more volume it'll be able to process. And we should, in another week or so, be able to get another pillar online, as long as the accumulation of power continues to go down this road."

"Progress!" Quinn said.

"That's got to feel good," Milaro said, giving her a wink. "Does feel powerful, doesn't it, Quinn? Knowing you've accomplished something grand?"

"If I didn't know better, Milaro," she said, "I would almost think you were being ever so slightly condescending."

He grinned. "Well, I am a—what do you call me, an elf?—Isn't haughtiness supposed to be typical of elves?"

Quinn cringed. "Yeah, some stories might have mentioned that. I see you've done some research."

"I'm only trying to live up to expectations, my dear," he said, giving her a flourishing bow and somehow suppressing the very real laughter she could practically feel emanating from him.

"Thanks," she said.

"Excellent." Dottie trotted up into the check-in desk. "Is that really a third filter I can feel?"

"Well, not yet. It'll kick in tomorrow, but it's been activated. It's just got to clean itself," Quinn said.

"This is fantastic. I am so excited." The little bench was practically dancing in the very cramped space. "You don't even understand how wonderful the Library is when it's fully functional, Quinn. Just you wait."

"I'm waiting, I promise," Quinn said. She couldn't help but be infected by Dottie's over-enthusiasm.

Quinn scanned the Library, watching as Eric and Geneva checked in another couple of books. She watched those patrons exiting the Library again, their heads were bowed toward each other as they exited, chattering, whispering amongst themselves. Maybe people were starting to understand that the Library really was back.

Hopefully, word of mouth would spread. They'd need to send out another pulse notification soon. The books weren't coming in as fast as she liked anymore.

She couldn't help but notice the look of skepticism turn into wonder whenever anybody actually entered the Library. She was surprised people still remembered how to get to it. Granted, time didn't pass the same in all the worlds, and not everybody aged the same in all of them either. Very few seemed to have the limited life spans of humans on Earth.

"What are you thinking about?" Malakai asked, suddenly standing next to her.

"You're practicing your ninja moves again, aren't you?" she asked.

"Just a little bit," he said, "but you look sort of thoughtful."

"Well, I think I expected the whole filtration-restoration thing to be a little bit more in-depth, perhaps even a little riskier." She shrugged. It sounded silly when she said it out loud. "It feels slightly anticlimactic."

"Really?" He leaned back so he could get a better look at her. "You feel like scaling a five-story pillar and spending seventeen-odd hours replacing all of the filters while fighting off miasma drones wasn't enough?"

"Well, when you phrase it that way," Quinn said. "But still, it feels almost too easy."

"Why did you have to say that," Malakai groaned. "Haven't we talked about this before?"

She shrugged, nonplussed. "I guess, we do still have to figure out what's wrong with Ashiron, so the whole filtration chamber issue hasn't been completely resolved, right?"

"There you go, silver lining. You've still got loads more work to do," Malakai said, some of those syllables dripping with sarcasm.

"That's my grandson," Milaro said. "Always a ray of sunshine."

"To be fair," Quinn said, "I believe I was currently being the ray of sunshine."

Milaro chuckled. "You can definitely be a ray of sunshine, Quinn," he said, his tone serious.

Quinn calmed down a little, the fun gone out of her at Milaro's rather serious tone. "Okay, that was a great compliment, but what's up?"

"Nothing," Milaro replied. "As I've mentioned before, I believe in giving credit where credit is due, and I don't think I would have reacted this well, being sucked into a world I'd never heard of, told that magic existed when I'd never witnessed it before in my life. Frankly, all things considered, you've dealt pretty well with it."

"Thanks," she said, not knowing what to say. There was something more in Milaro's words, though she wasn't sure what. Like there was something else she didn't know yet. She could feel the heat rushing to her cheeks. Quinn had never been good with compliments. Giving them, sure. Receiving them? Nope, not her thing.

"Anyway," Quinn said, changing the subject, "aren't you guys supposed to be figuring the rest of this whole subject infection thing out?"

"Yes," Siliqua said. "It was just exciting with the pillar reactivation and stuff."

She grabbed Harish by the arm and tugged him away toward their research room. Milaro watched them go, a thoughtful expression on his face, and then he turned back to Quinn.

"How have your dreams been?" he asked.

"Oh." Quinn thought it over. "Last few nights have been pretty uneventful. Not getting pulled into anybody else's dream, not having anybody appear in mine. The orb seems to be mostly stable, even if a little leaky, but I put a barrier around it and on top of it, so I'm hoping it sort of stays more or less intact."

"You put another barrier around it?" Milaro asked. "That was a pretty wise thing to do."

"I figured the more protection between it and the raw centers of my brain, the better?" Quinn half asked.

"Nice and logical. You are correct." He beamed at her, a hint of pride in his countenance. "Anyway, I wanted you to know that I haven't forgotten about what I promised to do for you. I'm still researching it. Dreams are not my forte. I can enter them and control them, to some extent, but it's not my area of mind magic expertise. In order for me to help you, I have had to reach out to resources that I haven't had the pleasure of utilizing prior to this."

"Okay," Quinn said. She raised an eyebrow at him. "You know, that's the first time I've heard you speak like a professor and not a grandpa."

Milaro laughed. "Ah, sometimes when I'm talking about my specialties, I'm often perhaps a little more zealous about them than I am about other things. There's joy in life and there are things that I find utterly fascinating and that require that I take them completely seriously. Dream infiltration is one of those things."

Quinn nodded.

Milaro flashed another smile. "I will leave you in the capable hands of my grandson, and Lynx."

"What about me?" Eric interrupted, calling over from where he stood, half sitting on the desk and glaring at Milaro.

"And of course, Eric, my dear fellow, you as well." Milaro's eyes were twinkling. Literally.

"Sure, sure," Eric said. "I've got my eye on you, king."

"Of course you do, Eric. I'll take my leave and go and do what I'm supposed to be doing." And with that, Milaro followed after Harish and Siliqua.

Quinn watched him go, her feelings at war with each other. She didn't know how she currently felt. And it wasn't about Harish and Siliqua or Milaro. It wasn't even about being here in a different world.

It was that this genuinely felt like a lull in action. In her list of things to do. Which she felt was a precursor to having too much to do.

"What's really wrong, Quinn?" Lynx asked.

"Yeah," Malakai said, nudging her, which had become an extremely annoying habit. But at the same time, there was also a certain level of comfort to the action.

"I don't know," she said. "I think I'm feeling a little . . ." She searched for the word and she couldn't quite place it. She wasn't feeling down. She wasn't bored. "Oh, I think I feel a little lost."

"What do you mean, lost?" Malakai asked. "You're in the middle of the Library of Everywhere. You're literally able to open a door to anywhere you want to go."

"That's not the kind of lost she means," Lynx said. "Stop it before you embarrass yourself."

"Too late," Malakai said, grinning at Quinn.

She laughed, still trying to search for exactly how to express what was bugging her. "Yeah, lost. But not in the sense of not knowing where to go. More of . . ." She shrugged helplessly.

"Can you tell us why you feel lost?" Lynx continued to prompt her.

"I'm not sure. We've just—we've done so much. The filtration system is working now. We've got the infected subjects almost figured out and almost all fixed. And the books we could already return have already been returned. We're getting plenty of returns still coming in. We went to a chaos-ridden world and got some slimy books back. . . . And in two days we're gonna have even more applicants for Library assistant positions. Speaking of which, can we delegate so we have more supervisors, so I can train my skills and spar with Malakai?"

Lynx shrugged. "Nice change of subject there. Sure, I don't see why not. I mean, you have the power to do that."

"Awesome." Quinn turned to the two winged assistants at the other end of the check-in desk. "Hey, Eric, Geneva, are you guys up for a promotion? Wanna be a supervisor?"

"Sure," Eric said. "What are the perks? Do I get a pay rise?"

Quinn glanced over at Lynx who nodded almost imperceptibly. "You do! You take care of all that stuff, right Lynx?" she said.

He laughed. "Yes. Yes, I do."

"Geneva?"

She pursed her lips and looked over. "I get to supervise others, like you all have done to us?"

"Sort of," Quinn said.

"Yes. I would like that." Geneva preened a little, her wings fluttering briefly even though she was sitting down. "I do like being in charge of things. You should probably ask Jim and Bob too. They've been fantastic."

"She's not wrong," Dottie chimed in.

Quinn smiled. "Okay, I'll ask them later." She really did like Jim and Bob. They always seemed ready to do anything to help. Eager and attentive. Even if they often finished each other's sentences.

"Now that your subject diversion is over," Malakai said. "Why do you feel a little lost?"

"I don't know. Maybe it's not lost; maybe it's just relief." She sighed, having hoped they'd leave it alone. "I mean, I don't feel like there's this cloud of doom hanging over my head right now. For the first time since getting here, it feels like I can actually relax. And not like, 'Oh well, I'll go and have a power nap and then absorb five books and then train and then see if I can go retrieve the books we need and then see if we can boot up the filtration system and then try not to get killed by a snake man in my dreams.' It's freeing."

Lynx smiled. "It's not always going to be like that. I mean, you've still got to figure out fines, you've still got to make more announcements about the Library being open, see if we can get a few thousand more books back, we're still waiting for the filtration system to completely kick it up a notch. Then you're going to have to go and retrieve some books if people aren't bringing them back. It's not like you can *relax*-relax, but I think I get what you mean."

She made a face at him. "Thanks for that."

Malakai grinned at her. "Quinn, does it appear that you have a little bit of free time on your hands?"

Quinn grinned at him, sensing a bit of mischievousness in his tone. "Why, yes, Malaki. It seems that I might have some free time on my hands."

Lynx groaned. "Oh no, this doesn't sound good."

"What are you talking about!" Eric said to Lynx. "This sounds brilliant."

Malakai ignored them both and focused on Quinn. "What is it that you would like to do, Quinn?"

She paused for a moment and took in the Library all around her. "You know, Malakai, I think I want to do everything."

19

AFFINITY DEFINITION

Everything, as it turned out, was a lot.

Despite the in-cahoots maniacal laughter she shared with Malakai when she declared that she wanted to do everything, Quinn really meant it. Now there'd actually be time to dive into the nitty-gritty of the Library, to build herself up. From everything she understood, the Librarian was supposed to be strong and able to defend the entire space all by herself.

Even though she had people who would fight alongside her, she'd never really had to depend on anybody else in her life, and it was difficult to start now. Even if, to some extent, she even thought she sounded a little arrogant thinking that way. The others might be there for backup, just in case.

"What are you thinking, Quinn?" Malakai asked as she stood in front of a massive listing on the HUD that extended to be taller than herself as she scrolled through it.

"Hmm, I mean, I could start with everything, or I could just narrow down a few things since Harish and Siliqua are almost done fixing the problem. I want to learn about combat affinities. I know I'm not the strongest person," she said to forestall Malakai's comments. "I understand that. But at the same time, I could become stronger by using the affinities. There are strength tomes, agility tomes, tomes on martial arts, on sword-wielding, and not just a bloody machete. Machetes are sincerely not what I thought I'd be fighting with."

"Really?" Lynx asked, sounding a little offended. "I thought they quite suited you."

Quinn laughed. "Seriously? Have you seen my coordination with sharp objects?"

Lynx cringed. "Fine. I won't take offense."

"Good. I didn't mean to upset you. But I was hoping I could maybe use a staff. Perhaps I'd be better with blunt weapons. I don't know. I've never used them." Quinn shrugged.

Malakai crossed his arms and leaned back against one of the counters. The three of them were completely ignoring the rest of the check-in desk. "I could see that. I can train you in blunt weapons. It's not quite at the expertise level of my sword, but I am proficient in bow and staff usage."

Quinn grinned. "Perfect. So you can help drill the knowledge into me."

"I can." The elf prince nodded in agreement.

But Quinn wasn't done yet. "I also want to learn about making regeneration food and energy replenishment food. I want to see if I can try and come up with new recipes. I'm not the best person in the kitchen, but I make pretty decent, okay-tasting food."

"I'm sure Cook will help you. They seem to have a soft spot for you." Malakai hesitated and then asked, "You know, okay-tasting food isn't really a good benchmark to brag about, don't you?"

Quinn rolled her eyes. "It doesn't matter. I want to absorb cookbooks. I want to have all the elemental knowledge, all the abilities and skills and spells and however the things I don't know about work. It's all necessary. Because you know they're going to come after me outside of my dreams if they can't get to me *in* them, right? Eventually."

"I'm sort of surprised they haven't yet," Malakai said. He scowled, deep in thought for a moment.

Quinn was still running through the massive list of books. She asked it to refine itself down to the specific areas she wanted to address.

"You know," Malakai said, "it's only been, what, four weeks since you got here? Considering they didn't realize that the Library would be able to get a Librarian at all, I would say the enemy is currently not in a position to continue their sabotage of the Library. They're probably trying to amass forces or to figure out a different way to get to you."

Quinn paused. "What do you mean by 'a different way to get to me'?"

Lynx cleared his throat very loudly so he could butt in. "Look, you two little trouble makers," he said. "At some stage here soon, you're going to have to retrieve books that haven't yet returned. That's probably the easiest opening for them to get you . . . or try to."

"Well, I'm going to take my bodyguard Malakai here and absorb all the knowledge in the Library so I can just obliterate them on the spot," Quinn said, attempting to laugh the threat off.

"Not quite how it works, but I like your gusto," Lynx said.

"Gusto?" Quinn asked, raising an eyebrow.

"Yes," Lynx said. "But that is food for later thought, because right now we still have ten days until the thirty-days fine grace period are up, and then we're going to have to send out warnings. Oh, it's going to be magnificent." He rubbed his hands together, the runes in his hair suddenly swirling like a vortex.

Quinn eyed the runes with some trepidation until they calmed down a bit. "Don't I have to send out another pulse to let them know to return the books?" There was probably a part of him that didn't want to give people more forewarning.

"Oh, yeah. No time like the present. May as well do that now." Lynx seemed giddy with the thought of being able to leverage fines again.

"Okay, shouldn't we wait until we have the other assistants in place?" Quinn asked.

Lynx blinked. "You know, that also sounds like a better and more logical idea. Get ready for the influx and all. You pick. You're the

Librarian. You managed the whole Library for several days while I was completely out of it. I know you can do this."

Quinn's eyes narrowed as she stared at the manifestation. "What are you concocting?"

Malakai spoke up instead. "He's realized that you're in danger, and now he's trying to figure out ways, without you knowing, to protect you."

Quinn raised an eyebrow. "Really?"

Lynx sighed. "You're no fun, darigháhnish."

"I know," Malakai said. "It's part of my charm."

"Charm, schmarm," Lynx muttered.

"Is he right, Lynx? Are you trying to figure out ways to keep me safe?" Quinn asked, her voice soft.

"I'm trying to figure out ways to keep you safe while still allowing you to learn all of your abilities. So . . . yes," Lynx answered begrudgingly

"Thank you," Quinn said, really meaning it. "I want to learn all the elements, horticulture and alchemy, and . . . I mean, my affinities helped me with the whole miasma drone thing. Maybe that'll kick in again." She paused. "Wait a second. If it exists as an affinity, then I have that affinity, correct?"

"Yes," Lynx said so. "Essentially, you can absorb every single book in the Library, if you so choose."

Quinn nodded slowly. "Doesn't that mean that chaos is also an affinity? I mean, it's magic of creation and destruction . . . right?"

Lynx blinked at her. So did Malakai, but the manifestation spoke first. "Well, yes, but . . . not just anyone can use that without being devoured."

"Kajaro uses it, right?" Quinn asked.

"Yes," Malakai said and rushed to head off anything else she might say. "And did he seem normal to you, Quinn? Did he seem normal?"

Quinn had the good grace to laugh. "No, he doesn't seem normal, but then none of this seems normal to me, although maybe it is here. It just means that my having the chaos affinity shouldn't be that much of a surprise. And Kajaro still had enough of his mind left to work out a pretty devious plan."

"Still, not normal," Malakai piped up. "It's not normal to try and implant dream control into your opponent's mind."

Quinn shrugged. "Well, it might not be normal, but it's definitely logical in a really weird magical sort of way. I mean, wouldn't we do the same thing if we thought we could get him to stop what he was doing? Or if we thought we could get in deeper and understand what they were doing? Or hell, if we wanted to stop what he was doing and we were strong enough in that dreamworld. I mean if I was strong enough in there . . . if I could use that magic effectively? I totally get it."

"You do have a point," Lynx said. "But still, Quinn, grappling with chaos is just not how things are done. There's a level of danger there . . . of losing yourself completely, of being overrun."

"Yes, but pulling somebody from a completely non-magical world into this one is also not done. It seems we're breaking all sorts of rules here." She sighed. "I'm not trying to be rude or to say you're wrong, because I have no idea what I'm doing. But at the same time, I think we can all agree that from the very start with the sabotage, the way things are usually done? That hasn't been a thing for a really long time. It's all changed and still changing."

Lynx looked extremely thoughtful at the comment and he shut up. Quinn returned to gleefully scrolling through the titles for the areas she was interested in and selecting those she wanted mentally. Wind and air and ice. She definitely wanted some more ice powers. She had a feeling that if she tried hard enough, she'd be able to freeze somebody from the inside out, even just using their veins to freeze the water content in their blood.

Quinn paused and looked for anatomy. Her jaw dropped when she saw the huge list of them. "There are books on every single species' anatomy, every single creature's anatomy. How is that magic?"

"It's not magic," Lynx said, like that answered everything.

Suddenly Misha materialized in front of them. "It is magical application. You see, for some types of magic execution, you must understand the creatures or the species you are fighting against."

"Know the makeup . . . and you know where its weak points are?" Quinn asked.

"Technically. If you know how something is made up and you can basically unmake them, destroy them," Misha said.

"Isn't that a very chaotic way to think?"

Misha blinked. "Was that not what you were just speaking of? It is a very unique way to use magic. Not everybody can unmake things. You, however, have the ability to unmake everything as long as you understand the theory behind it. As long as you don't give in to simply devouring it."

"Just me . . ." Quinn said, a little scared by the prospect of that type of power.

Misha's moon-like eyes flashed. "Currently from what I can extrapolate. Yes. Aside from the Library, that is."

Quinn suddenly found it hard to swallow and turned back to her catalog perusal. The Library too? More question for later. She paused, finding something else odd. "There's blood magic?"

"Of course, there's blood magic," Malakai said. "What? You think you can have water magic and fire magic and you can't have blood magic?"

"Wouldn't that be sort of evil?" Quinn asked.

"I can see your prejudice showing up there," Malakai said. "It's just like this whole 'elf' business with you."

Quinn blushed slightly. "I just—I was thinking vampires and stuff."

Malakai rolled his eyes. "Not this again."

Quinn was about to change the subject when Misha spoke up again, "What other elements are you looking to learn, Librarian?"

"Well, I sort of want exciting ones and ones that can give me immediate results," Quinn said, after some thought.

Misha somehow managed to raise one of their golem eyebrows. "Exciting ones? But you can eventually absorb them all."

"Well, yes, but some seem frightfully dull," Quinn said.

"Quinn," Misha said, "some might seem dull and mundane to you at first glance, but any information can be useful given the right sense of circumstances. Your ability to defeat the miasma drones is proof of that. What you currently find dull and mundane, could perhaps one day save your life."

"Oh," Quinn said, feeling sufficiently chastised. "I'll try to remember that."

She continued to leaf through and select the books that she wanted to grab. The constant being told what she needed to learn had dried up, especially since Milaro wasn't looking over her shoulder. She accessed areas of mind magic that seemed to lead on from areas she'd already studied. Then there were books on ice magic. And she took a beginner book on blood magic because she couldn't help but find it fascinating. And why wouldn't she be able to combine ice and blood magic? Surely there wasn't anything that stopped that. And that's when she turned to the species and picked out a manual on the Serpensiril physiology.

There was no way she'd ever let him get the upper hand again. Plus, perhaps she could find a way to stop him from coming back next time Malakai killed him. The thought lingered in her mind for a moment and she felt guilty for entertaining killing . . . but only for a second.

If someone wanted her dead, it'd always be better if she was the survivor.

"Do you think I can get all of these sent up to my quarters, please?" she asked, suddenly a little nervous about learning this much information. It'd be a lot to take in, a lot to absorb, and she'd definitely have to stop by the kitchen for applicable snacks. Quinn let out a long sigh.

"I still have two days, right?" she said, suddenly thinking of the pillars. "I don't need to be here when the twenty-four hours clicks over on the third pillar, do I?"

Lynx shook his head. "You don't need to be here for that."

"Hey," she asked, "those chaos books we retrieved. Where are they kept, and why aren't they on this list?"

Lynx clucked his tongue in exasperation. "You've already learned them, Quinn. Why would they be on that list?"

"Oh." She could feel the heat rising in her cheeks along with a flush of embarrassment. "Well, why aren't there any other chaos books on this list?"

"Because chaos books are a restricted item, and you're not looking at the right list for that."

"Well, surely studying the effects and nature of chaos essence is like the best way to incorporate it so that, you know, you can nullify it, right?" Quinn paused for a second making sure she'd said what she thought she'd said. "Doesn't that make sense?"

"Well," Lynx said, "we do have a restricted vault. We haven't showed it to you yet because most of the items in there are A, dangerous, and-or B, above the level you can currently absorb with your knowledge level."

"Oh." Quinn was mostly unfazed about not being able to absorb it yet. She got that she needed to rank up through the different skill levels first. "But I can probably absorb some of them, right?"

"Well, DeKarlyle's book is a restricted one. All of those initial returns were."

Quinn pondered that for a second. "Still though, we have like, a high-security vault?"

"Yes."

"Oh, now you're talking," she said. "You have to show me that."

Lynx sighed, and she knew where they were headed next.

Quinn really liked getting her way.

2 0

RESTRICTED

QUINN EXPECTED THE RESTRICTED VAULT TO SIMPLY APPEAR IN FRONT of her. Sometimes the Library seemed to know what she needed; hence, it made sense to her that the restricted vault might operate the same way and just appear.

However, as she followed Lynx through the Library, they passed the kitchen and dining room area, the magical plant section that Farrow attended, and the book infirmary. They even walked up the slight step and into the area where she'd first fought the bookworms, which now seemed like a lifetime ago. But they didn't quite make it back to the training room.

Lynx paused in front of a very different double door. This one went up about twenty feet, but each door was only about three feet wide at the most, nothing like the majestic front doors that were six feet wide per door. These were long and slender and had frosted glass as their main component, with wrought-iron filigree covering it.

"Oh, I thought this was one of the entrance doors that people came through when they wanted to visit us," Quinn said.

Lynx flashed her a smile. "Nope, this is the restricted vault. If you would do the honors, Librarian."

Quinn placed her hand on the door handle, and it swung soundlessly inwards.

She wasn't entirely sure what she'd been expecting, but she'd somehow thought the restricted vault would be much larger than it appeared to be. The room was maybe twenty feet wide and about fifty feet long, much smaller than she'd anticipated. It was also much cleaner and less cobwebby than expected.

It was actually beautiful.

At the far end, there was an extensive bay window that stretched from the bench to far above her and took up the entirety of that wall. There was padded seating all around the interior of the bay window.

The windows themselves had to be huge. And as she looked up, she couldn't even see a ceiling in here. It was too dark. From her vantage point at the entrance to the room, she could see little through the windows. But what she could see was a darkness that resembled the night sky with some smatterings of silver pinprick-y stars.

The view tugged at a sense of adventure she hadn't realized she possessed. She'd never seen the outside of the Library before because you only entered it through dimensional doors. It might be nice to see what the grounds looked like.

Quinn resisted the urge to run and gaze out, and instead turned her attention to the bookshelves. The books weren't laid out with a spine facing outwards. Instead, each book lay flat on a slightly inclined shelf that had a lip to keep it in place. The tomes revealed their covers to whoever perused them, but each book was individually locked behind its very own door. The small doors were made out of the same frosted glass and iron filigree as on the double doors that led into the room.

"Are these really secure?" she asked Lynx as she ran her fingers along one of the doors. It obliged by opening for her. She frowned.

"Yes, they're secure," he answered, but continued straight away, "but you're the Librarian, so these doors are already attuned to you, and you can take anything out that you want to."

Quinn turned to Lynx. "Aren't you worried that you might get a Librarian who wants to, I don't know, take over the universe?

Wouldn't giving them unrestricted access to restricted knowledge be sort of counterproductive?"

Lynx blinked at her. "Well, no, the Library screens that."

"How? The Library didn't even realize that I was mostly resistant to chaos until a few days ago."

Lynx flickered in and out his eyes doing that strange thing that they hadn't done for quite a while. "There are fail-safes in place. You wouldn't be able to become the Librarian should you have nefarious motives."

Quinn let out a little laugh. "You know, or even know about the existence of the Library of Everywhere, and have a whole grand plan in place just in case you become the Librarian."

"That too, that too," Lynx answered. Even so, he looked at her with a sideways glance and Quinn realized that he was probably mulling over exactly what she'd said. Because they all knew that just because someone was originally cleared by the Library to be a Librarian didn't mean that during the tenure as a Librarian they couldn't be compromised.

People changed. Quite frequently in fact.

Quinn shook her head, wanting to dislodge the thoughts in there. She didn't like the turn they'd taken. This wasn't about trying to figure out how the last Librarian had done whatever she'd done, or how other Librarians had might have secretly fed into it too, or how it had happened in the first place.

Right now—this was about Quinn being introduced to the restricted vault.

"Anyway," Lynx said, "this is our restricted-access vault. As I've said, all of the books in here are books that could alter the fabric of a world, that can ignite chaos, that can be used specifically to unmake creation in ways that may not require chaos knowledge. Some are the more advanced magic fundamental books—the ones that go into theory—that isn't necessarily something the majority of magic users who come to the Library will understand the scope of."

Quinn raised an eyebrow. "So you're telling people what they can understand."

"No, we are protecting knowledge that in the wrong hands could be devastating for the Library. Just because you can read it doesn't mean you understand it. Knowledge is powerful, but there is a line between deliberately using it because one is selfish, or because they are willfully ignorant. It's the latter we try to avoid." Lynx shrugged. "This is a self-preservation room, shall we say."

Quinn flashed him an understanding grin. She looked through the books and noticed that underneath each book was a little plaque with a name. There were a few cubbies that didn't have a door on them nor a plaque.

Finally, she made it through, studying the books on the left side of the hall and down to the end, where the glorious bay window was. She knelt on the window seat and looked out at the scene beyond.

It wasn't just a night sky. It was an inky, blue-black darkness speckled with stars. Some shone brighter than others, some shot almost like fireworks across the distance.

"This is amazing," she said. And even the hint of wonder in her voice was audible to her own ears. "That's so endless. It's like I'm looking out of a spaceship at the galaxy around me. This is breathtaking."

There was a vastness, an absoluteness, to the whole thing. For just a second, as she closed her eyes, she felt like the Library was breathing. Slow and gentle, as it too took in the beauty of its place in the universe.

But when she opened her eyes again, everything was still, and the wondrous galaxy in front of her hadn't moved. It was a very strange sensation. She turned back to Lynx.

"This has to be the best place to sit in the whole Library." She gestured outside of the windows. "That is inspirational all on its own."

Lynx was smiling. He appeared to be slightly amused, but not in a condescending way. "That's not the reaction most people have. Most think we're being unnecessarily restrictive. But I'm glad you like it."

Quinn grinned. "I love it. Now, how does the restricted section work?"

"Any person who wishes to enter the vault must first be verified and checked by the Librarian and Library," Lynx began. " Once they are, they are accompanied here and must peruse their books inside of the vault. They can only be admitted by the Librarian."

Quinn rolled her eyes ever so slightly. "Yeah, I got that by the whole 'only I can unlock it' thing."

"Well, yes, you or somebody you have specifically given permission to. Like me. They can take some notes depending on their level of clearance that the Library, or you, grant them. Depends on whether they're even able to absorb any of it. A lot of these texts are extremely advanced, so many people can't. The restricted vault doesn't exactly get a lot of traffic."

Quinn frowned. "If they have to read them in here, then how did the books on chaos get borrowed out by the Dabilians?"

"Oh," Lynx said, blushing slightly. "You see, that was a case of dire circumstance which the Library agreed was an exception. We stepped in after deciding the Dabilians would benefit most from sheer numbers of their people having intimate chaotic magic knowledge. Since they were all capable of understanding the books, we agreed to an indefinite term of borrowing. There are exceptions to every rule, and the Dabilian homeworld crisis was one of them. Also, someone like Milaro who has donated several of these volumes, has clearance for borrowing. There are several thousand families that do."

"What about the other books? You said the initial three were supposed to be in here too, right?" she asked, finally tearing her eyes away from the amazing view in front of her.

"Yes, they are. See." He pointed to *Mantis Leaf's Advanced Combat Strategy*, which was conveniently located right next to the window seats. "There it is."

"Milaro needed that for a crisis?" Quinn raised an eyebrow. She didn't quite understand what constituted a crisis, especially with a martial art book that required practice after absorption.

"No, like I said, there are exceptions. This tome was actually donated by Milaro's family, the royal lineage of the Seveshalls, and it was done so on the proviso that when they needed to train new descendants, they would borrow the book for a chunk of time. Which they did, and I guess they would have borrowed it again if the Library had been open and they'd been able to return it in the first place, so that they could train Malakai . . ." Lynx's voice petered out.

"Why don't they just make copies of them? If it's their family fighting style . . . I mean, isn't that their call?" she thought.

"No. Not with something that potentially lethal and transcendent. Not in the form of a tome anyway. Things like that are usually kept in blood-locked scrolls." Lynx replied so quickly she realized she must have been accidentally projecting the question outside of her mind shields.

"Blood-locked scrolls?" She had to know.

He shrugged. "Scrolls that can only be opened by proof of blood lineage. Offering up a drop of blood to read it."

Quinn raised an eyebrow and nodded thoughtfully, leaving that line of thought alone for now. There were so many ways that could be abused. Why did her thoughts have to go so dark? "What about the others? Or did they all donate them?"

Lynx shook his head. "No, they did not. *Tarlegish's Dichotomy of Herbal Evolution* was borrowed by Dinal because they'd discovered an encroaching plant virus that was trying to destroy their coastline. I do believe, because they're still there a few hundred years later, that they got something from it that worked."

"Well, what about *DeKarlyle's Thesis of Spatial Distortion?*"

Lynx actually scowled. "As seen from the memories that we managed to retrieve from Aradie, I think it is obvious that specific book shouldn't have been loaned out. Especially given Kajaro's history of reluctance to return any book at all."

"Yep, that seems pretty short-sighted to me. Pity you weren't around to stop it, but I sort of think that's the whole reason you weren't," Quinn said absentmindedly. She looked around, and pursed her lips as she noticed several nameplated books with closed doors that held no books. "Some of these are empty."

"Of course they are. The empty ones are there in the event that we need to restrict new text or there's a new affinity that is too far advanced to be put into normal circulation. There are always ways to look at these books but this is the section we keep the ones that are just a little bit too . . . edgy."

"Yes, I think that would be a very apt term. But that's not what I mean by empty." She gestured to an actually empty one with no door or plaque. "I get that that's available for potential new tomes."

Then she moved over one diagonally above it. She could see how it would be easy to miss if you weren't looking for it. And most people would come in here with a very specific agenda. But the shelf didn't have a book on it, even though the door was closed and presumably locked. It also had a name tag. "I meant this type of empty. Are any of them loaned out currently that you know of?"

Lynx shook his head, and his eyes began flickering as he searched his archives. "They shouldn't be."

"Well, I haven't approved anyone to enter here since I became Librarian," Quinn said. "But I've found three so far that have name-plates but they don't have books in them."

"No, you have to be mistaken," Lynx said, the denial very clear in his voice. As if he hadn't even thought it possible books might be missing before she pointed it out. "Perhaps they've been shelved in the wrong place."

But he stopped, reading one of the names and gasped. He read the name off as if he needed to breathe, gasping as he did so.

"*Chatfield's Force Fields of the Mind.*" And he moved to the next one. "*The Dean Principles of Immortality.*" Even being a manifestation of the Library, he seemed shocked.

In fact, Lynx managed to look panicked.

"I'm taking it some of these shouldn't be empty?" Quinn asked.

"Definitely not these two," Lynx practically whispered while his mind was obviously racing through something else.

"We'll get to the bottom of this, Lynx." She tried to reassure the panicked Library manifestation.

"The worst thing is," Lynx said, "none of these books should be missing or borrowed without me knowing of it. But I have so many gaps. I gave you the list of the three that needed to come back. They had specific properties we required to get us started."

He paused, looking around as if he might discover they'd accidentally fallen on the floor.

"Nooo," he said with a slight moan, running his hand through his hair runes "These? I should have known they were missing. I would have had you recall these as well. They might not have been vital to recalibrating the Library until we could get other things in place, but they are still vital. The power they give off. The energy. And there are . . . we need to catalog the ones that are missing and we need to do it now. These *have* to be found, Quinn."

Quinn sighed. "I should have known things were going too smoothly. Guess it's time to leave for a while."

Lynx shot her a withering glare. "First we have to figure out which books are missing, and since I can't do it from my system as well as I'd like, I need to retrieve archives. We're not going to be able to do anything until after the new assistants are hired . . . so consolidate your power. You're going to need it."

2 1

MISSING FRAGMENTS

Figuring out which books were missing was a lot more difficult than Lynx originally made it out to be.

At first, it appeared only a few books were missing from their cases. This was very easily determined by the relevant nameplate missing from the section. There were also twenty-eight new book slots completely available. No door, no plaque, nothing. Perfectly normal, all legit.

However, eight more shelving sections had a door, thus indicating that they *should* have had books. But the nameplate was completely missing. Lynx double- and triple-checked. Then he showed Quinn how to look up the restricted vault in the Library system.

"Can you see any other books that are missing?" he asked her, as if hoping he'd somehow missed it.

Quinn shook her head. "No, this is . . . this is really weird, isn't it?"

"Yes, the doors don't appear on the section unless there is a book slotted into it. Unless that book was destroyed. No, even if it was destroyed, the door should have disappeared because the book would have no connection to the Library." Lynx was practically muttering to himself. "I can't even be sure these are the only books missing now. If this was tampered with, who knows what else has been done."

"Wait," Quinn said sharply, trying to pull him out of the spiral he was in. "I thought you said books couldn't be destroyed."

Lynx gave her an uneasy look. "That really shouldn't be possible, but then I didn't think there was a way to sabotage the Library, and here we are."

Quinn just kept a level glare on him until he capitulated.

"Fine," he snapped. "But there's a very involved ritual involved in the destruction of a Library book. And it would sever the magical connection, so if the Library thinks a book belongs there . . . it's not gone, it's just been wiped from memory."

She thought that over, and knew there was still more he wasn't telling her, but odds were, he probably didn't even remember. "Is there any way for us to trace connections to the Library without knowing what the book name is?"

Lynx turned to Quinn. "I mean, sure there is. They all have a magic signature. There are some rituals, and other means I would guess . . ."

Quinn nodded. "Back where I come from, there's GPS. You can track like a whole heap of stuff, unless somebody manages to shut it off so that the main system can't find it. But I mean, it's something to go on at least."

"It's an excellent idea." Lynx's demeanor brightened ever so slightly. "I'll figure it out."

He still looked extremely worried and his eyes kept doing that flickery thing they did when he went off. Only this time, Lynx was multitasking much better than usual.

"It's okay, Lynx, we're gonna get it sorted," Quinn said.

"Yeah."

There was a light tapping at the door, and then again. Quinn looked around a vague sense of something missing. "Is that Aradie trying to get in?"

Lynx was now very involved in what he was trying to figure out within the system. So much that he didn't even acknowledge what she'd said.

She walked to the door and let her bird in, who promptly flew to her shoulder with an angry sort of chirp hoot.

"I'm sorry. I didn't mean to leave you behind. This was just a little bit thrilling." Quinn had been so excited to visit the restricted section, after all.

Aradie hooted reproachfully once more and the sound was enough to bring Lynx out of his mild trance.

"Oh, Aradie's here." He gave the bird a serious look. "Aradie, I don't suppose you remember what these empty book slots are for?"

Aradie, to the bird's credit, hopped from Quinn's shoulder and moved over to look and hover basically with a very light beating of her wings in front of the sections that should have had books and name plaques but only had doors. She hooted once low and mournfully.

"So you don't remember what they are, but you know there were books in them." Quinn crossed her arms and gave her bird a look. "We've kind of already established that, but thanks for your help."

This next hoot was definitely irritated.

"Oh, you can't remember the names of them but you know there were books there so we're not just guessing that they're missing. It isn't just malfunctioning. We've literally lost eight books some- where . . . from the restricted vault." Quinn groaned out the last part. "But there could also be others missing because the temporal displacement around all the cases has the wrong aura?"

The next hoot was affirmative.

"Okay," Quinn said, trying to tackle the first part of the message, "so at least we know we're missing: *Chatfield's Force Fields of the Mind, The Dean Principles of Immortality, Uglandia Theories of Mind Manipula- tion,* and *Sethrovian Rings of Dream Entrapment.* These ones sound pretty bloody important."

Lynx didn't give her even a glance. He was still concentrating.

"Fine," Quinn murmured. The subject matters seemed awfully suspect. She thought for a few seconds. "You know what, Lynx, I'm going to stay here. I want a table so that I can work on it. Added to the window seats. I'm gonna soak up some of this restricted knowledge and we're gonna figure this out."

"You're going to read the restricted books?" He raised an eyebrow as that thought disrupted his concentration. "Most of them are currently still too advanced for you." He said the latter almost apologetically.

"Not yet. I said I'm gonna soak up some of the restricted knowledge because . . . oh, I see how you got there." She took a breath and rephrased. "I mean I will stay here in this area because well, it feels thick with knowledge. I might get Misha to bring me the books that I had sent to my quarters. What do you think Aradie means by the aura is wrong?"

Lynx shrugged and then sighed. "Probably that there are more missing than is initially obvious."

"Ah." Quinn's stomach chose that moment to rumble. She blushed ever so slightly and held up a hand. "First up, I'm gonna go get some food. If I'm to absorb all of those books and increase my power like you keep saying I need to, I'm going to need food for sustenance and to replenish my energy."

"Cook should be able to make you something other than those energy balls by now," Lynx said. "We've begun to reestablish some of our trading partners. There are ingredients coming in."

Quinn looked at Lynx with concern. Despite his coherence, there was something off about his manifestation. He had very subtle static within him. "You don't look too good."

"I'm sorry, Quinn. I am attempting to run several different applications to determine if I can crack down on some of these weird restrictions that the reboot inflicted on me."

Even with that explanation, Quinn was still concerned about Lynx and the Library. With good reason, she felt. A lot was going wrong. She reached into her pocked at gripped her Library pebble. It leant her a sense of brief calm. Which was good, since this sabotage went a lot deeper than any of them realized initially.

"Okay. I'm going to go and get me food," Quinn said.

Aradie nipped at her ear, "Yes, we're getting you food too."

Quinn didn't really want to leave Lynx alone in the restricted vault. Not that the knowledge wasn't safe with him or anything, she just really thought that he was taking things a lot harder than he probably should. He was ancient, beyond ancient, like prehistoric ancient. That was a long time ago.

She wondered if he'd ever seen dinosaurs.

Of course we've witnessed dinosaur-type creatures; they're on several different worlds, the Library butted in.

"Are there intelligent Library-book-borrowing dinosaurs?" Quinn asked.

For a moment she thought the Library had stopped talking to her.

In a way, but not the type of earthen dinosaurs you're thinking of. These are a little bit more domesticated.

Quinn laughed. "Domesticated dinosaurs," she muttered out loud. "Like in little suits and jeans?"

But the Library didn't deign to answer. Quinn continued to chuckle as she made her way to the kitchen.

Aradie jostled up and down a little, as if she too was laughing. The Library shut off the connection with a little bit of a huff. Quinn would apologize to it later. She walked into the kitchen through the partially filled dining room that was bustling with people of all different species. She'd never get used to it and loved it all the same.

Cook was very happy to see her. She could tell from the way their facial expression barely changed at all.

Cook looked up from where they'd been preparing food to go out into the buffet-style area setup that fed visitors to the Library. The good thing about the dining area was that people who came to the Library to research or even just spend time, could eat if they needed to. It was a large enough area, with plenty of food. Not everyone in the universe could afford regular meals. Even if they weren't returning a book, with the Library open, there was always a good solid meal available.

It rarely got very busy, but there were more people today than Quinn had seen before.

Perhaps they'd eventually need assistance for Cook.

"Librarian," Cook said.

She blinked at them. "I'm so sorry. I was just off on a thought tangent."

Cook nodded. "Perfectly acceptable. I take it you are about to delve into learning more of your skill set. If so, you will be requiring energy and replenishment meals. Is that correct?"

Quinn smiled. "Yes, it is."

"Excellent. Excellent. Then I have a few things that I have pre-prepared for you for just such an occasion." Cook sounded pleased.

"When did you get the chance to do that?" she asked, smiling. Cook reminded her, maybe a little bit, of her father, if she remembered correctly. Those memories were getting hazier and hazier.

"I make time," Cook said enigmatically. "I thought you might like a little bit of chili, or perhaps a Hungarian goulash."

At the latter, Quinn's mouth practically dropped open and drooled. "Hungarian goulash? You can make a Hungarian goulash?"

The corners of Cook's mouth lifted ever so slightly, so much that maybe Quinn was imagining it, but she liked imagining it.

"I have been conducting further research."

Quinn raised an eyebrow. "That's a lot of research you've been doing on Earth. Does that take a lot of power?"

"No, not once the path was established to pull you through. An information transfer takes very little power."

"Okay, I'll believe you," she said.

"Excellent. Where will you be? I will have the Hungarian goulash brought to you, and in the meantime, I will send a few specifically tailored sandwiches with you. Now, you must eat these. One half at a time. They will give you, as you are absorbing books, a sort of energy-regeneration effect. It will not last more than fifteen minutes at a time. I advise you to not use more than one of these per hour. The rest of the time, you can spend percolating on the information that you have absorbed." Cook spoke plainly, and kindly.

"Got it," Quinn said. She was actually quite excited. "I will be in the restricted vault. Just have someone bring it there."

"Very well, Librarian. There are some treats in the bags for your night owl as well. I wish you the best of luck in your endeavors."

Quinn, on impulse blurted out. "Can I hug you?"

Cook nodded.

"Thank you," she said, giving them a very brief sidearm hug, and then hurried away. She didn't have the heart to turn around and see if they'd really hated the hug. She'd never been a big hugger, but Cook often made her feel warm and fuzzy.

Cared for.

Maybe it was the food component.

On her way back to the Library, she pulled up her information. Because it was a HUD, she could easily see where she was going, so she didn't trip over anything as she was going through her information.

Name: Quinn
Age: Irrelevant
Heritage: Earth, Sector 12942
Species: Librarian
Energy Capacity: 1018/1018
Mana Levels: 1214/1214
Alignment: 101%
*Affinities: 1722**
Tome Knowledge: 9
Affinity Level: 9
Determination: Rising
**As far as the Library can determine*

Her information had barely changed. Except for the fact that her species was Librarian now, which made little to no sense to her. Then again . . . she hadn't been absorbing many books lately, so that was probably why the numbers hadn't risen much.

So much to do and never enough time.

As Quinn let herself into the vault with her packaged sandwiches, she walked to the end.

Beneath the starry galaxy wall of glass, there was now, in fact, a table, just as she had requested. She turned around, wondering just what else the Library could modify if she asked it to.

I can modify anything, Quinn. It's all a part of me.

Quinn mulled that over. So many hints. She was starting to truly think she might be able to figure out what the Library was.

As soon as you know, come and see me. This time, the Library's voice was almost teasing.

"A little bit of entrapment there," Quinn muttered. There was no response from the Library, only from Aradie as the bird nuzzled against her head. "Don't worry, I haven't forgotten that Cook gave me treats for you, too. I only hope these sandwiches are okay because he seemed to want to make sure that I would eat them regardless. He hasn't fed me anything bad yet."

She sat down and pulled the massive pile of books toward her. Misha obviously had someone deliver them.

"Very well," she said, and pulled down the first one. But before she opened it, something gave her pause. Even in a computer, deleting things from history, actually wiping them off a hard drive was a very difficult thing to do. Apart from completely destroying the drive or running a complete scrub on them. But that hadn't happened, because the Library was still here, and so were the records of, well, what, ninety-eight percent of the books in the Library? So surely the information was there waiting to be retrieved.

Fragments of it hidden away to be pieced back together.

Quinn really wished she'd paid more attention in the basic computer classes that she'd taken. Although this would probably be an advanced situation.

And as the Library kept telling her. It wasn't a computer. Not in the way Quinn was used to anyway. She still side-eyed that bit of information.

Still, she sat down, looking at all of the books that she had brought here for her to work in an area that felt like condensed magic to her.

Mastering Your Own Thought Domain

Energy Requirement: 298

Mana Requirement: 152

Mental Manipulation: Getting Your Way is Just the Beginning

Energy Requirement: 197

Mana Requirement: 352

Conquering Fear and Other Maladies

Energy Requirement: 256

. . .

Combat Ice Magic 101

Energy Requirement: 199

Combat Air Magic 101

Energy Requirement 203

Magic Gravitational Force: Don't Let It Bring You Down

Energy Requirement: 326

She chuckled at that one. It made her laugh a little. And there was:

Up in the Air, You Should Care

Energy Requirement: 248

Shadows Are Your Best Friends (And How to Use Them)

Energy Requirement: 212

Mana Requirement: 298

Dream Acrobatics, Volumes 1-4

Energy Requirement Each: 178

The History of the Library

Energy Requirement: 99

Detailed Serpensiril Anatomy

Energy Requirement: 261

There were a lot of books.

And as she looked at the energy cost of them all, it made her cringe. A few of them even required mana.

"Oh well," she said and grinned at her bird. "No time like the present."

She was going to need all of the advantages she could get. There was no way she'd let herself get caught unawares again. She pulled the last one out. A bit of a heavy hitter, but something she felt she needed in her arsenal.

Ice and Liquid: Knowing What It Takes to Freeze Everything

Energy Requirement: 289

Mana Requirement: 332

Quinn wasn't sure if using these played into the hands of the people who'd sabotaged the Library, but she did know that she had to take care of herself before she could take care of others.

She grabbed the sandwich out. The crusts had been cut off and it looked suspiciously like white sourdough bread. When she bit into it, flavors assaulted her senses, but in a really good way. She chewed the first half, and watched as a notification popped up.

Energy restoration replenishment activated
Duration: 15 minutes.

"Well, then," Quinn said, "let's get started."

And she opened the first book.

2 2

SECOND WAVE

There were drawbacks to absorbing a lot of knowledge at once.

The first was that Quinn constantly needed to replenish her energy levels. The second was that even if she had food capable of helping her replenish her energy levels, absorbing so much information that she had to basically chain regeneration food and energy balls . . . had detrimental effects.

That much knowledge in such a short period of time had, in hindsight, been an extremely bad idea, if the pounding in her skull was anything to go by.

On the day the new Library applicants were due to arrive, Quinn stumbled down her stairs and into the kitchen, leaning on the counter next to Cook. Before she spoke, she realized she had somehow buttoned the shirt she was wearing in the wrong order. She breathed out, "It's gonna be one of those days" as she rebuttoned it.

Cook shot her a glance but didn't say anything.

"I see what you're doing," she said, her head pounding as if she had somehow drunk three bottles of liquor. She assumed that was the case, since the most she'd ever managed was a couple of shots. "Do you have anything to take this headache away?"

Cook put a cup down right in front of her with a resounding

clank. "I do believe you were informed, multiple times, not to overdo it with knowledge absorption."

Quinn shot them a minor glare, but even that hurt her head. It made her feel decidedly sorry for herself. "What's this? Is it like a tonic? Will the taste make me cry?" She sniffed it, but it didn't smell bad. In fact, it didn't smell at all. She eyed it skeptically and threw it back. It was very slightly sour but not in a bad way, more in a remnants-of-lemon-juice way. It tickled her throat, stung a little, and then it was gone.

A couple of seconds later, something like rejuvenation flowed through her, almost like a healing potion, with a side of refreshing.

Quinn looked at the cup in astonishment and then at Cook. "What was that? It was amazing." She could already feel the pounding headache subsiding. Not completely—there was still a little bit of a beat in the background—but it was more like she'd dialed down the volume on the bass drum instead of having it smashed directly into her head.

"That was what I believe you would refer to as a hangover cure, except in this world it is for magical hangovers." Cook's expression barely changed, but she did get the sensation Cook was lecturing her. "Overusing your abilities gives you the same type of reaction. Absorbing knowledge is simply like an extension of your magical abilities. Thus, it has the same effect."

"Oh," Quinn said, still relishing the mostly clear-headed feeling. "Well, I like it. Can I keep some of that on me?"

"Are you planning on regularly abusing your powers?" Cook said reprovingly.

Quinn blushed slightly. "No, but I just like to be prepared."

"Should you leave the Library, I will make sure one goes with you. But until then, you can come to me to get your cures. I do not advise you to push it, Quinn. You need to learn where your boundaries lie." Cook finished making whatever food was being prepared and bundled it up in paper before sliding it into a bag.

"Thanks, Cook," she said. She could tell Cook genuinely cared.

"You need to hurry up. I do believe the applicants are about to arrive."

Quinn glanced at the time in the corner of her HUD. It was earlier in the morning than she'd like. Sitting around seven in the morning. It seemed the new batch of assistants were over punctual. Quinn headed out, slightly rejuvenated now.

Cook hadn't been lying. There were already about a dozen people mingling around in front of the check-in counter, with Lynx standing directly in the middle. She shot him a thought. *Are these all applicants?*

Why, yes, I am so glad you're observant, he replied.

You're angry with me. It wasn't a question; Quinn knew full well from the waves of emotion emanating from the manifestation that he was annoyed with her.

Yes, I am, he said, multitasking as he took in applications from the people around him. They segregated into smaller groups, chatting amongst each other, and he turned to join Quinn, speaking softly as he did. "You overspent energy in a reckless way. You can't afford to do that. Promise me you'll be more responsible next time."

She'd never heard Lynx speak so vehemently before, and found herself agreeing quickly. "Promise."

There was no doubt about it; she felt guilty for having worried the people around her.

"Good." He took in a breath, "You are not conducting the interviews—"

But Narilin cut him off, suddenly standing directly next to Quinn. "Except for mine, right?"

Quinn blinked at the Salosier's arrival. "What do you mean yours? You're already our book doctor."

"I mean my relatives will be here shortly, and I was hoping that they would get the chance to speak to you directly, as I did. About the roles they could play here." Narilin seemed oddly hesitant in her speech, which gave Quinn pause.

Quinn frowned. "I'm sure I can talk to them about their applications?" Lynx gave her an almost imperceptible nod, and Quinn continued. "Is there anything I should know beforehand?"

Narilin grimaced slightly. "They are not all like me. Less studious, perhaps, although no less competent."

"No less competent sounds good to me," Quinn said. "So they're going to be able to heal up my books just like you can?"

Narilin nodded. "Perhaps not the most advanced ones, but the majority of them."

Quinn could practically feel the anticipation rolling off her book doctor. "I'll give them an interview. Is there anything else I should know about their applications?"

Narilin hesitated. "They are also specialized in areas I believe the Library currently needs."

"Good to know." Quinn turned and looked at Lynx. "What do you think?"

Lynx raised an eyebrow as he leafed through the rest of the applications. "That's acceptable. Malakai will be here shortly. Dottie and Geneva are also interviewing."

"What about Eric?" Quinn asked, glancing over at the imp.

Lynx crossed his arms. "Do you really want Eric to interview potential Librarian assistants?"

Quinn thought about the imp's idiosyncrasies and cringed. "Probably best he just stays in charge of the check-in desk."

"That was what I was going to do," Eric said, loud enough for them to hear where they stood, literally checking in books as he spoke. "I can hear you from here you know." He turned back to pay attention to the patrons, grumbling under his breath.

Quinn smiled and led Narilin over to the exact spot where she previously interviewed the Salosier. "How about here? What do you think?"

"Thank you, Librarian." Narilin took a deep breath. "I realize we have had some contention on occasion. I do apologize for this. Sometimes I am rather passionate about my work." As she spoke, the leaves in her hair gently rustled. "I do hope my siblings are amenable to your tastes."

Quinn raised an eyebrow. "Narilin, as long as they can do the job as well as you, I'll be happy. Even half as well as you."

Narilin gave a small smile. "I'm glad half as well is acceptable. I am the most talented among my peers."

Quinn had to suppress a small smile as they sat down. Narilin would never be called modest, but she could afford the confidence because she truly was excellent at her work.

Aradie swooped down to rest on Quinn's shoulder, nuzzling her ear. She absentmindedly held up some seed for her owl, which the Aradie gladly took. Then there was a light peck on Quinn's ear as Aradie sent her a mental image. There was an undercurrent of wanting attached to it. The night owl wanted a mouse or something a little fleshier.

"You can get that on your own time," Quinn murmured at the bird.

Aradie sent out a very displeased aura, and Narilin looked on slightly perturbed. The owl looked away from the Salosier as if making a point about her needs also being important.

Quinn took to watching the others interview the new intake while she waited for the Salosier family to arrive. More applicants gathered around. All of her assistants worked hard, dividing up all these different people into groups with Malakai, Lynx, Geneva, and Dottie.

Quinn saw a few new species that she'd never seen before. There were rock-like people. They had crevices in them and were black, almost like volcanic rock, she guessed. Some of them had beautiful streaks of what must have been gemstones running through them in blues, reds, and the occasional green as well.

She inspected them

Sedimentites

Sedimentites – Rock- and Earth-based creatures

Located in the: Illukai Region

Library Allies For: time immemorial

They had been with the Library since the beginning of time, and the alliance they held with the Library was firm. They seemed to be from the same region as the Aracnios. She wondered why the Sedimentites hadn't been among the first group of applicants. Another thing to ask Lynx later.

Or you could just ask me, the Library spoke up.

Of course, I could, but half the time you don't answer me, so it doesn't matter, Quinn thought back at it.

Shouldn't you be working?

I am.

Quinn looked at the next group she hadn't ever seen before. Not that she'd even scratched the surface of the universe. They looked like skittering praying mantises crossed with ants. And they walked upright. It was a very segmented body with elongated arms and long antennae. They only stood about three feet high, and they were called the Mantishia.

Mantishia - Anticular Mantis

Located in the: Efrium Region

Library Allies For: 15,629 years

When the remnants of her absorption headache weren't still trying to bash in the back of her skull, she was going to find research materials on some of the regions' histories. At least she now understood exactly what they meant by backlash and overdoing it.

Being stubborn sometimes had its drawbacks.

Okay, it often had drawbacks.

The next group of people to enter the Library really caught Quinn's attention. Narilin stood up and Quinn could sense an overall happiness emanating from the Salosier. It seemed she had missed her relatives. The three of them all looked very similar and yet, at the same time, extremely different.

One of them had white blossoms cascading down her hair and extremely dark wooden skin. The group of them reached out, grasping each other's hands with their elongated fingers in what seemed to be a celebration of reunion. They leaned in toward each other with a soft kiss to each other's left cheeks in some sort of greeting habit.

Two of them looked almost identical. Their skin some form of oak, more orange than red or brown. Quinn watched them as they embraced each other and brought their applications over, ushered by Narilin, who shook with barely contained excitement.

"These are my sisters. They're my seed-sisters," Narilin said in a tone of voice that Quinn had never heard from her before. It made her want to know more about the Salosier species, too. Apparently, being excited and with loved ones trumped any grumpiness that Narilin ever felt.

"Nice to meet you," Quinn said as she took the applications. "I'm the Librarian."

She stood up and reached her hand out to shake theirs as Narilin introduced them one by one.

"This is Arilin."

Quinn shook the hand of one of the oak sisters, dreading the next names.

"This is Marilin."

Quinn just knew it.

"And this is Jane."

Quinn stopped short, trying not to laugh as she shook the hand of the sister with the white-flowered hair.

"Excellent," Quinn said, knowing that she would remember Jane's name the easiest. She glanced at the applications, noting that Jane possessed fourteen of the sixteen affinities, while the other two had twelve each. Just like Narilin said. Not quite as good as she was.

She wondered if the two similar sisters were twins. But she wasn't sure it was polite to ask.

"Wonderful. Your applications are looking fantastic," Quinn said. They were all a little younger than Narilin. But their records were immaculate, just as their sister's, cousins . . . she'd look into the Salosier familial bonds. "Do you have any specific places in the Library you'd like to take part in?"

Jane raised her hand, her delicate nine fingers curling into a soft fist. "I would love to assist Narilin in the book infirmary."

Quinn nodded. "I think, at least for now, we definitely still need the help. That'd be fantastic."

Jane practically glowed as she inclined her head.

Arilin and Marilin looked at each other. "We would love it if we could assist in the growing of magical herbs and plants that you might need assistance with in the Library. Our specialty is, as you can see on our applications, horticulture. Is that acceptable?"

Quinn couldn't believe that they quite literally spoke in unison. Narilin saw her slightly shocked expression. "They are twins. They often speak together."

Well, that answered that question. Quinn glanced over at where Jim and Bob were helping Eric with returns.

"That's fine. I think we'll take you to meet Farrow and see how Farrow feels about having assistance. Farrow will, however, be your boss. She'll be in charge of you and you'll have to do what she says." Quinn did her best stern teacher impression.

"We accept," the twins said.

"Then I don't see a problem with this, though again, we'll have to talk to Farrow first, and then you'll all have to undergo the training to be a Librarian assistant. Sometimes people change their mind."

"Oh, I don't think we will," the twins answered, a beautiful smile on their faces.

Quinn glanced at Jane, who was simply sitting there smiling. They were all ethereally beautiful. It made Quinn wonder if that was a species-related element.

"What about you, Jane? Anything else?" she asked.

Jane just shook her head, the white flowers dancing merrily in her hair. "If I get to repair books, I don't see how I could be dissatisfied."

Quinn stood up and spoke. "Misha."

The golem appeared directly next to her. "Yes, Librarian?"

"Could you please take Narilin's sisters, Arilin and Marilin, to Farrow? Have them check in with her, and see if Farrow is needing any assistance with the horticulture section of our magical herb and plant growth."

"Very well, Librarian. Follow me." Misha beckoned the two to follow her and turned briskly to walk them to Farrow's domain.

Quinn felt quite accomplished.

Narilin turned to her. "I will take my sister to the book infirmary. Is that acceptable?"

"Yes," Quinn said and watched as they left. Narilin seemed much more amenable with some of her peers around—directly related peers, that is. Quinn mulled that over a little. Maybe that was a Salosier thing. Being close with each other.

That portion of the hiring process went very smoothly.

She turned to see that Lynx and the rest of them had begun dividing their people into even smaller groups and had, in fact, sent maybe two dozen people away. Quinn felt confident to leave it all in their hands. She was following the HUD's information stream as the new applications were entered into the system.

So far, it seemed another ten people, plus the sisters had been hired. Things were going well.

Quinn could even feel, by the thrum that entered her body through her feet, that the third filtration column's activation was making itself known. The power was almost tangible. Maybe it was just because she'd learned so much in the last couple of days that everything felt real, but she liked to think the Library was getting back on its feet again.

"It's going well, don't you think, Aradie?" she said as she petted her owl.

Aradie let out a long mournful hoot as if she was saying, *Why did you have to say that?*

Quinn scritched the bird's neck and laughed.

At least until a few seconds later when the Library announced a door opening related to recruitment.

Door B27, accessing recruits 83, 84, and 86.

Quinn watched with curiosity that immediately turned to horror when she realized that the next three recruits were Serpensiril, complete with filled-out applications they shouldn't have had access to.

23

———

SERPENSIRIL

Quinn wasn't entirely sure how to react to the fact that three
Serpensiril had walked into the Library. Her only personal experience
with them had been Kajaro, which made her hesitant. Unless she
counted that weird dream sequence and his henchsnake.

The Library itself posted a notification in front of her face as she
decided what to do.

Serpensiril - Reptilian species

Located in the: D'vor Sector

Library Relationship: Contentious – 1,681,852 years

Quinn took it all in as she walked over toward their unexpected
guests. They'd been riled up against the Library for a very long time, it
seemed.

Tenejorissimo (Tenejo)

Status: Contingent Leader

Species: Serpensiril

Faction: Ebolibia (Translation: Against the Library)

Caution: Antagonistic

Power Level: Intermediate (Active) - Progressive

Quinn did her best not to show a reaction to the information the
Library gave her. It was the first time she'd seen so much on an indi-

vidual. She pulled up the information on the others getting much the same, but their names were Narajo and Dijaro. She'd wait and see if they introduced themselves.

There was already tension among the people who worked in the Library, as well as the visitors back in the reading sections. She could feel it emanating from Eric and Geneva, not to mention Malakai and Dottie.

Quinn was pretty sure the flickering in Lynx meant he was annoyed as well. She tried to walk as authoritatively as she could, while using her mind-time dilation to speak to the Library. She needed to assess the situation as diplomatically as possible.

What are they doing here? How did they get an application? she asked.

The Library didn't sound angry when it spoke, just irritated. *We didn't send the applications to their homeworld. We don't invite non-allies or friends to be Library assistants, even if everyone has access to the archives. They shouldn't have one unless they went somewhere that did and took them. It should have been coded to their magical signature as well. This, like every-thing else recently, shouldn't be possible.*

Quinn got that. *Well, we're not telepaths, so I guess the only way to know why they're here is to ask them, right?*

We're not forceful *telepaths, Quinn,* the Library corrected her. *Asking is your best bet.*

Good point, good point. She was almost there now. *I'm going to try and get the information out of them and see if we can't have some sort of civilized conversation before I remember how close Kajaro came to killing me and that he has a virtual mind-bomb planted in my head. I wouldn't want to accidentally freeze every single drop of blood in their bodies.*

Quinn. The Library sounded somewhat concerned. *Where did you learn that?*

You know where I learned that. It's not like I'll do anything anyway—I'm still reeling from thinking I helped kill Kajaro. But I've got the books in my head. And a really bloody awful hangover from all that information I absorbed over the last two days. I can piece things together. Quinn might have sounded a bit smug.

Told you not to overdo it, the Library said.

Not helping.

Quinn plastered a smile on her face as she arrived directly in front of the visitors. They hadn't moved from where they had originally landed when all eyes turned to them. They were differing shades of green. One of them was almost lime with black stripes down the side of his arms that she could see poking out through his robes. He was different from Kajaro's type. He didn't have a snake-like hood under his hood that she could tell. Although, they still had forked tongues from how they darted out every now and again.

"Hello," she said.

The one to the left of Tenejo, in the middle, also had a lime-green coloring with the scales mottled with black in what seemed like almost even stripes. That one was Narajo. To Tenejo's right stood Dijaro, whose scales were a forest green type of color, but matte and not shiny. They all had yellow eyes, forked tongues, and the same snaky nose holes.

Quinn turned to the leader in the middle, after going over all the information once more before dismissing it. She refused to be ill-prepared or put on the back foot by people who shouldn't even be here. She was the Librarian, and this was her show.

Besides, the odds of someone else butting in, who didn't have all the information except for that pertaining to Kajaro, was very probable if she didn't beat them to it. A certain winged imp to be specific.

The leader gave a shallow bow before introducing himself. "Tenejo, Serpensiril. Full name, Tenejorissimo. Allied with faction Ebolibia."

"I know who you are," Quinn said, keeping a shallow smile on her face. She wondered if the name endings were species related. "Did you come here to introduce yourselves? I must confess I didn't expect to see you here. I do believe you shouldn't have those applications." She kept her tone even and a small smile on her face, while trying not to let on that she was absolutely scared out of her wits, and instead hoped that she portrayed a modicum of control over the entire situation.

The Library hissed in her mind and flashed across her vision:

Scanning intentions: just below hostile
Yellow alert
These three entrants are being monitored for changes. Should changes occur, the alert level will adjust.

Just as Narajo was about to open his mouth, Tenejo stepped forward. "I believe I have been remiss. Let me try again. I am Tenejo, son of Arishnemis. I have come here to plead our case. We are a distant faction of the Serpensiril. And we have decided that we do require the knowledge within the Library."

Quinn did her very best to suppress raising the eyebrow that she so desperately wanted to. Not only that, it was obvious they didn't realize the extent to which the Library could gather their information, which meant they had no idea that she was aware of what the faction they belonged to meant.

Nor were they aware that the Library could read their currently level of intention.

She cleared her throat, sending a thought to Lynx at the same time, for everybody to stop gaping and get back to their work. She could almost feel his hesitance and willingness to argue with her through the link they shared. But he turned around and made a motion to the others. They reluctantly began the interviewing process again. With the Library less quiet, it was easier for Quinn to relax.

"Excellent, Tenejo. So if you wouldn't mind following me into my office, I believe that would be the best place for us to have a discussion." It took a lot of willpower for Quinn to turn and allow them to follow behind her. She just trusted the Library to keep her safe.

Tenejo's eyes narrowed very briefly, which was odd in a snake who didn't have eyelids. Still, the hood portion of his head, sort of like a cobra, flared slightly. "Very well, Librarian."

Quinn could practically sense the animosity rolling off him. How the Library hadn't yet tweaked to throwing them out, she had no idea. She sent a mental image to the Library to make her office as small and sparse as it could. She wanted all books hidden, and for it to more resemble an interrogation room from the procedural dramas she'd seen back home.

Except she wanted a desk and chair for herself.

By the time she got to the door, she knew the configuration would be in place.

It was one of the best perks about a magical library. It could be whatever it wanted to.

Just as Quinn expected, her room had been transformed before she opened the door. A rudimentary metal desk sat where her usual one would be, with a decently comfortable chair behind it for herself, and three wooden stools arranged in a row before the desk.

Aradie swooped in to sit on her shoulder at the last moment, and she summoned Misha with a thought. Having the supervisory golem with her always made Quinn feel more secure, just knowing they were there.

She motioned for the Serpensiril to sit in the three seats in front of her. The entire room had been shrunken, or as Quinn was fairly sure had happened, this new creation was simply placed inside her original office. There was no way she'd give these spies, because she had no doubt that's what they were here to do, an opportunity to glean anything about her or the status of the Library.

"We apologize for our unexpected arrival, Librarian, and we greet thee," Tenejo said, after a brief exchange of looks between the three of them. "We were not expecting such a hostile reception."

Quinn raised an eyebrow, not even bothering to hide her disdain this time. "Whyever not? The Library and your branch of the Serpensiril haven't been allies for a very long time. I do believe it's approximately, what, just over a million-odd years of us not being allies anymore? Your faction has attempted to belittle the Library's works and purpose in the form of both protests and attempted theft before. And you sit here wishing to apply to be a Library's assistant after obtaining those applications in what I can only assume is an underhanded way because I know they weren't sent to you. So please, Tenejo, explain to me how your reception wasn't expected."

The weight of Aradie on her shoulder was one of the only things giving her the strength to be this forthright. Her soul was trembling. She only hoped they couldn't see it or feel it. Misha stood next to the desk, their hands behind them, their golem expression impassive as they watched the Serpensiril without blinking. Quinn's main hope was that they'd be off kilter because of how much she already knew, and wouldn't examine her too closely.

After an initial shock at her speech, Tenejo, to his credit, gathered himself well. "As I said, Librarian, my apologies. We are aware that one of our ilk did attempt to thieve a book from the Library. We would like for you to understand that this is not the stance of our species as a whole."

Assessing intentions: intentions still hostile
Yellow alert extended.

"Really," Quinn said, as more of the history pertinent to this specific situation scrolled up in front of her. Lynx flickered into the room now, too, lending the physical manifestation of the Library heft to the conversation. "So you didn't mean to take part in protests attempting to tarnish the Library's dispensation of knowledge to anyone who could access it?"

She shifted in her seat and leaned forward slightly. "Did I get your affiliation wrong? No, no. Nope. Says it right here: Ebolibian Contingent—hostile to Library operations. That seems to be the correct alignment. I mean, that's even how you introduced yourself to me. So, tell me, how did you get the applications?" she asked, again. Aradie let out a long hoot as if adding punctuation.

"We were visiting a nearby world where we obtained the application. As we do have twelve of the requisite affinities required for the position, and it didn't specifically rule us out as applicants, we did not think that applying was inappropriate," Dijaro spoke up. "We apologize if we have offended you. We merely wished to help and be of assistance to such a vast depository of knowledge."

Quinn's skin began to crawl. There was something about these three that she didn't like. More than just the Library assessment or their history with the Library as such. The danger emanating from them crawled up her skin. Even if the Library said they weren't actually dangerous yet. She knew for a fact that they were going to be one hell of a problem. One word that they didn't like, and this wasn't going to go well.

She was already on very thin ice with them.

And her gut instincts were practically screaming.

Although, even as she scanned them again, she realized there was something underlying their dispositions. As if they hadn't expected her to be so knowledgeable about the Library. It would make sense, if they'd come in already knowing about the sabotage. She decided to try and figure them out.

"So you're saying you genuinely want to be assistants. You realize it's a very long and involved process to become an assistant. And you're never out of our sight for the duration, correct?"

There was a hesitance in their next answer. But this time Narajo spoke. His voice was slightly higher pitched, and she wondered if perhaps he felt as nervous as she did deep down. "We would like to contribute to the Library and its greatness."

Quinn thought it sounded so fake, she actually cringed. And as if to punctuate that point, Aradie sent an image in front of her. One that told her that was an outright lie.

"Okay, so you know, I'm not buying that. I want another reason. And actual reason. Why should I even entertain allowing those who aren't even our allies—and have been at loggerheads with us for so many millennia, I can't even process it—why should I let you stay here any longer?" Quinn kept her voice as even as she could.

This time Dijaro spoke again. "We've concluded that the Serpensiril have been shortsighted, Librarian. We need the Library."

This time Aradie let her know that it wasn't a lie. Quinn frowned. Yeah, she could see it. They definitely needed the Library. It wasn't a lie, but their needs didn't correspond with those of the Library. And Aradie did not say that it was the truth. Just that these three in front of them believed in their need for the Library. There were ways to conceal the truth without lying.

"Yes," Tenejo added, obviously misinterpreting her wavering. "We'd like to learn about the Library. So we can give back to it." This time the lie was obvious. Even to Quinn's senses. She barely needed the confirmation Aradie gave her.

Just to be certain, she pulled up Tenejo's information again.

Tenejorissimo (Tenejo)
Status: Contingent Leader
Species: Serpensiril
Faction: Ebolibia (Translation: Against the Library)
Caution: Antagonistic - approaching downright hostile
Power Level: Intermediate (Active) - Progressive

He's gotten worse since I brought them in here, hasn't he? she asked the Library.

Much worse. It's almost to a cocky extent. As if they know something they think we don't. I'd hazard a guess that it's to do with assuming the Library still being in critical power mode.

Quinn stood up and walked around the other side of her desk. It was nice to have a small ace in the hole, one the enemy was unaware of. She crossed her arms, feeling oddly safe with Aradie on her shoulder, Misha on her left, and Lynx on her right. She could even sense Malakai standing just outside the doors.

"You can come in," she said, knowing he'd hear and waited until he was inside with the door closed behind him.

"You know," she said, now focused on the three in front of her. Their presence suddenly gave off an aura of uncertainty. All of that confidence they'd had when they walked into the Library was eroding. "You almost had me there. I almost felt generous, which I'm sure is something else you had a hand in. However"—Quinn sighed and flexed her fingers out of the fist she'd been keeping them in—"I don't believe you. And I think it's about time for you to leave, but before you do, some questions need to be answered."

All three Serpensiril stood up at once, their hoods flared, and their stances changed. Forked tongues flickered out and each of them began casting . . . at the same time as the Library issued an alarm.

Hostile entities detected.
Library is in lockdown.
Emergency Protection Protocols engaged.

24

THE KEY TO ALL STUFF-UPS

Malevolence rolled off the Serpensiril in waves. It boiled just underneath the surface, rippling through the three visitors.

Before Quinn could even think properly, an instinct, ingrained so deep inside her she didn't know where it came from, reacted.

"*Gravitas tenere,*" she said, hand outstretched toward her unwelcome guests. Visible strands of thick air surrounded the Serpensiril immediately, pushing them to the ground face first.

"Cateno," she said, biting the word off with clipped anger.

Warning:

Combined skill usage requires the following cost:

Mana per second: 2

Duration based on current statistics: 14 minutes and 28 seconds without experiencing backlash.

Please be advised to replenish mana regeneration before this occurs.

It was the first time Quinn had used a spell that had a duration on it. To weigh them down and secure them . . . she'd barely had to think. And there wasn't currently time to dwell on that.

Fourteen minutes wasn't that much time.

But she needed to figure out how she'd been so certain what she did would work.

This was *her* Library. She'd been given the responsibility to be its Librarian. She'd already waded through bookworm guts, been almost killed by a giant freaking cephalopod, ventured out to a world beset by chaos, and almost been eaten by a damn mimic, not to mention having to inhale copious amounts of chaotic sludge miasma in order to replace the filters downstairs.

Quinn wasn't giving anybody who wanted to hurt the Library a chance to do so. Plus, she needed to show them, and anyone else who sought to question it, that she was a Librarian through and through—not just in name, but in power.

It probably helped that the three Serpensiril hadn't been expecting her attack.

"*Clausura,*" she added, in order to lock down their minds. It wasn't infallible, and she only thought she'd understood correctly from absorbing the book. It should shield them from any telepathy being sent to or from them.

Lynx gaped at her.

Clausura's usage also flashed a warning at her.

Warning:

Clausura skill usage requires the following cost:

Energy per second: 1

Replenish energy as necessary.

Quinn didn't exactly understand why the mental lockdown cost her energy instead of mana, but she wasn't about to argue. At least that meant the other skill didn't have its duration shortened.

"That was amazing, Quinn." Lynx's runes were swirling in his hair, and his eyes had sparkles of enthusiasm.

"I guess we currently have hostages, or prisoners, or just people who really annoyed me." She could see three sets of reptilian eyes watching her. Watching her every move and interaction.

Misha moved forward several steps. "Well initiated, Librarian."

There was even surprise in the supervisory golem's voice which made Quinn somewhat proud yet slightly offended that most of the people around her expected so little of her. Still, now wasn't the time to address that.

She watched them struggle internally. Not that they moved externally, but she got a sense of their internal turmoil at having been stopped in their tracks. "Is there any way for us to rummage through their thoughts and extract information? I mean, there has to be a way to do that, right? There have to be books for that."

"Well, there are some books for that," Lynx said. "They aren't necessarily books you can manage right now."

"Really, Lynx? Does this look like something I didn't manage?" she said, cringing as she realized how cocky it sounded.

"I may have underestimated you, but there are approximately four more books you need to absorb before you can approach that level. Otherwise, there will be vast gaps in your knowledge, and any skills from those books can go horribly wrong, if you haven't taken all of the steps to get there. It's like going down a flight of stairs and having to skip five of them because they're broken, but not noticing and so you go plummeting to your death six stories down," Lynx spoke calmly.

"Oh," Quinn said. "That's a pretty good metaphor."

Lynx approached the three hostile Serpensiril.

Malakai moved with him, his sword out and trailing on the floor as he watched them. He brought it very close to one of their hands. "Hi," he said. "I don't like you guys."

Quinn could feel anger rolling off Malakai in waves. Anger that spoke a lot more animosity toward them than she'd expected, despite having almost been Kajaro's victims back in that cave. Yet another thing she'd have to explore later.

"So, do we question them?" Quinn said, noticing that she was down to about twelve minutes on her skill now.

"Well, we *could* question them," Lynx said, "or you could finally summon the Library guards and have them do their jobs."

Quinn blinked at him. "We have Library guards?"

"Well, yes," Lynx said. "If you summon them, we have Library guards."

Quinn shook her head. "Why did I not know about the Library guards?"

Misha sighed. It was a very metallic sound, almost ending with a bell-like flourish. "Same reason as always, Librarian. Yet another gap caused by your chip that never delivered the information correctly through your mind. You can summon the Library guards. Only you can summon the Library guards now that we are back in a mostly stable power mode. The Library and Lynx can only summon guards in emergency mode. You are in charge of that ability now."

"Very well," Quinn said, sort of scrolling back to the one brief mention in her mind of Library guards, which literally stated, *The Librarian, given the correct situation, may summon up to eight Library guards for the main branch. These are large construct golems who will take on the job of keeping the Library safe from threats. More may be summoned dependent on Library power levels.*

Quinn shrugged. "I summon the Library guards," she said, but it came out more of a question.

"How many, Librarian? Define them and do not phrase it as a question." Misha's patience seemed endless.

"Oh." Quinn blushed slightly, pausing to take a slight breath before speaking more confidently. "I summon three Library guards."

Three eight-feet-tall guardians, made out of the most polished metal armor she'd ever seen, stepped out of the back wall of the office. Quinn gaped at them. They were colossal.

"Oh, wow," she said. Upon inspection, they were referred to as Guardian One, Two, and Three. After this was all over, she was definitely giving them names. She refused to think her naming conventions might have gotten a tad out of hand.

Not to mention they were going to have to talk about the fact that they'd had Library guards this whole time and hadn't been using them.

Information scrolled up in front of Quinn's eyes. Like detailed instructions on how to instruct the golems and what specific functions they could perform. There was also a detailed listing of permission delegation that she'd have a long look at later.

First things first.

"Guardian One, activate imprisonment enclosures. Guardian Two, activate restraints. Guardian Three, activate mental broadcasting interference."

Malakai's eyes widened in awe. "These are awesome golems. Can I get some of these?" He looked at Lynx.

"No, Malakai. You cannot 'get some of these.' They're not play toys," Lynx replied.

"We won't talk," Tenejo snapped, now that the gravity sealing his movement had been lifted in favor of an imprisonment enclosure all to himself.

Lynx moved forward, slowly shifting from his human form back into his lynx-like form. This time, he was much larger, reminding Quinn almost of a saber-toothed tiger. His teeth were razor-sharp and he lingered just outside the reach of the Serpensiril' faces. Although they probably couldn't reach through their enclosure, she wasn't entirely sure it would keep Lynx out, given what he was.

She wouldn't want to be in their position.

"You don't need to talk," Lynx said, his voice purring smoothly. "All you need to do is continue to give away everything you've already started to. I don't think you realize how much your body language, word choice, and cocky attitudes have already told us about your faction."

Tenejo actually gulped audibly, but one of his co-conspirators jumped to his feet despite the pressure the prison around him applied.

"The Serpensiril will release chaos from your foul imprisonment!" Dijaro yelled.

"Stop them!" Misha yelled, but it was too late.

A loud cracking noise came from Dijaro's mouth a split second before an explosion rocked the room. Quinn fell to one knee, momentarily losing her footing as blood, viscera, and barely recognizable scaly flesh plastered itself onto the shield inside of his singular enclosure.

"Guardian One, activating stasis shield. Any movement apart from speech is halted, prohibited." The first guard spoke with a slightly metallic clang.

This didn't matter for Dijaro anymore, because his remains were currently liquefying into a mass of bodily goop inside the robe that he'd worn. The application they'd stolen and filled out for him lingered briefly on top of him as it was then dissolved into the liquid that he'd become.

"Well, I guess that's one choice to make," Malakai said, holding his nose. "Any way to get that stench out of here? Why don't those shields contain it?"

Guardian Two waved his hand impatiently, glaring at Malakai. In other circumstances, Quinn might have laughed at the situation, but not right now. She wasn't under any illusions as to what happened. These Serpensiril came here with an agenda, one they fully expected to result in literally destroying aspects of the Library.

Somehow they'd armed themselves with explosives. She should have considered it. Given the fact that Kajaro had implanted her mind bomb himself, this shouldn't have been a surprise.

Frankly, it should have been almost expected.

She and the Library needed to know why and how. They needed to know a lot of things.

Malakai put his sword away and strutted in front of them, next to Lynx, who actually came up to his waist. "Just so you two know, you're not going to have such an easy out."

For the first time since knowing him, Quinn watched him execute some type of magic spell that didn't appear to be linked to combat. Two cracks sounded, but not in quite the same way as the crunching that came from Dijaro.

An object floated out of each of the remaining Serpensiril' mouths that looked suspiciously like a section of jaw. Indeed it was, because a few seconds later, small sections of jaw ended up in Malakai's hands. He looked at them with disdain.

"I don't see why you'd do this. That's a stupendously ill-advised way to go. Your friend was in excruciating pain for a second or two." The pieces disappeared into Malakai's storage as he crouched down to speak to the other prisoners face-to-face. "So we're gonna do this a couple of ways. My buddies over here, Guardians One, Two, and Three, are going to help me make you talk."

"We're not going to talk," Tenejo spat again, but the strain from even trying to speak due to the restrictions was obvious in his voice.

"Well, guess you didn't get lucky, then," Quinn said, very glad her mana was replenishing itself already. "Would you like a cone of silence so they each don't know what the other one says?"

"Cone of silence?" Lynx asked. "Wouldn't a box of silence or maybe even a cylinder of silence be better?"

Shaking her head in disappointment, she said, "You don't get it at all. I'm extremely sad about this." No one here knew anything about any Earth television shows.

"We can move the interrogation room, Librarian," Guardian One spoke up. "We can have it excised from your office and moved over to next to it."

"Oh," Quinn said, glancing at Lynx, who was still grinning with very many pointy sharp teeth about a foot from each of the captive's faces. Considering Malakai's actions, she knew the manifestation could reach through to the prisoners, just not the other way round. She thought Lynx might be having a little bit too much fun with that.

"You can move the interrogation room after we've got something from them," Lynx practically growled.

"Like what?" Malakai said. "Do you see them talking?"

"Can't we just force them to reveal what they know? I mean, isn't there a way to make them talk like a truth serum, or something that gets them to just start talking and never shut up?" Quinn asked, not understanding why they couldn't just magic a solution.

Malakai looked at her and raised an eyebrow. "I guess they did plant a mind-bomb in your brain, didn't they?"

"Yes. Yes, they did. And it's still there. It's just under lock and key." Quinn was flustered. She wanted to know what these two knew. She wasn't even sure she should have said that with them there. What if they could communicate back home.

They currently can't extend mindspeech outside of the Library, the Library so helpfully added.

Quinn let out a small sigh of relief. If the captives had any idea what Kajaro, or the leadership of this group of protestors, was up to then she needed to know five minutes ago.

"Maybe we could do the same to them. You know, under threat of having a mind bomb implanted and being completely incoherent for the rest of their natural lives. We could do that," Malakai offered, his tone consoling.

Quinn sighed, knowing she was just frustrated and that made her less cautious. "No, we shouldn't lower ourselves to their level."

"Whyever not?" Lynx said. "That's a very human affectation, Quinn. They're trying to destroy both you and the Library. I'd say a little destruction aimed their way is more than warranted."

Quinn sighed and spoke softly. Their captives were currently behind barriers, but she couldn't be sure they weren't able to hear. "Yeah, but we already know that they think that the Library is about to tumble down. They came in assuming we'd only just begun to pick up the pieces and assumptions—they're the key to all stuff-ups."

No one said anything. So she continued. "Plus, in the meantime, we have to figure out a way to keep them from leaving and keep others from coming here. Any ideas?" she asked the Library directly.

I'd suggest a stasis chamber, but I'll give you a few options.

Several options popped up in front of Quinn's face. She frowned.

Stasis chamber: Inserted in between their door and our entry door. Shuts the potential entrants inside until they can be verified. Can be configured to a specific planet, or species signature.

Immolation chamber: Identifies potential threats based on banned species, people, planetary alignments, and eliminates that threat.

Escrilian Mind Bug Borers

Quinn refused to read anything further on the last one. *We don't need to torture people.*

Could be fun. It used to be entertaining a few hundred thousand years ago, the Library said.

If Quinn could have raised an eyebrow at the Library without raising suspicion that she was talking in her head to the other people in the room, she would have. She mulled it over even though she really didn't think it was much of a choice.

"Let's use a Stasis Chamber. I agree that's the best option. We can send guards if it's alerted. If the occupants kill themselves in the interim? Not my problem. Not my choice." She sounded a lot more confident about that than she felt.

"They're fanatics, Quinn. There's only so much you can do for them." Malakai fixed her with a surprisingly melancholy look. One of these days they'd get to sit down and chat about their lives.

"Okay, congratulations," she said to Tenejo and Narajo. "You just managed to put the whole of the Serpensiril species on the blacklist of the Library. For, I believe, the first time. Is that correct, Lynx?"

Lynx nodded and growled. "First time. The Library has never excluded an entire species from entry before and you guys and Kajaro just managed to do that."

"Don't worry, you can still come, but getting in is another question." Quinn decided not to correct Lynx. After all, if the Serpensiril who came next were genuinely not enemies, they'd be permitted entry, but their current "guests" didn't need to know that. She turned to the guards. "I think now is a good time to move the interrogation room away from me."

The guardians began to comply, and Quinn watched the walls warp as they moved away. Her knees shook and her head swam with knowledge, and she needed some alone time to figure out just what parts of her powers she'd tapped into.

2 5

INTERLOPERS

With the Serpensiril out of her office, a wave of exhaustion washed over Quinn, forcing her to sit against her desk, even as her office transformed back to its usual state around her.

It was mesmerizing to watch as everything shifted around her. The couch emerged from behind the wall that made the smaller office as it dissolved. The desk changed and slid back to its rightful place, despite the fact that she sat against it.

Magical fricking Libraries, eh?

She checked her energy levels; they were fine. Her mana levels were still relatively low, but not enough to drain her of energy like this. Her mind whirled, unable to stop analyzing every single event that transpired after she had taken the Serpensiril into her office.

The knowledge to restrain their hostile visitors simply popped into her head with action words that she was fairly certain were Latin, or at least Latin adjacent, a dead language on Earth even. She had no idea why Latin happened to be her trigger for magic. She didn't know the language and she certainly hadn't realized she was capable of the powers the words triggered.

Perhaps that's how the universal translating doohickey managed to present it to her. *Gravitas Teneri* loosely meant that gravity would hold them in place. *Cateno* restricted movement, or it was supposed to. And *Clausura* locked them in place, locked their minds down. At least, that was her understanding of what she'd done.

Quinn had, after all, never taken a Latin class in her life.

She knew all of this information theoretically because she'd only just absorbed the books. She hadn't spent any time practicing the elements that she needed to in order to have them under such good control. The sudden knowledge of how to restrain them and her intrinsic capability to do so was actually rattling.

She didn't look at Misha, nor Lynx. Malakai had left with the guardians.

She leaned more heavily on her desk and decided it was time to ask the Library just a few questions. *How the hell did I do what I just did?*

You mean leaning against the desk?

Don't be facetious, you know what I mean.

There was a hesitation before the next words. Almost like the Library didn't want to answer. *To be honest, I don't know.*

Quinn ran her hand through her hair. A chunk of loose curls had come out of her ponytail. She didn't feel like putting it back up. *You know, you seem to not know an awful lot for a Library of Everywhere.*

That's a little bit speciesist, isn't it? the Library said.

No, Quinn retorted. *It is precisely the truth and exactly right. So much has been revealed since the reboot. So much was stolen from you.*

That's also not exactly my fault, the Library said, sounding extremely defensive and perhaps mildly concerned. *I didn't exactly foresee these circumstances as they have arisen. I'm not prescient.*

Do you have any theories? Quinn asked, still absolutely exhausted.

The Library didn't speak for several seconds. So long that Quinn thought it was doing one of those "just not going to talk to her anymore" things. And then there was an audible sigh that echoed through Quinn's head.

Look, you take care of the interlopers, go and speak to the guardians, talk to Misha, learn what we're going to do in regards to retrieving the information that we need out of them.

I don't know. I'm not really into torture. Quinn really wasn't sure what to make of the Serpensiril, or how to deal with them. Or how to retrieve anything from them.

Yes, Quinn, we realize this. None of us are exactly "into" torture. We don't want to torture people, but we do need the information they have because they very obviously came here with an agenda. To the extent that they had explosives with them, inside of them even. If that explosion hadn't been contained by the barrier, that would have been very bad for the Library, Quinn. If all three of them had managed detonate those in the Library itself, that would have resulted in some almost irreparable damage.

We do have backups of the books, right? Quinn asked.

Yes, we have backups of the books, but I don't have backups of my internal organs, okay?

Quinn filed that little tidbit away but didn't say anything else. She sensed the Library wasn't done talking yet.

Look, you go with the guardians, take care of the Serpensiril, figure out what we're going to do. Then, take care of all of the new assistants that are out there waiting to see you, and hoping that this hasn't blown up in all of their faces. And when you're done with those things, I want you to come down to the core room because I have something very important to teach you.

You have something really important to teach me? Quinn prodded the thought as she had it.

Did I stutter?

No. No, you didn't, but you got really snarky, Quinn said defensively.

The Library paused again before answering. *Look, this has all gotten so far out of hand. I was supposed to fetch you and make the Library whole again. Easy. Except it hasn't been easy with you from the get go. From the likely genetic interference with the chip to your innate ability to adapt the magic you've absorbed. In the process of rebooting everything, we've lost such a plethora of information, and I have ridgy-didge, as you would say, gaps in my memory, which is not something that's ever happened to me before or even something that I'd conceived of as possible. So just indulge me.*

Quinn could do that, but she was still curious. *Why can't Lynx teach me?*

Lynx is a lot of things and can show you a lot of stuff. However, he is only my manifestation. He is not me. He is and has become a definite, mostly unique, individual. He is quite literally his own person, and one day I will get him a tangible body if he wants it. But what I need to teach you . . .

I think he'd love that, Quinn said.

Well, of course he would, but at the same time, I think he'd be a bit lost. Anyway, I digress. What I want to teach you requires more finesse because it deals with organics, in a way.

Okay, Quinn said. *I'll go wrangle the assistants and make sure that we figure out a way to deal with these interlopers, which, by the way, in case I didn't mention, is a much better term.*

I know, the Library said. *And when you do come down, Quinn, clear a few days.*

Done and done, Quinn said. She sensed that asking for more clarification right then wasn't going to happen anyway.

Misha approached her while Quinn still had her head in her hands, leaning against her desk as she finished up her conversation. "Librarian, what is the next move for the interlopers?"

"You've been talking to the Library, haven't you?" Quinn said, without moving a muscle, well, apart from her mouth.

"I am synchronized to the Library," Misha said, as if that explained everything.

Which it sort of did. Quinn sighed. "You are, aren't you? As for the interlopers . . . I believe it's best left to those who know how to deal with this sort of thing."

"If I may say so, Librarian, you did deal with them quite well." Misha's tone gave no indication to how the supervisory golem felt about that.

"Malakai's already there, correct?" Quinn asked, deciding not to pursue anything else awkward for now.

"Yes," Misha said, "I do believe we are fetching Milaro once he has finished his current tasks in his homeland."

"Ah." Quinn mulled that over. "Because of the mind-stuff?"

"Because of, as you so eloquently put it, 'the mind-stuff,'" Misha said. There was a slight twitch to Misha's lips as they gave a very brief grin in response.

Quinn chuckled. "Well then, what is it he'll be doing?"

"I do believe he can use thought extraction, or a specific type of mind wandering that he developed, but I would have to double-check that." Misha hesitated a second and then continued. "He will not be able to attend us immediately. It will be a few days before he gets here."

"Okay, well, while we set all this up, I think it best to go and check on the new assistants."

Misha's voice lowered until their words were soothing. "They are doing fine. I believe we have narrowed it down to nine new ones and the three siblings of Narilin's, giving us a dozen new assistants."

"That's a lot of new assistants," Quinn said.

"Having this many allows us to divide them into four shifts a day so everybody is working a maximum of eight and a half hours a day, so they have overlap with other shifts, and usually only a four-day week, only needing to work a fifth day once every five weeks I believe. Things will need to shift if someone needs a longer vacation than three days, but we will sort that when necessary. It leaves people less cranky, leaves them less likely to snap at the patrons and attempt to impose fines like Eric constantly does." Misha said with an echo of distaste.

Quinn raised an eyebrow. "Does he really do that?"

"Yes, Quinn, he really does that." Misha didn't seem to approve of Eric's approach.

"Should I go and meet them now?"

"Do you want to go and meet them?" the supervisory golem countered.

Quinn sighed. She still felt very drained and very confused. All she actually wanted to do was go down and visit the Library core. To hear whatever it was the Library wanted to teach her or show her. But she knew she had a couple of things to check on first. She looked over at where Lynx hadn't moved since the others left the room. His eyes were flickering, so she directed her words at him specifically. "Okay, let's go and do that, shall we, just quickly, and then I'll go and check on the interlopers."

The Library manifestation looked up, his swirling eyes steadying as he blinked.

"Very well," Lynx said, and nosed her out of the door.

It wasn't nearly as much of a hullabaloo beyond the doors as Quinn thought it would be. All the potential assistants were seated on the seats or around them, in the area she'd first interviewed Narilin. Eric, Geneva, and Dottie stood in front of the semicircle, going over a lot of information with the new assistants. Quinn could hear every word through her connection to the Library, even though they were a good fifty yards from her. She walked toward them, knowing they would sense her approach, or at least that Dottie would.

"Ah, here she is," Eric said. "Our wondrous, our fantastic Librarian from galaxies far, far away. I present to you, Quinn."

Narilin's sisters looked up at Quinn. Large deep green eyes and small smiles. The leaves that made up their hair rustled ever so slightly as if in a welcoming breeze. Quinn returned the smile, feeling more at ease because of it.

Everybody else seemed quite intimidated. One of them was a mantishia. It was all Quinn could do not to stare. Half of her brain wanted to dedicate time to figuring out how the different segmentation of body parts worked. But she flashed them a smile and turned to the rest, two of which were sedimentites. Their strong, dark-as-coal bodies rippled with contained heat.

Quinn was really excited to have them working in the Library. There were a couple more of Milaro's people, and two more of the Furionas like Geneva. She inspected everybody, gathering names that she knew she would forget as soon as looking at them right now. But it at least let her know, and keep them in her notes for later reference.

"Welcome to the Library," she said, feeling like the words were extremely hollow right now. She wasn't her usual self. Her confidence in what she was doing was flagging and she couldn't understand why. But she had accepted her place as the Librarian, and with that came responsibility.

The one thing that made it better was knowing that if she chose, she could simply open a door to somewhere and disappear.

Sort of.

The Library could probably find her again.

She kept the smile on her face, and tried to let it reach her eyes. "Does anybody have any questions?"

The sedimentite, whose name was Larry, put his hand up. "I just wanted to know if we get, you know, vacations to go home and see our family."

"Of course," Quinn said, glancing at Lynx for confirmation. He nodded his head almost imperceptibly. "While this is a job you get paid for, you're also technically Library volunteers. We appreciate everybody who comes and works in the Library. Of course, you can go home and visit. I believe most weeks you will have three days off. You're not stuck here seven days a week."

"Not all of us have seven days in a week, you know," Eric interrupted and then smirked at the glare Quinn directed at him.

She cleared her throat before continuing. "You can just hop through a door and get here. You don't have to live here. We have that option available because sometimes it's just easier."

Geneva nodded. "Yes, the dormitories upstairs are at your convenience. I've found them quite comfortable personally. You are not required to live in the Library."

"Right, then. Great," Larry rumbled and his lips curved into a smile. His molten eyes glowed for a second. "This is really great."

Geneva smiled at the obvious enthusiasm as she continued, "Now, please make sure you let Cook know if you have any dietary needs."

With that, Quinn sighed, turned around, and left the group. She'd put in an appearance. That was enough for the day. They were settling in. They'd be taken through all of the orientation they needed to become amazing assistants. And now Quinn had to go and visit what amounted to prisoners.

Her next stop was the new interrogation room. It had two entrances, but the one outside her office wasn't one she wanted to reveal just now. Instead, she decided she'd go through the door in the far back of her office. She took a deep breath and knocked.

When she entered, she walked into an antechamber, almost like a viewing room with a big glass window. She assumed it was anyway, since it was similar to the interrogation rooms they used in procedural dramas, where the people on the other side couldn't see those who were looking in and watching them.

Guardian Three, upon inspection, was standing in there, waiting.

"Librarian," it said, by way of greeting.

Quinn stared at the guardian for a moment. "I think you should be called Fife."

Fife nodded, and a subtle glow of blue permeated their body, changing it ever so slightly. The armor became more condensed, their build slightly thicker. "Fife is an acceptable name. Appreciated Librarian, do you wish to view from out here or would you like to enter the domain?"

Quinn shook her head. "Here is fine. Would you be a dear and get the others for me, please?"

He did so and swapped positions with them, keeping a watch over their . . . guests. Misha appeared in the other corner of the antechamber, watching silently.

"Uno." She pointed at Guardian One, knowing it was a little bit on the nose. "And Dale," she said to number Guardian Two as they entered from the other room.

Dale paused for a moment before altering slightly as well. He became slightly more slender and perhaps two or three inches taller, with masculine tinges to the armor he wore. Whereas Uno remained exactly as he had been.

"Much appreciated, Librarian," they said in unison. And they both disappeared back into the chamber.

Misha stood next to Quinn. "That made their day."

"I'd imagine being called into existence again after however many millennia it's been since they were last needed was probably the highlight of their day," Quinn said.

"Likely, but this made it even better." Misha flashed one of her golem smiles in Quinn's direction. "From being resummoned and then given an identity. I would think the latter would make this more distinctive for them."

They watched as the security golems enforced submission, while Malakai stood in a corner of the interrogation room watching. Quinn squirmed. She didn't like seeing anybody forced into a position, even somebody who seemed hellbent on blowing up the Library. Taking it down by conventional means apparently wasn't something that the Serpensiril were willing to do.

"I don't know what to do, Misha," Quinn said, feeling alarmingly out of her depth. Misha, while not motherly as such, or fatherly like Cook, or even grandfatherly like Milaro . . . was a solid presence Quinn was coming to depend upon.

"May I give you advice, Librarian? I have many eons of experience in my head, garnered from all the previous supervisory golems before me. I would like, if you would let me, to lend you some guidance."

Quinn paused and looked at Misha. "Fire away."

"Milaro is one of the foremost experts in the universe on mind magic. He does not know every aspect, as evidenced by the slipshod solution currently in your brain. But he is exceptional at interrogation."

"Could he cause them pain?" Quinn asked softly.

"Of course he could cause them pain. But Milaro also knows ways to extract thoughts from those who, A, do not wish to part with them, B, have been put under influence that might otherwise restrict them from sharing some of those thoughts, and C, he knows how to compel them to speak the truth. You might not know it from the friendly way he treats you, but Milaro is a formidable king. There's a reason he is in the position that he is."

Quinn listened, sobering up very quickly. She nodded. "Okay, we requested his presence, right?"

"Yes, we have sent a message, but I will let him know the urgency. He is currently dealing with a situation in his homeland. At this rate it will take some time for him to arrive."

"Acceptable," Quinn said. "We can do that. I have somewhere I need to be anyway."

"Excellent. Then I will see you when Milaro arrives." And Misha was gone.

Quinn glanced at the time in her HUD. It was late in the day, and she was very tired. She needed food. She wanted to shower and sleep. Her subconscious needed to digest the rest of the magic knowledge she'd devoured. All those books needed a lot more time to percolate.

And tomorrow? She thought she might just take some snacks and go and nestle in the boughs of the core for a couple of days. Not only did the Library have things to show or teach her, but Quinn also had questions.

After all . . . they were fast approaching the time when she'd be able to start leveraging fines. She had every intention of being completely prepared for it.

26

BEST-LAID PLANS

Quinn fully intended to wake up the next morning refreshed, informed, and recharged. She planned to grab some food, check in with Lynx quickly, and run down to the core.

However, best-laid plans are usually screwed up somehow. Her initial plans were, in fact, not actually possible.

The first thing she noticed was that Aradie wasn't in the room with her. Quinn reached out with her senses, which were slightly more attuned to the Library every day, and felt that Aradie was downstairs somewhere close to the check-in desk.

This was odd because the bird had been there when Quinn went to bed and didn't usually stray from her during sleep. That she knew of, anyway. There was so much to do, Quinn didn't think too much of it and decided to go and have a good breakfast downstairs, grab her bird, go down, and spend some cozy time with the Library, getting to know it better.

She could feel it. This was it. Her chance to really become the strong, kick-ass Librarian she wanted to be.

With positivity flowing through her, she raced downstairs.

And all of those thoughts flew out the window.

Aradie practically hovered in the air, squawking loudly at Harish and Siliqua. Lynx stood with them next to the check-in counter, speaking to the bird and the researchers in all earnestness. They all seemed to be conversing with the owl, which didn't strike Quinn as odd as it maybe should.

She'd never realized Aradie could speak to other people. Magical bird who spoke through telepathic images and emotions—and sometimes words—was probably able to communicate with anyone open to her type of magic. It made sense now that she thought of it.

Aradie, Harish, and Siliqua began practically yelling at each other, while Lynx couldn't get a word in edgewise. The elf couple spoke to Aradie and Lynx with loud hand gestures and words that Quinn couldn't quite make out because Dottie was trying to train the new recruits at the same time. Minus the Salosiers, that is.

The bench wasn't more than twenty feet from the check-in desk, which created a huge hullabaloo because there was a line of about twenty people waiting to return books to the Library.

It appeared that Eric was the only person checking in books. And the imp didn't look happy about that at all.

Quinn pinched the bridge of her nose and mentally counted to five. But the din didn't lessen.

She breathed in deeply and yelled, "Quiet!"

Everybody stopped, just for a second. But it was enough for her to make her presence known and walk down to where Aradie, Lynx, Siliqua, and Harish were having their heated discussion.

"I'll deal with you guys in a moment." Then she turned to Dottie. "Take the new recruits back a tad, away from the noise in the front lobby, okay?" She waved toward the couches and table that they used for some of their meetings.

"Fine, Librarian," Dottie said, sounding extremely put out, but she trotted away with the rest of the recruits following after her. The bench had proven to be such an amazing help since their first very awkward meeting where Quinn pretty much sat on her. She'd have to remember to thank her later.

Quinn then turned her attention to the four in front of her, but not before being interrupted by Eric.

"Don't mind me," Eric called over, "I'll just keep doing this all by myself the whole time."

Quinn sighed. "Okay, Eric, I'll bite. Why are you the only one at the check-in desk?"

Eric, it seemed, was brilliant at multitasking, because he didn't even pause in checking in books as he spoke. "Because you said that all of the Library assistants can take vacations. That it's as easy as walking through the door if they like. You said they just have to make sure to come back in time for their shifts after they've had time off. And voila! Danio, Jim, Bob, none of them turned up today. Except Finn, but Cook needed help so they're helping over in the kitchen right now. So here we are. Geneva has the afternoon shift, so I'm making sure she rests, but it's a little hectic here."

Quinn sighed. "I didn't mean they could just take off straight away without any prior arrangements. Plus isn't *this* their shift? I thought I was pretty clear about being here for their shifts. I guess I wasn't. We'll have to reword that. I apologize. I'll be with you in a few minutes to clear any backlog."

Eric grumbled under his breath, "Fine, I'm obviously making do right now." His hands moved faster than humanly possible, but then, Quinn guessed, he wasn't human.

"Okay, you guys," Quinn said, turning her attention from Eric. If she really tried, she'd be listening to his grumbling forever. "What gives? What's with the noise? It's a library, isn't it supposed to be quiet?"

Lynx raised an eyebrow. "What do you mean? Why would a library be quiet?"

"So people can concentrate on reading," Quinn said. "Every library on Earth has a rule, you have to be quiet in the library."

"Well," Lynx said, looking like he was really considering her words. "I mean, of course we don't want yelling or screaming or playing music or singing or whatever in the Library, but people are going to talk if they're researching. They're going to compare notes, they're going to want to have theoretical and theological discussions. We promote the sharing of knowledge, not the reading of it in your head all by yourself."

Quinn blinked at him. She actually much preferred that philosophy. "Still, you guys were being what I would call unproductively loud. What's the problem?"

"We have finally figured out how to fully cleanse the last subject sections of their virus," Harish said, not focusing on any one of them in particular. Aradie flapped her wings irritably and went and settled on Quinn's shoulder.

"Well, Aradie doesn't seem to agree with whatever your solution is." Quinn was about to say more, but the bird flashed a few images in front of her mind. Some of them were a complex melting down of books that Quinn wasn't partial to at all. "Wait, does this mean the solution is to withdraw a heap of books, melt them down, delete them basically, and then reconstitute them from the Library's archives?"

"That would be the best solution we've found," Siliqua said. She wouldn't meet Quinn's eyes.

"Why these books? Why are they so hard to, I guess, cleanse?" she asked.

"Yeah, *cleanse* isn't exactly the word I would choose," Siliqua said. "But it's close enough for us to use for the current topic. The detritus inside the books is, it's too far gone for us to magically—"

"Oh!" Quinn said. "Decontaminate."

"Excellent word." Siliqua continued from where she'd been interrupted. "These sections are infected. They're not salvageable; they're irreparable. We were going to approach Narilin with them and see if she agrees with us, but there's only so much we can cleanse from something rotten before it disintegrates or before it gives way to what is trying to infect it. Luckily, there are only fifty-seven books we've had to put in this category." Siliqua looked like she was fighting back tears.

Harish cleared his throat, obviously disliking his partner's stress levels. "We tried everything. We do apologize, but it seems this is the best avenue for us to take."

Lynx sighed. "At least we have a solution. Looks like it's time to go and talk to the book doctor."

Quinn completely understood their reticence to do so.

Narilin was engrossed in her work with Jane when the group of them traipsed in. The two sisters barely even looked up as Quinn, Harish, Siliqua, Lynx, and Aradie entered the room.

Quinn wasn't entirely sure how she had gotten roped into coming along, but here she was.

Aradie flew off with a hoot of dissatisfaction, settling among her brethren and cooing at them in what appeared to be a retelling of her very angry opinion about what was about to happen.

Quinn approached the desk and cleared her throat. Narilin looked up and blinked. "Oh, Librarian, I did not realize it was you."

"Who else comes to visit you here?" Quinn asked, forgetting her manners in all her curiosity.

"Sometimes Misha, occasionally Dottie, and every so often Geneva and Eric just to double-check on some books they have given into my care. Often they receive returned books that are in less than ideal condition. Eric seems very invested in how the books come back to us, so much so that he wants to know if they are indeed irreparable and if that means he can levy a fine. I have told him . . ." She paused, flushing a little. It was difficult to tell on a Salosier, but there was definite blushing. "I apologize. I do get carried away when it's about fostering good book etiquette."

Quinn couldn't help staring. She had never heard Narilin speak so much in the whole time she'd been at the Library, the whole like almost three weeks. "Oh, that's perfectly understandable. I'm so glad you and your sister seem to be doing well here."

Jane perked up at the mention of her. "This infirmary is fascinating. We have book infirmaries back at home but nothing on this scale, nor with all of these tools."

Narilin practically shone with happiness. It made Quinn wonder if the Salosier had been homesick.

"Anyway, why are you here, Librarian? I know you were not due to assist with book reparation today, especially since I now have Jane," Narilin asked.

Quinn nodded. "Sadly, it's not really book reparation we need to talk about. I'll let Harish fill you in. He understands it better than I do." Quinn stepped back, allowing Harish to step forward.

He glanced at Siliqua before clearing his own throat and speaking while his partner produced a thick, plastic-like covering to place over the table in front of them. Harish pulled out several books, laying them on a protective surface so that they were spread out.

It was highly obvious something was wrong with them. Their spines were mottled with a strange black substance that Quinn would have thought was black mold from Earth. But it was more insidious than that. She could practically see the rotting patterns all over the book as they moved, congealed, and spread out. As if it was alive . . .

Quinn instinctively reached out her senses toward it only to recoil like she'd been slapped. It felt . . . dangerous.

Narilin gasped in shock, her eyes going wide. Even the leaves in her hair shook in a way that wasn't attractive like usual but more scared.

"What happened?" she asked, pulling on some complex-looking gloves that were made for her nine-fingered hands. They went all the way up her arms and almost suctioned to her hands and elbows, appearing like a second skin that was magically protected.

"These are the books we have quarantined, some of the ones we found that were infecting part of the Library. We have fifty-seven of them, and they are, as far as I can tell," Harish continued, "beyond saving in the way they are now."

Over her shock, or at least appearing to be Narilin reached gently for one of the books. A melancholy frown passed over her face as she touched them. "Oh, these are—these are not the books they should be," she said. She looked at Quinn. "They are warped beyond their intended purpose and will serve no one anything but harm should they be allowed to continue. Do you wish my opinion?"

Harish sighed. "We were hoping you could let us know if we're doing the right thing in destroying these books and if we have the capability to recreate them with the current supplies that we have on hand."

Narilin frowned. "Well, yes, I can look them over." She placed both hands on the book and, as far as Quinn could tell, she looked *beyond* the book in a way that Quinn didn't exactly understand. Pulling herself out of the trance a moment later, Narilin sighed. "Even though at first appearance we'd think they are beyond hope, it is always better to make sure. You are indeed correct in thinking that these are beyond saving. I . . ." She paused, leaving the book and handing a pair of gloves to her sister. "Take a look and see what you think," she said as she moved around the workshop.

Quinn could never get over the contents of the book infirmary. Its sheer majesty was reflected in the reams of parchment, of beautiful binding thread, the leather for the coverings, and the leather balm to take care of the final product. It was a magical place, quite literally.

Narilin frowned. "I believe we are currently capable of reproducing thirty-nine of them. However, I could be wrong. That is just an estimation given the current predicament and the writing implements I have that can currently be employed. You will have to talk to Farrow about the bookworm, night owl, and silverfish interactions. My night owls have currently given us a lot more writing implements than I thought we would get at this point in time. It seems they aligned their shedding of them with the current urgency level of the Library. So we should be able to get most of the books redone straight away. But the other eighteen will take some time."

"How long will that take?" Quinn asked.

Narilin scrunched her face up very oddly. It made her skin look like old, withered bark for a moment. Quinn tried not to laugh and was barely successful. Luckily, it seemed the Salosier did not notice.

"I would give us about two to three weeks, perhaps a little longer. I would appreciate it if you gave us a level of urgency per book title and we can address that then."

Quinn sighed. "So wait, if we pull all of these books out of rotation and cleanse the area around them, then we can return the books to those specific subject sections without fear of them being further contaminated, is that correct?"

Harish nodded. Siliqua smiled. "That's exactly it. These books were part of the overall problem, having infected the Library during your shut down. We removed them as soon as we discovered them and quarantined them. The areas they were in have been cleansed, but these books . . ." She shrugged.

"So we could do that as early as today?" Quinn asked.

"We could do that as early as today," Siliqua answered, smiling. "Which, it's not ideal, but that's fifty-seven books. The Library has been operating without eighteen thousand for what, five hundred years?"

Quinn laughed. "It's not like we don't have hundreds of thousands more. Looks like we have a decent solution, then."

Siliqua nodded, even if there was a hint of sadness to it. "I will begin listing out the books for Narilin here, and Harish will go and begin the cleansing of the actual sections."

"Great," Quinn said, hopeful to get back on the schedule that she had originally had for the day. "Thank you. Will Harish let the check-in desk know when they are able to return all of the affected books?"

"Done and done," Harish said.

Quinn heaved a sigh of relief, excited that she might just have salvaged a portion of the day.

Narilin cleared her throat. "I will be needing your help, Librarian. I cannot authorize the destruction of Library property myself. And even though the books are ruined, the fact that we must destroy them, lest they become a danger to anyone who touches them, still remains."

She'd known it was too good to be true. Siliqua maneuvered a large crate out of her inventory and placed it on another mat on the floor. Quinn couldn't tell what the material was made out of, but it didn't seem like something they'd had on earth.

"Well, then," she said, taking a breath. "What do I need to do to destroy these?"

Narilin glanced at Lynx before speaking. "Siliqua has provided a granite crate, and I have given it the Abishu lining. But I am not capable or permitted to destroy a Library book, no matter how damaged."

Quinn raised an eyebrow in Lynx's direction. "Me, then?"

He nodded. "Just access your Librarian interface. Under your skills you want to access Book Creation. And then demand that it give you access to Book Destruction. It's a hidden field."

"Hidden, why?" Quinn asked curiously as the menu popped up.

"We don't want fledgling Librarians getting any destructive ideas," Lynx said begrudgingly.

Quinn wanted to say that person wouldn't be a very good Librarian. But she—wisely—didn't say it out loud.

Book Destruction

Criteria: Is the book damaged beyond repair?

Yes or No?

Quin indicated Yes.

Has the book been placed in an appropriate Granite Vessel with an Abishu base?

Yes or No?

Again, Quinn indicated Yes.

Text rippled in front of her eyes, like it was being plucked out of the air in front of her.

Book Immolation granted upon assessment of books.

Assess books now?

Yes or No?

Quinn walked over and saw fifty-seven books laid out in the crate in such a way that a piece of each of them was visible. She indicated Yes again.

Scanning

Scan Complete.

Books Qualified.

Book Immolation Level 21 granted. Brace yourself.
Activate Now?
Yes or No?
Quinn gulped and looked at Lynx who nodded ever so slightly.
Quinn chose Yes, and a wave of heat consumed her thoughts.

2 7

INCINERATION

Fire streamed from Quinn's hands in a pure, white-blue light. It hit the books, the covers, the pages, and the infestation contaminating it all, igniting them immediately and spreading throughout all fifty-seven books in the massive granite crate. The fire burned everything it touched, incinerating it.

As it did so, a squeal of high-pitched agony and anger reached Quinn's ears.

The sound came from the books themselves, as if the contamination within them was in pain. It didn't want to go. It didn't want to be dissolved.

It hadn't finished its job.

Everyone could hear it. Even the night owls thrashed their wings, hooting and squawking from their perches up above.

Quinn felt like her blood was boiling, but instead of consuming her, it lent her an energy with a strange aftertaste of ice, like heat and ice so cold it burned combined in her veins. The fire continued to stream from her hands. The screams continued to emit from the books, and slowly but surely, every single particle of them turned to ash.

When the last piece of ash disintegrated, the fire stopped abruptly, and Quinn fell to one knee, gasping for breath.

Messages flashed up in front of her face.

Ability to channel Library power increased.

Current capacity increased to 22%.

Warning, overextension has resulted.

Impending Backlash Onset within the next 18 hours.

"Quinn, are you okay?" Lynx asked, crouching down to her current level.

"Great," she said, gasping for breath again. That took more energy than she'd imagined. She plucked one of the energy balls from her storage and popped it into her mouth, raising her energy up another two hundred points. Considering it only brought her to two hundred thirty-five, she'd come very close to disaster. "You know, a warning label on using that ability might have been really nice."

Lynx shrugged. "You would have done it anyway."

"True, but it shouldn't be taken advantage of, and it's beside the point because if I had known I could have at least braced myself or eaten one of those energy foods that replenishes over time." It took a lot of effort, but she managed to push herself up to standing, shakily. She felt like her knees were made of jelly.

"Note taken," Lynx said, sounding contrite for once. "Apologies. I didn't foresee quite how much energy that would take. It might have served us better to split the books up into separate groups."

"In hindsight, that's very logical," Quinn said. She took a deep breath and calmed her mind, even though there were still remnants of pain racing through her veins. She moved over to lean against the workbench, watching as Narilin and her sister gaped at Quinn.

"I'm really okay," she said to them.

Narilin's eyes narrowed. "That was a lot of power to channel," she said. "I did not realize you had it in you."

"Thanks, I guess," Quinn said, not exactly liking the backhanded compliment. But Narilin had always been difficult to gauge, so she'd take what she could get.

"I did not mean offense. I just meant that you have only been here, in this world for a month or so, correct? Connected to the Library, at least. I would not have attributed that much energy to someone still acclimating to their powerset." Narilin might have been clarifying what she'd intended to say, but it still came across as mostly snooty.

Quinn chuckled. She was fast learning that Narilin's default was condescension. "To be honest, I almost ran out of power. Not sure what would have happened then. But it's all good, I'll be fine."

At least, she hoped she would.

Quinn pushed herself away from the table and focused on Siliqua and Harish, who were still in the room, talking amongst themselves. She walked up to them, ignoring the shaking of her legs as she moved. "So, is this all that's needed? Was there something else we have to do to get the Library fully operational again? You know . . . able to accept books, able to lend books out? What else do I need to do?"

The couple looked at each other and Harish spoke first. "We need to cleanse the actually contaminated areas, as in the sections where the books belong, the avenues through which they have passed. If there is a way we can condense the cleansing flame down to very specific areas without the need to worry about the fire spreading, that would be most ideal."

"Oh, that won't be a problem," Lynx said. "It can be a directional flame. As long as we use the correct type of burner to contain it, I should be able to finagle it so that the areas that are contaminated can be cleansed without affecting the rest of the Library."

"That's perfect," Siliqua said, a smile of relief lighting up her face. "Of course, it would be better to have that available to us sooner than later, if you don't mind."

Lynx flashed her a smile. "It shouldn't take long at all now that I know what to access and how to condense it. I should be able to restrict any strain it pulls from the user's mana. Now that Quinn has shown us the way."

Quinn flashed him a slight glare, but she didn't hold it against him because she knew exactly why he was saying that. Sure, there had been some pain involved, and what she was fairly certain was going to be a nasty reaction headache, but they'd got the job done. She'd been the perfect test subject. Sometimes, even with magic, it appeared they needed guinea pigs.

Siliqua cleared her throat. "Librarian, just so you know, we're developing a specific scan not only for the books to rid them of any potential threat to the Library, but also to make sure people aren't carriers as well. They'll be installed in the entryways."

Quinn raised an eyebrow. "To rid the Library of people?"

Siliqua blushed. "No. I mean to expunge any harmful elements they might bring into the Library with them. Milaro will go over that with you and with us. It was his idea to protect the Library and its contents from people who come and go, from assistants to potential applicants to even the visitors who come to see the Library. Hopefully, we can use this to avoid most dangers posed toward the equal distribution of magic."

"That's fantastic news," Quinn said, and she meant it. Except there was something that really bugged her and it wouldn't let her alone. "Equal distribution, though . . . how do you mean that?"

The elf blinked at her. "When magic isn't filtered, it'll tear apart most of the people seeking to use their affinities. That's not very equal."

"Good point," Quinn mused.

Still, they needed more than just preventative measures, more than just identification. They had to figure out who, apart from the Serpensiril, was actually behind the whole thing, because she was about 99.98 percent sure that the Serpensiril were not the masterminds. There was more behind this, and she hoped that her up-and-coming conversation with the core was going to let her in on a few little secrets . . . if she ever made it down there.

"So," Quinn asked, another thought hitting her, "does this mean we can start repairing the systems now? You know, the glitches and the gaps in information and whatnot?"

"We can cautiously hope that that's possible," Siliqua said, but the way she phrased it gave Quinn pause.

"That's not your area of expertise, is it?" Quinn asked.

"No, sadly, it's not. That's something that's for the Library, Lynx, perhaps Milaro, and maybe another couple of people, depending on the trust levels and whether they're still there." Siliqua sounded oddly defeated.

Quinn was suddenly very interested in who these other qualified people could perhaps be. And . . . why might they *not* want to help? Still, she was excited that maybe Lynx could start getting his memory back, that maybe they could unlock the different files that were hidden from them, that they could find the memories that had been quasi-deleted.

She smiled at Siliqua in what she hoped was a sympathetic way. "Well, that's cautious hope, at least. Am I done here for the time being? Is there anything else you need assistance with?"

Narilin shook her head, her silvery eyes giving off a thoughtful aura. Jane was engrossed in a book she appeared to be repairing and barely noticed Quinn's question. Aradie swooped down from her perch to sit on Quinn's shoulder, cooing in her ear in a very conciliatory way.

"We will get started on replacing the incinerated books right away Librarian. They have high priority," Narilin said. At Quinn's questioning glance, she continued. "While we have many damaged books, they are still whole in a knowledge capacity. Having books neither borrowed nor in the collection in any capacity is not acceptable. Jane will focus on repairs, and I will focus on replacement."

She smiled at Quinn, which gave Quinn slight pause, considering their relationship up until now had been marginally contentious. It appeared that Narilin having a sibling with her had allayed some of her pricklier tendencies.

"Thank you, Narilin and Jane," Quinn said as she turned and started walking out of the book infirmary.

"Well, I guess the first part of getting the systems repaired is to give you the window of time you need to go and talk to the Library," Lynx said as he fell into step beside her.

"That's very well, but I have some stuff I need to get done first," Quinn said, suddenly feeling tired again. Granted, she'd just channeled enough magical fire to obliterate a small town, so it was understandable. It started out as a solid day for her to get a very specific list accomplished, and as of right now, everything had come between her and that goal. Not that it mattered.

Such was the nature of life, even here in a magical pocket dimension.

Lynx stared at her as they walked, like he was trying to read her mind. Quinn was proud of her mental barrier progress and directional thoughts. At least she'd gotten better at keeping some things to herself.

The manifestation stopped staring and sighed ever so slightly before speaking. "You need to go to the kitchen. I believe Cook has something for you."

"I know," she said. She knew all of the responsibilities and everything she needed to do. Slowly but surely, it was starting to feel insurmountable purely because every time she went to do something, another ten things she needed to take care of were revealed. Quinn decided it was probably best if she magnified her ability to quick think. There'd be a path of books specifically for that. It should help her manage time much better. She liked solutions that were plausible . . . or at least plausible for a magical Library that could serve her abilities on a platter.

Quinn was lost in thought as she headed toward the kitchen. Lynx mustered up a dose of courage before pursuing his next line of thought. "Quinn, we need to speak about some other things too," he said.

She raised an eyebrow. "You mean the vacation statement I made, right?"

"That, among other things," he agreed. "Mainly that."

"Yeah, I'm so sorry. I didn't think that after a few weeks of working here, everybody would want to take off." She really hadn't given it a second thought. Frankly, she'd barely thought of her homeworld in the last few weeks herself and had simply assumed everyone else in the Library felt the same way.

After all . . . in such a short time period the Library had already come to feel like home. There was a deep-seated sensation right through to her bones that she belonged here.

"Realistically, once the new assistants are trained up, we're going to have a lot more time on our hands because we'll have more than enough to fill all the shifts. That way people can swap their shifts. It'll get a lot better," Lynx said. "However, right now, I need you to help me formulate how you would like to bring that across to everybody."

Quinn sighed and thought about the few jobs she'd had as a student, about how things had been worded. Ambiguity was not her friend. "Sure. How about something along the lines of: Vacation can be taken at any time as long as it doesn't leave the library short-staffed and is discussed with the supervisors and approved by the Librarian beforehand. Vacation must be requested with a week's notice so as not to put undue stress on other Library assistants, and may be declined if too many others have already requested the same time off. All efforts will be made to accommodate vacations where at all possible."

"That sounds reasonable and well thought out." Lynx beamed a smile at her. "Eventually we'll have enough assistants that it doesn't matter. But right now we're being very specific with the needs of the Library."

They'd made it to the kitchen. Quinn stepped inside. It was mid-morning. A good dozen library patrons were sitting along two of the long tables, eating what smelled amazingly like apple and cinnamon something. Quinn crept up to the counter. "Hey, Cook, did you make some apple and cinnamon stuff without telling me?"

"Very similar to what you would call apple and cinnamon, Librarian. I did not conceal it deliberately. You have been late in visiting this morning." Cook handed her a bowl of what looked suspiciously like an apple pie. She wasn't about to turn that down.

Quinn dug in and felt the flavors explode. It was divine. She shoveled in another bite before speaking. "They said you wanted to see me?"

Cook paused as they created another delicacy to hand out to patrons. "The Library has requested that I make a few snacks for you to take with you upon your visit."

"Okay. Is there something special about them?" Quinn asked, curious.

"You will need to eat these only when you are down there." Cook's focused gaze felt heavy. "Do you understand?"

Quinn gulped, the stickiness of the apple-like fruit almost making her choke. "Yeah, sure. Are these foods dangerous?"

"Not for you." Cook finally finished the food line and turned to look directly at Quinn. "But they must be consumed while you are in the presence of the core."

"Okay," Quinn said. "Nothing else I should know about them?"

Cook's expression softened slightly. "It will help your synchronization. These are specifically tailored foods to assist with such a high-level mental link."

"Perfect," she said, satisfied. "Take me through what they do?"

But Cook shook their head. "That is not my place to do. Your connection to the Library has grown tenuous with all the upheaval and changes. It's not a dire set of circumstances, but this food will enable a smooth resynchronization for all of us."

Quinn nodded, taking her bag of treats. "Consider it done." About to leave, she was surprised when Cook called her back.

"Quinn." There was a pause, as if Cook wasn't sure if they should speak. "Just remember, this is your place now. You are important here, and . . . to us."

Aradie hooted in agreement.

Quinn smiled, despite the soft hint of caution underlying Cook's words. "I know." She took a deep breath as she left the kitchen.

Now, at least barring all disasters, she should finally be able to get downstairs to the core. "You coming with me, girl?" Quinn asked, stroking Aradie's neck.

"Hoot," Aradie said indignantly.

Quinn chuckled as the translation became apparent.

Just try and stop me.

She really liked her owl.

2 8

———

WINDING DOWN

E̲very time Q̲uinn ventured down the stairs and into what she now thought of as an enchanted cavern to visit the core, a strange sense of peace washed over her. Maybe peace was the wrong word. It wasn't entirely accurate. It was more like the moment she set foot on that slightly spongy floor, she suddenly felt like she was coming home.

Like everything almost clicked into place.

The Library had echoes of the mother that Quinn was finding it more and more difficult to remember, of the family that she'd assumed she'd been loved in, that she swore she had glimpses of a happy childhood from. But the thing was, they were all fleeting images, almost like the ones Aradie gave her when trying to explain things to her.

It was hard to remember what her life had been like before she entered the foster system. She had vague recollections of a grandmother who baked and of parents who had given her the hugs and support, smiles and love. At least, she thought they had.

There were memories of the caring and comfort and safety to be who she was.

But when she was down here, they were no longer vague or just memories. That's what the Library gave her. And she clung to it eagerly.

Aradie nestled in the crook of Quinn's neck, somehow wrapping Quinn's ponytail around her like a blanket, but not in such a way that she became entangled. Quinn chuckled as she walked across the vast cabin floor and scratched Aradie's neck again.

"There, there, girl, it's all good. This is going to be long-awaited and productive," she said, pushing all the hope she had into her voice.

Aradie hooted like she was skeptical about Quinn's goals.

"No, really, it's going to be productive. Finally, the Library has some power, we've solved one of the worst problems, and we have a couple of leads to go off for the Serpensiril allies. I think I've been patient enough."

Aradie's next hoot sounded like the bird couldn't help but agree with Quinn.

There you go. The Library's voice echoed around her and in her head. *Trying to turn my own night owls against me, are you?* the Library asked, but it wasn't really a question. There was a definite humorous tone to the words.

The owl hooted again, like she was telling the Library that she was her own owl and belonged to no one.

Quinn's stress levels began to even out, despite the dangers to both herself and the Library that loomed on the horizon. Despite all of the shenanigans being orchestrated by whoever was orchestrating them. Despite whoever had been in cahoots with Kor and tried to destroy the Library in the first place, not to mention killing all the remaining potential Librarians.

Despite all that, Quinn's stress disappeared with the surrounding atmosphere, and both the Library and Aradie played a large part in that. Down here with the Core, she felt as safe as it was possible for her to be under the circumstances. Frankly, even *with* the circumstances, down here just felt right.

"I wouldn't have to steal them, or turn them against you, if you actually told me everything I need to know," she grumbled half-heartedly at the Library.

Ah, Quinn, we have had this discussion before.

"And we will have it again," Quinn said. "I know it, you know it, doesn't mean I can't be irritated by it."

Understood, the Library said. *I'm just grateful that you also realize that there are things that cannot be disclosed to you until such a time that you've reached certain milestones of knowledge and that the Library has reached certain levels of power. There is a lot that goes into my makeup. So much history . . .*

"You don't say," Quinn said. If the Library had been corporeal in nature and walking next to her, she would have elbowed it in the ribs. "I do understand, even if it's extremely frustrating to be constantly kept in the dark, even though not being in the dark could likely hinder me, or confuse me, or both. Probably both."

Quinn chuckled as she ran the conundrum over in her mind. Even with the threat still very real . . . as long as they stayed safe, they had all the time in the universe. Finally reaching the middle of the cavern where the massive core branched out from, she sighed happily.

"Ah," she said, "this is perfect."

Aradie hooted once softly, tugged on one of Quinn's hairs, and flew up to alight onto one of the branches. Quinn glanced around. "You know, it's very odd that a tree like you, with the all-encompassing quiet, is surrounded by so much darkness. I've always associated trees with light and the outdoors, but here in this place . . . it still feels right."

That's the beauty of a tree of knowledge, the Library said.

"Keep telling yourself that." Quinn grinned. "I've got a feeling there's a lot more to you than that."

The Library chuckled softly and then let out a contented sigh. The sensation rippled all through the room like a breath, a deep inhalation. If Quinn focused really, really hard, she was sure she could almost hear a heartbeat. Curiosity nibbled at the back of her mind. She had so many questions.

Well, Quinn, thank you for coming as I requested. I appreciate you going out of your way when it really is busy up there.

"Of course I'd make time. You asked me to come." She jiggled the bag in her hand. "Cook sent me with supplies. I didn't know you ate."

The Library chuckled. *I don't precisely eat in the way you're thinking. The food in the bag isn't for me, it's for you.*

"Something about synchronization, right?"

Yes, the Library said and for just a moment Quinn felt like something was peering into her soul. *"Something about synchronization" is accurate. But first, I think there are some things weighing on your mind. Talk to me, Quinn.*

Of course, I've got something on my mind. I've had something on my mind since you guys dragged me into this dimension, is what Quinn wanted to say. However, instead, she turned and patted the trunk. "What exactly are you?"

The Library seemed to hesitate. *Finding that out is part of why you need to stay for a while. There are concepts larger than you, larger than the Library, frankly bigger than all of us combined. And you need to form an intrinsic understanding of how this world was formed to fully comprehend how I came to be and what I am. Do you understand?*

"Well, obviously not," Quinn said, "because you didn't tell me anything. You just told me that I need to know more to understand what you haven't told me yet. Does that not seem highly convoluted and a roundabout way to say, 'Listen, Quinn, we're gonna tell you a story and then I'll tell you what I am'?"

There's a majesty to storytelling, Quinn. Let me spin my story the way I want to, please. The Library managed to sound ever so slightly offended.

This time, Quinn laughed. "It's okay, I understand. So," Quinn continued, putting the bag of food on her lap and fingering the fold-down section of it, she thought for a few seconds, trying to really summarize what it was she wanted to ask in the first place.

"So," she said again, "is this like a serious magical Library birds-and-the-bees talk then?"

The Library paused for a moment. *You know, Quinn, I think that's exactly what this will to be like.*

"Okay," Quinn said, mulling it over, "what exactly do you need me to do for this to work?"

Listen to and experience what I have to say, question me some, because I doubt that you couldn't. Then listen some more and trust that the synchronization process will work for us, will work for you and will bring some more clarity to the things that you don't yet know and overall to your position as Librarian.

Quinn analyzed the words. She knew the Library was deliberately leaving things out and being circumspect. Not only could she hear it, but she could feel it and yet there was no malice contained within. There was no ill-conceived purpose, simply the will to do it in the correct order of things.

"Why now? What's so different about right now?" Quinn asked. "Why couldn't we do this weeks ago?"

Is that really a question, Quinn? the Library asked, leaving the question open.

The thing was, Quinn knew it wasn't. They'd had so much to do, repairing the Library, getting rid of the bookworms, rediscovering some of the books, returning books, making the Library operational, gathering assistants, repairing the filters, boosting up the power levels of the Library. She knew the answer to her question.

"Yeah, I know," she said begrudgingly.

We never had the power before, Quinn. This is going to require quite a bit of that power. We had to wait until we got the Library to this level for us to synchronize fully.

"So we weren't before?" Quinn asked despite knowing the answer.

No, and you're fully aware of that fact.

"And this synchronization will make me a whole Librarian?" Because even now, Quinn knew there were elements of her role here missing. Like pieces of a puzzle.

I think that's an accurate description, the Library said.

"Well, is it going to be like Lynx was when he had to reset?" Quinn pushed.

The Library actually laughed. *No, you are not a manifestation of me, Quinn. You are my Librarian. I can't just absorb you into my being and have you come out fixed, or even come out fully formed. So no, I will not be absorbing you as I did Lynx.*

Quinn cocked an eyebrow. "You know, you would think that was an extremely comforting thing to say to a person, but oddly, in this set of circumstances, it really isn't."

Huh, the Library said, and then there was a pause. *I need you to know that some of what you witness, and some of the information you gain might cause confusion . . . it may even be upsetting.*

Quinn thought about that for a few seconds. "Is it something detrimental for me?"

You'll likely find it quite the opposite.

Quinn raised an eyebrow. "Is it something malicious?"

No. Never malicious.

Quinn nodded, mulling it over. "Then I will do my best not to react until I've had time to digest what is revealed."

Thank you.

"Is there a way I should sit? Should I eat now?" Quinn wiggled herself into the little divot she had for her butt. It really was oddly comfortable with the sponginess of the floor.

Take a breath, Quinn. I'm going to give you a very basic setup for this. Okay?

"Okay," Quinn said, slightly wary.

Just sit how you usually do. Lean in that little root area that you've made yourself, and lean against my trunk. Before we synchronize, I need you to understand where I come from.

"Well . . . okay, then," she said, leaning into the comfortable alcove of the tree. "Hit me."

What? the Library asked.

"Like, tell me, give me the information."

Oh, that's a rather novel way to say that. Anyway, as you can probably guess, I've been around a very long time.

"Can we skip over the bleeding obvious and get to the summary of what we're on about today?" Quinn drawled out in boredom.

Quinn, patience is a virtue.

"Yes, but not one of mine."

The Library chuckled. *Okay. Back when chaos ran rampant through the universe, creating, my kind was one of the first events. When we realized that chaos began devouring what it created, that it began feeding back in on itself, we realized that something had to be done. One of those solutions was the Library, which was spearheaded by my family. Of sorts.*

"Well, I mean no one disputes that you're the Library."

Becoming the Library required a lot of work, a lot of magic. Not just from me, but from others as well, and all of it ended up contained within me. This was done so we could spread magic equally, so that magic was available to everybody, and anybody, without the risk of destroying them, and without destroying that for which it had been used.

Quinn was silent for a second. "Okay, so the Library was created to make sure this expansive universe didn't eat itself and everything in it."

Do you understand how huge the scope of the service we provide here is?

"Yes." Quinn suddenly felt the true gravity of the situation. A wave of nausea hit her ever so subtly. "And I need to know this because . . ."

While you are synchronizing with me, there may be glimpses of things from my past that my brief history will help you understand and process.

"So we're talking large-scale, mind-blowing stuff?"

Very large scale, the Library answered.

"Okay then, how do we do this synchronization?"

Just settle in comfortably.

Even as Quinn moved, she could feel the floor morph into almost a mattress underneath her, one of those memory foam ones that formed around the body. It was like a big cloudy hug. It raised her ever so slightly too, so she wasn't directly on the ground anymore, but it was still cushy.

Are you comfortable?

"Yeah. Yeah, I am." Parts of the bed or the trunk that extended out and combed through Quinn's hair, lightly touching her scalp. "Okay. Is that normal?"

Yes. I need to have as close a connection as I can manage with you. How do you feel?

"Okay. Shouldn't I have eaten already?" Quinn was starting to feel ever so slightly nervous, and ridiculously drowsy.

You'll need to eat now. Grab the first one out. This trance you'll be lowered into will allow you to synchronize fully with me. I won't have many secrets, but at this point in time it is very important we risk this. You will need the power and understanding going forward. Each power level requires one of these synchronizations.

"Isn't it going to be difficult to eat sitting lying down like this?" Quinn didn't relish the idea of choking on her food.

No, that food will melt in your mouth.

Quinn, slightly skeptical, ripped off some and put it into her mouth. It did, in fact, melt. It felt like a dripping cinnamon sundae. It was amazing.

She felt her eyes grow heavy as she put the second piece in her mouth. She didn't even remember putting the third piece in. And suddenly she was floating in space along with the celestial bodies. And then everything took on an infinite nothingness, punctuated only by the occasional falling star.

<hr>

NOT LONG AFTER Quinn fell unconscious, the core lit up like a blue shower of sparks all the way through its branches, leaves, and right down to the trunks and all through Quinn.

Did you get it done in time? the Library asked.

A long sigh sounded from behind the trunk. "Barely. But I got what we needed."

Good. Our connection was tenuous at best from the start. We need to reinforce it.

"Are you sure this is wise to do now?" Milaro asked, stepping out from the shadows. His long blond hair lit up with faint white highlights from the blue lighting.

You told me it was necessary. Have you changed your mind? the Library countered.

Milaro shook his head. "It's definitely necessary. She can't access all of her powers yet, all of her abilities. And we're in too dire a situation to maintain the slow pace we have until now."

This is slow? She's barely been here over a month. For anyone else, in any other time, this would be acceptable, even speedy Librarian progress.

"But this isn't any other time. This is the now we have. Do you think she'll understand?" He pulled a small bottle out of his pocket, idly toying with it.

I have high hopes. And she has promised not to react immediately. I still don't understand why you didn't tell me as soon as you walked through our doors again.

Milaro closed his eyes for a few seconds, and didn't dignify the last comment with a response. Reaching out with his mind to make sure Quinn was deep in the synchronization trance, he spoke softly. "She's almost ready. Almost deep enough."

Then it must be done now, the Library said, a trace of melancholy in her tone.

"Very well," Milaro said, and he took a dropper from the bottle and let a single drop of liquid onto Quinn's tongue through barely parted lips. "Let's just hope she's as prepared as you think she is."

The blue lights of the Library continued to flicker.

29

MILARO

The glow from the bough of the tree suffused through the small connectors, and flowed right into Quinn as if she were simply a part of the greater whole.

Well, the Library said, manifesting as a shadow as it moved out from behind the tree, taking on no more than a vague human semblance, *that is entirely more compatible than I hoped for.*

"You should have known she'd be at this level," Milaro said absently as he focused his senses on reading Quinn's reactions to the power spreading through her.

To be honest, the Library continued, *I did not expect a theoretical experiment to work this well. We spoke of it before Lynx activated shutdown mode, but I didn't think it could go this far. To be honest, I didn't expect it work at all.*

Milaro actually turned to the specter of the Library and raised an eyebrow. "Really? You should know, more than many of us, quite how far Seveshall magic can take things."

That is *true*, the Library conceded. *You've been allies for longer than I care to remember.* The Library paused for a second, watching as the lights fed down through Quinn's entire body. *How many of you did it take to enact such a "plan," shall we call it?*

Milaro sighed, noting down several things into what appeared to be a journal. It was more like a notation device attached to the system, similar to the map Quinn used on her first venture to find books.

"The whole council took part. The same people you appointed once you realized you didn't have a Librarian recipient. Myself, Siliqua, Harish, Escadril, Nishpa, my son, and Hal . . . sort of." Milaro paused his entries for a second, still able to remember the day the Library disappeared from his immediate senses. It was a feeling that stayed with him always."

Hal agreed? The Library's shock was evident.

"Technically. He was a bit busy; he sent Ikeshal in his place. Anyway. When you shut off, we were lost. Being cut off from so much power, only having a trickle left, and that trickle being heavily tainted with chaos . . . it didn't bode well for the magical community. You know that as well as I do."

The shadow nodded. *I know it more than you can possibly imagine.*

"Probably not," Milaro said, distracted by the levels of power emanating from Quinn as her body began to suffuse with the Library's power. "I have a pretty good imagination."

The shadow chuckled. *Truth, you do have a way with minds, Milaro.*

"That I do, that's why they pay me the big acorns," he muttered, his attention mostly consumed by the readings.

Big acorns. This time the Library's shadow laughed. *I forgot what a delight you can be when you try. Much like your grandfather.*

"Thanks," Milaro said. He moved to the side and held a hand over Quinn's torso, muttering under his breath, words without true meaning fell from his lips like raindrops. Gold droplets of power entered the blue that suffused her entire body, dripping down like a spiderweb into different sections. "Okay, that should help," he said, stepping back to admire his handiwork.

What exactly are you doing?

"Don't you know everything?" he quipped, still calculating the train of Seveshall power he'd mixed into the synchronization.

I'm a magical Library, not a god.

"Well, you're not really just a magical Library either, are you, if we're going to nitpick." He flashed the Library a mischievous grin.

You know we don't speak of that . . .

"But maybe we should." This time his look was a glare. Milaro knew the Library was more ancient than most things in the universe, but sometimes the grand sweeping statements got a little stale. "You realize there was no other way to get genetic material except for the samples that we had from you. We were damn lucky we had some on hand."

You weren't supposed to use those remnants in that manner, the Library said, *but I, for one, am desperately glad you did.*

"It was touch and go there for a while. We had no idea if the concept could even become reality." Milaro sighed fondly, melancholy mixed in his tone. "Miyago had his best idea yet."

Did your son really come up with the plan?

"He really did." Milaro heaved another sigh, this time it was filled with sadness. He remembered his son very fondly. How brave he had been, how stubborn, and how utterly brilliant he was. If only he hadn't gotten involved with that wretched woman and left him Malakai to raise on his own. Still, Malakai was a great kid. He had a lot of fire in his soul.

"We haven't exactly chance to chat on our own since you got back, have we?" Milaro asked, softly.

Well, now we're doing something we have to talk about. He couldn't tell if the Library was amused or reticent.

"Using your traits and genetic makeup to create a virtually impeccable replacement was the most out-there concept I'd heard, but Miyago was adamant it would work." Milaro smiled at the memory of the arguments they'd had. When something was theoretical and the only desperate option left. . . . He shrugged and continued. "But he was right. Look at her."

The lights, weaves of bright blue with pale golden threads, wound through her passageways, lit up her entire set of magic pathways. More than any one person had a right to have. "She has every single affinity you have and can ever have. She has the ability to adapt to every single affinity there ever was or will be. And you know, as well as I know, once we can upgrade her neural network, she could probably just absorb the entire Library at once."

He paused and then added for emphasis. "Much like you did."

Just because she can *do something doesn't mean she should,* the shadow said, a hint of protectiveness in the words. *But I see your point. Maybe we are being a little too cautious with her.*

"No, she still thinks that her whole life has been normal. And that this all here is something fantastical." Milaro fell silent and the Library didn't interject.

He really wondered if he'd done the right thing, creating a life specifically to become a Librarian, and save magic as they all knew it. To save the universe. He shook his head. What was she going to do when she found out? "I wasn't completely sure at first, you know," he said.

It took me a while too.

Milaro watched the coursing of the magic through her veins.

Do you really think we should tell her? the Library asked after another few seconds of silence.

"Have you met her? Miss 'ultraviolet light.' If we don't tell her, she'll figure it out herself. Besides, wouldn't you want to be told if it were you?" Milaro posed the question right back at the Library.

I think I really would. And if we don't tell her, she's never going to be able to come to terms with what she is and what she has to do. Have we just doomed her to a life she didn't choose?

Milaro shook his head from side to side, but he wasn't entirely certain. At the time it had been the only solution. Even now, there was still no other option. "That was never the intent. The intent was to make the Library, and thereby the universe, continue. In all our desperation, I'm not sure we were thinking straight at the time."

Milaro closed his eyes and guided the golden light deeper through Quinn's magical channels. He hit different pressure points throughout her body, dissipating into thinner lines, entering her veins and suffusing her body. He guided it, weaving it to become a strength for her with the ability to tap into potent knowledge. These were all avenues she could work toward as she found out who and what she was and why she'd been created.

And hopefully realize she could still entirely be herself.

He had regrets, many regrets. Most of all, not immediately telling her why she was in the Library amidst all of the confusion that she was going through when she'd first arrived. Perhaps it would have been kinder to reach out with a lifeline as to *why* things had happened. But she seemed to be doing so well, adapting faster than he'd ever assumed she would. Then again, that could have been some of her predisposed makeup.

Not to mention, it took him several days to cement that she was who she was. He'd only really clicked when he'd helped her with the mind bomb Kajaro planted.

He frowned.

What's wrong? the Library asked, concern in their tone.

"You weren't created to be a Library. You were simply part of original creation. Correct?" Milaro asked.

You know that's true, the Library said flatly.

"I was just wondering. You got to decide that you would be who you are. Yet we created and decided that for Quinn."

Technically, that's right, the Library said. *I have to thank you for what you accomplished, or none of us would be here. And frankly, she could always choose differently. I wasn't originally created to be this either. You did what you did with the best of intentions.*

"Isn't Halschius paved with those?" Milaro chuckled to himself. He knew Quinn would have appreciated the pun. She wasn't stirring to laugh with him though. Even though it was part of the whole synchronization process, he sort of missed her laugh.

"How is it going on your end?" he said.

She seems to be perfectly in control of the power coursing through her. The Library paused for a second. *It's going extremely well. How did you get this so . . . right?*

"Told you. We came up with a plan to mitigate side effects, and Miyago tweaked the blueprints. We sent her somewhere nobody should have been able to find her, so her genetic mash up could settle.

She should have been safe there. And technically, Quinn was safe. Her caretakers, not so much." Milaro still hadn't forgiven himself for allowing three of his best operatives to fall while in service.

Is that how she lost her parents?

"Parents, bodyguards . . . we had fail-safes in place to activate different countermeasures should they be compromised or else destroyed." Milaro shrugged. "As you can see, they didn't make it."

Could you track her? Could you keep an eye on her? Was she left alone? The Library sounded quite distraught. Milaro couldn't fault them for that.

"She was the only chance we had. I may be connected to you through a blood bond so old there are stars younger than it. But I couldn't connect to you in the way you needed to save you. None of us could. This was the only choice, and we built-in powerful fail-safes that would trigger at certain points of maturation." He turned an irritated glance on the Library shadow. "This is what you get for not making time to see me since you went back online."

You can scold me later. Make sure you don't drop the energy transfer right now, and keep talking.

Milaro smiled, tweaked the energy flow through Quinn and continued monitoring it while he kept speaking. Arguing with the Library had never gotten him anywhere, and things weren't about to change now. "The magic evolution in her needed to hit a saturation point where every single affinity was open to it. You should have found her years before you did. I'm not entirely sure what happened there. But if you couldn't find her, that's why no one else could either, and that's how you found her when Lynx scanned that one last time."

We cut it so close, the Library said.

"Don't dwell on what is now mostly in the past," Milaro chided as he smoothed out an energy bump.

It's very difficult not to. I spent almost half a millennia simply hibernating, unable to do anything and watching as everything my siblings and I built, everything that we'd poured into my creation, poured into this Library, as it all melted down and almost disappeared. All in barely the blink of my eye.

"Now it's not going to disappear," Milaro said. "Or at least we're going to do our damnedest to make sure it doesn't disappear."

Do you think she's ready?

"No," he said. "I don't think she's ready. And at least at first, I don't think she'll thank any of us for what we did."

Don't look at me. The shadow stepped back, hands in a defensive position. *I wasn't the one who came up with this harebrained scheme.*

"No, but you were one of the original council who helped develop multiple fail-safes should no Librarian be found. And if you recall, this was our last resort. Voila, look at your last resort." Milaro spread his hands out in front, indicating Quinn. "Isn't she magical?"

Why haven't you told her yet? the Library asked. *You two have such a compatible relationship. She looks up to you, like a grandfather of sorts.*

Milaro chuckled. "It's probably the blood-line bond. We had to use several magic essence distillations in order to combat the side effects of your genetics. Can't send a full-blooded cosmicisodracus to a world devoid of magic. How would she have sustained herself? And we couldn't make a human shell. Not with the volume of magic she'd need to channel sooner than a human would be able to acclimate to her true blood. We took the familial abilities from the Seveshall, Nishpa, and the fey, and a drop of imp blood from Ikeshal, and some of the book magic essence from Escadril, representing the Salosiers to make sure the chaotic connection was solidified and didn't just come from the samples we had from the Library. Her genetics might be majorly yours, but . . . we had to give her balance that would help her exist as a human."

Magically implode? The Library laughed softly. *Yeah, that makes a lot of sense. What is it we do now?*

"Now," Milaro said, and wiggled his fingers in the way that Quinn loved so much. He chuckled at the fact and hoped that he wasn't about to irreparably ruin the relationship he'd started to build with her. "Now I dive into her mind, only to the areas she's already given me access to, and hope I can help guide her synchronization with you."

There was a brief pressure on Milaro's hand as he went to close his eyes. "What?" he asked the Library, curious. It was very rare that the entity reached out for physical contact with anybody or anything.

I just . . . she has to know on some level. She has to be questioning some things by now, like why and how she'd been able to fight off Kajaro's mental insertion at all.

Milaro pondered that, which was likely a very apt observation. Quinn did have his blood, after all, and Milaro had always had a strange mental fortitude. From birth, his mental powers were lauded. As a Seveshall, he was immediately linked to the Library as a guardian. Just like every crown prince in the Seveshall line. His fascination with the Library had developed into friendship and respect, until everything went wrong.

When the council decided to figure out a long-term plan because of the lack of Librarians, this one had been so far on the back burner, such a far-reaching probability, he hadn't even really considered anything of agreeing to give his blood to the project.

He was certain she'd inherited his mental prowess. It's what made devouring those books and applying them so easy for her. That's why her mental barriers were advancing at a rate of, well, much higher than anything he'd ever witnessed. Levels that took people, even people adept at mental manipulation, years to traverse. It was taking her mere weeks.

Maybe distilling the overall essence of those abilities had been a bit of an overreach. But if it kept her safe?

And so, he was worried about her, and he was sure that even on some subconscious level, she may have drawn the occasional parallel, maybe. The synchronization process was going to reveal so much to her. It would undoubtedly give her even more questions than she already had.

How would they explain to her why she'd been created? Just how easy was it to explain that because of her near identical signature to the Library, most searchers would simply assume that she was a part of the Library, because for all intents and purposes, she was a child of the Library.

Essentially a child of the cosmos.

She hadn't been a "chosen one" at all. Quinn had been engineered, created, specifically to save the Library.

In a way, she was a weapon.

"I don't know," Milaro finally answered, a cold lump settling in his stomach. "We both know she's caught wind of some things . . . I can only hope that she will understand the desperation that led to what we've done. And I really hope she has the forgiving heart I think she does."

3 0

SYNCHRONIZATION

MIND-RELATED MAGIC ENCOMPASSED MANY AFFINITIES, ALL OF WHICH Milaro was more than adept at. From dream creation to mind manipulation, protection, projection, manifesting, and influence. There were other lesser-known specialties of the mind, but those were the main ones.

Quinn, not entirely to Milaro's surprise, had handled all of them remarkably well when thrust unexpectedly into the dream trap created by Kajaro. Her mind, at least on a subconscious level so far, could operate with a scope that spoke of vastness. It surprised him the first time he attempted to go to her aid.

Mainly because, while he'd had his suspicions, he hadn't been completely sure.

Milaro's main hope was that the protections he left in place while restricting the orb Kajaro placed in her mind were enough to prevent the Serpensiril from figuring out exactly what Quinn was. If some of their opponents figured out what Quinn was before they were able to get her training up to speed . . .

He shook his head. Not ideal at all.

Just like the information transfer not taking place when she was pulled into the Library wasn't ideal either. Milaro still wasn't sure how that had gone so very wrong in the first place.

Perhaps it was Lynx not realizing she was part Library . . . the transfer would be so different for her because of that.

And considering the difficulty she'd had in absorbing the prepared information package that Lynx imparted onto any new Librarian . . . Milaro couldn't help but marvel at the fact that Kajaro managed to slip a destructive quasi spy orb in under her defenses inside of a split second during combat. It spoke of a level of control that Milaro hadn't realized someone like Kajaro possessed.

That sphere was designed to lift any of the Librarian's thoughts and intricate knowledge that it could seek out once it grew and spread its tendrils out. Eventually, given the energy it required to feed on, it would have destroyed her and thus the Library. It was only Quinn's natural affinities that allowed her mind to detect it in its stasis form.

This was yet another reason he had to help her get this synchronization right. She needed to tap into the powers of the Library and the Librarian more fully before he could impart more of her history and legacy.

Milaro was getting ahead of himself. Right now, he needed to remove that sphere, and to do that, he required the elixir he'd used already on Quinn as well as the Library's power and aid. Having her in stasis in order to complete power-sharing from the Library system was paramount to being able to exert enough control to remove that damn orb.

Not only for Quinn's safety but ultimately for everybody's.

Navigating himself into the locked area they kept the orb in, Milaro was quite surprised to see the amount of reinforcement Quinn had worked around the orb. She'd told him she'd been working on her mental barrier skills, and she hadn't been kidding. He was accepted in this space. It knew him. It sensed no danger from him. Which he needed because he didn't think he could tear down her walls quick enough otherwise to achieve the end result they currently needed.

He took a breath and reached out, dissolving the outermost wall. There was a flicker, almost like a vision of Quinn. Almost like a question mark. "I'm destroying the orb" was all he said to the image, sending out a sensation of safety and self-confidence so that Quinn would know that he was doing what needed to be done. He paused for a second, waiting to see if she accepted the reasoning of the intruder in her mind.

Considering the level of trance she had to be in so that she could fully synchronize with the Library, Milaro found it disconcerting that enough of her mind had been aware of his presence to check on it. Though in hindsight, he had to admit to being grateful. They should be able to beef up her personal security so no one could ever intrude again.

Slowly, acceptance leaked into him from the surroundings of her mind, and he reached forward to dissipate the next wall and the next, and then the final residual one they had originally built together. He was glad she'd put so many more around it, because this wall was crumbling, and he could feel the power from the orb trying to batter against Quinn's defenses.

There was malevolence in that bomb. A hatred so vile for the Library and everything it stood on, everything it stood for, that it made Milaro recoil. He wanted to banish it, but that wasn't going to be enough for this. What he needed to do was reinforce the walls around it and then assert enough control over it until he could grind it into a nothingness.

As he did so, flashes of Quinn's battle with Kajaro flickered before Milaro's eyes as he reinforced the containment field. Fleeting memories taken from the actual event that gave her the foreign object. Shots of exactly how Kajaro managed to touch her face just long enough to initiate the contact that immediately transferred the orb to burrow in past her defenses. Luckily, it seemed to have taken a while to reach where it needed to go but it did leave Milaro with the sensation that the Serpensiril had been much smarter than Kajaro's level of chaotic corruption would have indicated.

A part of him wanted to believe that Quinn's natural defenses saved her, or perhaps pure luck. But there was that overly jaded and skeptical part of him that came with age . . . he didn't believe in coincidences. That part of him—no, it thought the orb was more like a test.

Had he not seen it for himself, Milaro would never have believed that this was indeed instigated by that specific Serpensiril, which meant perhaps they were underestimating the whole bunch of them. Underestimating an opponent never worked out well.

Even as he worked to free Quinn's mind of the potential mind bomb, Milaro could feel the Library's power prickling at his skin, starting to tear at the very fabric of his being.

While his relationship to the Library allowed him to enter the core area, it was with restrictions and for limited amounts of time. In order to stay longer, he too required specifically designed sustenance to boost his natural defenses to the pure power that lived there.

He deftly opened an inner robe pocket, pulling out a resilience mint that he popped into his mouth in an almost trance-like state, considering he was still elbows deep in Quinn's mind and couldn't afford to break the contact at all.

Finally, after much pressure, the sphere's power capitulated. The walls Milaro had been reinforcing snapped inward toward each other, as if fired from a shotgun, and annihilated anything left of the orb. Milaro sensed the backlash of power as the orb was obliterated, but the sender shouldn't know any details aside from its destruction.

Hopefully, Kajaro would assume it was Quinn's doing.

Maybe, with any luck, the backlash would kill Kajaro. Milaro could dream. After all, the Serpensiril had been in bad shape the last time they'd heard anything from him, or from Quinn's dream observations at any rate. It would be nice to have one enemy they knew out of their way. However, that would interfere with tracking down the rest of the conspirators.

Milaro had too many suspicions and not enough time to locate proof.

He took great care scouring the area of her mind where the orb had been contained to make sure that no minuscule bits remained. Tiny fragments could potentially continue to infect her or surreptitiously bury their way into parts of her mind, giving Kajaro a form of reentry.

Milaro had once witnessed something similar, and it wasn't pretty. Fragments of corruption could fester and warp a person into somebody that no one around them recognized.

Once Milaro was completely sure that her mind was in the clear, he gave her consciousness a gentle nudge and enabled her ability to fully synchronize. It required visiting the two places that he had before in her mind and activating them as a wealth of knowledge and as a means of learning. While the orb was still present, her entire mind had been on lockdown, required to defend her mind from potential incoming assaults and dangers. Granted, it could serve as both once she mastered those abilities, but right now she needed to be open to receiving the Library's full bond as well as the complete Librarian package.

Once that was done, he did another sweep, just to triple-check. By this time it was probably a quintuple-check, but that didn't matter. It was always better to be safe than sorry, especially in matters of the mind. Once he was completely satisfied, he withdrew himself.

It was disorienting, being back outside of her mind. The atmosphere inside it almost felt like a dense fog that was desperately holding things in place.

Milaro still stood in exactly the same position, right next to the raised bed, his hands held over her body but not touching it. He knew his shoulders were going to pay for that if he didn't treat it with a tonic. As he cracked his neck slowly back and forth, the shadow representation of the Library stood and watched him. He wondered, sometimes, if the Library would ever take on an actual, human-like visage. But it wasn't where his mind needed to go right now.

He realized that he was sweating. A sheen of perspiration covered his face, something he hadn't experienced in millennia.

You look like that took it out of you, the Library said.

"You're one to talk," Milaro answered. "You're already losing more power than you anticipated."

The Library's shadow shrugged. *Well, we did only just pass the threshold of this level. It may have been wise to wait a few days longer.*

"Oh, now you agree with me," Milaro said. "You made me rush to get the elixir. There's no way I could have helped her fully synchronize if I hadn't fetched it, and you know I don't like being rushed."

The Library remained silent, but he could practically feel it's silent laughter. He'd been around the Library too long; it knew far too many of his secrets. He cleared his throat. "Still, it's not like we couldn't just synchronize her again later if you need to. It's probably going to be best for both of you to synchronize regularly, given the nature of your relationship to one another."

The Library turned to look directly down at Quinn, which threw Milaro off slightly, considering the Library was currently everywhere around them. A singular soft pulse of sensory inquiry pulsed out.

"Are you okay?" he asked.

Yes and no. I always thought that my gift to the universe was knowledge and the ability with which to use it. And the magic that wouldn't damage people and kill people any longer, or devour planets because we managed to contain the destructive element.

"That is your legacy," Milaro started, but the Library interrupted him.

No, now I have two . . .

"There's Quinn and technically she's a part of you, almost like a clone." He was desperately trying to cheer the suddenly melancholy Library up.

She's nothing like a clone. Genetic makeup doesn't predetermine the being, the Library said. *In fact, she's nothing like me. I'm old and vast. There are parts of me that should likely have been long dead, Milaro, but I continue on for reasons we all know are important and yet Quinn gives me more hope than I had even millennia before the whole disaster.*

"Well, that's good, then," Milaro said. He considered his next words carefully before speaking further. "I mean it, that it's great because I would hate to think that you ever thought you were unnecessary."

There was a trickle of laughter like a happy spring creek rushing over the stones after an ice thaw. *Oh, Milaro, I know that I am necessary, but sometimes I am simply tired.*

"Oh well, join the club," Milaro said, taking one of the phrases from Quinn's world that he'd enjoyed learning about.

Is it just me or is she glowing brighter now? the Library asked, switching the subject entirely.

Quinn was indeed glowing, much brighter than anticipated. Milaro smiled as the gold and blue threads wove themselves together through her body instead of remaining separate. They became brighter, suffusing into her skin, into her veins, into her very being, becoming a part of her. All of her different magical heritage mixed with the Library's presence the predominant one.

Now all they had to do was hope she wanted to stay a part of the Library.

How long do you think this will take? the Library asked, a sense of wonderment in its voice, which was amazing considering the Library had been around since the beginning of time.

"I would think perhaps another day," Milaro said. He shrugged, realizing how dreadfully bone-weary he'd become. His energy levels were dangerously low, as was his mana. It was then he realized that he hadn't moved yet, largely because he didn't think he currently could.

"I may have overdone it slightly," he said, "but with the Library's power up, her connection is now secure and the synchronization will finally work. I think . . ."

You think?

He shrugged. "Hey, it's all still theoretical. I haven't done this before either. The transition *should* be smooth, and I think when she wakes up, she'll have access to most of her powers."

Will she remember what she's seen and heard? There was hesitance in the Library's tone.

"Maybe. Probably." Milaro shrugged again. "Highly likely."

I'm guessing she'll probably have questions.

"Definitely, but what she is doesn't change who she is." Milaro said, smiling at the low hum of power as the synchronization began in earnest. "You should probably answer some of those questions."

He was pretty sure the Library scowled at him.

Milaro chuckled. "And opinions. Don't forget she's chock full of those too."

3 1

DISARRAY

Quinn opened her eyes, not in that sudden awakening way where you sit bolt upright, but in that languid opening of the eyes because you're still super tired. She felt as though she was still half in a dream. There were stars above her, flickering like fairy lights or, well, like stars. She wasn't exactly sure why. She knew she hadn't gone to sleep outside.

The lights had a blue tint, and it tugged at something in a memory. Her mind was still valiantly trying to go back to sleep and coaxing her brain to do the same. But that was when she realized she'd been seeing stars the entire time she was asleep.

Different stars, odd constellations. Given that she was no longer on Earth, that made complete and utter sense, but for some obscure reason, it had escaped her for the last two minutes—ever since she'd woken up.

Her head felt foggy, like someone had grabbed handfuls of cotton wool, soaked them in water, and shoved them inside her ears, maybe in place of her brain. Was her brain okay? There were so many weird sensations running through her.

She didn't actually feel like she'd slept, but she knew that she had.

She struggled to sit up. When she did, and the entire world went the wrong way up, dizziness flooded through her system.

Quinn clutched at her head as all the information came rushing back to her.

Aradie flew down to sit on her shoulder with a soft hoot by way of greeting, to ask how Quinn was.

That was the whole thing, really.

Quinn wanted to answer that question, but she had no idea how she currently was. Furthermore, she had no idea why she didn't know how she felt. There was just so much to process. She wiggled her toes, wiggled her legs, jiggled her arms, and realized that everything was still intact.

There was a strange lingering sensation in her body like she'd just gotten over pins and needles.

Quinn looked around again. She was indeed at the core, on the bed the Library made specifically for letting her rest. Apart from Aradie and herself, only the core trunk was there.

She felt rested, yet still tired, disoriented, and yet somehow oddly connected to everything around her right now, including Aradie. There was something more there now than there had been. Like she could reach out and pluck it from one of the owl's feathers. There were deeper sensations than images or broken words that she interpreted from her owl—a deeper connection now, something much more solid and emotional.

And not just to Aradie, but to the entire Library—all an extension of herself.

Quinn peered around again, and realized that she had, at some stage, dropped the bag of food she'd brought down with her. Aradie obliged to her thought, instantaneously, by swooping down to pick it up and deposit it back on Quinn's lap.

You should really eat that second treat right now. It will help you regain some of your equilibrium. The Library's voice almost sounded hesitant, like it wasn't entirely sure it should be speaking to her yet, or maybe that it wasn't entirely sure that it was welcome to speak to her.

Quinn frowned. There was something that she should know.

Something she'd just experienced but it was just out of her reach. Something she might even have been upset about?

"Yes," Quinn said, belatedly registering the Library's words. She reached into the bag and pulled out a pastry that looked suspiciously like an apple turnover. As she munched on the delicious delicacy, Quinn looked around, surprised at how much brighter it seemed down here.

But not a brightness that emanated from the lights above her, nor from the core right next to her, but more simply brighter. It was her eyes. Somehow her vision had changed ever so slightly.

She munched another bite of the pastry, thinking as she slowly chewed through it that she was going to have to thank Cook, because she could feel the energy rushing back into her body, filling her back up to where she should have been. She'd checked her energy levels, but they were full.

1395/1395

That wasn't the problem. She'd rested and replenished her energy and mana levels. She was eating, too, which took away some of the tiredness.

"You know, this is really good," she said, as she popped the last bite in her mouth and crumpled up the paper. A sliver of resentment passed through her connection with Aradie, and she made a mental note to herself to give the owl a taste next time.

How do you feel? the Library asked, that same hesitance from earlier in its tone.

It was very odd behavior on behalf of the Library, something Quinn hadn't witnessed yet. She wanted to know more about why, but her brain kept darting here and there and not focusing well.

"I think I'm feeling okay," Quinn said. "I'm just a little disoriented. And like you said, my equilibrium is pretty much gone. I'm not entirely sure why, but I feel like I should know."

That's all part of it, Quinn, the Library said. *It's a long process. It'll take a few days for it to sink in. It took almost three days to experience it.*

"What, already? More than two days? It felt like I'd only just closed my eyes." Quinn still couldn't grasp the passage of time. Her mind was still wading through mud.

Oh no, it definitely took a few days.

"I have to go. I . . ." Quinn shook her cotton-wool head. "Milaro will be here soon, we have to question the . . . don't we have to question somebody?"

It's okay, Quinn, you've still got time. We're not quite ready to question them yet. You need to re-synchronize yourself first so all the information flows together in the way that it should. I imagine you're rather discombobulated at the moment.

"That's a good word for it," Quinn said absently, racking her brains for the strand of something she could feel tugging at her memory, but couldn't quite grasp.

Oh, how she hated this fragmented sensation.

"How is our patient feeling?" Suddenly, Milaro was there, standing in front of Quinn.

She blinked up at him, her mind a whirl of confusion. How was he even here? "Did I black out?" she asked, still confused.

"No, I just came down to see you right at this moment." He smiled, in that kindly grandfather way that had come to feel like safety.

"But I'm sure you were already here, right?" she said, knowing at the same time that it wasn't quite right. And yet, she scrunched up her face. "Ah, this is woeful. I can't stand this feeling."

"Well, tell me, how do you feel?" Milaro asked, echoing the Library's hesitance in his tone. Quinn liked that even less. She felt like there was something just beyond her reach, maybe. She sighed.

"Look, it's not that I have any comparison, but I think the synchronization went well." Except as soon as she said the words, Quinn regretted it.

Pain ripped through her whole body, starting in her mind like an arc of what being struck by lightning probably felt like. She could hear the scream torn from her throat that went hoarse seconds into the sound. It sounded so far away and yet echoed through her skull at the same time. Her back arched, her head pounded, and she fell against the bed, trying to heave in breaths that wouldn't come. She could feel her body twitching.

At the same time, her mind went completely blank.

Until images began to assault it.

They were memories. Of her and her parents. They weren't parents. They were bodyguards. They were caretakers who loved her, who swore to fiercely protect her. And Quinn? Quinn was *not* normal. She didn't know why. And then, the caretakers were gone, and the foster system took her in.

She'd been lucky; she knew all about that. But there was always something in the back of her mind, telling her how to be. How to pass under the radar in her new environment. How to avoid being given undue attention by the foster system. And how to keep to herself. Those self-preservation tactics were always there.

Throughout school, the part-time work she'd had, the different homes she'd gone through. Everything mushed together into pure, instinctive survival mode. To make it through, so she could build her life and be herself.

On the day she was choosing her major, something inside her flicked a switch. That she had to choose what it was she *wanted* to do. Not the pragmatic choice, but what she would be best at. What would be the greatest fit for her abilities?

What was something she'd always loved?

Only now she realized that compunction didn't mean academic. It meant something entirely different. That a part of her was missing, and just needed to slot back into that part of herself it belonged to.

The Library felt right.

Everything about it fit.

From the first moment she'd been dragged here. Even though she'd ended up in an entirely different galaxy, she hadn't questioned much.

Well, not too much, anyway.

Something hazy came back to her, grazing her thoughts, tickling her memories.

Just recently. Just now. While she'd been asleep, or in stasis, or whatever. She had senses she didn't even realize she possessed. Things that sat with her, observed for her. An outer element to herself. She knew, instinctively, that Milaro had been there to talk to her, to soothe her through her synchronization. That familiar voice, with its calming properties and that safety element.

Her mind seized on the fact that he'd been there, that he'd stuck with her, guided her. The Library was a being as far as Quinn had determined so far, but they seemed so far removed from the mortal coil.

Not Milaro—he was solid, someone to lean on.

Wasn't he?

Now she had something to focus on instead of the pain. It helped her ignore the spasms as everything she'd achieved through synchronization began to level out.

Flashes of civilization before it existed flitted through her mind, right through modern societies, to ancient and then futuristic ones. So many different worlds, different stages. All these different species and planets and homes.

Created.

Destroyed.

Evolving.

Thriving.

And then, a sense of a time before time. When there were only a few. A few who had made choices that the rest of the universe would depend upon for eons.

Just as suddenly as it began, the pain stopped completely.

Quinn was up and off the bed within a fraction of a second. She felt faster. More in tune with her body, and everything around her. Information streamed into her mind in such a way that it was disorienting. Dizzying.

Yet, at the same time, exhilarating.

Everything around her felt vibrant, alive, humming with a whole sense of magic beyond the finger waggling. She couldn't keep the wonderment from her voice. "What? What did you do?"

Milaro cleared his throat. "What do you mean?"

"What did you do in my mind when I was out? Did you . . ." Quinn closed her eyes briefly examining herself. "Thank you. Thank you. There's no remnants of that damned orb. Now I'm completely connected to the Library."

She paused, able to run through everything in her mind in such a short order, in such a quick fashion. All of the books she'd read, everything made sense. Ways to harness the energy she now knew instinctively how to control.

She even realized now that she didn't even need to utter an activation word. All she needed was a simple thought. Better for her to picture what she wanted really.

"Quinn . . ." Milaro's words seemed distant as he spoke. "Are you okay? You could be experiencing overload."

"It's . . . it's okay." She felt like she was above everything, looking down on a puzzle that was herself finally seeing all of the pieces fall into place. Especially now she could remember what she'd heard while in that trance.

Was she shocked? Yes. She was definitely shocked. Was she angry? Definitely. But she wasn't entirely sure where to direct that anger right now.

This was something that would take time for her to fully process.

A lot of time.

Everything clicked into place once she'd connected to the Library. A sense of belonging she'd never had anywhere else. That was the one thing giving her pause.

The only thing holding her back from unleashing her anger. It tempered it. Mildly.

Even if she didn't fully understand the hows and whys. This, right here, was why she'd felt so out of place her entire life leading up to now.

She had a reason.

Quinn looked at her hands and realized they were glowing with a blue-gold tint. And she tamped down on it, taking in a deep breath, able to grab onto an equilibrium and just relax, leaving the anger simmering in the background.

The room around her became still, the blue lights up above from the core blinking in synchronization with her breathing.

Or that's how it felt, at least.

She turned to Milaro. "You've been so kind ever since I got here. But"—her voice took on an icy edge—"did you know?"

"Did I know . . . ?" It was like he didn't know what to ask. "That it was you?"

Quinn waited, her eyes never dropping the gaze.

Milaro shrugged. "Not at first. I couldn't be sure until . . ."

Quinn held up a hand to forestall whatever else he wanted to say, taking in a deep breath. The power under her skin flared, and she could feel some sort of change stir within her. She counted to ten. "I want to make one thing clear. This whole thing is not okay. I am not okay with it. But . . . right now, I don't have the time or the capacity to deal with it."

Milaro gulped visibly and looked away. "I'm sorry."

"We're not even close to the apology stage yet," Quinn said, calling two small balls of ice into her palm. She ran them around her hand, letting the cold soothe her mood. "Just so we're clear. This is not done. I am not happy right now. I'm angry."

The ice balls shattered as if punctuating her sentence.

Milaro paled ever so slightly and nodded.

"But I'm also grateful for your guidance." Quinn refused to overanalyze it. There was so much information floating around in her mind right then. So much that just made her entire life make sense even if it made that life far less organic than she'd imagined.

She couldn't control the past. All she could control was what lay in front of them. Whatever else there had been, she would process her anger over time. She cleared her throat. "I have to ask you some questions, and I really hope you'll answer them honestly."

"Anything," Milaro said. Even though she could tell there was some reluctance in his tone, he continued, "Within reason, within my power."

"I need you to wait until I truly process everything before you ask me how I am again. Can you do that?" She gave him a very pointed look. "Because right now, I'm resisting every urge to just open a random door to anywhere, and leave this whole fiasco behind never to return."

"Yes." Milaro didn't even flinch. "Understood."

Maybe there was a tone of apprehension there, but Quinn knew he'd honor her wishes. Which was good. Because she needed time. Overreacting or underreacting weren't going to help anything right now. And if she reacted, she was fairly sure she'd do some lasting damage to her surroundings.

She held up her arms, blue and gold entwined strands still lighting up underneath her skin. "Now I need to understand what I can truly do as the Librarian. Show me?"

Milaro nodded, some of the tension leaking out of him. "As you wish."

32

ACCLIMATION

The next day, after some rudimentary control measures, and a deep restful slumber to make up for the exhausting rest she'd had while synchronizing, Quinn's training began in earnest.

Quinn sat on the massive, mahogany-like desk that served as her place of work in her office. In front of her was a massive, ornate mirror. It was ringed in silver intricate knotwork that reminded her of Celtic imagery back on Earth.

The special thing about it was that she could watch the way her mana and magical energy circulated through her system. The glow moved through her veins, every single one of them, and occasionally seeped out through her pores leaving faint traces of a scale-like pattern behind.

At first, she'd been shocked. The synchronization had wrought unexpected changes.

Well, unexpected for her. The thought still made her scowl, even if the results fascinated her.

Not to mention those blue-gold traces reached her eyes, and swirled like small whirlpools mixing with her original dark brown whenever she circulated her mana for any extensive period of time. At least she'd got something out of it all, right?

Quinn sighed and shifted her focus back to the mana circulation techniques. If nothing else, Milaro was an excellent teacher.

Generally, the mirror gave her an excellent estimation of how to meditate and allow herself to get used to the flow of magic within her. She frowned at the image, pushing to maintain the current circulation level.

Since the synchronization caused a much higher level of compatibility and gave her much more power than she'd had, she needed to be, somewhat cautious about how she used it. The recent power acclimation was quite sensitive.

Now that she could sense absolutely everything around her to such a heightened degree, it meant that mana and magic circulation, as well as the attunement and tempering of the chaotic elements she was so attuned to, took on a much larger role within her body and her mind.

Previously she'd been able to feel the Library all around her, but now it practically ran through her veins alongside the magic and mana. Complete and wholly a part of her. There was energy to feed off everywhere, and at least right now, the power practically burst from her whenever she wasn't actively maneuvering it.

She had a sneaking suspicion that she wouldn't need to eat those energy balls as much anymore.

Hopefully. She felt like she'd overdosed on them lately.

"Quinn, pay attention," Milaro said, cutting through her thoughts. "Your mind is wandering again."

She glared at him, disliking the tinge of guilt she felt for not grasping the task yet. "It's really not. I'm trying my best to—"

"Quinn, I can tell when you're lying. It's one thing you're, unfortunately, really going to have to learn to do. And well." He stood with his arms crossed, returning the glare.

Quinn resisted the urge to yell at him to do it if he knew how to so well. Not that he didn't deserve it. He might have become the perfect teacher once they left the core, but she was still processing a lot.

"Now, focus," he chided gently, and she knew the care in his voice was genuine. "You need to master how your mana circulates so you can do it subconsciously. Make it a constant thing, always ready, always circulating, always replenishing all of your different energies. When you replenish your body, mind, mana, magic, and energy as a whole, it becomes much more difficult to best you in any type of fight. But it needs to become second nature . . . muscle memory."

"It's as exhausting as building my mental walls was," she said. And that was just it. She got it. She understood what he meant. It made her sort of like an air conditioning system pushing air through the ducts of a house and making sure that every room in that house had the same air pressure entering it in order to leave it at the same temperature as all of the others. "Magic is sort of like air conditioning."

"What?" Milaro asked. "Air conditioning?"

"Yes, and I'm like, my veins are sort of like ductwork." She blinked at him like he should totally understand what she was saying.

He pinched the bridge of his nose and took a deep breath. "You know, Quinn, if that helps you analyze, assess, and apply it properly— I am all for you explaining it in whatever way works for you."

"That's good. Because I wasn't going to explain it differently," Quinn said before she fanned out her hands to put them on her knees so that she could enter a meditative state again. But in doing so, she somehow managed to create a gust of wind that knocked over a massive stack of books that had been waiting for her to repair. They flew all over the floor with some of the loose pages coming out of them.

She groaned and got down off the desk to pick the books up. "Narilin is going to have my head for doing this to the books," she muttered.

"No, she won't. She'll be happy you decided to help her," Milaro said. "However, once you finish that, make sure to get back to what you were doing, or you're never going to control offhand incidents like this."

Quinn sighed because it definitely wasn't the worst thing that had happened so far. And when she had come up from the core cavern yesterday, she'd emitted a gust of wind so strong it sent Carty racing through part of the Library, and knocked a few chairs over on his way, simply by not understanding how to control the magic that leaked out of her.

Right now, they were concentrating on her meditation, so that her magic might be maintained within her spirit instead of joyfully leaking out and latching on to anything and everything it could. It seemed that some of her inclinations with magic were mischievous.

"Your synchronization took well," Milaro said. "But we're going to have to get a handle on your ability to wield the power that you now possess."

Quinn raised an eyebrow at him as if to say "No shit, Sherlock," but she limited herself to the action and didn't say the words. Everything she wanted to say still formed angrily in her mind. She hadn't passed that stage of the revelation yet. Although, interestingly enough, denial hadn't even been a blip on the radar.

She leveraged herself back up onto the desk to continue the lesson.

Milaro had spent more hours in her head with her than she'd ever thought someone would. He guided her through meditative exercises, including multitasking, mind control, leveling up her mind barrier to level five, which took barely any time at all. He'd given her drills to help strengthen her resolve. Willpower and mental fortitude went hand in hand. It didn't matter how much potential someone had if they had absolutely no trust in themself.

And he couldn't have found five minutes before synchronization to talk to her?

She'd never had anybody this close to her before, so shaking that sting of betrayal, even if it wasn't technically accurate, was difficult. Maybe she wasn't meant to have anybody that close.

There were so many human aspects to her upbringing that it was difficult to think of herself as other than that. But in a way, she'd always known there was something different about her. She'd just assumed, in a very human way, that it was more about her being an orphan.

Everything around her felt like it was on a hair trigger, even with Milaro there to guide her. Maybe especially because of that.

One false move, an out-of-place thought, a snappy temper, or impatience, and she could blow a hole in the space-time continuum for all she knew.

Although probably not.

Although maybe?

"Stop that train of thought." Milaro's voice drifted across to her. "Calm it down. Condense your focus and remember that everything about you can result in a weapon now if you so choose it. Control your reactions."

Quinn shuddered ever so slightly. Weapons.

She hadn't relished in killing Kajaro, at least when she thought she'd killed the snake-man. But sometimes, she realized, she'd have to use force to retrieve what somebody else was trying to claim as theirs when it belonged to the universe as a whole.

"Yeah, I know," she said feeling a little melancholy. "Sorry, I lost my train of thought for a second there."

"It's perfectly okay. We'll get back on track." He was smiling, she didn't even have to have her eyes open to know that.

And he was right because she had at least that much control over herself. Meditation, focusing inwards, acclimating her body to the way the power felt and moved. She entered a trancelike state and only Milaro's soothing tone roused her out of it.

"I want you to try and communicate with parts of the Library at different times, mentally, without having to speak out loud," Milaro instructed. "There is so much more you can do with just a thought, and all of it so much faster than by speaking."

Quinn mulled that over and opened her eyes to watch him. He definitely had a point. "Yeah, that's really true, but, you know, I still like to speak to people."

Milaro crossed his arms and raised an eyebrow at her. It was the sternest he'd looked at her since she warned him yesterday. "And you can still speak to people, but you're going to find that with the retrieval of books and the fines being levied, the fact is that we still have to find out, expose, and stop the culprits who sabotaged the Library in the first place. Not to mention that because there are culprits who sabotaged the Library, this also means you, very specifically, are in danger. You're not unkillable. Technically you might get to live forever if somebody doesn't kill you. So we need to make sure that you are safe, and in order to cram as much into your training and your survival as we possibly can, you need to be able to multitask at the speed of light."

Quinn gaped at Milaro. It was probably the longest speech she'd heard him give. Not only that, there was a level of passion to his words that couldn't help bring a smile to her face.

"Thanks," she said. "I appreciate the reality check."

His tone softened and he looked away. "You're at your weakest right now, at your most vulnerable. This time, right now, is when someone will most likely attempt to remove you."

Quinn nodded, not trusting herself to respond.

She scoured the connections she felt, getting used to them, feeling out every nook and cranny, knowing the parts of the Library that she could reach, the parts that were still a little hazy, how much distance she could cover with it. One of the best things she discovered was that she knew exactly what doors to the Library were being opened and where they were coming from. Granted, she didn't understand the sectors, quadrants, and whatnot yet, but that would come with time too.

Everything fed back into her mind, all of it compartmentalized in such a way that it was a little bit overwhelming, and yet, at the same time, completely and utterly eye-openingly awesome.

She took in a breath and closed her eyes. *Misha, are we ready to question the prisoners yet?* She sent out a simple question to her supervisory golem, simply to test the bounds of the telepathic link.

Misha didn't appear in front of her like they usually would have when she called out their name. This time, Quinn could practically hear the amusement over the connection.

Thank you, Librarian. I will let you know as soon as the prisoners are ready for you and the king.

Are you preparing them? Quinn asked, thinking that she might just prefer telepathy for the Library. Maybe.

Misha paused, and for a second, Quinn thought she wasn't going to get an answer.

There are barriers that the guardians can wear down so that your interrogation of the prisoners is easier. Right now, those have almost been broken through. Milaro has used a different approach that should work much better. We're almost there, Librarian.

Thank you, Quinn said. Telepathic communication was swift. The entire conversation took a blink or two. Quinn opened her eyes and smiled at Milaro. "I see why you and Malakai use the whole telepathy thing so often."

Milaro didn't even try to hide his grin. "You haven't even discovered the half of it yet."

Quinn laughed.

Milaro stared at her thoughtfully. "I have to admit, you're taking this all very well."

Quinn frowned at him, her defenses up immediately. Meanwhile, she checked on the status of the Library books that were being returned, how Malakai, Dottie, Eric and Geneva were doing with training the new assistants, and checked on Cook to see if they were making anything nice for lunch.

Then she scowled. "I told you not to ask me that. I'm alive. That's the positive. Everybody comes into the universe in some way. Some are born. I was created. And the people who created me kept it from me when it made a lot more sense to inform me earlier than during a risky power amalgamation. Don't push it. Don't bring this up again until I'm ready."

Milaro blanched, and let out a sigh. "Apologies for overstepping."

Quinn spoke after a few seconds. "I could do a lot worse than being a magical Librarian, but you don't get to dictate how I process the revelation."

Milaro turned away, and Quinn went over her words in her mind just to make sure she hadn't been unintentionally mean. With all of the information in her head, and the new experiences, she might have been nasty and not realized it.

She'd been honest and to the point. And she didn't have time to dwell on it any further.

Besides, truth be told, she liked being the Librarian. She wanted to know more about the universe—everything. He just needed to let her be for a while.

Quinn enjoyed the connectivity and the power that came with her position. Even though the danger of chaos lingered everywhere. She could feel it trying to lull her, trying to pull at her and coax her. It had this entrapping quality, but it was a signature that she could hold at bay. Once seen, it wasn't something that could hide from her. She had no intention of letting it fool her into anything.

Milaro finally spoke again. "I think perhaps it might be a good idea for us to double down on your multitasking training." He cleared his throat and wouldn't make eye contact with her.

"Multitasking is fine," she said.

He dove into her mind with her. What began as a way to divide her mind and allow her to think faster than she had learned in that book, which seemed a lifetime ago, had moved to a new level with the synchronization. Even though it could get noisy in her head if she tried to have more than one conversation, the point was that it was technically possible to keep track of multiple conversations at once.

It would have been the coolest skill to have as a kid. She could have eavesdropped on *everyone*.

"You're getting off track, Quinn." Milaro spoke through her mind. "Focus."

"Fine," she said and laughed.

Perhaps the most significant change in the whole synchronization process was that Quinn no longer needed the Library pebble. She kept it because she found it soothing to sometimes just rub her thumb over it. Sort of like a fidget toy. But now, no matter what was happening, who was nearby, or how far away she was, she could sense everything about the Library's core. It was just there as if she could reach out and touch it.

Heavy and steadfast.

"Excellent, I think you've got the hang of that," Milaro said, "at least for now."

"What next?" Quinn asked.

He flashed her a small smile. "Now you need to work on your stamina. Malakai will take you through some endurance training."

"But like . . . can't I just magic stuff?" she asked, wiggling her fingers to break some of the tension.

"You know that's not all there is to it. I don't know why you ask that." After a brief hesitation, he wiggled his fingers right back at her. "You're not the most physically imposing Librarian we've ever had. And you need endurance to be able to wield the almost endless power you'll eventually have."

She sighed. Milaro opened his mouth to say something else and closed it as Misha appeared in front of them.

"The guardians request your presence, Librarian," Misha said with a brief bow. "The prisoners seem ripe for talking. Very relaxed in their environments, in fact."

Quinn raised an eyebrow. "Really? That sounds like fun."

Milaro rolled his eyes. "Give a Librarian a bit of power . . ."

"And she'll get to the bottom of a conspiracy theory!" Quinn finished off for him. "See? I'm learning."

She ignored Milaro's groan as they headed toward the containment cell. They'd be fine. Everything would.

33

———

OBSERVATION

The holding chamber—or jail, as Quinn had come to think of it—had undergone several changes since the last time she'd seen it.

Where, before, it reminded her of those interrogation or questioning chambers they had in every single procedural drama she'd ever laid eyes on in her life, this one was now quite different.

As she looked through the glass window she could see each side of the room had a bed, and basically a small living area for each of the prisoners. Guests. Whatever they were. Both Tenejo and Narajo were in their respective spaces but didn't seem to understand that the other was just feet from them. As if they were sequestered in their own little worlds.

If she reached out tentatively toward them with her heightened Librarian senses, she could see the space felt like it was separated. Must be a part of what the guardians and Milaro did in preparation.

She watched through the now-expanded antechamber that had explicitly been set up for viewing. It, too, was larger, with several seats for observing from, as well as a desk and, from what she could tell, monitoring crystals.

"Are those what they look like?" she asked.

Milaro glanced at the crystals. "If you think they're recording every movement and action of the people we're holding—then yes?"

"Oh good. Yep. That's what I thought." Quinn frowned as she looked back through the one way window into the cells . . . the cells that really didn't seem to be keeping prisoners, even if the Serpensiril within didn't quite appear to be guests either. She moved closer, focusing on the bed Tenejo had. It didn't actually look like a bed but more like a nest on a different-colored stone floor than the rest of the room. "Is that . . . a nest?" she asked, her voice belaying her surprise.

Milaro nodded, his eyes focused and yet not as he stared through the observation window.

"Yes that we have them staying in nests?" she asked again, not entirely sure how to take that.

The elf king blinked and turned to Quinn. "Serpensiril are cold blooded. Their habitats are generally cave-like and dug down to get the warmth from the earth. They bring in any type of material that allows them to absorb and maintain that heat and thus keeps their body temperatures even. So in order to make sure they're comfortable, the guardians provided heated stones because, well. In here, we don't have earth for them to burrow into. Not all of them are like Kajaro, who had or *has*, enough magic to keep himself the perfect temperature no matter where he goes."

Quinn mulled that information over. After synchronizing properly with the Library, she assumed she'd have so much more information available to her. That she might actually know everything. But that apparently wasn't the case. All it gave her was this blood-and-bone-deep connection, where she could feel everything in it, around it, and connected to it.

Okay, that was a pretty awesome "all."

And something told her that when she did gather new skills from some more books, she was going to have a much easier time adapting to the contents. She couldn't wait to explore exactly what this deeper level of synchronization meant for her and the Library as a whole. Now the magic swimming inside her veins no longer felt foreign—it simply felt like an extension of herself.

"So, basically, we're trying to make them as comfortable as possible?" Quinn asked, still a little confused, but finding it a relief that it was easy enough to push her anger at Milaro aside in order to get stuff done.

"Of course. Just because they might want to unleash unfiltered chaos back into the universe in the hope that it creates more than it destroys or at least doesn't destroy their species . . . that's neither here nor there. We're not about to go around killing people for kicks." Milaro smirked. "Although I do know people who'd do that."

"But these guys, these Serpensiril . . . are they all like this?" She watched as Tenejo rose from where he'd been curled up on his nest—bed, whatever—and moved to get something from a small box that, upon opening it, appeared to be like a magical refrigerator. He sank onto the couch in a way that only a snake-like creature probably could. Fluid and graceful, with a hint of deadly.

"I'd think not. I met a few researchers from the Serpensiril species, oh, several centuries ago. They seemed intent on proving the opposite of the fanatics we've encountered thus far since you arrived. But . . . I daresay those are the minority." He paused, frowning as his eyes took on a sudden golden hue and he sighed. "It seems these guys are completely brainwashed however. I was hoping Tenejo at least, from what I'd already heard about him from the guardians, might be a good starting point. He appeared to at least have thought through his own standpoint. But we'll see, I guess . . ."

"How can you tell from this distance?" Quinn asked, not sensing anything mentally from the Serpensiril in question at all.

Milaro's eyes narrowed as he looked at her. "I can tell because I'm looking at it from a sort of vibrational frequency. Another piece of information about Serpensiril mind waves. It's one of those many things you're going to have to learn. But we've got time now that your connection to the Library is solid."

"Can't the Library sense when people are hostile toward it?" Quinn asked, quite certain she'd heard that as early as when she'd first entered the Library well over a month ago now.

"Yes, which is why the alarm went off when they entered."

"But it didn't," Quinn said and Milaro looked surprised. "No, seriously. It let them in, and they even spoke to me before the alarm blared."

Milaro stroked his chin thoughtfully. "They might have had some sort of concealment device for their intentions, or else not have had their minds quite made up about their intentions before they entered. In that case it would take the Library sensors some time before they triggered the true intent of the people who entered. But no matter when . . . the Library will know if someone within it, means harm to it."

"Then how did the last Librarian screw things up so badly?" Quinn muttered, half expecting Lynx to pop up and defend Kor . . . but he didn't. She really needed to check in with him.

Milaro shook his head. "I have no idea how that happened, but eventually, we're going to figure that out too."

"Hope you're right," Quinn said with a sigh. "What do we do next?"

"We go in and interrogate them." Milaro flashed her a tight smile, one that told Quinn he didn't enjoy this part of the process.

"They don't really look like they're ready. I mean, they seem relaxed and quite content. Happy, even. Comfortable." She gestured toward where Narajo was sleeping and Tenejo was relaxing on his couch. "Hell, they don't even look like they can see each other.

"That's because they can't. For all they know the other is gone. They are alone, they have sustenance and shelter but are cut off from friends and family."

"But didn't the guardians say they were ready for interrogation. Shouldn't they be more . . . I don't know, despairing?" She shrugged, spreading her hands out wide. This just didn't look like the type of questioning base she'd been expecting them to perform.

Her head was filled with all sorts of action movies and spy thrillers.

"Really?" he asked, genuine shock showing on his face, so much so his eyebrows almost hit his hairline. "Why on earth would we have them despairing and—if I'm reading your expectations correctly— perhaps beaten up?"

"Yeah. Downtrodden . . . practically begging to tell you what they know?" she said, "That's how torture is done, isn't it?"

Milaro blinked. "We're not trying to torture them. We're trying to get information out of them. How in the universe would you expect anyone to give you truthful information if you scare them and hurt them so badly it scars them for life?"

"Um . . ." Quinn had the good grace to look away. She'd never thought of it like that. "I've just never seen anyone get information from an enemy in any other way."

"And by seen?" Milaro raised an eyebrow even farther somehow. "You mean you've witnessed this yourself, or on one of those boxes that give you visual stories?"

"Well, you've been in my head, what do you think?" She crossed her arms and glared at him.

Milaro sighed. "Look. That's not how this works. We can't just lower ourselves to the same level as someone like Kajaro. Two evils do not make a right. He planted a literal bomb in your mind that we barely managed to contain and then dispel. I couldn't do that to someone else. Frankly... I wouldn't do that to someone else. Even if it was something I resorted to, it's more likely the prisoner would lie to give me the response I want to avoid more harm. These guys in there? I'm pretty sure they're low on the totem pole as far as information goes. But we have to try and extract something useful in the least invasive way possible."

Quinn gulped, seeing his reasoning and completely understanding what he meant. At the same time, she knew they needed to under-stand who exactly their enemies were, or they were never going to be free of the threat that hung over the Library and the ill-advised release of chaos en masse into the universe.

Then an idea struck her. "Wait. Shouldn't we, like, have their permission to enter their thoughts, then? Isn't that extremely invasive?"

Milaro ran a hand through his long blond hair like he wished he could just disappear into the questioning room. "Yes. Yes we should. But I'm not about to break down walls, or tear their minds apart.

These are hostile people, and these are uncertain times. I will extract what I can from what is floating in their minds given the relaxed and comfortable state we've managed to bring them to."

"Are they despairing?" Quinn asked, splaying her hand against the glass to really peer in the best she could.

"Not necessarily. It's more like a quiet defeat, with a hint of having resigned themselves to torture. Because that is what their species excels at. When we offer an alternative that is not pain, it's usually met with relief and sometimes suspicion. For most people in times like these, we attempt to retrieve pertinent information in the least damaging way. For all of us."

"It hurts you too if you have to be more forceful?" she asked softly.

It took a few seconds, but Milaro eventually answered. "It hurts in more ways than you'd think. I hope it's not something you'll ever have to experience." A sad smile lifted the corners of his mouth and Quinn wracked her brains trying to think of a way to change the subject.

Which was the perfect time for Aradie to hoot.

"I believe your owl is impatient," Milaro said. "You may bring her; she will serve as an extra judge of truth. Sometimes, even mind to mind, depending on the level of manipulation they've undergone, lying is still difficult to determine. Especially if the subject believes what they're saying to be truth."

"You want me to come in there with you?" Quinn asked, slightly taken aback.

"Whyever would you not? How else will you learn? Why would I have brought you here with me in the first place so close to your synchronization otherwise?" The elf king smiled again, but this time it held his usual smirk too. "Relax, Quinn. We aren't about to go around planting mind bombs in people's minds like certain other individuals. We're simply trying to extract what they know in the most humane way possible."

"That still sounds like a justification," she grumbled, because while it did, it also had some sound logic backing it up.

"Maybe," Milaro mused. "Justification is, after all, a means to an end. A way for us to convince ourselves that what we're doing is a worthwhile pursuit. But there are an awful lot of boundaries I'd push if it means I can save trillions upon trillions of lives from some scheme meant to purify the universe of weakness."

She mulled that over and shot a thought to Aradie. *Are you able to dive in with us and tell if the information we're getting is truly helpful or if it's a hidden plant.*

Images flashed in front of her eyes, but slowly turned into a message. *I can help you define what is real and what is fiction. What has been presented as such to the recipient.*

Quinn frowned. Okay, so that meant her owl could tell what these guys believed based on what they'd been told. It wasn't quite what she wanted, but it was better than not knowing at all. *And can you tell Milaro—can you communicate that with him too?*

Yes.

She looked up at Milaro and nodded. "I guess we should head in and see if we can't prevent a chaotic cleansing, right?"

He nodded. "We just have to wait a few minutes. Right now only Narajo is ready. Tenejo isn't quite there yet, but if you watch him, how he's almost to that relaxed point; he'll be ready any moment."

Quinn watched, still feeling uneasy. Still feeling like maybe this wasn't the most ideal way to obtain this information, but she couldn't see any other options available right now. They didn't have time to the resources to place their own spy. Plus, wouldn't they sort of expect that?

She'd have to reserve judgment for how Milaro went about it. After all, despite having the opportunity to, he'd never pushed further past anywhere in her mind than she'd given him permission to.

It was one of the reasons she was able to bench her anger, able to look at this all logically.

For the most part, anyway.

Who knew that five weeks into coming to another world she wouldn't even bat an eyelash at the fact that they were about to go swimming in someone else's head.

What a crazy universe it was.

34

DETAILS

QUINN FOLLOWED MILARO TO THE ENTRANCE DOOR, GIVING A NOD TO
Uno, the guardian who remained behind, silently observing and
managing the crystal on the table. If anything happened they'd be able
to enable proper spatial memory recollection. Which was basically
just a record of everything that happened in the . . . interrogation
room.

It was always best to have a backup, just in case.

Aradie accompanied Quinn, sitting very solemnly on her shoulder,
her wing mixing with Quinn's messy bun and lightly tickling her
cheek. In a way, it was soothing.

As they stepped through the doorway, it was like all the air around
her had been sucked up, and out. And all it left behind was this dense
sort of fog. Almost like they were flying through clouds.

A ripple of isolation passed through her but seconds later, and it
was only Aradie's presence and the quick translation of it into words
in her head, that Quinn avoided nerves. It seemed her bond with the
owl had also deepened with the synchronization.

*This is the state into which we bring them. Those who would not other-
wise give us answers willingly.*

Quinn raised an eyebrow at her owl, which was promptly ignored.

But the words sounded archaic and important, and even regal. Which, Quinn guessed, was how the owl carried herself most of the time. Perhaps Aradie was playing to the gravity of the situation.

Quinn nodded instead of commenting telepathically.

She had to admit, this whole atmosphere in here was calming. Soothing, even. Given some time in such a space, she could see relaxation taking over. She could see herself coming somewhere like this to unwind when everything got too much.

Aradie swatted her gently with a wing. *That's not what it's for.*

Milaro's voice reached her ears like it was tunneling through cotton wool. There was a flat quality to it instead of the usual gentle melody that wove its way through his words. "I'll do the heavy lifting, but I need you to observe. Use the information you got from *Mastering Your Own Thought Domain* and *Detailed Serpensiril Anatomy.*"

She narrowed her eyes ever so slightly. How had he known what books she'd taken out in the first place? He wasn't always there. But she nodded anyway. Then again, he was always talking to Lynx and the Library.

From the way he'd moved with ease in the core chamber where she thought no one else could really go, to the revelation she was still struggling with internally, she realized there were a lot of things she still didn't know about Milaro. She wasn't sure how she felt about that.

"Excellent." His flat tone continued. "I need you to see if you can sense anything off. Out of place. Something that shouldn't be there . . . or else, something that is there *too* convincingly."

Sure, that wasn't clear as mud at all. But she sort of got it. At least she thought she could follow his train of thought, anyway.

With that, he nodded once and moved into the cubicle that housed Narajo. From inside it, she couldn't see anything else, not like the fog-like substance outside had helped her see anything either.

But the walls of this were like opaque double-paned glass with smoke and clouds fed through them to conceal what was inside. To give a feeling of serenity of a dream-like surrounding. There was no way for Narajo to know that Tenejo was but feet away from him. No sound got through, no sight. Nothing.

He was completely cut off.

The cubicle itself was maybe twelve feet squared or so. Much larger than she'd initially thought, especially considering they had two of them in this room. Naturally, nothing should surprise her anymore when it came to the Library's ever changing interior.

Narajo was, quite obviously, asleep. His slumbering form seemed oddly relaxed and reminded Quinn startlingly of those little snake videos that went viral for a time back on Earth. She could almost picture him in a little top hat.

Almost.

Milaro waved a hand and a stool appeared, onto which he lowered himself carefully. She shook her head when he glanced at her, opting to stand for now. Then he reached that same hand out to Quinn, which she took without hesitation.

The man had been in her mind more than she had.

She might not know him as well as she wished yet, but his intentions toward her were based largely around the fact that she could help prevent the Library from destruction. And, if he'd wanted to hurt her, he'd had a million chances already.

Logic bought a lot of leeway.

He then locked eyes with her briefly as if to say "We've got this" and touched his other hand's pointer finger to the temple of the slumbering Serpensiril.

Quinn was immediately pulled into a cloudy, even more opaque area. Except the clouds here were more grey than white. It wasn't a troubled sensation, but a resigned one. Where the owner of this space felt that they'd done everything they could and there was no more escaping who they were now, nor what they'd done.

She thought she could even detect just a hint of remorse in the surroundings. It was barely even a thread but it was there.

Before she could think of anything else, she was tugged toward a memory. Her body wasn't solid here, not like Milaro's, but instead she felt sort of spirit-like, ghost-like even. Aradie sat on her shoulder, feathered arms gripping tightly as she concentrated. It was only then that she realized her owl seemed to be a cross between a humanoid and a bird of prey, and it was oddly beautiful.

Just in this space. The voice spoke into her mind as Aradie gave her a slight smile. *Easier to navigate.*

The images around them kept changing as Milaro delved into whatever he could to find what they needed to know. There were images of times in school—classes of chaos. Where they were taught the importance of chaos in the history of the Serpensiril and how bad people had taken away their opportunities to prove how strong, how much of a warrior or wizard they were.

Even here, Narajo didn't seem to care beyond doing well enough to not get in trouble. The friends around him constantly changed, flickering in and out as he grew up. Nothing he was taught or shown resonated with him in any particular fashion. But he did as he did, because to not do as he was told, was to bring dishonor and shame to his entire family. That was the way he was raised. It was the way they all were.

It continued in such a fashion as they sped through these memories that jumped around. Until there was one glimpse, a very vivid image in what had otherwise been a landscape awash with apathy, of Tenejo.

"Come with me," the other Serpensiril captive had told him. "I've been tasked with something very important. Something we have to verify."

"Sure," Narajo replied.

"We've been tasked with verifying the success of a plan placed into action millennia before we were born." Tenejo's eyes shone with a fervor that made Quinn shiver.

And then the two Serpensiril moved off, and the memories dissipated, turning into a sigh of white smoke that lingered around until it blew away to reveal the Serpensiril still asleep as Milaro blinked his eyes open.

Milaro grimaced briefly, and Quinn could tell the information wasn't what he'd been looking for. Not that she could blame him. None of that helped any of their leads. It left them all cold.

She felt a pang of sadness for Narajo's life.

But it did show them that Tenejo was probably the leader. It caused her some relief as she'd been afraid the one who blew himself up might have been leading them.

They moved beyond Narajo's cubicle and were able to speak briefly again.

"Not exactly what we were after." Milaro sounded more sad than irritated.

"You were expecting more?" she asked, speaking out loud in this strange dead space for the first time.

Milaro shook his head, pausing outside Tenejo's room. "No. Not like that. Just . . . I think, if given different opportunities, I don't believe Narajo would have chosen to be our enemy, or anyone's."

"Yeah," Quinn said. "He seemed very much about survival."

Milaro nodded. "Ready?"

"As I'll ever be," she said.

Another chair was summoned, they joined hands, and dove in. Exactly the way they'd initiated what she'd experienced with Narajo.

Except Tenejo was a whole other ball game.

As soon as she entered as the incorporeal spirit, she could feel the density shift. This wasn't some wishful thinking "I just have to survive" lair. No . . . this was dark.

And dangerous.

This mind haze was different. Tenejo's entire presence was filled with elements of zeal, of righteousness. In his classes when he was called on, he knew the equations of theories Quinn couldn't even begin to fathom.

The darkness of his clouds, the opacity of his inner sanctum was so many shades of charcoal it made Quinn feel like tinder.

Aradie flashed an image that shot down the bond shared with Milaro.

Truth.

This was reality for Tenejo. He was the one who'd been given the task to come to the Library in the first place. Milaro doubled down, and pushed a little harder than he had with their other subject.

They worked through the memories, the glimpses. From where Tenejo was praised and lauded for his understanding of the Serpensiril culture. To only make friends for one reason: leverage and loyalty.

It was the latter that led him to Narajo, who was unwaveringly loyal to the one friend who'd ever stood up for him.

Quinn felt a moment of sadness but knew it belonged to her and not to the mind she was observing. As far as Tenejo went, there was no remorse, no attachment-based emotion contained within the man. He was clinical, cunning, and he was ever so fanatical in his belief that chaotic energies wouldn't harm him

She could feel the ice cold that ran through his veins, in more ways than one.

His school life was exemplary, and he'd been conscripted at an early age, from what she could tell because she didn't quite understand how the Serpensiril even aged. He'd served with zeal and fervor.

Flashes of memories to him slitting a throat of a species she couldn't identify, before moving on to the next target or victim. The way the blood bubbled made her gag briefly.

Aradie pushed toward Milaro and the vision changed to the next.

This one involved taking out a few of his own species, and Quinn's blood ran cold. She could have sworn one of them was adolescent at most. Bile rose in her throat, and she clenched her eyes shut, upset to realize that in spiritual form, she could still sense everything.

Another push, and the images changed again.

But this time there was no blood. He sat on a padded bench in a wide hallway outside of what appeared to be a rather ornate door. It was at least twelve feet high, with double door handles and intricate wooden carvings that were accentuated at intervals by iron studs.

He sat, his forked tongue darting in and out, his cloak hood pulled up to hide his face in the shadows.

"Tenejo. You may enter now."

Tenejo started. The doors opened without their target even realizing it. He stood, smoothed his cloak down and slithered into the room. The vision changed with the entrance.

They now stood in a large rectangular room. Books lined the two sides of the walls, while the back wall was one huge window. But contrary to the gorgeous view Quinn had in the restricted vault, this showed something akin to lava and brimstone. Something that reminded her of the Dabilian home world before it solidified into igneous rock formations.

The large desk in front of the window was at least six feet wide, and the chair was pushed back as someone stood, gazing out of the window.

"Do you see this?" the sibilant voice said, strong and proud.

And oddly familiar to Quinn.

Tenejo's eyes took on that fanatical gleam. The emotional sensations rippled through the dream space, threatening to take those in it, with it. The destruction of chaos right in front of him seemed to get the Serpensiril off. "I see it."

"We're slowly approaching our goals," the man said, "and now that you've proven yourself, my assassin, I need you to check and see just how successful our set up has been."

Tenejo nodded, barely keeping the glee from his face. "I will kill anyone you ask of me. Just direct my blade, your lordship."

The figure waved him away, but the posture changed, and Quinn could tell he was pleased. "This is more of a reconnaissance mission. And you will need to do it once I have taken care of something myself. You need to be ready to face this within the next month."

"As you wish, your lordship." This time Tenejo bowed so low, he almost scraped his head.

"Enough of 'your lordship.' After all, you should be calling me uncle." And the master of Tenejo's whole world finally turned around, revealing Kajaro's face, and an evil smirk.

"Then I will do as you command, Uncle. I'll bide my time." Tenejo's words were filled with such resolution, such blind faith in the man before him, that it sent shivers down Quinn's spine.

"See that you do," Kajaro said. "And when the time comes, I need you to be a thorn in their side."

Aradie sent out the sensation of truth again, and Quinn suddenly felt very vulnerable. After all, Tenejo was right here, inches from Quinn.

The vision blanked out, briefly, and turned to Tenejo getting ready with his two accomplices as they prepared to acquire the applications. Tenejo's head snapped up from where he was writing, his reptilian eyes seeking out something beyond the memory . . .

Milaro broke the contact and ushered Quinn out of the enclosure, and out of the room.

As soon as they entered the antechamber again, Quinn started shaking. It wasn't out of fear, but out of certainty that there was a lot more to what they were dealing with than she'd thought.

"Are we safe?" she asked Milaro as soon as he'd sealed the door.

Milaro didn't answer immediately. He checked the door and the seal and turned to Uno. "Triple-check that they're locked down. That there is no way of reaching their inventories or each other."

Uno nodded and a brief hum echoed throughout the room. "We already extricated their storage devices. They have been placed in containment."

The elf king then turned to Quinn and half smiled. "I wish I could say we're safe. But I can't help feeling I've played right into their hands. I only hope I broke contact before he saw you."

"Is it even possible for him to see me when he's in that state?" she asked, tamping down on her fear.

"Probably. Maybe? It's not exact; there are so many variables when dealing with the mind."

"Would Kajaro know what you can do?" Quinn asked, dreading the answer.

Milaro shrugged. "He knows the Seveshall family generally have very strong mind magic affinities. He probably has some inklings."

"How secure is that?" Quinn asked, gesturing over her shoulder at the holding bays.

"Right now?" Milaro said. "They're as strong as we can make them, and considering we got ourselves out of critical power mode, we at least have that on our side. I'm not about to say we're safe, but we're going to bring reinforcements and lock down what we have."

"Great," Quinn said, suddenly itching to get out of the interrogation area. "Then I think I deserve a donut."

"That's not the response I anticipated," Milaro said, a small smile crossing his face.

"Stress sometimes makes me want sugar," Quinn confessed.

"He was not what you expected, was he?" Milaro asked after several seconds.

She shook her head. Because for some reason she'd thought Tenejo might actually not be bad. Perhaps the whole Serpensiril being evil was a schtick. But she'd been wrong. She had to get harder. She had to stop giving everyone the benefit of the doubt because she really wanted people to be nice. "He was definitely not what I expected, and now I can't help but wonder if we've played into a clever trap."

"True," Milaro said. "But we can try to make sure we're at least shielded as best we can be."

"Yeah, at least I don't have a bomb in my head anymore." Quinn sighed, reached up and petted Aradie. "Let's go grab some donuts. I miss Cook."

Quinn made her way to the kitchen, unable to shake the feeling of foreboding. She couldn't get the sudden recognition in Tenejo's eyes out of her head.

She couldn't help wondering if the thorn had already been planted.

35

FRANTIC FOOTSTEPS

As much as Quinn wanted to concentrate on the power she could feel bubbling just below the surface since she'd synchronized more intimately with the core, there were other priorities.

Library Fine Leniency Period over in 96 hours and 27 minutes.

Would you like to issue a system wide broadcast to remind people to return their books before Fines are levied again?

Yes or No?

She suppressed a groan. What she wouldn't give for a time stasis chamber, or even just a damn break so she could spend some time familiarizing herself with all the new senses and abilities she'd gained.

She guessed she could just partition that off in her mind and work on what she could. But it wasn't a good solution.

Despite wanting to figure out how they were going to approach the Serpensiril problem they seemed to have, not to mention finding those who were in cahoots with them, Quinn knew they had to make sure the Library ran efficiently enough that it could continue to increase its power levels. They weren't out of the woods quite yet.

Almost reluctantly, she chose Yes.

There was a brief pause, almost like a jolt to her surroundings and suddenly a message played in front of her, and she could only imagine also in front of every single person who'd borrowed a Library book, or had one in their possession at that moment.

The Library of Everywhere requests your overdue book return.

The Fine Leniency Period ceases in 96 hours and 12 minutes. Please return your books before this deadline if you wish to avoid a fine.

And for almost four days . . . the Library was full of a different kind of chaos.

Quinn gripped the check-in desk, taking in deep breath during a rare lull.

"We're almost there," Lynx said, back in feline form, perched on the top of the desk. Not being a housecat should have meant he was too big for the surface, but he really wasn't. Probably another form of the Library adapting to suit its inhabitants needs.

"You mean we're almost back to imposing fines, right? Because we're sure as hell still a long way off from having all the books back," Quinn said, as she glanced at the long overdue list she kept handily minimized in the corner of her vision for easy access.

Lynx did a weird shrug roll of his feline shoulders. "Imposing fines helps keep the Library replenished in funds and power, and reminds people that they can't just take the knowledge without sharing it."

Quinn frowned. She got that, she did. What she wanted was some time where she could just focus on her new powers. Right now her attention to them was minimal, and thus her learning had been slowed to a trickle. Granted, she was much faster at implementation now.

"This would be much easier if I could just stop time for a bit to catch up," she grumbled, as she sorted several books through the cleansing devices they'd installed.

"You shouldn't even joke about that," Lynx said, grooming himself for all the world like he was a big lynx.

"I swear you only transform back into cat form when there's too much work to do." She shot him a glare.

"Whatever are you implying?" he asked with a smirk.

Quinn wasn't angry at him; she just felt tired at this point. "Do I have to go and start collecting books straight after this, and leveraging out fines? What about the restricted ones? We're not any closer to figuring out their location, right? And how am I supposed to find time to train with Malakai when I have to go and get all of these books?"

Lynx sighed as he morphed back into his human form. It was as if the space in front of her rippled, confusing her senses ever so briefly until he stood in front of her the way she'd got so used to seeing him.

"Stop it. This isn't rocket science. You're a Librarian. You'll go retrieve some books for some specific reasons, also known as the difficult ones, and then you'll be able to categorize the ones that require your direct attention and the ones you can delegate—or 'pawn off'? I think that's the term—to your supervisor subordinates." He paused, as if mulling something over.

"What is it? What aren't you saying?" Quinn crossed her arms. She'd been here long enough to know when the manifestation was checking on other things. She just didn't have the energy right now to balance books on his head while he was off with whatever vision he was looking into.

"We do need to open some of the other branches. And the key books that allow that are really coming along. But there is a golem type we can send to retrieve the books that don't appear to be near inhabited areas."

"Books not near inhabited areas?" Quinn raised an eyebrow. Because why in the universe would books be somewhere no one could read them?

"Sometimes depending on species survival rate, or fallout between clans, that sort of thing, books can be misplaced. While the tug of the Library's power can help them begin moving toward the destination, they do require a physical presence to open a door to here." He paused again when he noticed Quinn was staring at him rather blankly.

Clearing his throat, he approached it differently. "They need a person to open the gate and retrieve them, or walk them through. They're just books acting on a homing beacon. And golems can retrieve those. The specific type of retrieval golem is actually well-adapted to that specific task. As long as it's just an ordinary book that is."

"They can't just go off and get the restricted books we're missing back? So we just create and send a few golems to find stray normal books?" Quinn asked, wondering why he'd made it so complicated.

"Well." He looked down for a moment. "Sure, you could say that. But we do have to verify that it's actually a book that's gone missing and not, well . . . setting a trap for us."

"Ah, I see." And now she got it. Which showed her just how tired she was that she hadn't quite caught onto that during the conversation.

"In the scope of the Library's age, almost five hundred years feels relatively tiny to me." Lynx spoke quietly. "But for a system to be functioning on only an emergency level of power for that long, for it to lose access to many of its functions . . . that makes almost five hundred years seem like an eternity. I just didn't realize it at the time."

Quinn shrugged and patted his shoulder. "You know, it's not like you'd done a full power down before. You'd never needed to. You can't blame yourself."

"Oh, I can," Lynx cracked a smile. "But that is futile at best. What we can do is simply move forward and make sure we don't let them get their teeth into us again, right?"

"Speaking of which, have you heard from Milaro?" Quinn asked hesitantly. Enough time had passed since her synchronization that she thought she was almost ready to give him a piece of her mind.

Although not literally.

Lynx shook his head. "No. He had several things to attend to after the interrogations."

"Don't you mean mind gleanings or something?" Quinn cut him off. She had so many questions about mental manipulation for him, but since the king needed to get back to his actual job, she found herself tempted to find out the answers by researching herself. Except even she could hear the alarm bells in her head telling her not to risk it.

"Don't be pedantic," Lynx muttered.

Library Doors A 27, Q 41, B 35, F 19 have been accessed.

Quinn groaned as she glanced at the list as it flashed in front of her face and minimized the information. "Back to work. We still have a few hours."

So many books had been returned since Quinn sent out the last warning. They'd sent one every twenty-four hours since, although Eric complained the whole time.

"What's the use of telling them constantly? We're just wasting away the fines we could be leveraging already! If you'd just taken my advice, our power levels would be way past where they are right now." It was a constant tirade he kept up under his breath whenever no patrons were around.

"They wouldn't be way past where they are," Quinn chided gently.

Eric grumbled. "But they'd be better!"

"Stop being so grumpy. I've seen you half smile at some of these patrons." Quinn nudged him as he got ready to check in the books brought to him from a group of four people with hooded cowls who, for all the world to Quinn, looked like they might be assassins or wraiths.

Sicarae—Wraith-bound Species, Mind Leaning

Located in the: Fountains of Halschius

Library Relationship: Allies—Eternal

She made a note that they came from the same region as the imp, and perhaps that's why he seemed extra grumpy today. It probably meant he sort of cared about them. Quinn noticed he got particularly grumped when he actually gave a crap about things.

Between the four of them, they brought back approximately eighty-one books. Quinn was astounded as she began cleansing them, surreptitiously listening in on their conversation with Eric.

"I don't know why you had to leave this until the last moment. I told you it was legitimate. I've seen the Librarian in action. What did you think, I was lying?" He sounded very affronted and slightly put out.

"It wasn't that we didn't believe you. We had hoped the grace period would be extended. I don't believe we've located all of the books, but these were what we could find." The Sicarae that spoke was named Atrecea, and her words sounded like a chilling whisper meant to send even goosebumps running.

"Should have put more manpower on it," Eric said, his words short. But Quinn could tell he was slightly mollified by Atrecea's admission.

Aradie sent back amused images to Quinn as the owl flew through the Library keeping an eye on everyone there. From the patrons returning books to those who were newly browsing the Library. There was a vibrancy in the building. A sense of things coming back to the way they should be.

And yet, given the circumstances, Quinn couldn't help but worry.

She'd never been a fan of things going smoothly, and that hadn't changed just because she'd synchronized to the core in a meaningful way. In fact, it had just gotten that much worse.

But this was one more thing they needed to check off their ridiculously long list. Get as many of the books back, and then she could go over that damned list and figure out what next steps to take from there.

And maybe squeeze in a self-advancement break.

The timer clicked down in her peripheral vision, new species she'd never seen before began to haze her vision. Quinn got into a routine that helped cleanse every single book they returned now. So ingrained into their check-in system over the last couple of days that it was simply second nature to perform it now.

So far, none of the alarms had gone off, and they'd easily scanned through two thousand books.

Harish and Siliqua kept a constant watchful eye on the system just in case.

And finally, the damned clock ticked down.

Remaining Library Fine Leniency Period: 59 seconds.

Quinn scanned the books.

More Library doors opened.

Frantic footsteps ran into the main chamber.

Books were returned, plopping into the chute to be cleansed.

Remaining Library Fine Leniency Period: 32 seconds.

More Library doors. More footsteps.

Quinn's shoulders ached, and she shrugged them.

00:03

00:02

00:01

00:00

Library Fine Leniency Period over.

Future fines can only be waived by the Librarian.

Quinn snapshotted the people in the Library at the end of the countdown and reassured them over an announcement. "Anyone who made it into the Library will have their fees waived. You made it on time. Anyone coming in after you will be fined."

She couldn't help the tingle of anticipation running down her spine at that thought. Finally, she'd get to do some cool stuff. Like— no, your book is overdue! You dogeared a page!

This was going to be fun.

But maybe she was also just very tired. She sighed as Eric handed her one of the first of about a hundred fifty books that had made it into the Library during the last moments of the time limit for her to waive the fee.

He nudged her. "Come on. Just these ones. I can see how eager you are to get to the fines. You can't hide that from me."

Quinn laughed. "You could be right, you know."

"Oh, I know." He winked and flew back to his station.

Maybe he'd rubbed off on her. But Quinn decided that might not be a bad thing.

After all, leveraging fines wasn't just going to be fun, it was going to help get her answers and increase the power of the Library.

It was time for them to stop always reacting. Now it was finally time to act.

After she waived these last fines, of course.

36

POUND OF FLESH

QUINN WOKE AFTER WHAT SEEMED LIKE WAY TOO LITTLE SLEEP. HER eyes felt crusty, and she couldn't remember how much of a break she'd taken at all since the final countdown of the book return saga.

Frankly, with Aradie still obviously slumbering at the top of her headboard, Quinn couldn't even figure out how she'd woken up in the first place. The grime in her eyes started itching, and she finally pushed herself up in the bed, painfully aware of just how stiff her shoulders felt.

That's when she noticed pounding on her door. It was light enough to call a thud, really, and she groaned, knowing instinctively who it was through that pesky old deeper connection that she needed to investigate along with everything else.

"Come in, Lynx," she said, smiling to herself. It was amazing how easy it was to feel at home in a place she'd been made for. It bothered her that she'd been so accepting of this fact. She supposed some people had inborn talents for art, music, or sports. Quinn happened to have an inborn talent for becoming the Librarian. Even if it was deliberate.

That was something to delve deeper into at a later time.

Lynx pushed into the room, his styled hair with its runic accents in far more disarray than she'd ever seen before. But his usually dark purple eyes were just shining. And in his ever more frequently solidified hands, as they had been since the filtration system was set to a third filter . . .

Wait—had they opened the fourth yet?

She pinched the bridge of her nose in a bit of frustration. She was losing her trains of thought here. They were derailing.

"What is that?" she asked of the massive tome he dumped on the foot of her bed. The thing had to be easily a foot thick or more. Its pages were yellowed with age, and that was even without opening them. The leather seemed to have a perpetual layer or grime across it, and was tattered, worn, and obviously very well-loved.

"This," he said, his eyes continuing to shine with a gleam she thought might even verge on maniacal. "Is the *History of Fines*."

Quinn frowned. "*History of Fines*." She looked it over and tried to tug it up to her. "That is heavy."

He smirked at her. "Of course it's heavy. It's a handwritten history."

"That thing is sincerely handwritten?" She tossed him a bit of a skeptical look at that comment.

"Well." Lynx stared at it for several seconds. "I mean, it started out that way, but as the stock of books increased, the affinities increased, and then—of course—the fines multiplied. Sometimes it's *magically* handwritten?"

Quinn laughed, despite still barely feeling awake. "And why, pray tell, have you brought the holy tome of fines up to my quarters instead of waiting for me to meander down for food?"

Lynx blinked, in that oddly reptilian way he sometimes had about him. "Because you've been asleep for over a day and I didn't want to wait any longer."

"What?" Quinn asked, quite sure she'd heard him wrong.

"We didn't want to wake you. You worked through the whole ninety-six hours the Library was counting down. Everyone thought you deserved some sleep." He shrugged, like it was self-explanatory.

"Oh." Quinn felt oddly touched and slightly embarrassed. Still. "That's a lot of sleep. How do I still feel like so much crap?"

Lynx shrugged. "That I can't help you with, but I can tell you that we're not being that nice. You should come and eat and help get everything back in order. Plus! Now we get to levy fines! We haven't been able to take any books back because you didn't set up the system first."

"Have there been a lot of people turned away?" Quinn asked as she jumped out of bed, worried.

Lynx chuckled. "No. I activated a brief hold on new intakes while we organized the new changes. At least I could do that. I think we had all of ten people try, and those have been noted by the scans you and Misha put in place to weed out any other potential threats entering the Library."

"All right, then. Give me ten. I'll be down." Quinn shook her head, still unable to believe she'd slept that long.

"I'll have Cook prepare your favorite breakfast and put it in your office." Lynx left, hefting the massive tome with him, a slight skip to his step. The Library manifestation appeared to be in an oddly good mood.

Quinn showered and dressed in record time and pulled on some simple soft jeans, a pair of sneakers, and a light button down shirt before tossing her still-damp hair up into a ponytail and taking the steps two at a time down the three flights of stairs.

She could already smell the cinnamon coming out of her office as she traipsed in. "I should have gone to get it from Cook myself. I swear I haven't seen them in ages."

"Cook isn't going anywhere," Lynx said, barely able to contain his excitement. "You, on the other hand . . ."

Quinn scowled. "Really?"

"Well, not straight away, but soon. You'll get to go see worlds. I'll actually get to come with you sometimes." Lynx sounded so content-edly happy that Quinn almost missed it.

"Wait. You can leave the Library now?"

"Yes! Well, shortly. But soon!" Lynx literally beamed. "Thought you might catch that. Now that we're at this power level, as long as we fix my memory, I can actually go places. Well, that is if we maintain and continue to increase power."

"That's the plan." Quinn felt a whole lot better knowing Lynx could would be able to leave too. Not that doing things on her own was bad, or with Malakai, but there were times when having the Library closer would be more comforting.

It also made her ponder just how far away she could be and still speak with the actual Library.

She sat down and pulled up her console interface while biting into a massive piece of what appeared to be cinnamon toast. It was thick-cut white bread and dripping with butter. Cook really knew how to match her moods perfectly to the food. It was like their very own magic.

Quinn fiddled for a few moments with the console.

Library Fines Level One

Minor Fines

Standard Fines

Permission Levels: Not set.

Quinn mulled that over for a few. It made sense to allow the supervisors access to leverage minor and standard fines to start with. She indicated so by adding their names to the list of supervisory staff.

Library Fines Level One

Staff permissions required: Supervisory Roles Within the Library

Supervisory Staff further broken down: Malakai, Dottie, Lynx, Misha, Eric, Geneva, Jim, Bob.

Lynx leaned over her shoulder. "Not going to add in Narilin?"

Quinn raised an eyebrow. "Would you give her the power to smite someone who had dogeared a page?"

Lynx cringed. "Yeah, no. That's perhaps a wise decision."

"Just giving Eric fine access is already touch and go," she muttered as she double-checked the permissions.

Lynx chuckled. "He does seem eager. He's got a wee bit of a justice streak going there. Odd for an imp, but strangely perfect for him."

"That's a very accurate assessment," Quinn said as she accepted the changes. "Do you think those are enough to start with?"

"Well, as much as I'd like to think thirty days was enough to return books, there might have been extenuating circumstances. We should probably wait another few weeks before we start taking pounds of flesh." There was a cunning gleam that passed ever so fast through Lynx's eyes, making Quinn wonder just how kidding he was.

"Is that a literal fine?" she asked hesitantly. Sometimes she wasn't sure she really wanted the answer, but curiosity got the best of her.

Lynx winked at her. "It can be."

Quinn shuddered slightly, now seeing why Eric was perhaps so eager to levy fines. "But these levels should be fine, right?"

"No pounds of flesh yet, Quinn. I promise." The Library manifestation grinned in that awful Cheshire way.

Quinn made a mental note to check any future unlocking of fines a lot more diligently. She paged through the massive book, her alarm growing increasingly.

"Seriously?" She pointed at one line.

Fine Levied on failure to return Fire Power Prowess and Incineration Techniques.

Book was being used opening during a battle, pages were singed. Overdue messages ignored.

Fine Levied: Mana depletion 4x monthly for one year. No borrowing rights for that year. Monetary fine for recklessness with Library property: 150 Dimensional Tokens.

"That seems excessive. Doesn't mana drain mean they had to come and donate their energy and mana?" she asked.

Lynx nodded, a smug smile in place now. "Yep. You'll also notice that the person responsible appears numerous times in the book—he should actually be in the system itself too. Always late. Always pushing the boundaries for no good reason but that he could."

"So the fine depends on the reasons it was late, the person borrowing it, and their attitude to returning it?" Quinn spoke slowly as she reasoned it out in her own mind.

"Mostly," Lynx said. "Although you're missing the nuance of how they were using it, where they were using it, and if they were putting the book in undue and deliberate danger."

"Oh." Quinn turned her attention back to the tome and the console. "Fines are set for now. Those ten people who tried to return their books have had their fines lifted. We don't need to be chasing those down yet."

She mulled over what else lay in front of her, knowing she also had to get stuff crossed off her massive lists. She frowned at the sheer number of books still missing when a thought occurred to her. "These are just the books still missing, right? Like . . . the Library has hundreds of thousands more books right?"

Lynx raised an eyebrow. "Of course it does. We'd be a pretty crap library if we only had like twenty thousand books or something."

"Yeah. Good point. Only . . . I mean it always feels so endless in here." She reached out with her heightened senses—to all the doors, the portals, the different rooms and potential branches. So much yet left to explore. "What about the branches? They're sealed, right? There are books in there too?"

Lynx nodded. "Yeah. There are a lot of books in those too. The main branch only houses the very beginner texts of the other branches. Once we've retrieved the books required for them to open up, there'll probably be even more missing. But right now I can't access those files, as the branches were sealed off to protect both our power base for the main branch and themselves."

Quinn suppressed the groan she could feel trembling at the back of her throat. That meant once they had all these books and opened all the branches, there'd still be more to collect. She bit into her cinnamon toast with a bit of viciousness that surprised even herself.

"Hey," Lynx said softly. "I hate to tell you this. But there will always be books to collect. Some will require your direct intervention . . . others will not. Some will be simple. Others will get lost. Some fines will be boring, and others will bring you all sorts of joy." He grinned ferally at the last.

Quinn chuckled. "Fine. I get it." Then she blinked . . . and laughed. "Get it? Fine?"

He groaned. "I should not have woken you so early, it seems."

She shrugged. "You've changed a bit. Since we got the Library back online power-wise, since the timer ran out . . . since I synchronized more intimately with the Library. What gives?"

For a whole moment he just watched her, his eyes flickering in that strange way. She almost thought he wasn't going to answer, when he surprised her. "Before the filtration system was fixed, before the power helped us synchronize on a deeper level, I didn't think any of it was going to happen. I thought I'd doomed the Library to a fate worse than death, and if you ever see chaos unmake something, you'll understand exactly what I mean by that."

He shrugged this time, uneasiness in the action. "For almost five hundred years, I thought I broke the Library. I really thought I'd ruined us. Even not knowing what happened with the sabotage, I simply assumed it had all been my fault. I—well, the Library and I—made the decision to lock people out, to preserve what we could when I found no signatures that could help us."

"But you're the Library too, doesn't that make you simply responsible for yourself?" Quinn tried to keep her voice gentle. She'd had no idea he'd been going through this. Perhaps once she'd just simply thought of him as an algorithm attached to the Library, but she'd long since realized the Library wasn't a machine of any sort.

"You would see it that way, and really, most would." He looked at his hands. "But I'm not only the Library, as it is also not only me. Shutting it down after Korradine dissipated was one of the hardest things I've ever done. A thing I could only do because she dissolved. I had no way of knowing, not after years of already searching, if we'd ever come out of limbo again. What if I'd doomed the galaxy, the universe, billions of species of people, plants, and planets?

"Now, though . . ." He smiled without that sense of Cheshire mischievousness. It was the first real smile Quinn had seen on him. Not a half-one, or a smirk. But one filled with hope. "Yeah, now there's actual hope. Sure, there's a few downsides too, but overall, I didn't doom everything."

"No, you certainly didn't." Quinn smiled back at him, and once again got that odd sensation of belonging. Of that heartbeat connected to hers, lingering in the back of her mind. "I'm glad too, because this synchronization has been great, but there are a few things I'm going to need to work through."

"Yep," Lynx agreed, and pushed the fines tome in front of her, his Cheshire grin back. "And one of those is the Great Fine Tome of Doom . . . or so I like to call it."

"You're having far too much fun with this," she said, pushing it to the side. "We have other matters to deal with first."

He raised an eyebrow and then pouted. "Fine. You're no fun. Let's check on the book numbers first, and then we can get to the fines."

"So tell me," she asked, suddenly more serious again. "How are we coming with the books missing from the restricted vault?"

Lynx's face fell. "Yeah, those. I was hoping we could forget about those for a while."

"Why?" Quinn was legitimately confused. "I thought they'd be the most important."

"They are," he said. "It's just that with portions of information still missing in their entirety, it's more difficult than I'd like to ascertain approximate locations or even a definitive list."

Aradie hooted.

Quinn turned to her owl. "Really?"

Aradie nodded solemnly.

"Problem solved, sort of. Aradie say the owls can retrieve memory replays for you to peruse and see if we can locate them that way. Or at least get some hints."

Lynx blinked, and some of the tension leaked out of his shoulders. "That's a bit of a relief."

"Excellent. Then . . ." Quinn grinned up at him. "Shall we get started?"

3 7

BOOKS STILL OUTSTANDING

SEVERAL DAYS INTO NORMAL LIBRARY OPERATIONS, ALSO KNOWN AS THE post-fine-free period, Quinn was already at her wit's end. She'd always been a little bit more of the history and story buff, and definitely not a statistical and mathematical person. The amount of math that appeared to be involved in running this specific Library irked her no end.

She had a gazillion lists she had to get through, some of which the Library set up for her, and some of which she'd set herself, but the most daunting list of all was the as-yet-still-unreturned books.

Sure, they'd managed to return a substantial amount of the missing ones, but the problem was the opening of branches. Those required specific volumes to be returned to the Library in order for those avenues to be opened up. Which meant that there were high levels of combat and alchemy that she couldn't access until they received the necessary missing beginner level books.

Not having access to those branches made her, and therefore also the Library, weak.

Quinn didn't like the idea of being a weak Librarian when there were whole species intent on wiping the Library and its purpose from the face of the cosmos.

"Focus," she told herself, turning her attention back to the long list on her HUD that she'd been staring at for the last half hour.

Books still outstanding: 9,925

Books returned: 8,117

Books currently being reproduced: 57

*Restricted Vault Books missing: 12**

Alert Level: High

Requirements for Library Branch openings. Defined by relevant book and/or ingredient count only.

Horticulture: 412/720

Bardic/Music: 492/897

Culinary Arts: 277/282

Crafting: 399/730

Alchemical/Medicinal: 241/384

Combat: 522/837

Academy: 461/785

Total: 18,042 Books/Tomes/Codices

**As far as the Library has been able to ascertain*

Numbers, numbers everywhere and . . . and just so many books still to go.

On the bright side, they were only missing five more of the Culinary Arts books, and she knew one of those was being reproduced.

"You don't seem like a happy Librarian today," Malakai said from where he'd stopped to lean against her doorway, which she'd left open because she hated being confined to a stuffy office. Not that the Library wouldn't adjust the appearance for her if she so asked.

"I'm not a very happy Librarian today," she grumbled in agreement, running her hand through her annoying curls that refused to stay up in the messy bun today.

"You skipped this morning's training, but I figured you were probably sore. Now I find you here poring over . . . lists?" He moved in, all his usual swagger left at the door. Malakai actually appeared to be concerned.

She raised an eyebrow at him, squinting up at him. There was so much more she could sense from people now, ever since she'd synchronized. "Your grandfather asked you to check in on me, didn't he?"

Malakai shrugged. "He did, but I would have anyway. I take it you've been up all night with this." He gestured wildly around her head. It wasn't like he could see her HUD from where he stood.

Quinn chuckled, finding herself automatically relaxing. She reached her arms up and stretched. He was right, after all. She had been up the entire night. Again. Going over all things Library. Her shoulders were stiffer than a board, and she had a mild headache that threatened to spill fog across her vision.

Shaking her head she pushed herself up. "Enough of this. We're close to opening the culinary branch, but we need a lot of the ingredients for it. Come with me to chat with Cook?"

Malakai grinned. "Which gives me an excuse to eat Cook's food? You'll have to twist my arm."

"Nope. All Cook's food belongs to me," Quinn said, partially serious.

"Probably should go to Farrow to talk about the ingredients we're missing for the opening, though, don't you think?" Malakai suggested.

Quinn thought about it and realized she should probably get some sleep. But Cook had a variation on caffeine that tasted less bitter and helped pick her up just as much. That would do for now. "I'll just grab a drink off Cook first."

Malakai rolled his eyes, as if he knew it was just an excuse to visit the kitchen and potentially also get food. He was a bit of a smart elf.

Her tiredness was more from an overload of information than anything else. It appeared that aligning up more with the Library was giving her more perks than just a deeper connection.

They stepped out of her office and into the majesty that was the Library.

Since they'd passed critical power mode, everything within shone with this light of hope. She wasn't certain how to describe it, except it felt like a spring day was constantly shining down on them through shafts of light that made it through the windows.

Granted, power levels weren't completely out of the woods yet, but it was slowly getting there. Although the recuperation rate had slowed to a trickle since the fine free period was over. With the extra filter going there was increased capacity. Things were definitely looking up.

Quinn glanced around toward the massive check-in desk to see a jolly Eric supervising a couple of their new recruits as they checked in a few straggler books. The imp had a huge grin on his face, and his wings appeared to be fluttering extra excitedly.

He caught Quinn's eye and flashed her a huge wink.

She had to suppress a laugh. He'd been wanting to impose fines for so long, she'd been a little worried to let him. But so far he hadn't incinerated anyone, so she figured that was a win.

His eagerness was contagious, and his little assistants were very forthright in the way they carried out the approved fines. They were nothing serious so far. Monetary fines here and there, but generally, they asked for energy donations. The Library was still recovering, after all.

"He's having a ball, isn't he?" Malakai asked.

"Yeah. I think he has a lot of respect for the books."

Malakai raised an eyebrow. "Or he likes a bit of a power trip."

"Or both," Quinn conceded. "I guess he's in his element."

To Quinn's surprise, as they made their way toward the kitchen, she could still spy many patrons strolling through the Library. There were golems assisting, assistants helping, and people from all different species sitting and chatting quietly in all the little seating alcoves and areas available to them.

The carts slowly shelved and reorganized sections, books flying to and from shelves with trails of happy magic. Or at least, that's what it looked like to her.

The whole scene gave Quinn a sense of peace, of comfort, and serenity. She refused to think of it as a lull, but more of the way it should be. Tempting fate was never a good idea, regardless how little or much one might believe in it.

She turned her attention from the main part of the Library and beckoned for Malakai to follow her into the kitchen. The warm fuzzy feeling continued to grow once she got there too. The dining hall had at least a dozen people not employed by the Library in it, as well as some assistants.

They were all eating and chatting merrily. As if everything had gone back to normal.

Which it had. Sor of.

But only for the last several days.

Quinn frowned.

"Uh-oh," Malakai said. "What are you thinking about?"

She shook her head, not wanting to say anything out loud yet until she got a real handle on what it was that bugged her. "I'm thinking about how much I need some of that drink Cook makes me." Perhaps she was just feeling tired, and a little out of her depth.

Sure. That was it.

A hum sounded under her feet, and she looked around surreptitiously to see if anyone else noticed it. It was very soft and subtle, nothing like when she'd been pulled into the world. Or even when she'd synchronized.

Malakai appeared oblivious, as did the rest of the dining hall. Cook was bustling with what appeared to be two cooking helpers behind the stove area. She'd never seen Cook appear so alive . . . so real.

Was that it? Was the fact that the Library was finally coming into its element just something to get used to?

Cook waved her over, making direct eye contact with her. "Librarian. You will be wanting this mirta tea. You said it helps revitalize you. I can see that you have little energy this morning."

The humming that vibrated through the soles of her feet made them feel heavier, even tingled her bones a little bit. Perhaps she was just over-tired. That was a thing, after all. "Thanks, Cook," she said, smiling appreciatively as he also handed her a donut.

He paused as he did so, his deep eyes practically boring into her own. "Watch you do not get swept away" was all he said.

"What?" she asked, blinking rapidly.

Cook nodded. "Exactly. Do not get too bogged down in your

thoughts. Look and see and feel. Your connection is stronger now, and you have to make sure it does not bog you down. Does not drain you too much."

"Oh." Quinn smiled and checked her energy levels.

Energy: 1285/1894

Yeah, that appeared to be draining fast. She frowned, tapping into her connection to the core. *Hey, slow that drain down a bit. You've got a lot more of your own energy now.*

There was a pause before the Library answered. *I wasn't draining you. You were subconsciously pushing that toward me.*

Quinn blinked. Odd again, but not unfathomable. To be fair, highly probable given her current state of mind. *Sorry*, she said

The Library chuckled. *Don't be sorry. If you don't tell me, I'll take anything you're giving me, especially as we're transitioning. Here, I'll place an emergency-only on it for now. Help you gain that equilibrium.*

Thanks, Quinn said, and immediately felt the strange hum lessen. But it didn't disappear entirely. She glanced at her hands with a frown, resolved to get these new sensations under control.

She munched on her donut as she snagged Cook's attention again. "Do I talk to you or Farrow about the ingredients the culinary branch needs?"

Cook's interest definitely wasn't in her imagination. Their whole facial expression changed. "Farrow and I have been working on the list, but she would be better equipped to inform you of the status, Librarian. Are we close?"

There was so much hope in their voice, Quinn couldn't help but grin in return. "Yeah. We're getting pretty close, I think."

She waved goodbye and trundled over to Farrow's area past the dining hall and on the way to the book infirmary. Malakai toodled after her, also snacking on multiple donuts. Quinn was happy that people liked them so much. It should mean they'd be a staple for a long time to come.

But as soon as she stepped past the dining hall, part of that humming sensation came back. It could just be that her connection had grown that much stronger, but something nagged at the back of her mind anyway.

Misha stood with Farrow, going over the rows of planter boxes in their massive indoor greenhouse. It had come a long way from being cramped into the kitchen when Quinn first arrived as the Librarian.

Massive terrariums for all the different bookworms were spread out in one section. Their rainbow hues gave beautiful lighting to the whole area. She scowled at them briefly. She'd probably think they were cute if they hadn't spent half a day trying to devour her in their engorged forms.

Next to the far wall were darkened holding tanks that she could only assume the silverfish lived in. Quinn walked over and peered in. They were very similar to the insects she'd thought they'd be like. With six legs and long antennae, one could argue they were exactly the same.

But from what she could see, their bodies were made out of a brittle, glass-like substance that glowed with different iridescent colors. She felt a momentary pang that these little guys provided the ink.

The rest of the vast area, which was a lot larger than she remembered initially, was filled with raised planter beds and myriad herbs, plants, spices, and weeds. Quinn could even feel the power emanating from them. The doors kept all this concealed from the passageway to the rest of the Library.

More magical aspects.

Magical medicinal plants.

"Ah. Librarian." Misha inclined their head. "Have you come to see the progress?"

Quinn nodded . . . still feeling like she was walking in a dream. As if everything she'd listed in her head to do today was happening without any effort on her part. Which it was. Completely and utterly. "I wanted to talk to Farrow and you about where we stand on the ingredients for opening the culinary branch."

It felt like déjà vu. And even though she'd had much the same question for Cook . . . that didn't account for the strange sensation running through her. Acclimating to a new level of power was certainly tiring.

Farrow stepped forward, all willowy grace and dignity. She bowed briefly before reporting. "We currently have 240 of the 287 ingredients necessary to enable the opening of the branch. I will have the other forty-seven ready within the next week or two. I'm hoping for one, but I will ask for two should I run into any unforeseen circumstances."

Even her voice sounded like a song.

Quinn found herself smiling in response. "Excellent. Looks like we'll be able to open that one soon."

"But not before I have finished recreating the one culinary book we had to burn." Narilin's tone was harsh as she came toward them from the direction of the book infirmary. "That will also take several more days to be reconstituted. We were short some of the correct ink. I apologize."

Quinn nodded. "That's perfectly fine." She blinked around as Aradie hooted softly, coming in to land deftly on Quinn's shoulder leathers.

She turned and looked at the owl, who head-butted her with concern.

"No. I'm really okay," Quinn said, scratching the back of the owl's neck. "Even if I don't look like it."

But the owl kept rubbing a wing against her cheek like she was trying to say something more.

Quinn blinked and turned around, eyeing Malakai, Misha, Farrow, and Narilin. "How did you all know I'd be here?"

"In this room?" Misha asked, confusion coloring their tone.

"Yes. How did you know I was going to come through here asking all sorts of questions about getting the culinary branch up and running." Quinn's head felt like it was spinning now. The hum sang through to her bones. The Library felt like home.

Everything felt much too easy.

And she was so very tired.

Malakai stepped forward. "Because you mentioned it to me."

"Not you. You, I told. But the rest? How is everyone here . . . instead of my coming to find you?"

Narilin paled slightly, and Farrow simply crossed her arms, but it was Misha who spoke.

The supervisory golem cleared their throat and spoke somewhat haltingly. "You called us here. We can tell where you are going if you let us know now. Did you not mean to?"

Quinn shook her head. "I didn't know I was broadcasting my intentions." She groaned. That was yet another thing she was going to have to learn to tamp down on.

Except that wasn't the only thing. She sighed. And she didn't want to say the words. "I just think there's something we haven't thought of . . . and all of this feels way too much like the calm before another storm."

Malakai groaned this time. "I thought you didn't like it when people did that."

"I don't," she grumbled. "But it had to be said."

"No. You could have said, 'Hey I'm tired and I'm broadcasting. I'm going to sleep now that I have answers.' But instead, you just tempted the doom and gloom." Malakai held his hands up. "Nope. You taught me this, remember? Whatever happens next, it's all your fault."

He flashed her a wink, but Quinn couldn't help thinking he was right. Even if she hadn't known she was broadcasting.

Now all she had to do was figure out what was about to happen before it did. And she could forestall the gloom.

Right?

But first she needed to sleep.

3 8

GOES BOTH WAYS

The next days were super frustrating for Quinn. Try as she might, she couldn't get her broadcasting over general Library waves under control. It wasn't even a matter of intentionally sending out a signal. It was more that the Library knew where she was headed and gave everyone a heads-up unless explicitly told not to.

"Is it like a system setting or something?" she said angrily gesturing at the HUD in front of her that found no urgency in her actions whatsoever. All the angry emoting only made her feel marginally better anyway.

She tried multiple different options, such as privacy settings . . . which gave her crickets. Then she attempted roaming options, but again, there was nothing. Why couldn't it just be nice and easy like the internet settings on her phone used to be?

"Are you okay in here, Librarian?" Dottie poked a part of her bench around the mostly open office door, like she wasn't entirely sure of her welcome into the space.

"If I said no, could you fix it?" Quinn asked, collapsing into her chair with an exasperated sigh.

Dottie took that as an invitation to enter the room. "No, I don't believe I could, but I can listen and maybe help that way." There was a happiness to the words as the bench trotted over, like she was excited to maybe be able to help.

Dottie was Quinn's favorite surprise to stem from the Library. Well, other than being in a universal Library, that is.

"Don't suppose you have any idea how to adjust it so I'm not constantly just broadcasting where I am and what I'm doing to everyone within the Library?" Quinn leaned forward, stretching out her hands underneath her HUD and focused on the bench. "I basically expect an announcement next time I use the loo—Librarian is on the toilet."

Dottie snorted a laugh and then angled the head end of her seat somewhat. "I'll be your bouncing board if you want to vent."

"Sounding board," Quinn corrected absently.

Dottie ignored it. "I'm not the only one who can listen, you know. We all care. But I am here right now, if you need me."

"Thanks, Dottie." And Quinn meant it. She groaned again though as flashes of information made their way through her head. "It's a pity it won't just tell me everything I ask it, especially since it seems set on overloading me with information I don't necessarily need right at this moment instead."

"What do you mean?" Lynx asked from the doorway. He walked in, taking deliberate and very physical steps. Ever since the power upgrade he seemed to have forsaken being incorporeal most of the time. Now he only did it when it suited him. He approached the desk, a frown on his face. "Well?"

Quinn flashed him an irritated glare. "So much information that I haven't been seeking is currently just traversing through my mind."

"Like what?"

She raised an eyebrow at him. "You surely should know."

"I think we've long since established that I do, in fact, no longer know everything I should or need to. However, I can estimate that you're currently getting a heap of Library operational functions and manuals. Not to mention specific golem relations and specifications, and probably also a briefing on exactly what it is the Library is currently in need of as far as establishing supplies and more person-nel, including golems. Am I right?" He looked smug.

"No," Quinn said, just to see the confusion on his face at her answer.

His brow furrowed and he went to talk but stopped himself.

Quinn relented shortly thereafter. "And yes, but there's no need to be such a know-it-all when doing so isn't helpful to either of us." She grimaced. "It's like I instinctively now know how to craft the golems, what's required when they're required, but I don't know how I know or why? It's like there's a disconnect."

Lynx sighed. "Yeah. I know."

Surprise, surprise and they were back to square one.

Quinn tried to figure out how to break the awkward silence that arose. Dottie cleared her throat, which still always caught Quinn off guard—because where was her throat?

"Is there a way you can use the information you're being given to sort of trace back any of the problems? Like following a string?" Dottie sounded genuinely curious, not like she was asking something she already knew the answer to.

Lynx spoke before Quinn could completely follow. "Not quite, but the idea has some merit. Backtracking can often lead to finding entrance points we've overlooked. Still, this isn't that. But thank you, Dottie."

It was the most polite way Quinn had ever heard the manifestation speak to the bench. Maybe he was finally starting to feel himself again. Guilt did weird things to people.

"How can I tweak my broadcasting through the HUD, or the inter-face? Do I need to go back down to the core to do something like this?" Quinn asked, pulling Lynx out of his contemplations.

Lynx shrugged, and his eyes did that distant focus thing he usually did when he was looking into something. Quinn glanced at one of the books to her left but didn't have the energy to stand up to balance it on his head.

"I'm not completely out of it. I'd have noticed if you put the book on my head this time," he muttered in her direction.

Quinn groaned. "I'm even broadcasting my pranks now."

Lynx actually chuckled. "Actually, I've just gotten used to your tricks. Anyway, we'll get this fixed, it's just going to be more involved than I remember. Keep in mind, the initial influx of information never reached your brain and you started out a little behind in knowledge and application ability. This is just all going to take time."

"But I have direct access to the system now, right?" Quinn asked. "Doesn't that mean I should be able to access it and just download all the things now?"

Lynx shrugged. "In a way, yes, but only to a certain extent. Also, that means you have to know what it is you need to do in order to rectify whatever is glitching."

"What aren't you telling me?" she asked, not even bothering to look at Lynx. "Come on. We've got the Library back to a decent standard, but we have a long way to go. And I know you always think you're protecting me by not telling me stuff."

"We should probably just check with the core to see what it thinks." Lynx sighed. "We don't always agree on everything."

Quinn just needs to give the core and HUD proper access to her mind, beyond her walls.

Quinn blinked at the statement that floated in front of her eyes. The answer seemed so simple. Here was the Library trusting her with copious amounts of power and an age-old legacy, and she hadn't even let the damned thing in past the mental walls she'd built.

"You haven't let the connection propagate?" Lynx asked incredulously, turning his full stare on her.

Quinn didn't even need to look up to know his gaze was locked on.

"Maybe," she mumbled into the desk, suddenly feeling extremely silly for not having thought of it. In all of Milaro's teachings about building up her mental barrier, she'd never come across the option to let a friendly foreign presence back in.

She moved back and sat in her chair, centering herself. Reaching in, she pulled through to her mental barriers and felt the thickness of the walls. So many levels thick to protect her mind from the attack by Kajaro, and now, she had extremely dense protections.

All it took was one simple thought, and she could feel the core so much closer to her. All of the control reverted back to her instead of outside of her, and everything immediately became simpler.

She sat up straight, opening her eyes in surprise. "It was that easy?"

Lynx shrugged and the Library practically pulsed with laughter.

Quinn tested the connection once more, and felt the flooding of information come toward her. But this time it was controlled, and coherent.

It shouldn't have taken her days to come across this. *Why didn't you tell me sooner?* she asked the Library, somewhat put out.

There was a pause before it replied like it had weighed its answer heavily. *I won't always be able to help in the moment. Most times, yes, but sometimes you're going to have to figure out things yourself. Think outside the box more often. Or, in this case, within it.*

That was cryptic. Quinn pouted.

Sometimes a little cryptic is good for all of us.

Quinn ran a hand through her disheveled hair. The messy buns and ponytails just weren't keeping her loose curls contained anymore. It had gotten so much worse since she'd synchronized. She'd have to check and see if any other part of her appearance had changed too.

Well, apart from when the excess mana overlaid her skin with glowing scales. But she'd get to that another time.

Your eyes change too.

What? Quinn thought at the Library, too shocked to say it out loud.

Just when you're using magic.

The Library fell silent again and Quinn digested that for a moment before slotting that information away and moving on.

"Now that's sorted." She turned to look directly at Lynx. "I believe we have some information to go through. We have to fix all of these holes in your memory, in the Library's memory, and frankly in my instructions. Where should we begin?"

Lynx radiated uneasiness and Aradie swooped into the room like she'd been summoned, landing with a soft hoot on Quinn's shoulder and dropping a bag into her lap.

Quinn swore the bird knew when she was suddenly starving. The bag held a sandwich and one of those apple-like fruits. "Thanks, girl," she said, reaching up to scritch her neck.

"Now, no avoiding Lynx. Talk." Quinn ignored the sense of foreboding she'd begun to feel once more. This time it resonated through her head instead of the soles of her feet, telling her she wasn't radiating concern out to the rest of the Library at least.

No, this doom and gloom was all in her own head right now.

"You have to understand that this isn't one of your computers," Lynx began, but Quinn held up a hand.

"You've told me this about twelve times I think. I could be mistaken; it might be twenty. Either way. I know the Library is not a computer. We've been over this. Stop stalling."

He frowned briefly. "It's an all-encompassing neural network."

Quinn kept her temper, pretty sure they'd been over this before too. "Like a brain."

"Almost exactly like a brain," Lynx answered, still sounding too evasive for Quinn's liking. "And right now there are areas of it that require healing more than it requires restoring, if that makes sense."

Quinn's eyes widened as she connected the dots. "So that means we need to apply mind healing, right? Sort of like when Milaro helped me with my own . . . issues, thanks to Kajaro."

"In a way, yes. It's just that." Lynx paused for a moment. "I did send for Milaro yesterday when you were having issues. He should be here soon, so it'll be easier for us to address this."

"You know he has a kingdom to run, right?" Quinn quipped. She'd been glad that he had actual duties, it had given her a few days to avoid him and her own complex thoughts.

"But this is a part of his council duties too, so technically, he also has a Library to help." Lynx winked at Quinn.

"Remind me to ask about that council one of these days," she said, the niceness oozing from her in a completely fake way. They were almost like her parents after all, and she had no idea who all it involved.

Lynx raised an eyebrow but, perhaps wisely, didn't comment.

She smiled and pushed the council business to the back of her mind. Not too deep. She needed to figure out all that crap sometime soon. The least of all because of the new heritage she'd discovered. "Okay, so mixing mind magic and healing together would give us elements of mind healing that should allow us to retrieve or repair some of those fragments of missing . . . brain? For want of a better phrase?"

"In theory," Lynx said, not sounding the most convinced. "I mean, healing goes both ways."

Aradie hooted that Milaro had entered the Library and was on the way. Quinn didn't need to ask the owl about it, considering the night owls all lived in the rafters and generally had the run of the entire Library.

They saw everything.

All the time.

It was an excellent information network that none of the patrons seemed to notice much.

"Have you guys had any luck piecing together what the other missing books from the restricted vault are?" Quinn asked her owl softly. Aradie shook her head and pushed the soft feathers of her face into Quinn's cheek for a moment. "That's too bad."

"Well, that's part of the whole dilemma." Lynx took the conversation and ran with it.

"Oh, do fill me in. I love me a good dilemma." Milaro swept into the room, his long robes flaring out behind him for dramatic effect.

Quinn narrowed her gaze. He was awfully good at perfectly timed entrances.

Lynx rolled his eyes. "The problem is that the books we require that would most likely work the best for healing the missing parts, are all from the restricted vault."

Quinn groaned. "And let me guess, they're all the ones we're missing?"

"Three of the four we've identified, yes," Lynx practically whispered, even though his voice managed to echo through Quinn's office.

She closed her eyes for a moment to collect herself, and then pulled up the listing in front of her. "Essentially, we need: *Chatfield's Force Fields of the Mind, Uglandia Theories of Mind Manipulation,* and *Sethrovian Rings of Dream Entrapment.*"

Milaro nodded. "And that's really just the start. I'm actually quite certain we're missing two more. Mainly because I wrote two of them. *Seveshall Lineage of Mind Healing and How to Break It* is the first one. I have to admit that if I were to develop those tactics today, I would not share them with the universe. I would bury them so deep that no one else could get access."

"You know knowledge shouldn't be restricted," Dottie snapped disapprovingly.

"But just because it can be done, my dear Dottie," Milaro said, his tone melancholy, "does not mean it should be."

"True," Dottie said begrudgingly and fell silent again.

"You said there was a second book?" Quinn prodded, filing away Milaro's regret to examine later.

Milaro nodded and frankly, he paled. She'd never really pegged him as the type to feel fear. "*The Ashelan Mind Capitulation Device.* It's a magical engineering book that creates a device. Well, I mean, it's in the title. We should have locked it up and thrown away the key."

"Hindsight is always great." Quinn tried to reassure him, but she could see it fell flat.

"It really is," he muttered. "Anyway. I only know that those two are missing from the list of available titles that Lynx gave me to peruse. And again, I only know because I helped with their contribution. But if those are missing, I don't like the chances of what else was likely taken and is probably floating around out there."

Quinn groaned. It kept getting better and better. But that was the thing right? She pushed herself to stand. "Okay. We have direction."

For the first time since the synchronization, her head felt full but clear, focused and with a purpose. "Aradie, I need the owls. Dottie, I need some assistant volunteers to help us scour memories. We're going to find out what the other books were, and we're doing it now. And then we're going to get them. Meet in the training room in an hour so we have more space."

Milaro smiled, falling into step with her as Quinn marched out of her office to get more food. "I like this plan. I will assist you to the utmost."

"Of course you will." Quinn half-grinned at him. There was still a tiny bit of resentment simmering in her. "After all. This is kind of, sort of, a little bit at least . . . all your fault."

Okay, maybe a little more than a tiny bit of resentment.

"How do you figure?" The elf king raised an eyebrow.

"You keep writing really dangerous books and someone is eventually going to use one."

"Can't fault your logic," he said.

She knew it wasn't all going to be as simple as that, but they had to start somewhere, and they may as well start now.

As she bit into the food Aradie had brought to her, Quinn was determined that this time at least, she wasn't going into anything with an empty stomach.

39

IN THE LOOP

Lynx and Quinn stood in the training room.

Or, at least, what she'd once used as a training room.

Quinn blinked as she took in her surroundings and realized it wasn't what she'd expected. After all, she'd been in the room with Malakai numerous times to hone her skills, practice her reflexes, and beat the ever-loving knowledge she'd gained *into* her sad little reflexes.

Now, however, it was an entirely different space.

Where there'd been copious mats on the ground and training dummies, there were now tree-like perches growing out of the walls and floor so the nightowls would have comfortable spaces to sit upon while they helped the Library figure out what transpired.

Granted, Quinn wasn't entirely sure why the nightowls' information wasn't simply immediate Library knowledge, but any time she tried to ask the question, the answer was very specifically sidestepped.

It was like Aradie could read her mind too, because she'd simply look away when Quinn wanted to inquire about it. Perhaps the nightowls and the Library had a special agreement or something.

Quinn had started to wonder just how much the Library had truly lost and how dire the peril was when they finally fetched her. From

339

the state of it when she got here, even to now, little things get itching at the back of her mind—so much didn't add up.

She was still getting used to the way the entire mechanism worked. Even with the extra reach, control, and sensations she'd amassed since realizing how close she was to the Library, Quinn still needed time to practice. Time to get used to everything.

Time to get stronger and understand just how and where that strength came from.

Lynx watched her, a frown on his face. "I don't know why you seem so astounded by the changes in here. You did ask for them. You've seen what the Library has done on a whim and a request before. Like your office, the jail cell . . . you know it can transform at whim. It's sort of our thing." He grinned widely at her.

Quinn sighed. "It wasn't that I wasn't expecting it, I guess, I just didn't think all this would happen." She waved her hand around as the hall continued to transform into something almost like a cinema. It was obvious she needed to start thinking in broader terms, in ways that were more encompassing than her human habitation on Earth led her to believe.

After all, the scale of things that concerned the Library was quite cosmic.

Eric flew directly in front of her face to hover there, his impish grin dripping lava into his mouth.

"I won the coin toss," he said smugly.

"Coin toss?" Quinn asked, despite being fairly sure she knew what he was talking about.

"Geneva got stuck with the front desk."

"She volunteered," Lynx pointed out.

Eric flashed him an annoyed glare. "Fine. Finn is absent today, and Geneva volunteered, but I won the coin toss anyway."

There was a pout to his words.

"Let me guess," Quinn asked, "Double-sided coin?"

"Maybe you know me too well, Librarian," Eric laughed and darted back out of view to the other side of the training hall where Dottie and the aracnio twins had gathered.

"Sometimes I'm not sure if he's on our side," Quinn mused. She frowned at the small gathering. Jim and Bob were standing slightly apart from the others. She'd never noticed a tendency to do that before. They appeared to be chittering amongst themselves. She hoped everything was okay.

Misha chose that moment to pop into view. "Excellent. I knew I would find you here." Misha blinked those pearlescent eyes rapidly, like they were accessing reams of information.

Quinn took a step back. "Should I like how happy you are to see me?" She crossed her arms and regarded Misha suspiciously.

"I simply have several reports that only you can go over with me," Misha stated. "Your connection through the console is no longer entirely necessary for anything other than dire circumstances. In which case you could also link directly to the core, given your unique set of circumstances."

Quinn blinked at the sudden onslaught of words. Misha often had a lot to say, but didn't necessarily do so with a lot of words. Resigned to having more work to do while waiting to do other work, Quinn sighed. "Fine. Show me what you need from me."

She could have sworn Misha smiled outright.

A list began to pour out in front of Quinn's eyes. She hadn't realized how much her access had been refined since the synchronization. Sure, she'd been able to pull up her lists, but this was a lot more information, and far more detailed, than she'd expected.

Malachite shards on hand: 3,789,043

Expected expenditure per day rounded for the next week: 12,761 daily—up to 89,327

Note: As daily expenditure will increase as the Library branches open, it is recommended to reach a minimum of 10,000,000 shards in perpetual stock and not fall below this threshold.

Do you wish to set up delivery to correspond with these goals
Yes or No?

"What's the cost?" Quinn muttered under her breath, knowing the system would answer her.

Current market pricing has risen due to increased demand that wasn't present for the last 465 years. This brings current market pricing to a total of 1 generic Library coin, to be configured into the local relevant currency per shard purchased. Bulk purchases are recommended to curtail costs.

Do you wish to proceed?

Yes or No?

Quinn glanced at Misha out of the corner of her eye and saw the supervisory golem just nod their head. She chose yes. Several pages of information flashed before her eyes so fast that she couldn't tell what was on a single one of them.

Purchase orders initiated. Delivery estimates will reach reserve levels within ten days.

Quinn blinked. This put bureaucracy back on Earth to shame. Maybe they all just needed systems to run everything for efficiency levels.

I'm a Library. It doesn't work like that.

Quinn cringed at the offense in those words. *Sorry.*

The Library didn't reply, but Quinn got the feeling it wasn't holding a grudge. Maybe. Hopefully.

Golem Components

Phosphorus clay required as an upgrade component: 32,985

Insidious clay required as an upgrade component: 18,958

Quinn stopped reading the list to look up at Misha. "Are you just having me approve a heap of spending for purchase orders?"

Misha looked away, and didn't make eye contact. "It is one of the duties of the Librarian that you must oversee the finances and supply runs for the entire Library."

"There's no way for me to delegate this?" Quinn said, finding that very difficult to believe. "Not to mention that I thought we were short on funds."

Misha turned back, momentarily having forgotten they were trying to avoid looking at Quinn. "We have never been short on money. Only on power levels."

Quinn didn't quite get it. "But isn't money how you . . ." She shook her head. Money didn't necessarily buy power here. It was knowledge and access to it. The things that the Library gave freely that others wanted to stop. She got it. "Anyway. Can't I just okay this within a certain budget?"

For the first time ever, it looked like Misha was going to pout. "Of course you could, but don't you want to know all the details and how to go about outfitting and supplying the Library?" There was a certain note of incredulousness to the golem's voice that made Misha seem almost volatile for a moment.

"I'm granting you permission to make the purchases you deem necessary as long as they don't exceed . . . what's a reasonable amount?" She turned to Lynx.

He shrugged. "How am I supposed to know? I've never taken care of that. I'm a Library manifestation, not an accountant."

"Who's perfectly aware of the content of what I'm sure are hundreds of thousands of books about histories of magical civilizations including some of their economic dealings?"

"Well . . ." Lynx sighed. "Fine. I'd say not surpassing ten million of local currency in Library equivalent."

"Per purchase?" Quinn asked, still trying to get her footing on how the money worked.

"Of course per purchase. Misha wouldn't even be able to get the clay required with that as the sole budget."

Quinn digested that and activated the relevant settings in the interface. Then she looked up at Misha and was slightly shocked to see the supervisory golem appeared to be a bit melancholy. "What's up?"

"Nothing. I just thought that would take more time." Misha looked out over the progress of the training area. "It is a good thing to be kept in the loop about all of the goings on of a magical Library. Especially as the Librarian of such an establishment."

Misha gave Quinn a very pointed look as they uttered those words, so much that a shiver went down her spine. "Got it. In the loop is good."

Misha nodded and then it seemed some of the tension drained out of them as they spoke. "But it does appear we are close to being able to start on the memory data. I will get to organizing this and see to the rest of the supplies after we are done with today's session."

Quinn put out a hand to stop the golem from leaving. "Do you think it'll take more than just a session?"

"Of course it will. These memories will likely have to go back over months and years. Any owl who thinks they might have something has been gathered by Aradie." Misha gestured up to one of the perches. There were at least two dozen owls on it. "Those with the most pertinent information will go first, and then we may have to delegate for others to comb through the remaining projections."

Quinn gulped. She hadn't really counted on it taking up more than one day. But the more she thought about it, the sillier that seemed for her to have done. They were going to have to go over years, decades at the very least. Time where all the books were supposed to be there. Time when other books might have been there. And figure out where the missing pieces of time had been removed from the recollection of the Library. Especially those books Milaro mentioned.

"Got it," Quinn said, and cast around a glance for the elven king. He wasn't there yet, but his grandson was. She waved Malakai over. He rolled his eyes but trotted to her from where he'd been chatting with Dottie and Eric.

"What?" he said, crossing his arms.

"Is Milaro coming?" she asked.

"I'm not his keeper," Malakai snapped ever so slightly, but then his expression softened. "But yes, he should be here shortly."

"Good. He's the one who knows what he's looking for."

"So do you." Malakai leaned forward, a frown on his face. "Why do you seem to lack confidence all of a sudden? This was all your idea and it was a good one. Take ownership."

Quinn blinked, barely having realized that she'd been getting down on herself while she'd been acclimatizing to all of the new information, and the HUD access, and all the money the Library could practically just give away. "You're right. I let myself get sidetracked."

"Sidetracked is a bad thing," Milaro said, doing that appearing out of thin air thing again.

Quinn scowled at him. "I thought you said you couldn't do the Library teleport thing."

"I can't." He laughed and waggled both his fingers and eyebrows at the same time to comical effect. "But I can do my own teleport thing."

Quinn rolled her eyes and focused on Aradie who flew to her shoulder. She frowned. "You think there's something we should see before any of the other visions?"

The owl nodded and gave a hoot.

"Okay, then how do we do this?" Quinn turned to Malakai and Lynx. "Do we like, plug an owl in . . ."

"Into what?" Lynx asked, curiously. "Oh, you mean placing it on the visual pedestal?"

"Sure. Let's go with that," Quinn said, doing her best not to roll her eyes again. Instead, she focused around the room and saw what, for all intents and purposes, looked like a crystal ball, on a pedestal just in front of the perching tree. Yeah, she'd call the weirdly woven dead branches a perching tree.

Heading over to the ball, she realized Malakai, Milaro, and Lynx had fallen into step behind her.

All of the eyes of every single bird on that perch followed her too. Those owls and their pesky neck range. *How to Feel Like You're Always Being Watched 101*. Now *that* should be a book the Library had.

Aradie sent out a series of hoots that blended together in a sad way.

Quinn watched the branches intently, trying to spy the owl that was called. Nightowls were such an array of different colors, and she'd never seen a one that was the same shade of midnight that Aradie was.

Granted, apparently Aradie was also older than, like, Earth.

A tiny little one hopped to the very end of the branches and dove down to stand next to Aradie and the stone. This little owl couldn't have been more than eight inches tall. It had eyes that looked so big on it, Quinn almost thought it was a stuffed toy. And its pitiful little hoot was about two octaves higher than Aradie's melodic one.

Don't be alarmed, came over her connection from her nightowl. And Quinn could feel panic already pitting in the center of her stomach. Whoever said they weren't alarmed when someone told them not to be was a liar.

After some coaxing, Aradie ushered the little owl to sit on a small divot in the crystal ball. To Quinn's surprise, it pushed in ever so slightly with whatever slight weight the owl had, and suddenly the wall beyond them was a hazy trail of images, just like a movie screen. It took several moments for them to clear up, for them to sharpen.

This is an image array. Memories retrieved from parts of this owl's mind.

Quinn couldn't help but love the sound of Aradie's thoughts as they whispered in her mind.

How far back memory extends depends on the quality of the picture and the ability to recollect. It is purely due to luck that this little owl hibernated most of the Library's shutdown, and thus its mind's vision has clarity.

"What do you need me to see?" Quinn asked, her voice barely even a whisper, but then she didn't need to ask anything anymore, because it was right there in front of her.

"Oh," she breathed out. "No."

There, on the scattered image in front of her, playing like an old silent film was Lynx, and a book—a book they hadn't even known was missing until Milaro mentioned it.

The Ashelan Mind Capitulation Device.

The image stuttered, like it wasn't fully realized. And then Lynx's eyes glowed purple, and he disappeared.

Silence fell in the room and Quinn turned to look at her side where Lynx stood, frozen to the spot, his mouth open in a large O.

"I don't remember any of that," he said, his voice suddenly weak and forlorn. "But that looks like me."

40

PRACTICALLY FLAWLESS

Recognition.

Recollection.

Any type of reaction.

That's what Quinn looked for when she watched Lynx immediately after realizing what the vision had shown them. Or tried to show them.

Even now she could recognize the cracks in the image, the static . . . interference.

The only difference in Lynx's countenance was that he suddenly looked lost, like this forlorn little being just standing there with his entire world ripped away from him.

Shattered.

Confusion and loss. That's all that echoed from every single pore of his being. Or light refraction . . . or however the manifestation worked.

"Lynx." She turned to him, focusing all her attention on him. "What did you do?" she asked, regretting the words almost immediately. They sounded so accusatory.

He turned to her, his purple sclera flickering in that way which meant he wasn't completely there with her. He was doing his own searching now. Not that she could blame him.

"Why would you ask me that?" he asked her.

She blinked at him and took a step back. The runes in his hair were swirling with a hint of violence.

"Do you remember any of this?" she asked softly, because her gut told her, right then and there, that either it *wasn't* Lynx in those fractured images, or he had no recollection of what he'd done. Because one of those was the only logical answer.

"I don't remember doing any of this. None of it." Lynx's voice got stronger as he spoke, as he delved into memories he was trying to retrieve. "When was this?"

Aradie hooted softly and Quinn scowled at the bird. "You could have told us that to begin with."

I needed to see the reactions with my own senses. To understand what has happened.

Quinn could see how that might be best, but her owl needed to learn a little bit about tact. "Still. That was unnecessarily cruel."

She could have sworn the owl shrugged at her.

Milaro frowned at the memory-reading crystal like he was trying to figure something out about it. The little owl on top of it was shaking, and Quinn reached forward, gathering it in her arms before turning back to Lynx.

He fixed his gaze on her with clear purple eyes. "That shouldn't have been possible. That can't be me. At that point in time, I should have been recuperating in the Library's core."

Quinn nodded. She'd thought as much. After all, it made sense that for those years prior to the Librarian resigning where Lynx was essentially hibernating to have been the ones where his guard—and the Library's guard—was down most. But that didn't take away from the fact that something had tampered with the vision that the night owl produced.

Either by utilizing Lynx's image, or taking control of his manifestation. And the latter was a terrifying option.

"When exactly did this happen?" Quinn asked, turning to Milaro, who was still looking at the crystal.

The older man shrugged and pulled out a cylindrical device that he peered through into the crystal. "From everything I can figure out, I think this happened when Lynx was out of commission. So it wasn't actually him but perhaps an illusion. A powerful one at that."

"I've been telling you that," Lynx said, a little bit more strength entering his voice again now that he was regaining confidence.

"Is the vision itself tampered with?" Quinn asked. Aradie shook her head.

Milaro did the same, but elaborated. "The vision itself wasn't tampered with; it was the perception. I'm unsure if this means the person who retrieved the *book* was tampered with, or if that means they delved into this little guy's head and made adjustments there. Either way, it's concerning. It wasn't just done on a whim. It must have been planned."

"Does this mean Lynx is compromised? Is everything compromised?" Quinn asked.

All of the crap definitely appeared to be rising up. They had too much still to do for this to sink them all. She really wished Aradie had warned her about it in advance. Surely she had to have known, because she arranged all of this.

Which made Quinn wonder if perhaps her nightowl hadn't thought to check how others responded to the information.

"I'm not entirely sure. I'd need to delve into deeper into the facts," Milaro said. "But I wouldn't think manipulating Lynx to act, especially while he was slumbering in the core, would have been possible. I'll summon Siliqua and Harish again and see if they can help us out as they have been. And Siliqua is wonderful with animal analysis. This should prove no different. Both of their insights into the neural functions and the system integration should at least help us figure out the how."

"But not necessarily the when, or the why?" Quinn pinched the bridge of her nose. She was starting to make that a very bad habit.

Lynx spoke up. "I should think the *why* would be obvious. Discrediting me, and disrupting the Library."

The vision is fake. I can guarantee you were sequestered in the core when this occurred.

Quinn was relieved to hear the Library speak up, because Lynx still looked glum. "Okay, so it's good to know you were in the core at the time. Think about it. Who is going to benefit from this disruption? The normal every-day patrons wouldn't even catch wind of it. Librarians choose when they retire, is that correct?"

"Yes," Lynx said, "when they've had enough of, I guess, serving the universe or they've just sort of reached a point in their lives where they no longer wish to continue."

"Being killed is the obvious exception," Quinn said.

"Yes, of course, unless they're killed," Lynx said and his eyes opened wide as he caught on to what Quinn was saying.

Milaro and Lynx moved in closer to listen, while Malakai trotted over to the group, his interest piqued.

"Why did the memory show stop?" he asked when he got there, a big grin on his face. "We even bought snacks to eat while we watched them."

"There are other more important matters we need to address right now," Milaro said, his tone short.

But they didn't need everyone to delve into this. Not to mention the fact that Quinn couldn't trust every single assistant yet.

"Can you take over? Go through all the owl memories we have with the assistants?" There we go, she was being a great and delegating Librarian. This way they'd still get today's viewing session done on top of starting to figure out how and when all the sabotage crap started.

Maybe.

Malakai scowled. "You know, one of these days you're going to realize I'm far more useful than just running errands."

Quinn nodded. "I know you are, that's why you're in charge of the whole watching memories party now."

Malakai opened his mouth to speak, narrowed his eyes, and let out a snort. "Fine. But you're coming clean to me as soon as you're done here."

"Promise." Quinn meant it, too. It looked like a lot more had been done to the Library than she'd initially thought and all of it way before they'd ever considered it happening. Having a few people she could trust on her side, really helped. At least, she was pretty sure she could trust them anyway.

"Should we do this elsewhere?" Milaro asked, glancing around the large training hall.

Quinn shrugged. "May as well just take a seat here. We've trusted these people to scour the memories of the birds with us. If we weren't going to share the findings with them, we shouldn't have let them come in the first place. They were going to learn about some of this anyway."

"Very well. Do you care to elaborate on your comment about Librarians being killed?" Milaro's eyes narrowed almost imperceptibly. As if the subject was highly distasteful for him.

"Not really. It was simply an observation that meant if *potential* Librarians could be 'taken care of,' then I'd assume so could Librarians." Quinn shrugged and promptly sat down on the floor, which was partially squishy like the ground around the core. She was tired, and it was far easier to sort herself if she could keep this shaking little owl in her lap and soothe it while talking. "Why is it so upset?" she asked Aradie.

The owl hooted and Quinn frowned.

"So some of its memories might also be overrides of the original and its head is hurting?" Quinn bit her lip. That had some potential, and if this little fella was cooperative and they could make sure not to hurt him, they might even be able to find out more about the override. Perhaps even do away with it to see what lay underneath.

But she couldn't get ahead of herself.

"We already know that Korradine was, at least at one point in time, in cahoots with Kajaro. Correct?" Quinn was going through all the information she'd gathered so far since coming here. Piecing together the small bits she'd got from Lynx's references.

"Well, from what we've seen, anyway," Milaro commented cautiously. "But right now, I'm uncertain if seeing is actually believing. I would never have thought so much might be altered if I hadn't begun witnessing it with my own eyes."

Quinn fixed her gaze on him for a second. For a millennia-old elf, he was sure naive sometimes. Apparently no one in this universe had ever heard of a deep fake. They'd be appalled by Earth. She tried to figure out how to phrase it best for their understanding. "Okay. We have that previous connection. But—and hear me out here—is there any way this memory was orchestrated?"

"You mean in another way than simply replacing what was originally there?" Milaro asked, his expression thoughtful.

"Was the owl's memory tweaked, and given how much this little guy is shaking, I think this could be a highly possible outcome." Quinn shrugged and moved onto the next, much less attractive, option. "Or could Lynx have been manipulated while in stasis?"

I said he didn't leave the core.

"But your memory hasn't exactly been reliable lately either," Quinn shot back at the Library, and could almost feel it pout in response and then she turned to Milaro. "Well, what do you think?"

"I'm not . . ." But that was just it. Milaro stopped short and looked back over at Quinn, as if he had a hundred things running through his mind right then. "I'm not entirely sure, although I could delve into it in more detail from a mind power angle. It'll take some time. When it comes to system command, Lynx has always been our expert on those things."

Lynx sighed from where he'd taken his seat next to Quinn. "I'm still here, I've just lost so much information at this stage. I don't even know if I'll be any more use."

"True. I'd hardly say you're a reliable witness at this point in time." Quinn gave his arm a squeeze. "It's okay. I actually have some pretty cool ideas."

"Then let's hear them," Milaro said. "We're not getting anywhere just sitting and mulling them over."

Quinn held up a hand and mentally summoned Misha, making

sure the supervisory golem was there with them too. She felt it always served to be overprepared. "Thanks for coming."

"You are welcome, Librarian." Misha sounded positively enthused. As much as a golem could, anyway.

"You're the only one here from your council, Milaro?" Quinn started, fixing her gaze on him directly.

He blanched slightly and nodded. "I am, but I have sent for Harish and Siliqua too."

"They were a part of the council too?" Quinn asked, petting the sick little owl. "That's good to know." She hadn't liked being out of the loop on everything, but she figured getting information gradually was better than an initial overload she'd only have to sort through.

"Then I have to direct this question to you. Was my genetic material extracted *after* the whole 'no Library affinity' thing was already underway?" Quinn finished the question with bated breath like she couldn't believe she'd had the audacity to ask the question. Especially when she still wasn't entirely certain how she felt about the whole "being genetically engineered" thing.

"Eons. Before, I mean." Milaro paused, like he was trying to figure out why she was asking this in the first place. "Frankly, it's about as close to the original form as we could get it. We had to be sure the affinity acclimation would be able to take properly, and mixing it or removing it too far from its original almost perfect state would have made you vulnerable to affinity sickness and a host of other things."

"Oh, you mean like alien species trying to kill me because I exist?" Quinn raised an eyebrow.

"Sort of," Milaro muttered, and it was the first time Quinn had really seen him contrite.

Time kept being snatched away from her. No matter how many lists she had, they just seemed to get longer. "Okay. With this sample of—I guess with *me*—doesn't that mean I'm uncorrupted? I'm an original portion of the Library that is currently invulnerable to, or outside of, whatever is being done to the Library's genetic makeup. Or have we already infected me by synchronizing?"

"No, not necessarily. Your synchronization is deeper, but you haven't fully connected yet. The Library hasn't reached full power." Milaro shrugged. "I guess in a way, you're closer to all of the others. So, technically, yes. I know for a fact that you haven't been corrupted by whatever it is that's impacting the Library's genetic makeup. Yet, anyway."

Quinn took a deep breath. She wasn't entirely sure how to phrase the next part of what she wanted to say. She'd never been a computer major of any sort. She'd known how to boot one up, use it, put it to sleep, and play games on it. In fact, she was proud of having been pretty proficient with them, despite not fully understanding them. She could also completely and utterly have all her facts backward and have no clue what she was about to say. "Lynx, I need you to listen to me. Look past whatever is going on with you and cling to the parts of you that you still recognize."

The manifestation righted himself from where he'd been slouching on the floor. "Got it."

"Do you think we can use some of my sequence to override any changes that have been made?" Quinn waited, hoping she was making sense, and not that she was going to inadvertently repopulate the world with dinosaurs.

Lynx blinked at her. "I have no idea what that means."

Damn it. She'd really been hoping he'd get it, that he of all people might understand. Then again, while they'd been through a lot in a short time, Lynx didn't have her background. So she attempted to clarify. "My genetic sequence."

Milaro sucked in a gasp. "That's too dangerous."

"But is it? I mean, you made *me*, right? Wasn't that all sorts of dangerous, and look how well I turned out." She gave him a wink, trying to lighten the heavy mood.

For a moment Milaro struggled and then gave into a smile. "Fine. Keep going."

"You've admitted it yourself. I'm the reason we still have a Library at all. I'm here specifically for that reason. The Library is organic, and thus will have a similar genetic sequence to my own. If we can, I don't know, cut out the offensive section that is corrupting the whole knowledge base at this time, couldn't we just replace it with a new section based on the original and thus practically flawless heritage and have it all recalibrate?" Quinn was talking out her ass right then, but in her mind it made logical sense to take out the infection and replace it with new and rejuvenated flesh. That's how she was looking at it.

Remove the corruption.

Quinn waited, but Milaro seemed lost in thought as he went over her idea. Aradie practically wrapped her wings around Quinn's head with joyous little pats.

But that wasn't who Quinn was waiting on. She needed to see if Lynx agreed.

"I guess it's worth it to give it a shot," he said, a glimmer of hope in his eyes.

Quinn felt a thrum of energy from beneath her feet, indicating the joy the news gave to the Library.

I'm sorting through the footage we're extracting from memories. There seems to be more than just that one Lynx abnormality. I haven't forgotten about you up there.

I know was all Quinn thought at it. "I know I had the idea. But, sort of like the ultraviolet light, I'm unsure how to implement it."

Milaro actually laughed. "That's okay. Siliqua will probably have a hundred ideas."

41

HEAVY CONSIDERATION

ONE OF QUINN'S FAVORITE THINGS ABOUT HER OFFICE WAS ITS ABILITY to morph. Essentially, it was a Library treat. The Library could become anything she needed or wanted at any time, depending on what she asked of it.

Quinn sat on a daybed on the far wall of her office, looking up at Siliqua, who had her arms crossed. Her wood elf features narrowed as she studied the Librarian.

Quinn sensed myriad emotions emanating from the elf. There was a sense of trepidation, a cautiousness about her. Quinn wasn't entirely sure why Siliqua suddenly felt so uneasy around her. If she were to venture a guess, it probably had something to do with the synchronization and all the revelations it had brought to all of them.

Not to mention it had now been days since Quinn had very definitively not addressed the whole elephant in the core room.

"What?" Quinn asked her.

Siliqua paused, bit her lip, and then took a breath. "Are you really okay with everything?"

Quinn raised an eyebrow, and deliberately misanswered. "Well, I thought the whole sequencing thing was my idea, so we should probably see if it's even going to work to help the Library in the way we need to."

"No, that's not what I meant," Siliqua said, and showed signs of actual frustration in the way her eyes twitched.. "You know that's not what I meant."

Quinn let out a sigh and mulled over exactly what she knew Siliqua meant. She thought about it while Siliqua busied herself in the office to prepare whatever it was she needed. Quinn grew quiet even as her thoughts tumbled over one another. "I mean, that's a loaded question, like super baked-potatoes-with-everything-loaded sort of question. It's not easy to answer."

Siliqua nodded as she continued her preparations, and Quinn fell into quiet contemplation.

Was she okay? Ever since the synchronization, she had just kept going full speed, because that was the choice she made. It was pretty easy to keep doing something she'd already been doing. Was it shocking to realize the real reason behind why she had all of these magical affinities?

Yes. Yes, it was.

But the synchronization had taken days. And at first she'd felt a little bit pissed off, floating in that weird abyss of stars in her head. How could people have lied to her her whole life? That made her angry. But realistically, *had* they lied to her?

No. They just hadn't told her.

Even if lying by omission was a whole other kettle of silverfish.

As time went by during the synchronization, she'd been a little angry. But the more time passed afterward, and as she amalgamated more to the core, learning more about how the Library functioned and what elements of it she could control, well, she had sort of mellowed. Her anger began to fade because she wasn't angry at the information, but at the fact she'd been there so long and Milaro hadn't told her beforehand.

She'd been at the Library for two months. That was barely a blip in her own life, let alone in the vast entity that was the Library. That was like a fraction of a fraction of a second.

And what did it change? What did her getting angry about a situation that was beyond everybody's control change?

Absolutely nothing.

Not to mention that everyone came from somewhere. *Everyone* was created in some way.

Even if her parents weren't actually her parents, they'd acted as such. They'd shown her affection. She could still remember her sixth birthday. She'd really loved that vanilla cake. It was amazing, with strawberry mango frosting. She remembered her father very vaguely having some of that frosting on the tip of his nose and pretending, for all he was worth, that he didn't have frosting on his nose. She'd laughed so much, it almost hurt to remember.

Those smiles, they'd been genuine. Those interactions were what she'd built her entire life on. They weren't manufactured memories. They were experiences she'd had.

How did that make her creation any different from a couple who had just really, really wanted a kid and had to go above and beyond to get one, to require treatment or surrogacy to have one, or to adopt one?

The Library really needed a Librarian. In desperation, a group of people helped make a hundred-percent guaranteed Librarian. Quinn wasn't entirely sure what that entailed, but she guessed that that meant she had been wanted and needed by a lot of people, in a lot of ways. And that was more than hundreds of thousands, even millions, of kids ever got.

Heck, in this universe . . . probably even trillions or some number she wasn't aware of.

Her parents had helped her form goals and morals, things that she still lived by right now, that helped her become a person that she didn't think was too bad. Her mother had encouraged her to do what she loved and to make sure that she took care of those who were less fortunate. They had essentially equipped her in her first dozen years with the know-how to make decisions that would affect her for the rest of her life, to make decisions that would shape her into the person she would become.

That she was a last-ditch effort to save the universe from basically devouring itself—didn't change how she'd been raised or loved.

It didn't change who she was or how she'd become that person. She still had her mottos. Help those who have less, don't pick on the weak, and don't be a dick, which was basically a tenet to live one's life by, no matter who you were, how you got here, or who you were raised by.

Frankly, if she'd gathered everything right, not everybody in the Library had known.

Lynx didn't originally know what she was. He just knew that they needed the Librarian's signature, and that's what he reached for. The Library, with all its holes in its memory, hadn't been part of the council plan when the experiment was put into action.

When she was retrieved, they didn't know. They couldn't even have known.

And then there was the cherry on top. She still had a choice. She could always still say no, and that's what was important. Just having these affinities, it didn't make her the Librarian.

Choosing to *become* the Librarian, that was her choice alone.

Technically, if Quinn wanted to, she could take all this power she'd been given. She could absorb every single piece of knowledge in the Library and then abandon it. If that was her choice, that's what she could do.

Frankly, it was an option. But she didn't want to do that. She loved Dottie and Misha, and all of the golems. She'd grown so attached to them after giving them their names. She liked Harish and Siliqua. Malakai had become a friend, sort of anyway. She even liked Narilin and her oddly willow-esque ways.

And Aradie, now. There was a bond, infuriating sometimes, that she had truly grown to appreciate. Aradie gave her that closeness that she had been missing in her life back on Earth, here, in the Library.

Quinn had access to worlds. She had access to knowledge. And frankly, she had access and power to do whatever it was she dreamed of. And these people, these beings and species that she'd met in this

Library, they were all individuals with the same dreams as her. And without the Library, everything would cease to exist.

So, she *could* leave it, but that would make her not the person she wanted to be.

Was she okay with being the universe's answer to the next Librarian?

Yeah, she really was. Was she a little pissed at Milaro because he'd kept this from her? Sort of. But how do you insert into conversation, "Oh, by the way, you're kind of sort of genetically related to the Library completely, with maybe a little bit of ability essences extracted from some other species, including my own. Hi, I'm sort of kind of like your creator, but only in a magical laboratory way"? Yeah, that wasn't exactly everyday conversation. And she got that.

Would there be some emotional upheaval for her? Probably. She was pretty good at pushing emotions back. But for right now, for where she was, where they were, this was where she needed to be. Being the Librarian was who she needed to be.

But that didn't define who she was or how she did it.

That, that was all Quinn.

"I'm so sorry," Siliqua said, pulling Quinn out of her contemplation. "I shouldn't have asked you that. That was intrusive and very disrespectful of me, Librarian. I ask for forgiveness."

Quinn laughed. "Why on earth would *you* asking me if I'm okay require forgiveness?"

Siliqua shrugged. "You asked for time. I pushed."

Quinn sighed. "I get it."

"We . . . we did what we had to do. We had no idea if it would work in time," Siliqua added hesitantly.

Quinn nodded. "Yeah, I know. I understand that. That's the whole sapient-sentient thing, you know? I understand. And I mean, if I wanted to, I could just pick a door, any door, go anywhere and never come back, right?"

Siliqua frowned. "Yes. Yes, you could do that."

"But I'm not going to," Quinn said. "I kind of like it here. It's calming and fun."

Siliqua's expression softened and she smiled. "That is very welcome news, Librarian."

"Anyway." Quinn clapped her hands together. "I'm okay. So how do we go about this idea that I had which I have no idea will actually work or not?"

Siliqua laughed. "Well, we're basically going to be grafting a portion of your sequence, I guess, to the Library."

"And couldn't we just take that from the original sample? I assume it's kept in some sort of magical stasis?" Quinn asked.

Siliqua nodded. "Yes, and we will, because we need to draw a comparison between it and yours and see if any of the adjustments made in yours are helpful."

"And what does that entail?" Quinn asked. Not entirely sure that she liked the idea of grafting. Wasn't that like peeling skin off and then putting it over other destroyed skin? She didn't think that sounded like the most painless thing to do.

"Well, we need to delve into the Library sequencing and see if we can actually identify the specific areas that have been infected. And because we have yours and a portion of the original sample to compare to, we should be able to establish a baseline." The excitement in Siliqua's voice was contagious.

"But aren't I a mix? I'm not just Library, right?" Quinn asked, hoping not to dampen that enthusiasm.

"True, but we can separate out that sequence as well as including it so that hopefully it gives us a round view with other potential solutions if this doesn't work."

"Okay, that's good."

"And once we have that figured out, we should be able to technically, theoretically," Siliqua qualified her statement, "be able to readjust it back to its previous state."

"Well, that doesn't sound difficult at all," Quinn said, sarcasm peeking through.

"Well," Siliqua said, like she didn't want to admit what she was about to say. "This requires a certain type of healing. I am not a healer. It's not actually my specialty. Identifying foreign elements in an already established sequence is something I am fantastic at doing, but healing them and bringing them back to their former state of glory, when it doesn't just require a basic disinfecting wash, is something I am not equipped to do. Would it be okay if I call in a colleague to assist?"

Quinn watched her. "Why are you just bringing up this colleague now?"

Siliqua hesitated before speaking. "Because they might be a slightly controversial choice to assist you at this point in time."

"Slightly controversial, how?"

"As in, their species is not one of the Library's immediate allies."

"Oh," Quinn said, "let me guess, they've got a sort of snake-y vibe to them."

"Sort of," Siliqua said. "Not Serpensiril, but they are related to the Serpensiril, and thus partially hostile to the Library."

Quinn thought that over. She couldn't condemn a people based on association only. "What about this person in particular? Are they hostile?"

"Oh, no. Oh, no, Cadre is very different from the rest of his species. He's, shall we say, an odd duck, I think, would be the way to describe him."

Quinn smiled. "And how's Milaro going to feel about this?"

"Actually," Milaro said, stepping into the room as if he'd been summoned. "Cadre is one of the few people I have no problem bringing into Library business."

"Well, now." Quinn flashed him a scowl, wondering how long he'd actually been there. "That sounds intriguing."

Siliqua glanced between Quinn and Milaro. "I'll go and contact him then, shall I?" she asked the mostly rhetorical question.

"Sure," Quinn said, flashing a smile in Siliqua's direction. "Do you have what you need from me to get started?"

She nodded. "I do. Thank you, for everything. I mean it."

With that Siliqua disappeared, leaving Milaro with Quinn in the office. He paused, like he wanted to say something, but wouldn't meet her eyes.

"You know this reticence of yours makes me angrier than anything I learned in synchronization. I said I'd talk about it when I'm ready," Quinn said somewhat flippantly. "I guess I'm ready."

Milaro let out a chuckle, but it sounded forced. "I wasn't sure if we'd succeeded when I first saw you. For all I knew, we'd just gotten lucky and finally retrieved a Librarian. I had no idea what to expect."

"But you were fairly certain, right?" Quinn asked.

"Yes. I was. There is such a thing as coincidences, but a human, from Earth, with all the affinities? That would have been too big even for a coincidence." He sighed and ran a hand through his ridiculously long hair. "I'm sorry I didn't inform you sooner."

Quinn accepted the apology, but found that it was mostly unnecessary now. "It wouldn't have changed anything, you know? Not really. Except for the fact that now I feel there is more purpose behind my having all the affinities."

"Does it feel like a weight?" he asked, almost whispering, like he didn't want the answer.

Quinn gave the question heavy consideration. "Maybe? No more than my college making me choose a major before I felt I was ready. There I could just drop out. Here, I can technically just take a magical doorway somewhere and choose never to return. So no, on second thought, I don't feel like it's an obligation. It's not weighing on me."

Milaro raised an eyebrow and smiled genuinely this time. "That is good. A burden is never fun."

"You're not actually genetically related to me, are you?" she asked, really hoping he wasn't. It would make certain ideas she'd been having very awkward.

He chuckled. "No, not genetically. All I did was extract the species-defining abilities from a few integrally important friends and distill it down to a pure essence so you would have heightened strength in those areas."

"Oh." Quinn blinked. "That's all."

Milaro laughed. "That's all. Though I do feel a sense of grandfatherly care toward you, it's in no way genetically related."

"Excellent," Quinn said standing up and stretching her arms above her. That was definitely a relief to know. "Anyway, like I said. This whole thing isn't a burden, it's something I can do. And if I don't, then I don't get to play in this magical world anymore. And that? That would suck."

"I like your logic." The tension had leaked out of his shoulders now, and he seemed much more Milaro. "We're good?"

Quinn nodded emphatically. "We're really good. But you owe me a Milaro-cooked meal."

"Oh, that's easy."

"A week."

He scrunched his brow. "Okay."

"For the rest of your life, Grandpa." Quinn flashed him a grin and darted out of the room. She didn't hold a grudge, but she'd milk it for some of his amazing food anyway.

4 2

WITH A VIGOR

Later that evening, after her stomach was extremely full from her first-owed Milaro-cooked meal, Quinn sat down in the Library to go over the lists that the Library had been intermittently making for her over the last couple of weeks.

She was amazed by how much better it felt to have her thoughts on the synchronization matter sorted, spoken out loud, and relatively discussed. Sure, something might pop up later that would make her backslide or maybe even have to deal with the emotions as they had come through originally. But overall, she felt pretty comfortable with her place in the universe.

She had a massive roof over her head, ridiculous amounts of knowledge, books, power, and food. Any type of clothes she wanted were made by the Library. It was like living in a dream where she didn't actually have to spend money to get anything. Just power, energy, mana, and stuff that she'd been raised to believe wasn't even real.

How magical was that?

Maybe things would be different once the novelty of magic wore off, but just being able to do something because you said so? She didn't think that was ever going to get old. The lists in front of her though? Those were definitely getting old. There was so much that she still had to do.

She opened the priority listing for her as the Librarian and frowned.

Priority listing—Librarian: Quinn

Prioritize:

Strength—progress halted—immediate attention required

Fine Definition—in progress 18%

Pillar Activation—in progress 3/10

Task Delegation—in progress 21%

Library Returns—in progress

Energy Amplification—missing components

HAHA VERY FUNNY, she aimed the thought at the Library. *I'll get to strength when you give me a moment.*

The Library, perhaps wisely, didn't comment.

Quinn had to prioritize all of those things. And then, well, how was that even a listing? She totally understood some of the designations on these. But the whole energy-amplification-missing-components thing? That she didn't get at all. What components? Probably something she needed to ask Misha.

She flicked through trying to pull up the other listings and finally found the one she wanted.

~~Repair the filtration system.~~

Calibrate and find the corrupted and missing files.

Book return status, including all of the branches.

New assistants required.

Replenish building and operational supplies.

Train in defensive applications.

Train in offensive applications.

Train in mind magic applications.

Well, she'd already repaired the filtration system, and she'd acquired new assistants, too. Although the latter appeared to be an ongoing thing.

She'd also spoken to Misha about replenishing, building, and operational supplies, but the rest of the stuff she was never going to get to crossed off at this rate. Calibrate and find the corrupted and missing files? She still had no idea how to go about finding all of that, even though they were trying.

And there were so many books still to retrieve.

She clutched her head trying to force some semblance of productivity into it. She added several things to the last list. Okay, open the culinary branch specifically. That was the closest one. And then she added activate the fourth filtration pillar, because she'd already activated the third and the fourth was pretty much ready now.

"So I might have to talk to Lynx about that."

Lynx is currently out of commission. The Library spoke into her mind.

"What, again? I don't like him being absent," Quinn said before she could think about what she was actually saying. But if she pushed a little into her expanded awareness, she could feel him there, like he was fast asleep.

The Library sounded like it was smiling. *I only answered because you were speaking out loud to yourself. If you'd been speaking in your mind, I probably wouldn't have heard you.*

I'm getting better at my control. As in much, much better.

The Library was silent for a moment before speaking again. *Also, I hate to have to remind you of this, but you are going to need to talk to the Serpensiril some more, especially Tenejo after what happened last time.*

"Yeah, I thought we might have to," Quinn said, although she was extremely irritated by the fact. She couldn't help that gut feeling that there was something she'd missed. Which, considering she'd been here for all of several weeks, was highly likely.

There's something bothering you, Quinn.

Quinn shrugged. "I don't know. We have so much to do. Not to mention we have to find and locate the restricted books."

How about you just identify them first? the Library said in a soothing tone. *We have a lot more time now. Now that we're out of immediate danger of depleting our energy, the returns and fines will bring in more power. Not to mention the filtration system is operating fully again. And we have you. You just need to make yourself a master list and work through it one thing at time.*

"You know, lists are always a great idea, but I'm very bad about ticking them off," Quinn grumbled.

Let's take today and see if we can rectify that. Anyway, how's it looking?

"Okay, I've added: Open the culinary branch. Activate the fourth filtration pillar. Talk to Tenejo. Name the restricted books. Find and locate the restricted books. Retrieve the restricted books." Quinn frowned at her list. It felt like a broken record.

Don't forget that you also have to retrieve the relevant culinary books in order to open the actual culinary branch.

"Yeah, I know." Quinn leaned back against the couch and propped her feet up on the coffee table as she went through more of the information in her HUD. "Okay, well, how about all of my abilities?"

Your abilities are leveling fine, Quinn. You don't need to check them every couple of days. They're not going to make that big strides just because you're constantly watching them boil.

Quinn laughed. "You almost sound human sometimes," she said to the Library.

I don't know whether to take that as a compliment or an insult, the Library said. *I've got work to do with Lynx. I'll send him back in a few hours. We're working on some ways to ensure he isn't still compromised, or that if he is, he can't compromise anything else.*

"Thanks," Quinn said. "It sounds weird, but I'm kind of used to him being around and things don't feel right when he's not within popping in when I least expect it distance."

I understand, the Library said. *Trust me, I understand more than you realize.*

Quinn smiled as she felt the Library's presence slip away to the back of her mind. It was never gone anymore. Nothing was ever gone. It was all compartmentalized throughout her mind with different allocations to keep the information sorted. Just like she could tell at this very moment, two dimensional doors were opening at exactly the same time from completely different areas in the universe.

Now *that* would never stop being fascinating.

Malakai cleared his throat, and Quinn looked up from where she lounged on a couch in the middle of the Library.

"Not in your office, couldn't knock on the door," he said, crossing his arms as he looked down at her.

"I felt like being surrounded by the Library, in a very literal sense," Quinn said. She peered up at him. "What's up?"

"It's very difficult to train you when you don't turn up," he said, snapping off the last word. "And to be frank, you're probably going to need to be able to defend yourself and the Library sooner rather than later. We all know that, so can you just make an effort to be on time, Quinn?"

She raised an eyebrow. She'd almost forgotten her own name; everybody kept calling her Librarian. She liked that Malakai called her Quinn.

"Sorry, lots on my mind. In my mind. You know how it is?"

"You have a very encompassing mind, Quinn, especially now. I'm sure you can partition some of it," Malakai said with a wink. He fell into the seat beside her. "Come on, talk to me. What's up? What are you doing?"

"I'm trying to be productive," she said, dismissing the lists in front of her as being too full of frustration to actually help her be the productive she was aiming for.

"Sure you are. You know you can't avoid training forever, right?" Malakai said, nudging her.

"I'm not avoiding it. I just have a lot to do." She could feel everything swirling in her head. It was overwhelming.

"How is Lynx?' Malakai asked, sounding concerned. The sudden change of subject made Quinn blink at him.

"'How's Lynx?'" she echoed the question, even though it was what had been asked of her. She reached out to sense him again, but apart from currents of power running through him and the Library obviously doing whatever it did in calibration . . . she could discern nothing. Which only meant she didn't understand yet what was happening.

"I don't know. The core is currently trying to figure out how much we can trust Lynx with, how deep the interference lies, if and how much he's being compromised, and it's just a big cluster." She sighed and tugged at the curls that refused to stay in her ponytail.

What was with the loaded questions lately? Everyone was asking her big things, like, "How is Lynx?" and "How do you feel being a genetically modified person?" She sighed. She felt pretty great, actually.

Overwhelmed wasn't the right word.

She'd been alive a relatively short time. In that time, there were things that she needed to accomplish. Finish school, get into college, finish college.

But now she was her own person and her own guide to her destiny. So what she needed to do was figure out the order in which she wanted to do things.

"You know, Malakai, I'm really glad you came to find me," she said, idly making two smooth ice balls appear in the palm of her hand. They were like fidget toys. She'd recently found they soothed her when her mind went into overdrive. Which had happened relatively frequently since the synchronization.

Malakai raised an eyebrow. "Really?"

"Yeah. So how about you sit here with me and help me figure stuff out?" Rare though it was, the downtime in the Library with the hum of people all around them, learning magic, discussing texts and methods . . . yeah, this was what made the Library home.

"You realize I'm sort of a sword-wielding, jumping, and killing-things person, right? Not necessarily your intellectual type of delver."

Quinn laughed. "I think you're a lot more than you're giving yourself credit for."

"Fine," he said, a small smile playing on his lips. "I'll take you up on that. What, pray tell, my dear Librarian," he said with a flourish of his hands, "would you like my wisdom to assist you with?"

Quinn laughed. This was just what she'd needed, a breath of fresh Malakai. She didn't have to do everything herself, despite the fact that she could literally tap into everything. Because even if she tried to do everything herself and take everything up on herself, it would A, defeat the purpose, and B, exhaust her to a point where she'd probably become useless.

And very likely put her in a really bad mood.

Yay for logic.

"Okay," she said, clapping her hands together and pausing as Dottie trotted up to them. "Hey, Dottie."

"I thought you might enjoy some company. Both of you." Dottie added the last as an afterthought as she spied Malakai. Aradie chose that point in time to swoop in and sit on Quinn's shoulder.

"Where have you been?" Quinn scolded the bird. "I've been going nuts trying to figure out how to approach some things, and you've been galivanting around."

Aradie looked her pointedly in the eye.

"Fine. I'm very glad you were taking care of our little friend. Is he doing okay?" Quinn was genuinely worried about the tiny owl.

Aradie nodded. She didn't even hoot.

"Okay. First things first. We have to identify the missing restricted books and see if we can trace them, and thus, if that's going to help us fix the system. So, Malakai. What did the assistants see? How much did you guys gather, information-wise?" Quinn dismissed the ice balls and got down to business. Maybe it was odd, but she missed their cool presence as soon as they were gone.

She'd been feeling rather overheated lately. Maybe it was all that brain processing power.

"We have three new book names apart from the ones that we already had. There are some more memories that we're going to have to filter through, but overall, here are the three names. *Chmilenko's Guide to Dimensional Complacency, Channeling Elemental Energy as Life Force,* and *Creation's Bane of Chaos.*"

Quinn cringed because none of those books sounded like they were particularly friendly to their current cause. "Well, that's three of them. How many more do we still have to identify?"

"Well, apart from the two Milaro listed, we still need three? No, I think it's five," Dottie said. "I believe there are another five of them missing, although through some recollection piecings, we're still delving into a few of the shelves we aren't entirely certain about."

"Have you been in the restricted vault?" Quinn asked, somewhat surprised that the bench got around so much.

"Multiple times," Dottie said proudly. "Many, many years ago, but I do believe there are a couple more missing. I'll gladly take on this task."

"Really? Awesome. I'll put you in charge of it. You can take that, and Malakai will teach me how to kick some butt and take some names." Quinn grinned despite already feeling fatigued at the prospect of how much work he'd make her do.

"Kick butt, take names? You're not making any sense, Librarian," Dottie said. "Sometimes I think you don't eat enough and there aren't enough electrons running around in your brain."

Quinn laughed. "Oh, I think Cook would definitely disagree with you on the eating front. I eat more than my weight in his creations."

"Anyway, I'll take on the missing books," Dottie said.

Quinn could tell that the little bench felt very important for doing so. "Thanks, Dottie."

"No problem. I will enlist a few assistants and we will methodically go through the rest of the memories. Rest assured, Librarian, you can count on me."

That gave Quinn room enough to breathe. "Fantastic! Okay, so that means we have to list out the culinary books. Can you access that, Malakai?"

"Yes, you're missing . . . you're looking at *Honor Among Pies: Culinary Regeneration at Its Finest, Making the Most on the Road: A Field Cook's Guide to Culinary Reinforcement, Emergency Supplements and the Taste Palette*, and then the last one I think we're missing is *Dire Consequences of Misusing Monster Parts: How to Avoid Pitfalls.*"

Quinn blinked at the complex names of the cooking books. She turned her attention to the HUD and frowned. "Okay, and if we ask the system to locate where the books are, they don't seem to be anywhere being kept by any singular person. It could be a whole plethora of things. I guess the last few centuries could have seen the ancestry die out, or get robbed . . . who knows."

But she sat back contemplating her lists of actions. Dottie would take on the memory delving for titles with the birds and assistants. Malakai would help her train, and locate the last of the culinary books. They'd gather all the books, figure out what the deal was with Tenejo, and everything would start clicking into place.

She jumped up from the couch with a vigor she hadn't felt for a while. She had direction and purpose with clear goals set out now. "No time like the present to get stuff done!"

That was the plan, anyway . . . and Quinn didn't have the best track record with plans.

43

FILTRATION HAS FINALLY BEGUN!

With a ridiculous amount of tasks on her to-do list, Quinn had been doing her best to maintain a regular sleep schedule, eat healthily, bathe, and generally take care of herself. She knew that these self-care routines would give her the energy reserves she needed to get every-thing done. The bed was comfortable, and although she often went to sleep late, she thought she could probably sleep in most mornings.

However, ever since Lynx had returned from being double-checked by the core, he'd somehow gotten it into his head that he needed to overcompensate for his past malfunctions. As a result, he woke her at the crack of the nebula, because in the dimensional pocket of the Library, time of day was what they said it was. He apparently had decided he needed to manage her day.

Quinn was not amused. "Lynx, just let me get up an hour or two later. I was up till all hours making those lists," she protested.

"But there's so much to do today. We've got enough power now to activate the fourth pillar, I've got a book location, and I'm currently running a diagnostic on the filtration system's distribution," Lynx replied.

Quinn sighed, even though a shot of excitement ran through her at the prospect of activating yet another pillar. Didn't that mean the

Library was getting closer to being fully functional? She pushed herself out of bed, trotted into the bathroom, and emerged ten minutes later, mostly presentable.

The jeans she'd pulled on were soft and reminded her of some of her favorites just before they began to fall apart. But the beauty of magic was that these ones weren't going to fall apart.

"Fine, come on, let's go," she said.

Down at the check-in desk, Lynx was all business. "Okay, so my advice is to activate Byron," he suggested.

Quinn looked at the diagram and frowned. "Yeah, that's probably our best bet, right?" Byron seemed to be their best choice because they couldn't activate Ashiron. But with another five pillars to activate before they got to Ashiron, they at least had a good chunk of time to figure out what the hell was wrong with it.

While she was refamiliarizing herself with the activation process, Lynx began to read through reports. "Okay, so the filtration has finally begun to clear the backlog of ley lines. The encrusted remnants of chaos and the miasma are beginning to thin, so that's great. Ley lines throughout the universe are beginning to see a substantial increase to the trickle of mana entering them, and the pools are filling back up. So we've done it, we've rebooted the Library, and hopefully, some of chaos's presence will begin to recede again." Lynx's voice hitched ever so slightly at the end of his enthusiastic report.

Quinn glanced over at him, somewhat concerned. "You know nobody is blaming you, right?"

Lynx sighed. "I'm blaming myself, Quinn. I'm obviously missing memories that we can't retrieve yet. Something happened that I can't remember. I did things I don't recall. Or at the very least someone made it seem that way." He turned to her, his expression pleading. "Do you understand how that feels for me?"

"We all forget things sometimes," Quinn said, her tone soft as she attempted to be soothing.

But Lynx shook his head emphatically. "That's just it. I don't forget. I've never forgotten. Give me three seconds and I can retrieve almost anything anyone in the Library has ever said, borrowed, or discussed.

Hell, I can probably tell you how many breaths they took while they browsed the halls. But I have gaps now. Spaces where something has been forcibly removed or blanked from my mind. Blocked out from all the data I can access."

"I'm so sorry," Quinn said. She reached over and gently squeezed his forearm. "But you know, right? You didn't do that to yourself."

"Didn't I?" he asked bitterly, his voice soft and full of self-recrimination. "Who else could have accessed my mind? I'm a part of the Library. Did my being here enable all of this to happen? For all I know, there's something else in my head hidden that maybe it would be best if the Library just, you know, got rid of me. Replaced me. I'm just a manifestation."

Quinn blinked at him. "You're not *just* a manifestation, Lynx. You're you. You've been alive for millions of years. You've been the Library's faithful companion. I don't think a tiny blemish in the last, what, five, six hundred years is going to make the Library or anybody else inclined to delete you."

Lynx flashed her a sad smile. "That's very kind of you to say, but I also think, given the circumstances, that it's foolish."

Quinn didn't know what to say. How was she supposed to make him feel better about this? "I might be foolish, but I think there's another way. And I know we need you. So let me worry about all of that."

He watched her for a few seconds and then gave a reluctant nod. "For now. Anyway, let's see if we can't retrieve the necessary books for the culinary wing first."

Quinn nodded. "Okay, so let me just activate the pillar, and we'll look." She went to place the heel of her palm in its spot on the console.

"You don't need to do that anymore. I probably could have just had you activate it from your quarters, but I was excited." Lynx smiled. "There is good news. I haven't had this much good news in so long, Quinn. I just . . . I'll try not to get you up quite as early next time."

Quinn laughed. "Maybe I'll try to get to bed thirty minutes earlier." She closed her eyes and visualized the map of the pillars, willing Byron to activate. The message popped up in front of her:

Filtration process functioning at 100%
New pillar activation permissible within these parameters.
Filtration Chamber Energy Levels: Medium-Low
Suggestion: 4th Pillar Activation
Do you wish to activate a fourth filtration pillar?
Yes or No?

Quinn chose Yes.

Pillars still requiring activation:
~~Ashiron~~, Byron, Cylion, Esheron, Farinon, Ishiron,
Activate pillar: Byron
Yes or No?"

"Yes," she murmured, noticing that the format had changed slightly. Was it because the Library's level of communication with her had grown since the synchronization?

Flushing Filters.
System Activation Process: 24 hours
Another pillar will be available in 336 hours or 14 days.
Should the power requirements be met prior to this, you will be notified.

"Well," Quinn said, "that's that. Okay. We'll have four pillars activated. What else do you have for me?"

"First culinary book has been located. It was a lot easier to find than I thought it'd be," Lynx said.

"Did you expect them to be difficult to find?" she asked, curious.

Lynx nodded. "To be perfectly honest, yes. The thing is, when a book isn't with a person, if it's been lost through time or other methods, the locators don't always work. Could we reproduce them? Sure, we could, although that gets more complicated the more intricate the book is . . . but right now we don't have the materials to spare especially if we can retrieve them instead. It's going to take a while. Retrieval is important, especially when it comes to books that help us open the branches."

The whole magical tome creation deal felt complicated to her. She knew eventually, as things settled, she'd get the hang of it. "Well, which book is it?" she asked.

"Oh, uh, *Dire Consequences of Misusing Monster Parts: How to Avoid*

Pitfalls. And it's located right here." He pulled up a map of a region that looked suspiciously like a video game Quinn had played once. It had floating islands all throughout the skies and what appeared to be no fixed landmass.

"Wow," Quinn said, "that looks difficult to traverse."

"This is one of the fae regions—dimensional portal L24. So it's one over from Geneva's home world. However, because it's another fae branch, we're going to send Geneva with you in order to mediate, as well as Malakai and Aradie."

"To mediate?" Quinn asked. "Is that really necessary?"

Lynx frowned. "It's better to be safe than sorry. Milaro wasn't incorrect to say you're at your most vulnerable. You're more powerful, but not into your full power. And the Library is also not even halfway back to peak functionality. Malakai and Aradie will guard you. And if all else fails, you'll have to take one of the emergency portal pods with you."

"Emergency portal pods?" Quinn raised an eyebrow.

"Malakai will bring one with him. He should be here shortly. I've already got Geneva coming in as well. We've delegated their shifts because this is a little more important. We need to start getting the books back, branches open, and power replenishment solidified."

Quinn frowned. "We still have to wait for Farrow to have some of the plants grow, right? Have I lost track of time?"

"Slightly, perhaps." Lynx smiled, and some of the sadness was gone. "Farrow should be done in a few days. It's just better to have the books and wait on the herbs, isn't it?"

"That makes sense," Quinn said. "Sure, I guess we're going on a field trip today, but how the hell am I supposed to get between those islands to find the book? Doesn't look like it has a rail system."

"Ah, yes, you should probably learn how to fly," Lynx said, as if it was a part of everyday normal conversation for everybody everywhere.

Quinn blinked at him. "Excuse me, did you say I need to learn to fly?"

"Well, how else are you going to keep up with a Furionas?" Lynx laughed loud enough that the patrons returning books looked over at him. He lowered his voice again. "Malakai will be fine, and Aradie already has wings."

"How is Malakai going to fly?"

Lynx blinked at her. "What do you mean? He's part Darigháhnish. Why wouldn't he be able to fly?"

Quinn pinched her brow, racking her brain to think of any information she'd ever read or simply was in the basic database of the Library about his species, but came up blank. Nothing in there told her that he could fly. "Fine, get me the book."

"Already have it. Here it is." And he plopped down a book that was about the size of letter paper and about four inches thick. "It'll feed off the hovering you've already been using for defense. You won't be able to fly non-stop, as it consumes energy, but your regeneration and your levels were boosted when you synchronized, so you should be fine."

"If you say so," Quinn said.

"*Schinhofen's Flights of Fancy* will be your ticket." Lynx patted the book.

Quinn glanced at him. "And how long do I have to learn how to use this ticket?"

"Oh, I think Geneva will be here in about two hours, so you should absorb it now and practice like the wind." Lynx grinned at her, a bit of a mischievous twinkle in his eyes.

Quinn sighed. "Fine." A little shudder of excitement worked its way up her spine. She was about to learn to freaking fly.

"Excellent. While you go and retrieve this book," he said, "Dottie and I will locate the other three culinary books. At least we will once we delve further into the owl memories. There's been some difficulties with several of them."

"Do you need Aradie to stay for that?" Quinn asked, trying to examine Lynx surreptitiously to make sure he wasn't just hiding his previous melancholy behind a mask. He seemed okay. She'd make sure to check on him as soon as they returned.

"No," Lynx said. "It's going to be fine."

"Very well, then." Quinn promptly sat on the floor in the check-in desk area, ignoring the fact that people were working on the other end of it. She absorbed the book without any rigmarole whatsoever. It was like air trying to push through her skin and into her body. It hurt, but not like other affinity related books she'd absorbed. It was trying to squeeze the life out of her for only a split second. And she gasped air in when it finally released her.

She could feel a tingle all through her body as the new knowledge settled into her veins.

Flying, it seemed, was much different to what Quinn had assumed it would be like. It was very closely related to hovering. She took in a breath and let herself hover above the ground, just like she did when she needed to dash out of the way, when she used it as a defensive mechanism. But even as she did, the blue and gold glow of her magical energy suffused her skin, coating it in those scale-like properties again, all up her arms.

It was one of those times she wished she'd had a mirror. She was pretty sure it wasn't only on her arms.

There was a soft gasp from the other people in the check-in desk area. She turned, still hovering, wobbling a little bit because keeping balance was quite difficult when you were literally standing on air. And she looked. There were three people checking books in. And her two Library assistants had apparently forgotten about them, because all five of them were gaping at her.

She sighed, lowered herself down very gently, and the blue and gold seeped back into her skin. "Sorry for the distraction. I'll go and practice this in my office."

And it was in her office that Geneva found her, just under two hours later.

"Librarian, I'm—"

Quinn was maneuvering around the room. She maneuvered back and forth and up and down, sideways. Above the desk, over the desk, around the desk. She turned to face Geneva. Prior knowledge of hovering had definitely given her more measure of control than she'd expected. "Hey, Geneva, I am not feeling very confident about this."

"It is okay. There are fail-safes. If all else fails, I do believe Aradie will be able to assist you."

"Aradie can assist me?" Quinn asked, raising an eyebrow at where the nightowl perched on the back of her office chair.

Her bird hooted at her.

Quinn lowered herself onto the floor and walked over. "Why didn't you tell me you could assist me?"

Another, longer hoot.

"What, do you mean I didn't ask?" she said.

Aradie let out what suspiciously sounded like a chuckle.

Quinn glared at her owl. "Well, I guess we're about as ready as we're going to be,"

Malakai stood talking to Lynx when they arrived at the check-in desk. They weren't exactly whispering, but they were definitely not speaking loud enough for everyone to hear.

"Is your world dangerous, Geneva?" Quinn asked

"Well, this is the neighboring fae world. It belongs to our distant cousins, the Esposians. But it shouldn't be dangerous," she said. There was a flicker of something in her eyes, maybe a little bit of fear.

"Are they not overly friendly toward you?" Quinn asked.

"It's not like that. It's something you're going to have to see. You'll understand when we get there." Geneva hesitated before continuing. "Not all fae are as friendly toward outsiders as my people."

Quinn frowned. "Thank you for the forewarning."

Quinn was glad Geneva told her. After the synchronization, she was pretty sick of people withholding stuff from her. Everything around her was more vibrant since she'd synchronized with the Library, including her read on people's auras or souls or whatever it was. She just hoped that Geneva wasn't underplaying the danger.

"Ready?" Malakai grinned at her, his bow slung over his shoulder.

"As I'll ever be. I can fly now." She nudged him in the side as they walked to the doors.

"Good thing. I don't think I could carry you across the divides."

Quinn almost punched him. Aradie swooped down to sit on Quinn's shoulder, and Geneva followed quietly behind.

"I like leaving from here. It feels grand." Quinn grinned at Lynx as Geneva sped forward and activated the double doors with her tiny fae hands.

The double doors swung open and the scent of humidity in a rainforest during summer swept into the foyer.

44

CASCADING WATER

Rainforests have a distinct scent. They're musty but fresh, humid yet somehow cool as water tends to mist down through the leaves and trees to the foliage below. The whole area has a vibrance about it. It's filled with the sounds of all the creatures, the birds, the trees, the scavengers that rustle through the bushes. Snakes, centipedes, insects, everything. Rainforests are teeming with life and a wondrous sight to behold.

Thick vegetation spread out from the doorway that opened from inside a massive tree's trunk. Quinn paused planting both feet firmly on the spongy ground as the Library doors closed and vanished behind her leaving the majestic tree's trunk intact once more.

It finally allowing her to breathe in the air fully. She took in a deep breath, relishing the freshness of the oxygen entering her lungs, the sounds around her, and that glorious smell of vegetation.

Maybe other people didn't like the dampness of rainforests. Perhaps they weren't fond of the humidity. Quinn found the whole ecosystem fascinating.

Rainforests were a magic all of their own.

She no longer needed the small palm reader she'd carried on their first couple of book retrievals because her HUD showed her everything she needed to know now. The power extended out to her through ley lines and pools and whatever magical wards the Library had activated and began to fuel in the universe. It made all her hard work feel like it was worth it.

She pulled up the map and frowned. The location of the book seemed to have shifted from where remembered it when Lynx had shown her back in the Library. She was almost certain.

"Quinn?" Malakai poked her somewhat gently with a finger. "Where's the book?"

She waved a hand at Malakai to get him to stop. "Patience. Give me a moment, okay?"

He frowned but stopped speaking.

Quinn scanned the area. There was something off about it but she couldn't quite figure out what. It was just another one of those gut feelings, that whole intuition thing.

Also the fact that she could spread her senses out to check for magical signatures and sensations was a huge boost for her since the synchronization.

Somewhere close she could have sworn there was a faint trace of pure chaos.

Not all the time, not even consistently, but this strange sort of interference that didn't seem to stay in the one spot. She couldn't pinpoint it.

Quinn shifted around and actually took stock of her surroundings. Belatedly, for sure, but everything looked very fresh, alive, and not at all chaos necrotic like.

She looked up into the canopy.

"That's where the village is," Geneva said, noticing her movement. She hovered next to Quinn, her tiny hands clasped together. "I expected we would be greeted by a standoffish delegation, but many of these trees and their homes appear to be empty."

"They're empty?" Quinn said. "I thought the village was inhabited."

"That's the last record the Library had. It's also the last record that my people have, which begs the question why we wouldn't have known the extent of abandonment." Geneva frowned.

"Is nothing left here, then?" Quinn asked.

"Oh, no. There are some of the Esposian fae here, but they are a little more secretive and not as social as my people. Right now they've remained concealed, but usually, with such a visitor, they would have greeted us. This is still unexpected and out of character," Geneva said, pursing her tiny lips. Even her iridescent wings seemed duller than usual.

Quinn studied all of the beautiful homes high up toward the canopy. She could see the little houses built into the trees and thought it would be basically impossible to retrieve a book from within one of those rooms if they didn't at least have Geneva or perhaps Eric with them. Although, given Eric's disposition, Geneva was definitely the right choice to bring with them.

"Is no one here, Quinn?" Malakai asked, frowning, his hand resting on his sword that hung from his hip.

Quinn shrugged. "I can feel a few large presences—well, Geneva-sized presences—in the trees, but other than the wildlife that flows through this forest anyway, I can't locate others. And on and off, I swear I'm getting a sense of chaos magic."

"Chaos magic? If there's chaos magic then the forest should be dying," Malakai said, whipping around to make sure he hadn't missed anything.

"It doesn't look very dead to me," Quinn said.

Geneva flitted back and forth from tree trunk to tree trunk. She even went so far as to fly up into the branches of the massive trees and knock on one of the doors. She waited. Quinn squinted up at her, wishing she'd brought binoculars, but Geneva flew back down with no answer.

"So are they just not talking to you?" Quinn asked.

Geneva shrugged. "I guess not? If nobody is answering, perhaps we should just go and try and find the book."

"But I thought it was in this village," Malakai said. "Isn't it supposed to be in this village?"

Quinn shrugged. "Well right now it says it's several clicks in that way."

Geneva blinked at her. "Clicks?"

"Miles?" Quinn half asked, half said. "Flying is faster, right?"

"Flying is faster." Malakai laughed. "We need to head through the forest and probably to another island, right?"

Quinn nodded. "I'm not precisely sure, but it's in that direction and if we run out of this island, I guess we're going to have to jump to another."

They set out with Aradie swooping ahead, easily soaring through the trees and dodging all the foliage as she scouted out the area in front of them. The bird hadn't said a word to Quinn yet, which wasn't unusual, but given the situation Quinn wished she'd have said something or shown her something. Still, she would tell Quinn if she spied anything in advance.

As they made their way directly toward where the map said they should be, Quinn kept glancing behind her because she felt something. She felt off. The area behind them didn't feel right. So much that she felt like she was being watched.

"Do we have to come back here to use that tree?" Quinn said, disliking the weird foreboding sensation around her even less. It flickered on and off, like it had bad reception. Or maybe she did.

"Not necessarily, Librarian," Geneva answered, still flitting about, a worried expression on her beautiful golden face. "We do have the emergency teleport . . . if we can get enough power to it."

"But it would probably be good if we came back and checked just to make sure that everything's okay, right?" Quinn prodded further. She really didn't want to resort to the emergency teleport if she didn't have to. Especially with the weird power fluctuations in the area.

Geneva flashed her a grateful smile. "Yes, I believe returning so that we can use the portal we know works to regain entrance to the Library is probably the best idea, Librarian."

As they trudged through the undergrowth, Quinn turned to Malakai. "I hear you can fly."

"Well, technically. Only for short bursts. It uses up a lot of my mana. And, to be fair, it's more like a constant double leap. You know, like I did back with the octopus." He grinned at her.

"Cephalopod," she corrected him absently. "Why did Lynx say you could fly, then?"

"Lynx says a lot of things, and if it's relatively short distances, then it is pretty much flying," Malakai said.

"Oh," Quinn said, "I feel less left out, then."

"What do you mean left out? You can literally absorb every single book in the Library. You have the ability to know every single recipe, every single combat style, every single magical tincture or potion or spell. You shouldn't be jealous of anything." Malakai laughed, but it sounded a bit forced.

Quinn blinked at him. "I can, can't I? Like, do it all."

"I didn't say you'd do it well," Malakai said.

She punched him playfully in the arm. "Thanks."

In the background, Quinn could hear the rushing of water. That soothing *shhhh* that she adored. The sound of water was one of her favorite things. But she couldn't see even a glint of it through the thick underbrush.

It was a bit of a traipse through the forest, but there was no lack of things to see. Quinn enjoyed the surroundings, the views, even if it was punctuated by odd power fluctuations here and there.

The sound of water grew louder and louder the closer they got to their destination. And then the canopy broke free, showing a massive body of water that simply ran off the edge of the island.

Quinn stood watching the cascading water, unable to contain her awe at the sight. The fact that she had no idea where it ended up felt like a massive waste of water in her mind. However, the scene was beautiful. She could see other islands not far away, maybe a mile or two at most. It was breathtaking out here, clouds at the same level as other islands. In the distance, she could see one with a massive structure. She would love to go and visit it. Some of the islands were small, others seemed large even though they were far away.

"Quinn," Malakai said, breaking her focus on the view, "we should probably get to the next island."

"Oh," she said. "Have you seen this before?"

Malakai blinked at her. "Yeah, it's an island floating in the sky."

"Malakai. It's an island floating in the sky." Quinn emphasized each word.

"Well, yes, that's what this world is." He seemed puzzled.

Quinn blinked at him. "This defies every single law of physics I have ever heard of in my life. I don't really *understand* physics, but I know that islands aren't supposed to float in the sky."

"Well, these ones do," Malakai said, shrugging.

In a magical universe, people apparently just accepted things as magic.

Quinn rolled her eyes, pushing down on the itch to figure out how this all worked. Magic was magic. "Fine. We have to jump across. We're pretty close to where we need to be. It should be that tiny island in front of us from the directional bleeping I'm getting."

Malakai frowned. Aradie hooted and landed on Quinn's shoulder.

"There's a tent over there," Quinn said. The bird nodded. "Well, I guess we're going. Did you look for the book at least?"

Aradie cocked her head to one side.

"You just came back to tell me there's a tent there. Probably could have saved us all a trip. Yes, I know you're not my servant." Quinn wished the bird could speak out loud so others would hear too. One sided conversations always sounded odd especially when she gleaned the information through images.

Geneva chuckled, her wings moving so fast Quinn could barely see them now. "Come on, Librarian. Let's get this done."

Quinn activated flight mode, trying to push down the fear as she stood at the edge next to the beautiful waterfall into nothing. A shudder swept over her as another flash of that chaotic mess lingered on her skin for a second. Then it was gone again.

After another few seconds, Quinn stepped off after the others. She was only mildly surprised that she didn't plummet to her death and continued to sort of jump walk across to the small island.

Moving this way was much faster than walking and they managed to cover the distance in a ridiculously short time.

The island in question was maybe thirty feet squared. It was tiny with a little copse of trees on it and a fire pit and a tiny little body of water that should really have been stagnant but had no algae around it at all.

Another example of magic.

Quinn frowned and approached the tent. "Hello," she called out. There was no answer. "Is anybody there?" Again, no answer. The coals in the fire pit looked like they were ancient. She sighed and took a deep breath before opening the tent flap. She didn't want to be right, but she'd still expected it. There, right smack bang in the middle of what used to be a sleeping bag on a cot, was a practically mummified corpse. It was more Quinn's size, far larger than any fae she'd seen. It had been there for a good many years.

"Oh," Malakai said, "that's a little anticlimactic."

Quinn scowled at him. Geneva pointed. "That's—that's the book. That's the cooking book."

Quinn grabbed it, lifted it up from where it sat next to the cot. "Yep, this is it. *Dire Consequences of Misusing Monster Parts: How to Avoid Pitfalls*. Huh." She stowed it away in her storage and looked at the other two. "Do we just leave the body here?"

Geneva stared at her. "Of course. You'd only disturb a body if you knew who to return it to. We should research and see who he belongs to, and perhaps let them know where to find the corpse."

Quinn blinked. Definitely different ways of doing things here. "I guess we head back?"

"Yes," Geneva said, suddenly a lot brighter than she had been for the rest of the trip. "This was a lot easier than expected, Librarian. I'd love to come with you on these little excursions."

Malakai groaned at the same time that Quinn sighed. "I wish you hadn't said that."

Geneva gave them both a very odd look, but they flew back to the other island and Quinn watched the river gushing down into nothing wistfully. She knew she was awake, because she could feel the light spray from the water hitting her skin as they landed. But she still sort of wanted to pinch herself, just in case it was a dream. Waterfalls were one of her favorite bodies of water. Never-ending ones were simply a cut above.

As soon as she put her foot down on the original island, that strange, ominous, foreboding feeling washed back over her.

But this time it was stronger.

"Hey, guys," she said, taking several steps forward immediately as she landed. There was a pull here. Something tugging at all her Librarian senses, at her mind. Like maybe there was another book. Maybe there was something here that she needed to get that the Library didn't even know about yet.

"I hate to tell you this," she said, "but I don't think we're heading home quite yet. There's something here."

Like magic, as soon as she said that, five Esposian fae appeared directly around them.

They were the polar opposite of Geneva's brightness. Where she had golden skin and luscious golden hair, they were pale and ghost-like. Where her wings were rainbow iridescent, theirs were so pale as to be almost invisible,

And where she usually had a pleasantly, almost happy demeanor, the group that surrounded them bared their teeth.

In all of the tales Quinn had read about faeries—don't tell them your name, don't accept a gift, never thank them—she'd never been told that they had mouths full of razor-sharp teeth.

"You are not welcome here. Hand over the book and leave," the one closest to Quinn spat out.

This definitely wasn't a welcoming party.

45

DIFFERENT DEFINITIONS

For some reason, being surrounded by five of the Esposians didn't scare Quinn. Instead, she fought back the urge to summon ice balls and tried to calm herself down. She was angry, yet sort of excited by the confrontation. Probably because she'd been cooped up in the Library for weeks.

What the hell were these guys even thinking, surrounding them and saying they weren't welcome? They'd come to get a Library book. Wasn't that like her thing? She needed to sort her thoughts out, because if she didn't, she was probably going to act rashly, and that wouldn't be good under any circumstances.

She knew she could think fast, but the amount of information she needed to process would still take time. How much did they really want to fight? Their countenance didn't scream violence or readiness to wreak mayhem and bloody murder. No, there was hesitation in the way a couple of them stood. They held what looked like bone daggers in their hands. A brief thought occurred to her that they couldn't hold metal weapons without harming themselves. Was that part of the myth actually truth? She glanced at them.

Their stances were a mess if what Malakai had taught her was anything to go by, and their grip on their weapons looked weak. They were definitely reluctant. All of them seemed to have some sort of expectation of a fight, but there was also a hint of fear coming from each of them.

She could feel it emanating like a bad smell.

Quinn automatically attempted to identify them because she'd been doing so with every new species that walked into the Library lately, and it was almost second nature now.

Esposian—Fae species – distantly related to the Furionas fae

Traveled from: Dimensional Portal L24

Ally status: 471,000 years

Current status: Regarding you with desperate hostility

Quinn frowned at the last addition to the information. Desperate hostility? That was oddly descriptive. She knew she had to interact as soon as possible, but still, the Library's reach had expanded exponentially. The hostility they were being shown didn't sit right with the Library's reputation. Had it seriously been so badly damaged in the years of absence?

Not to mention she couldn't get over the fact that she now had access to everything in the field. All the screens, the inspections. The system was expanding its reach and functioning properly now it had more mana flowing to it.

She pushed the inspection function just that little bit further.

Name: Varyn

Quinn took a deep breath and spoke. "Why are we not welcome, Varyn?" she asked.

"We do not speak to humans." The one in the middle practically spat on the ground when he spoke. If he was surprised that she knew his name, he didn't let on.

Quinn could have kicked herself. She knew they'd brought along Geneva for a reason. She was a fae Furionas and therefore should be able to at least speak to the Esposians. However, as she glanced at Geneva, she realized that her Library assistant was still in shock. She didn't seem to be taking this confrontation well.

Quinn continued, "Well, I guess it's a good thing that I'm the Librarian."

Whatever Quinn had been expecting to happen, it certainly wasn't what happened next.

Two of the five moved toward her so fast she could barely follow it with her eyes; their knives held out in front of them. The only thing that saved her was Aradie dive-bombing one of them, drawing blood and a scream, and Quinn's ability to think outside of time. She barely dashed to the left-hand side, missing the blade so closely that a few of her hairs got caught by it.

Two thick curls fluttered down.

Quinn crouched down on the ground, watching the Furionas and trying desperately not to lose her temper. Even Malakai arrived a split second too late to help her against one of those damn daggers. She racked her brains for something to say, for anything to say or anything to do. She hadn't expected to be attacked by Furionas when the Library itself was supposed to be on fantastic terms with them. The two who were now in the middle of their group, and the three who were still outside of it, were difficult for her to keep track of all at once.

Aradie squawked, hovering up above, keeping herself in place through magic and movement of wings. Somehow, the breeze from them managed to soothe Quinn and allowed her to think clearly, even as the other three of the Esposians started to move.

This time, they weren't darting in; it was like they were coordinating efforts telepathically, which they very likely were. Quinn kicked herself for not having thought to do the same, which led to yet another thing on her list she had to master. That anger boiled in her gut, threatening to come up.

She was pissed off. What the hell? All she wanted to do was open the bloody culinary branch. How could anyone begrudge the opening of that section? She'd maybe understand it if it was combat or alchemy based.

Even as she had the thought, the Esposians began to lunge toward Quinn again.

Geneva recovered. It had maybe taken her twenty seconds, which was a long time when people wielding sharp bone knives were trying to kill you.

Geneva yelled and her voice encompassed them all. "That is enough. What has gotten into you?"

The Esposians dropped their knives to cover their ears and screamed for a second as soon as Geneva spoke in that loud, resonant voice. Aradie shot up to the canopy just before the fae Furionas spoke. Quinn spared a very fast glance at Malakai, who gave her an almost indiscriminate shrug in response. He had no idea what Geneva's voice had done, but Quinn had an idea that it was a frequency that birds and, apparently, Esposian fae did not like.

The Esposians were pushing the heels of their hands against their ears, their weapons and grievance momentarily forgotten.

Finally, Varyn turned to Geneva. "We have to stop you."

"What's the matter?" Geneva asked again. She looked bewildered, lost almost, her eyes a little wild. "I don't understand why you attacked us."

Varyn scowled at her, baring his teeth. His eyes looked like they were almost on fire, with a yellow-orange tint to them. They were filled with fervor and desperation leaked out of his very pores. "We can't let you go any further."

The other four of the Esposians began to fidget. A couple of them went to retrieve their daggers, only to have Malakai loose an arrow right in front of their feet. They darted back, scowling at him.

"Why do you have to stop us from going further?" Quinn repeated, in a low and very menacing tone. Her patience had just run out.

The cantankerous little Esposian scowled at her, baring his teeth again. Three of them, completely disregarding Malakai's loosed arrows, sat right in front of their daggers and darted in to fight, their fingers extended, their nails just like claws. This time, Quinn was ready. She cast two streams of ice at them, hitting one in the foot and one in the hand. They yelped and darted back, but the other three rushed toward the Librarian and Geneva.

The Library's Furionas fought deftly, so fast that Quinn couldn't keep track of her. Not that she had time to.

Aradie flew at them, pecking at the attackers madly, but one of the two approaching Quinn almost reached her. She shot out more ice at them, even as Malakai was taking care of the one Aradie pecked at.

"Don't kill them. It'll only make things worse," Quinn called out.

They were coming in so close that Quinn almost touched them a couple of times while casting her ice. It was so cold she could practically hear it blister the almost translucent skin of the Esposians. But still, they only crept out to recover for a few seconds before darting back in.

A few scratches got through here and there, but Quinn kept her self-healing active and thanked Malakai and her lucky stars that she'd insisted on learning the self-healing book when she had. She got into a quick rhythm of dodging and casting ice shards, ice bullets, and a plethora of other ice waves. It was a lot more difficult to use her powers when she was deliberately trying to hurt her attackers the least.

Frankly, the ice had been harder to summon the last little while. She put that down to not practicing enough. She really needed to get on that.

Geneva let out a cry, and Quinn's attention wavered only for a split-second, but it was enough for her ice blast to go slightly off target.

Her ice caught one of her attackers' wings. The membrane froze so fast, Quinn could practically hear it crackle. The scream of pain emanating from the Esposian's mouth almost shattered Quinn's eardrums. She could feel fear and fury and this horrible, complete and utter sensation of despair.

"Damn it," Quinn said. "I didn't realize the wings would be that sensitive."

"Have you not seen my wings?" Geneva said. "Do you not see how transparent they are and how fine they are? Can you imagine something like that? Freezing. Do you know how much ice . . ." But she stopped, dashing down to help as their attackers stepped back for a moment, concern and bewilderment in their expressions.

"I'm sorry, Librarian," Geneva said as she landed. "I can just imagine how much pain she's in."

"Yeah, I get it. I get it." Quinn acknowledged her assistant. The injured Esposian seemed almost doll-like. She was still and paler if that was possible as she lay on the ground. "Mal, can you hold her down just in case she wakes, and heal her?"

Malakai raised an eyebrow but did as he was told and held the little Esposian down gently at its feet and shoulders. They were so tiny. It wasn't difficult for the six-and-a-half-foot man. Even as Malakai muttered his heal out, the tiny little Esposian didn't wake up, but her breathing evened out. Quinn wasn't surprised. Healing required energy from the body being healed as well and not just the healer.

Quinn brushed herself off as she stood up while the other four stared on, their faces still a little bit full of anger and fervor and a decided willingness to stab them if they could find an opening.

Quinn stood, hands on her hips, and gave them her own scowl. "That's enough. Now I know I can hurt your wings. If you try and stab me again, I'm going to ice your wings. Okay? So how about we just stop this and you tell me why you decided to come and attack me and my group with a bunch of knives. I don't get it. We didn't hurt anything in the forest. I've just retrieved the Library's property. That's all we've . . ."

"You've retrieved the Library's property?" Varyn asked, his voice high-pitched for once, almost in panic as he asked the question.

Quinn frowned. "Yes, I just retrieved *Dire Consequences of Misusing Monster Parts: How to Avoid Pitfalls*. Of course I'm taking it back. It's one of the four books left so we can open the damn culinary branch. Why don't you want us to open the food branch of the Library?"

All of the despair leaked out of the Esposian. "We didn't realize that was the book you came for," he said. Now his eyes darted around, not meeting her own. The fire was gone. The passion was gone.

Now he was being secretive.

Quinn liked that even less. "Okay, so you were just willing to kill me for taking a book with me. A book that *isn't* the book that I went and retrieved. Why is that?"

"I don't know what you mean," he said, and made to fly away. But

Geneva muttered under her breath. And he was stuck in place in midair.

"How dare you use one of the punishments on me," he said, snapping at her, some of that fire returning to his gaze.

"I dare," Geneva said. "You have given affront to the Library and its Librarian. I'm of a mind to report this behavior. You owe us answers, and you're not going anywhere until we've got them."

Panic flitted through his eyes. One of the Esposians made a run for it, but they didn't get very far. Aradie swooped down, pecking the top of their wing. It would be easily healed. But the thing about wings is when one is injured, flying can become painful or impossible. Quinn didn't like resorting to hurting somebody who was supposed to technically be an ally of the Library.

However, in this case, since they'd flown at her with sharp things, trying to stab and claw her to death, she figured she had the right to be just a little bit retaliatory.

"Malakai, you good with keeping an eye on the other three?" she asked him, her voice low.

"Oh, very. I'm sure Aradie will help me," he said, focused on the others. They shrank back ever so slightly.

"Will they fly away?"

Geneva shook her head. "Oh, no, I have seen to the fact that they will not fly away."

"Okay, Varyn? How about you tell me why you attacked me?" Quinn asked, trying to keep the angry tremor out of her voice. Involving emotions didn't usually help things, but she didn't like being ambushed by a supposed ally.

A sudden pulse rippled out from the center of an island like a stone dropped into a lake. Almost like a locating beacon. Varyn shuddered as it came into contact with him, and then he sighed. Two of the others fell down to the ground, wordlessly.

"Are they okay?" Quinn asked.

Malakai checked. "They're breathing, just unconscious, I think."

Quinn scowled and turned to Varyn. "Spill it, now." She didn't like the sensations crawling over her skin and up her spine. It felt like somebody was trying to intrude into her, through her, trying to read her mind, trying to figure out exactly why they were here and who they were.

And how it could devour them.

"You've got about sixty seconds, Varyn, before I really lose my temper and use some of the mind stuff that I've been learning from King Milaro." It was sort of an empty threat, but he didn't know that.

He trembled ever so slightly. "It's not the cooking book. We don't care if you open the culinary branch, but if you come and find the other book, they'll kill all of us."

Quinn perked up at that. Who the hell were they? "What do you mean they'll kill all of you? Who are they?"

Varyn shook his head rapidly. "I can't. I can't tell you. I've said too much."

His eyes darted wildly from side to side. He started shaking in the air, convulsing almost. Geneva lowered him down so that he could sit on the ground.

"Varyn, calm down. It's okay. It's okay. We just need to know what's wrong. We can help." Quinn attempted to soothe the Esposian.

"No," Varyn said, "you can't help. Nobody can help. That's why there's nobody here. They've been killing us off this whole time. Don't you see? We're sacrifices. And that book. They're never going to let you go now," he said.

"What do you mean?" Quinn asked.

But before he could answer, his mouth opened in a silent scream as he began to disintegrate from the hole that emerged in his throat outward. Spiraling around that point, the disintegration was almost hypnotizing.

Quinn looked around wildly to see the other four suffering the same fate.

Their bodies slowly turned into nothing. The smell of rotting flesh lingered for several seconds before it too had disappeared. Nothing but the dropped bone daggers on the ground left any trace behind that they'd been confronted at all.

Quinn gulped as uneasiness spread down her spine. Now she felt like she was being watched, and as Geneva and Malakai shifted uncomfortably, she knew they felt it too.

"Well. Shit," she said and sighed, turning toward where the ripple had come from. It was very obvious and easy for her to track that magic. So much so, that she was fairly certain it was a trap. "I guess we have to go find out where that ripple came from now, don't we?"

Malakai nodded, a grin spreading across his face. "Now this is much more interesting than a cooking book, don't you think?"

Quinn rolled her eyes. "You and I have very different definitions of interesting."

46

WATCHFUL EYE

QUINN COULDN'T SHAKE THE IMAGE OF VARYN AND THE OTHER Esposians' deaths from her mind.

The disintegration of each of them started with their vocal cords, as if the force behind it didn't want them to speak, to give anything more away. Whatever executed them knew they'd been on the verge of revealing information they apparently weren't supposed to have. That thought alone chilled her to the bone.

She felt guilty because part of her was relieved the executioner hadn't been able to do the same to her party. Logically, this meant that whatever was responsible could only influence those it already had control over. Those it had already made some type of relevant contact with.

If it couldn't reach her or her companions, at least that meant this wasn't something already present within the Library. And that gave her even more resolve to figure out what had done this.

The group remained silent as they moved through the forest, now painfully aware they weren't welcome for reasons other than they'd originally expected. Geneva, in particular, was distraught. Quinn could tell by the way she wrung her hands and her eyes darted from side to side as she clung to Malakai's shadow. Her wings moved in an almost staccato rhythm, as if she was expending more energy than usual to stay afloat. Even her countenance, usually vibrant in gold, was paler than Quinn was used to.

Quinn kept a watchful eye on the Furionas and Malakai as Aradie shot off ahead to scout their way forward. She could still feel the powerful unease that permeated the air around them. There was a quietly malicious undercurrent to everything. It was more amplified than when they had first arrived, more noticeable. Before, it had tried to hide, as if camouflaging itself meant they wouldn't notice anything. And, to be honest, a week or so ago, Quinn probably wouldn't have noticed.

Sending Varyn to make sure Quinn and the others weren't there for whatever book they were talking about had been a mistake. It gave Quinn pause, because she had lists of all the missing books. And any missing book that the system had given them information on would have been visible on the map if it was here. That meant it had to be a book that either didn't belong to the Library, or else *did*, and the Library had lost recollection of.

The latter could only mean it was one of the missing tomes from the restricted vault.

Given the ominous energy leaking all around her, it seemed more and more likely as time went by.

As the group moved slowly and deliberately through the forest, Geneva eventually fluttered closer to Quinn.

"I am so sorry, Librarian," she said, her usual vibrancy subdued.

"It really wasn't your fault, Geneva. None of this is your fault," Quinn said, speaking as softly as possible.

"But had I reacted faster, instead of freezing in place from shock at their actions, I could have held them in place so much sooner and maybe prevented—"

"No, Geneva, this wasn't you. And hindsight is always twenty-twenty. You had nothing to do with what happened to them." Quinn used her best quiet soothing voice, but it didn't appear to work.

"But maybe I could have stopped them from attacking you. I'm just . . . I wasn't raised to fight, Librarian," Geneva said, looking down.

"You know," Quinn said, "neither was I. How about we look forward, move past what just happened, don't assign anybody blame. But we also don't forget the individuals that were just lost, and we work on figuring out how and why it happened."

Geneva held her gaze for a few seconds, which made navigating the underbrush vastly more difficult, and nodded ever so slightly, a small smile playing at her lips. "Thank you, Librarian. I forgot myself for a moment there. Let's get this solved."

They continued on in the eerily silent forest. Apart from the subtle pulse that echoed through the ground like a heartbeat, there was no movement, and no sound.

"I've got a feeling," Quinn said, as they came upon a sturdy tree. She paused in front of it. "That we can't go back to the Library just yet."

"What do you mean?" Malakai asked, stopping and speaking low enough that his voice almost got carried away by the wind.

"This." She placed her hand against the tree trunk and spoke. "Library, I need you."

Nothing happened. There was no pulse, no recognition of her magic, no sign that the door could fit in this tree.

Nothing.

"See," she said.

"Does that mean we're trapped here?" Geneva asked, her voice higher pitched than usual.

"Well, I mean, you've got wings, so trapped is kind of subjective," Quinn replied.

Malakai frowned. "I didn't expect this. Even enabling my grandfather's teleport token here isn't guaranteed. It functions utilizing a portion of the Library magic too. Plus, if it *does* work, there's no guarantee we can get back here. And, to be honest, I think we need to check this place out. We owe it to those Esposians."

Quinn nodded, trying to run through everything logically in her head. She didn't like the way fear crept up her spine. It always clouded her judgment. They couldn't afford that right now.

"I guess the only way is forward," she said, tamping down on the sensations threatening to engulf her and wrapping her logic and senses around her like a security blanket.

Aradie hooted.

"I know, I know," Quinn said as the bird dived low and then up into the canopy again, scouting from the air. She intermittently sent Quinn back images, ones that showed no evident life, and yet even those exuded a sense of being watched constantly, as if something was observing them all.

Quinn, as they moved, extended her senses, honing in on the center of the foreboding sensation that pulsed like a heartbeat throughout the island. It emanated from somewhere past the area they'd first arrived in.

"We need to keep moving," she said, glancing around. The silence was almost scary in its prevalence.

Aradie, she thought at her bird, *be careful.*

Even as she scanned the area with her abilities, Quinn felt multiple presences extending out, clumping together. But then, as if they were singular to start with, they blended into each other and away from their group as they moved. Those same distinctive presences moved both toward the power center, and away from it. There was no rhyme or reason to the way they maneuvered.

It was bizarre.

Quinn couldn't tell whether these were beings amalgamating and separating themselves, or if this was a false power signature or something that was intended to lure them somewhere, perhaps into a trap. The farther they went, the less Quinn liked the entire setup. The constant pulses of foreboding didn't help.

Before synchronization, she wouldn't have had a hope in hell of sensing any of these presences, let alone tracking them. But her mind was able to pinpoint them now, all of the different types of magical signatures, even insofar as to see them separating and then converging on each other again.

They didn't appear to be Esposian fae. They were some sort of being she hadn't yet encountered. She had no doubt that if she'd had more time to spend acclimating herself to her new abilities, she probably would've been able to recognize them. As it was, all she could do was steer her group through these beings and hope they weren't about to get ambushed.

When she accessed the well of power inside her, viewing it, seeing it, really looking at it, as they scoured the forest, she could see the depth of access she had to something she didn't think she should yet. There was so much magic within her now . . . such potential. She was like a powder keg.

It made her even more cautious. Which was probably a good thing.

Making sure they weren't stepping into visible or obvious traps was easy. The magical energy signatures were almost like a second sight to her when she concentrated. If—no, she corrected herself, not if—when they got out of this and back to the Library, she wasn't letting herself be pulled along by others anymore.

Once they'd opened the culinary branch, Quinn would take the time for herself before she got someone else killed, because Quinn was under no illusion that Varyn and those other four nameless Esposians would still be alive if she knew even half of what the hell she was doing.

Geneva definitely had no reason to feel guilty.

Quinn had access to the power; she had the abilities. Hell, now she knew she even had the heritage. There should be nothing stopping her from becoming powerful enough to protect not only the knowledge in the Library, but those people who were attached to it, those people who needed protecting.

This floundering around because she had so much to get done was no longer acceptable. Once they solved this, once they got the immediate danger out of the way, once Tenejo was dealt with, once that trap was taken care of, she was taking time for her own development and nobody was stopping her.

She suppressed a sigh as she realized it was probably still a couple of weeks off if she was being completely optimistic. Right now, they still had things to do here.

Somehow, on the way back, the forest seemed bigger, emptier. It took them so much longer.

The underbrush was silent. There wasn't even a cricket-like chirp to fill the air. Nothing, not even the leaves on the trees seemed to rustle in the breeze. It was only their soft footsteps that gave any indication at all that sound wasn't immediately swallowed in this place.

Quinn gulped down a very difficult breath. Goosebumps ran up her spine. The pulse was closer. It resonated through her legs, almost shaking her bones as it went up through her body. She didn't like the sensation. She could tell the others were uneasy. Except Geneva. Flying definitely appeared to have its benefits. Except being on the ground allowed Quinn to, somewhat at least, tap into the power she could feel and trace it.

She frowned. "There are multiple beings around here."

"Yeah," Malakai said. "They're watching us, every move, tracking us."

"I knew this was a trap," Quinn said, resisting the urge to say "I told you so."

Malakai shrugged. "What you gonna do?"

"Seriously? Are you gonna blow people out of the way with your super bow?" Quinn asked incredulously.

He shrugged. "Maybe not, but we are about to see this book Varyn mentioned. Tell me, Quinn, aren't you curious?"

He was right. He had her there. She was almost completely certain this was one of the books they were missing from the restricted vault. Although if it started out this ominous, she wasn't sure why it existed to begin with.

From the menacing aura emanating from wherever it was hidden, and given the way that Varyn and the others reacted, it was very obviously being guarded by whoever or whatever it was that was watching them, following them, and basically herding them towards certain doom.

The group finally came upon the village they'd originally arrived in. Now, it was darker all around them. The sense of unease in the area was, well, much worse. And the air around them felt like it'd been sucked out of the vicinity, not to mention the light was fading.

Quinn didn't relish the idea of being stuck here at night, but right now it was looking unavoidable.

Upon closer inspection as they passed through it, Quinn realized that the doors in the trees up above them were ringed in a strange, almost matte black substance that reminded her remarkably of the chaos sludge they'd encountered in the filtration chamber.

She frowned. "Do you see that?" She pointed up above them.

Malakai nodded, his own frown deepening. She could tell just by watching him that he was unsettled.

Great, it wasn't just all in her head. Quinn decided to strengthen her personal shielding, wrapping it around her, sealing it tight. She felt a sensation of ick trying to crawl up her spine from the amount of chaos that was now pulsing along with the rest of the power throughout the entire island. It was getting worse by the moment.

And, unlike when they'd first arrived, it no longer seemed to be trying to hide.

"Geneva, can you tell me if those doors are ringed in chaos sludge?" Quinn could speculate, but she wanted confirmation.

Geneva nodded.

"Were they before?"

"No, Librarian," Geneva said, her eyes darting around once again. The forest had grown even darker.

"Does the sun set abnormally early here?" Quinn asked.

Geneva shook her head, "It shouldn't. Dimensional Gate 24 isn't much different than Dimensional Gate 25 in that respect. This is an unnatural sunset."

"Fantastic," Quinn muttered, "That's just what I wanted to hear."

Geneva raised an eyebrow.

Malakai shook his head. "Don't ask."

Past the village now and the sensations all around her were thicker, cloying. She felt like she was marching toward an inevitable gloom.

Quinn found herself questioning whether she should have Malakai try to teleport them out right now anyway. Thing was, it was obvious that the Esposian fae were under an attack of some kind, under coercion, and that would make her a horrible person to leave any of their species that were still able to function behind with something that was trying to control them.

Because she had no shadow of doubt that they were being forced.

Upon pain of death.

Literally.

Her group approached a cluster of trees, and Quinn paused outside of the circle. Part of her resisted the urge to check any further. That part wanted to escape. Quinn had never wanted to exercise her logic this much in her life.

"It's in there, you know," Quinn said, gesturing beyond the trees. "Do we want to step through?"

"Do you want Aradie to have a look first?" Malakai asked.

Quinn shook her head and beckoned to her owl. "No, we should go in together. Safety in numbers, right?" she added as Aradie swooped in to settle on her shoulder.

The four of them stepped through into a small clearing circled by tall willowy trees. In the middle sat a dark, twisted tree glowing in a malevolent red.

Its bark was blackened and withered, and blood seeped out from between the cracks between each piece. It smelled pungent, of rotting wood, flora, and fauna. Quinn turned her head to the side and gagged before she could get her senses under control.

A film of deep red surrounded the base of the tree, similar to the miasma cloud present in the filtration chamber. Except this was more than just a mist; it writhed and churned as if it had a mind of its own.

Quinn gulped and regretted it instantly. Aradie clung to her shoulder, and even Malakai paled.

She could feel the presences she'd tracked on their way here, all converging on this spot and she knew, without a shadow of a doubt that they shouldn't have come here.

The tree groaned. Not as in the wind blew through its branches and made it creak like any old tree. No, this was a humanoid groan, guttural and unsettling.

Then its branches moved, shaking themselves as if trying to be rid of dirt or dust mites, or some other pest.

And then two eyes and a gaping, serrated-toothed mouth opened up in a wide grin.

When it spoke, the sound resembled the grating of nails across a chalkboard. "We've been waiting for you, Librarian. Won't you stay a while?"

47

HOSTILE COPSE

Quinn, Malakai, Geneva, and Aradie stared at the bloody-barked tree. Quinn's response to its request for them to stay a while sat on the tip of her tongue. She had to fight against saying, "No, I don't really want to stay a while, thanks so much." Instead, she took a deep breath and concentrated on cataloging their surroundings while she tried to think of a somewhat more diplomatic approach to telling the creature in front of her to sod off.

Even as she studied their surroundings, she noticed that the forest floor was full of blood-soaked leaves. If she inspected the bark on the tree closer, she could see the pale, ghostlike wing membranes sticking out from between the cracks, bloodied and tattered, some hair here and there, the occasional toe or finger. It was all she could do to not gag.

A sinister pulse rippled out from the tree, giving a sensation of impatience, causing Quinn to shudder.

Shadowy figures emerged from the surrounding trees that now appeared to be farther behind them than before. It made the copse appear much larger than she'd originally thought, as if they'd somehow traversed a great distance. With time slowed outside of her mind as she rapidly observed everything around them, Quinn realized that the Esposians might have been sacrifices for whatever this was.

This tree wasn't natural on any world.

She paused. A breeze had ventured through its branches. Through its dead, partially broken branches, some of them dripping bloody sap.

That's when she noticed the rustling, which was strange on a bloody tree that had absolutely no foliage whatsoever. Instead, she realized there was a book embedded into it. And its pages were what rustled in the wind.

She gulped once more and again wished she hadn't. There was the stench of blood in the air, of rotting corpses, and of rotting vegetation. It was cloying, and the taste lingered in her mouth like bile.

She had to keep it together, even though she could feel the color already draining out of her face. The pale and ghost-like wings that hung in tatters from the tree leaked very slight power, as if they'd almost been completely drained.

They weren't alive as such, as far as she could tell. It was an amalgamation of spirits that turned into one, that fueled the tree and the book. It had power in it, locked in place by the branches, as if perhaps at one stage, maybe it had been a wooden altar. Perhaps whoever was using the book didn't understand how.

"Well, Librarian, you haven't answered me yet." There was a hint of ego in that voice, of impatience, as if the tree honestly thought it was a person.

The shadowy figures behind them shouldn't have been able to exist. Quinn glanced around and observed through Aradie's own projected images into her mind. These shadows weren't people. They were extensions of the creature in front of them. Vaguely humanoid, sluggish movement. But everything the blood touched withered away. Quinn made a mental note that coming within their reach was probably a very bad idea.

Them. The tree. The fact that the book was horribly stained and obviously damaged. Not to mention the fact that the tree was also filled with rotting corpses.

Something inside Quinn snapped into place.

It was a sudden anger, a cold calm that suffused her entire body. She knew without a shadow of a doubt that she possessed the power to figure this out. To bring this whole fiasco here to a close. Confidence returned to her where she'd been nervous only moments earlier.

She faced the tree and put her hands on her hips, cocked her head to one side and said, "No."

Malakai tried to tap her arm but she pulled it away.

She glared at him and then she glared at the tree again for good measure. "I said no." Her voice was clearer this time, ringing out through the clearing. "We will not be staying a while. I have far too much to do to waste too much time here with you."

The tree rumbled. It was a low, guttural growl. Like it had also swallowed a tiger.

"What did you say?" its voice practically screeched.

An explosive silence settled over the clearing.

Even the shadow figures were shaking, which made Quinn even more positive they were an extension of the tree standing in front of her. With her senses, she could see that they did belong to it and yet didn't quite understand how. There were no roots sticking up to fuel them. They didn't have runic carvings or insignias engraved into them either.

At least not visibly.

It made her wonder if it was a form of telekinetic magic or perhaps . . .

That's when she noticed. In the center of the creatures was a group of leaves, bloody leaves, that gave them their core of power. Knowing the location should make them somewhat easier to destroy.

She hoped.

Quinn sighed again. The sound was very loud in the hostile copse. "We are needed elsewhere. Somewhere vastly more important. I am certain you're aware that You. Don't. Belong. Here." She clipped the last few words in that last sentence for impact because the tree was easily baited.

Rumbling started to shake the ground, like an earthquake, far beneath Quinn's feet. It moved up to reverberate through her entire body. Only the shielding she had around her managed to keep her completely safe. Even then, she almost lost her balance. The tree's voice mumbled, the loud, high-pitched screech portion of its voice now gone.

"I am a creature of chaos," it said. There was certainty in its voice, knowledge in what it was.

Quinn raised an eyebrow. "Are you *really?*" she asked. She had no clue where this newfound, deadly calm inside her had come from. This absolute knowledge and certainty that she was right and would be able to deal with what was in front of them. Because she could, because of who she was, what she was, and the fact that she could now draw on the Library's strength, on its knowledge, on its vast age and experience.

It lent her a confidence she'd never had back on Earth.

Unease rang through to her from the rumbling in the ground that slowly subsided. Finally, the tree spoke again.

"What did you say?" it asked, stumped.

If it had had a face that was visible, Quinn thought it would have been looking at her skeptically, confused. As it was, it was just a gnarly, bloody, twisted death tree.

"I said, are you *really* a creature of chaos? Because you kind of seem like more of a thing than a creature," she said.

Quinn wasn't entirely certain whether it was wise to be taunting a tree that had obviously massacred hundreds, if not thousands of people. And yet, here she was.

Perhaps it stemmed from wanting it to get so angry it made a mistake. Missteps could only be good for her and her companions, right?

Power began to swell all around them, reacting to what she'd said, reaching around her whole group. The shadow figures began to move again as the power swelled, filling them, reaching the core inside. They moved toward the group.

Quinn sighed. She'd really been hoping to avoid any type of

combat. Then again, it wasn't like talking to it would make it back off. It seemed quite set in its destructive path.

Aradie launched herself up into the air with a loud hoot. Quinn pushed her shielding outwards to encompass each and every member of her team, to lend them strength and make sure they weren't going to be harmed more than absolutely necessary. It wasn't something she'd been aware she could do even ten days ago. But now? Quinn realized that every book she absorbed was just a guideline, a sense of how to initiate something.

All she had to do was push the boundaries. She knew there had to be a catch, but for now she'd do what needed to be done and deal with the consequences later.

Her owl familiar dive-bombed one of the closest shadows, aiming directly for the bunch of leaves that made up its core in its chest. Only she discovered that there wasn't as much give in the walking shadows as they'd assumed. Aradie turned tail and darted back into the sky, getting ready for another attempt as Malakai readied his bow and began loosing arrows.

"Where am I aiming for?" he asked Quinn.

"They have a core, approximately where a human heart would be." Quinn pointed at her chest.

"I know where you guys have hearts," he muttered, but the arrows didn't appear to bite deep enough into the shadows. Malakai scowled, and a soft deep blue glow suffused him briefly. The next arrow bit deeper. She'd have to remember to ask about that later.

Quinn kept her focus on maintaining the shielding until it had completely surrounded each of their bodies in a fine layer of defense. She focused on the tree in front of her, pulling from books that she'd read, like *Mastering Your Reality Through Chaos: Mental Manipulation* and *Recognizing Mental Manipulation and Its Effects*.

Despite everything else, how the power felt that emanated from this tree, how it looked, the blood that seeped through every single portion of its being, the aura spoke of tortured souls, of barely conscious remnants of life that gave it blood power. This monstrosity must have pulled some sort of mind trick over its victims, over the people it sacrificed.

There was a deep chuckle from the tree. There was none of that chalk-on-a-blackboard sound from it anymore. No, when it spoke this time, it was with deep intonation.

Commanding.

Terrifying.

"You think you've figured me out," it said. The voice was deep and resonant. Nothing like the Serpensiril she'd encountered. None of that sibilance to it.

This . . . this was a voice Quinn had never heard before. Something was speaking to her through the tree as if through a medium.

"I see you understand the situation now."

Quinn raised an eyebrow and began to form an ice ball in her hands. She wasn't doing it to distract herself or calm herself. This time, she had a more offensive idea in mind.

"Tell me," she said, "who are you?"

"Ah, Miss Librarian, that would be giving it away, wouldn't it?"

"Well yes, that's why I asked you to tell me," she said, as if he was five years old.

There was a derisive snort from the tree, and it shook like it was laughing. Blood dripped down as it did so, plopping onto the ground with sounds that shouldn't have resounded through the clearing but did.

Shadows leaked from its branches in vague shapes that resembled the Esposians as they had been in life. The shadow bodies slowly filled with blood, overflowing to the extent that it dripped from their wings and their fingers.

Geneva looked pale, but being as resilient as she could, she too was attacking the shadows all around them. The corpse-like blood dolls of the Esposians and the tree, they were all focused on Quinn.

"What do you want?" she asked, making the ball in her hands rounder and rounder and larger and larger, until it was almost the size of a basketball.

"I want you to disappear," the tree's new voice said.

Quinn was certain that this voice was a projection. She wanted to know more about voice and presence projection, she was certain there were books on that back at the Library.

"Get rid of me? Haven't heard that today yet, but the whole concept is getting old," she said. "So how were you going to do that? Got a villain monologue for me?"

The tree practically roared at her. "Villain! We are no villains. It is you who seek to contain the true power of the universe, who seek to limit chaos. You are the misguided ones."

Quinn raised an eyebrow, still gathering power. "Guess I hit a sore spot, eh?"

Three of the shadow people around them had already fallen, Aradie used an ability Quinn didn't understand; it was almost as if she had laser eyes. She was going to sit down and have a talk with that owl, one of these days, in all of that spare time she seemed to have.

"You located their weak point?" Even the possessing voice held incredulity.

Quinn paused and smiled. "What, like it was hard?"

There was a guttural roar from the tree, a mixture of whatever was channeling through it and the tree itself.

"See, I knew you weren't really a creature. You're just a puppet, aren't you?" Quinn said, taunting the thing even more than she had before.

She went on autopilot as the tree lashed out and shadows and blood-puppets attacked. She knew the other three could handle themselves, but still spared a glance as she watched Malakai cleave one of them in two with his sword, favoring it over his bow for the close-quarters contact.

Aradie dive-bombed and shot out her laser ability, clearing some of the way for Geneva to finish them off by piercing them through the heart with surprisingly accurate throwing stars.

Quinn, on the other hand, raised her arm and threw the solid ball of ice to float up into the air.

Meanwhile, she tackled the puppets the tree sent out for her. The remnants of the Esposians, who were already dead, long gone. It still saddened her to have to blast them away with ice and water. The latter of which was very effective at diluting the blood and dissipating the entire corpse puppet.

She didn't feel any exhilaration, only sadness underneath the anger at the sheer audacity to have sacrificed so many lives like that. And for what? Power?

The more of them came at her, the more she realized just how many had been sacrificed to create the tree. And the thing was too busy flinging out puppets at her that she hadn't gotten a definitive answer as to why.

And no villain monologue, either.

At least that could have been nicely enlightening.

But with each puppet she dissipated, with each one that she destroyed, the tree grew lesser. It had less power, less presence, less clout.

And then, just as the branches holding the book began to lose cohesion, she allowed the ice ball to drop. It cast blizzard over the entire trunk, freezing it solid in one go. The tree couldn't move. The last remaining blood puppets splashed to the ground, only to be frozen as the liquid rebounded.

"You will pay for this," the terrifying voice said through the ice.

Quinn shrugged as she walked forward to begin delicately, gently, freeing the book from the frozen, dead branches. "You know, I don't think I'll be paying for anything."

Reaching up, Quinn had to stand on her tiptoes to reach where the book was resting and was only able to because it had shrunk significantly as it withered under the ice.

Just as she was about to touch the pages, Malakai called out. "Don't touch it with your bare hands!"

Quinn paused and looked back, frowning. He made sense. Why hadn't she thought to protect herself? After all the crap they'd just gone through to cleanse the Library from the infection of chaos sludge, she'd almost potentially contaminated herself.

She examined her train of thought, finding a fog there she hadn't noticed. Perhaps the puppet master had an effect on her after all. Next set of books she needed to absorb were going to be all about possession.

They were probably in the restricted vault.

Quinn concentrated for a second, sheathing herself completely in a layer of shielding. "Thanks. Should be safe now."

Malakai nodded, a frown on his face, like he still wanted to keep her from danger.

Boosting herself up with a bit of earth manipulation, Quinn went about the delicate task of extracting the book from the evil tree.

4 8

MORE THAN ORDINARY

QUINN UNMADE THE SLIVERS OF ICE WHERE THEY TOUCHED THE BOOK, still embedded halfway into the foul tree. The blizzard she'd used was of such a high caliber that it had frozen everything. And while she'd tried her best to direct the frigid spell, she'd still managed to encase some of the book.

The whole tree-creature itself was frozen solid, right down to the blood oozing from it. The entire trunk and all the bark. The twisted, dead tree with all of the half-devoured body parts was in stasis.

No voice emanated from it now.

Not a breath.

Not even a trickle of power.

Quinn liked ice. Knowing in detail how to create ice also allowed her to unmake it. Doing so while attempting to extract the book enough so she could even identify it was a very arduous process. She wasn't entirely sure what Malakai was up to, but Aradie had perched on one of the outer circle trees and was keeping a watchful eye over everything.

Geneva went to scout out the once large village to see if she could uncover any survivors at all. That, and perhaps the remnants of the

418

bloody puppets and the bits of body hanging out of the tree itself, might have been a little bit overwhelming for the Furionas.

"You need to be careful with that," Malakai said.

Quinn raised an eyebrow but didn't bother to turn around. "Oh no, I was planning on diving in blindly. Thank you so much for saving me," she deadpanned.

Malakai laughed. "Well, you almost sort of did."

"Touché," Quinn said.

Finally, after leveraging and freeing the book from its last sheet of ice, Quinn managed, with shield-covered fingers lightly touching its magically dry pages, to inspect the book. The system brought up the identification in front of her. Quinn frowned at the results.

Machmüller's Theory of Dimensional Dissolution and Disintegration Through Ritual Sacrifice

Location: Error

Borrowing Rights: Error

Quinn blinked. "Well," she said to Malakai, sharing the information with him, "this book sounds just positively evil."

He grimaced. "Yeah, that's . . . why would we even have that in the restricted vault?"

Quinn shrugged. "I mean, technically, according to the inspection, it's not."

Malakai sighed and pulled out a cleansing bag from his inventory. He held it out to her. "Here, I brought some just in case. I tend to carry them with me all the time now. We never know when we might encounter a book that needs it. Hell, we can probably put the cookbook in one too, just to be safe."

He was right, there was no need to place the Library at needless risk when they could easily prevent it.

It took several more minutes to free the book completely. There were icicles stuck all around it and she had to not only break off the icicles, but break off parts of the tree that had attempted to intertwine themselves with the book. Quinn took the bag from him and inserted the book after gently removing it from its place. She sighed as she sealed the cleansing bag and popped it in her own inventory.

Geneva chose that moment to return. From the look on her face, the tears she'd rubbed away leaving dirt smudges on her cheeks, as well as the tears that streamed down her face, Quinn knew that there wasn't much good news she had to share with them.

"Did you find anyone?" Quinn asked.

Geneva nodded, but then shook her head. "I found three. Three households full of potential survivors. That's all out of almost nine hundred."

Quinn swallowed. "Oh, Geneva, I am so sorry."

Geneva sucked in a deep breath, nodded again. "Yes, I have to go and fetch some healers."

"I can heal," Malakai said. "Take me to them or bring them to me."

But Geneva shook her head. "It's not that sort of healing. All fae require more than ordinary care. Our physiology is very specific when it comes to healing, and our souls are deeply intertwined with our vascular system. Thank you for wanting to help, but I must get one of our doctors."

"You can use the Library to bring them here," Quinn said. "Give us just a moment to make sure this tree is done for and we won't unintentionally harm the Library by opening another doorway here."

With all of the items accounted for and the book safely stowed away, Quinn activated Blizzard again. This time, she dialed her power up, coating the tree even more, frosting it so much that it became brittle like a piece of freeze-dried fruit. Then she stopped and pulled back from it.

"Hey, Malakai, shatter the tree for me," she said.

He grinned. "As you wish."

The elf withdrew his sword and leveraged himself into a wind up. Power condensed in that deep blue form around both him and his sword, and he released all of that power in one massive strike, shattering the tree into thousands of tiny, icy, fragments.

Aradie followed up by lasering all the fragments into oblivion.

"Well, that's that. Let's get back. Make sure to bring them through the Library. It'll be a lot quicker." Quinn smiled.

Geneva's tears rained down her cheek again. She smiled at Quinn.

"Thank you. I might need . . . I might need a little bit of time off in order to get this all sorted. I'm so sorry."

Quinn shook her head. "Don't be sorry. Take the time you need; we'll figure it out. We have a lot more assistants now. Do we have everything we need?" Quinn asked, double checking that the book was in her inventory with her. She had everything she'd come with. She double-checked for the cookbook too. "Okay, are we missing anything else?"

Malakai shook his head. "I don't believe so."

Geneva shook her head and Aradie swooped down to sit on Quinn's shoulder. "Okay, well, let's just go back and use the tree we arrived here through."

It was very somber in the village as they jogged toward the tree. Quinn didn't want to waste any time, and she had to be certain that they could get back. She placed her palms on the tree and said, "Library, we need you."

GENEVA TOOK off immediately as soon as they entered the Library. Quinn could only hope the Furionas could make it back with the healers she needed in time. She'd given her permission to use the Library as a quasi-travelling system. It wasn't meant for that. If people used it like a bus terminal, then they'd be in all sorts of trouble and congested like peak-hour traffic. However, in a case like this, an emergency, Quinn thought they should be able to utilize the Library in a function that could save lives.

Back in the Library, Quinn, Malakai, and Aradie moved to the left-hand side of the massive check-in desk. They unpacked the two books from Quinn's inventory.

Lynx fussed over them. "This trip took a lot longer than I expected," he said, worry coloring his tone.

Quinn raised an eyebrow. "That's you and me both. I thought we were just dashing in, grabbing a cookbook, and coming back. Not stopping a people-sacrificing, blood-cult-magic-dimension tree thing."

"Wait. Tell me the whole story about this book?" Lynx asked as he looked over it as best he could with it still in the bag.

Quinn gave him a quick rundown, then sighed. "Speaking of this book, have you heard of it?"

"No," Lynx said, "but it is a Library book. It's stamped. I don't . . . I don't understand why it's throwing errors in the system."

"Because it's not a Library book?" Quinn asked, clinging to logic.

"No, but it is." Lynx gestured to the stamp on the spine that they could see through the window in the cleansing bag. "This is definitely a Library book. But it must exist in that glitch portion of our memory. Because while the system can read what it is, which it couldn't do if it wasn't in the system, it can't catalog it, which it should be able to do if it's part of the system."

Quinn's head spun ever so slightly. That was a lot of information to take in, even if, at the same time, it didn't answer anything. "Well, it's gotta be one of the ones that's missing out of the restricted vault, right? With a title like that?"

"Yes." Lynx nodded emphatically. "I'd say that's a very strong yes."

"And are we completely sure it's not on the list that we've got?" Malakai asked with tentative hope.

Quinn frowned as she went through the list of restricted books. "Nope, it's not here. How long has this one been gone?"

Lynx shrugged. "You're asking that like I don't have a glitching memory."

The Library chimed in as well. *It's stamped. It's our signature. But I have no recollection of ever having it, yet a distinct impression that I should.*

There were doors constantly opening in the Library. Quinn received copious notifications that they were being opened. She looked over the whole check-in desk area and frowned. She was about ninety percent sure that the desk had expanded. This made sense, because normal patrons came here to drop off their books, to check out their books, or to be fined occasionally, or try to weasel their way out of their fines, which it appeared a lot of people were starting to do.

As they stood there at the far side of the check-in counter, Quinn attempted to figure out the puzzle. Not only the fact that the Library was obviously functional enough to adapt to the volume of intake it was currently experiencing, but also that it had gaps in its memory data that were so huge they could fully forget a book.

Now this was a conundrum.

Malakai sighed. "I don't understand. It was so embedded in that damn tree, like it was trying to pull power from it."

"The tree or the book?" Quinn mused half to herself, but no one answered her.

"That's part of the restricted vault's charm, I guess," Lynx said, crossing his arms. "I mean, the books in there are powerful. There's a reason we needed a few of those books very specifically, because of the power they generate all by themselves. But in order to regenerate that power, they need to have been out in the world. And to have been being used, and thus replenishing their energy. The ones that just stay in the Library still generate power, but it's a low mana frequency, sort of like ambient mana."

Quinn nodded. "And when we first opened up, those three books I had to retrieve, they were the ones that the system flagged because it recognized that it was missing books from the vault, correct?"

"Yes, you were there."

Quinn took a deep breath. "Sometimes, Lynx, you use sarcasm wrong. This wasn't the place."

"Oh, teach me, great one." He grinned. "Sorry, I'll be serious. I think I'm nervous."

Quinn stopped and looked at the Library manifestation. "Have you not been nervous before?"

"Not like this." Lynx's eyes flickered briefly, as if to punctuate that he wasn't operating at optimum capacity.

"What's that doing there?" Eric asked, as he meandered over from supervising three assistants who were managing the check-in desk.

"What do you mean *that*?" Quinn asked, easily irritated right then.

"Oy, like, why is it out in the open? That book should be hidden away, never to leave the Library's restricted vault. Drop it in a cement block down a deep dark hole to hide it—that sort of concealment." Eric glared at them all. "That was the whole purpose of bringing it here in the first place."

Quinn blinked at Eric. Lynx followed suit.

"What do you mean? You know this book?" she asked.

But Eric continued as if he hadn't heard her, and it was obvious he wasn't joking. "Is that a cleansing bag it's in? Why—why does *Machmüller's Theory of Dimensional Dissolution and Disintegration Through Ritual Sacrifice* need cleansing right now?"

Quinn shrugged. "Because we just discovered it and found it in the middle of a ritual sacrifice and so we wanted to cleanse it before we put it back in the Library."

"Sorry?" Eric did a double-take. "Excuse me, what?"

"What do you mean?" Quinn was puzzled, and mildly annoyed at all the beating around the bush.

"It's one of the five-dimensional break books." Eric's wings flapped faster in annoyance before he tried to clarify himself further. "For universe dimensional maintenance, you know? It's restricted for a reason."

Eric looked at their blank stares. "That *DeKarlyle's Thesis of Spatial Distortion* is also one of those."

"Okay, so what? It's part of a set?" Quinn asked.

"Yeah, it's part of a set of five. I don't know the other names off the top of my head and I only know de DeKarlyle's because I know you guys brought that book back. Like, what's happening? These aren't books that should *ever* be taken out. That was part of the reason that my faction gave them to you. They're supposed to be kept safe in a Library." Eric was really getting worked up. His wings dripped brimstone onto the floor of the check-in area, he was so irate.

Lynx sighed. "Well, the Library was supposed to do a lot of things, but the last five hundred years have proven that that's not always possible."

"Sorry," Eric said. "I realize that some really screwed up stuff has happened to the Library. I get it. I'm angry on your behalf. I know how to figure out the names of the other books so you can check them. I'm starting to think maybe the other three are gone as well."

"Yeah, all signs point to that, don't they?" Quinn said. She was tired now. Everything was converging to make one huge mess.

"Okay," Eric said. "I'm going to flit away, grab that list, and bring it back."

"Can't you just, like, retrieve it?" Malakai asked.

"No, this is . . . the glitches are obviously neglecting to list all the books. And these ones are nasty shit," Eric said matter-of-factly. "Builds dimensional warp zones through ritual blood sacrifices and other unpleasant stuff."

"I mean, well, we stopped the ritual blood sacrifice," Quinn said.

"Did you? The book only needs to be part of it *while* a dimensional rift is forming. Not once it's fully realized. So you might have stopped this one, but that doesn't mean they didn't use the book to create others prior to this."

"Oh, great," Quinn said.

"Don't you worry, Librarian. I'll go visit my uncle and get that list of books. Maybe we can still lock onto the location if we know what it's called." Eric said. "You owe me. My uncle and I aren't on the best terms right now."

With that, the imp vanished.

Quinn blinked at where he'd been but seconds ago and sighed. Could everyone but her teleport?

She pulled the cookbook out and scanned it for infections, and then entered it in the system, feeling oddly anti-climactic that she now only had three books left to go.

After all, opening a culinary wing when there were probably *three* dimension destruction books floating around the universe that shouldn't be?

That just put a whole new spin on things.

4 9

—————

OUT OF SORTS

Geneva managed to retrieve the victims she'd found with the help of the Library and healers she'd brought with her from her own Dimension Gate 25 and that of the Esposian capital in Dimension Gate 24. The Furionas Fae was taking some time away from the Library to help tend them.

In the meantime, Quinn and Lynx spent the better part of the next day working on cleansing the restricted tome they'd retrieved.

Now that the Library had more power, they didn't have to rely solely on the cleansing bags, although they vastly contributed to transporting the book safely. Quinn eyed the next three books on her culinary list. It felt oddly anticlimactic to be even marginally focusing on opening the culinary wing when she knew that some of the rogue restricted vault books that were running around out there were more dangerous than she'd ever anticipated. Although, considering they were in the restricted vault to begin with, it really shouldn't have come as much of a surprise to her.

They *were* restricted for a reason.

That's when Lynx piped up. "*Making the Most on the Road: A Field Cook's Guide to Culinary Reinforcement.* That's probably going to be the one that's easiest for you to get to next," he said. He was perched on her couch in her office, curled up almost like a cat, except he was in his human body. "It's in a friendly quadrant on the homeworld of old allies who haven't died out."

"Are you spying on the information I'm pulling up yet again?" Quinn asked.

Lynx shrugged. "Hard not to when you're using one of the main systems I'm attached to. And I'm a little bored."

Quinn checked her storage, frowning. She hadn't forgotten anything. Then why did she feel so out of sorts? She'd eaten her food when she was meant to, she'd taken her supplements, and she'd unloaded any books she had to. But something was playing on her mind. It was tugging at her, pulling at her consciousness. She frowned at the information Lynx shared with her. "That book does seem easy. Are these the right coordinates you've sent me?"

"Yes," Lynx answered. "I didn't think it would be a good idea to send you the wrong coordinates just for a joke."

"Wow, you are really testy today," Quinn said. "But this isn't *too* easy, you think? I mean, didn't we think the last one would be easy, too?"

Lynx paused and frowned. "We didn't think it would be too easy. I mean, you had to learn to fly or you wouldn't have been able to access the island. There were things we had to get done in order to retrieve it."

Still, Quinn mused, "What if this one is also like hidden-evil-cult-revealed Easy?"

Lynx paused. "Well, I mean, unlikely that that's going to happen twice, right?"

"How do we know that the culinary books don't attract the restricted vault books?" Quinn said, on a whim, putting it out there, even though it was wildly unlikely. She also conveniently ignored that Lynx had just placed a major jinx on them.

His eyes grew distant for a moment. Quinn quickly searched for something to balance on his head and realized how much effort it would take for her to pick it up, walk over and place it there anyway.

By the time she'd gone through that train of thought, he was already back with her.

"I highly doubt they're linked," he said. "But do you feel that?"

"Feel what?" Quinn started and paused, reaching out her senses. No, it was there, just a flash. Something subtle and soft, with an ominous tone, with a hint of desperation behind it, as if it was trying to seep through the floor and reach up at something. And then it was gone.

Quinn frowned. "That was really odd, right? Is the gloom coming back?" she asked.

Lynx shook his head. "No, that's not how gloom feels. And it's not something connected to the parts of me that I can't seem to access properly. It's separate."

"Well, that's a small blessing, right?" Quinn asked.

"Maybe," he said, contemplative.

"Anyway," Quinn said, determined to change the subject, "shouldn't Eric be back by now?"

She was starting to get worried. He'd been gone since they came back the previous day, determined to get the list of books from his uncle. But Lynx shook his head.

"No. It is a really, I would call it, complex trip to get back to Halschius. He will probably be back soon. But this isn't late yet."

Quinn nodded. "Okay, I just . . . I found it worrisome. We have doors to everywhere. I didn't think it would take him long."

"Yes, but Halschius only has three possible doors. And the place is massive," Lynx explained.

"Wait." Quinn tried to make sense of his words. "Why does it only have three openings?"

Lynx cocked his head to one side, as if he was trying to figure out just how descriptive he should be. "Let's just say there are only three surfaces in the entire area that can accommodate a door."

"Seriously? Three surfaces? That's it?" It sounded highly implausible to Quinn

"Yes. Brimstone is one of the few substances that the Library cannot automatically turn into a door. Thus, there are simply a few areas that were specifically modified so that the Library could appear in Halschius once we had, I guess you could say, rescued them."

Quinn couldn't help the slight feeling of panic that she felt. She'd genuinely grown fond of Eric. "How did that even happen? Like, it says since time immemorial, and is that since the beginning of time?"

"Technically," Lynx responded. "It's time immeasurable."

Quinn glared at him. "So the imps have known the Librarian since the Library's inception."

"Yes, since before there was a Librarian, actually," Lynx said and paused for a second before adding. "The Library, back then, saved the imps from a fate worse than death due to the rampaging of chaos."

"The Library is an entity," Quinn stated.

"Yes," Lynx said, even though he really didn't have to.

"And thus, wouldn't the ruler of Halschius also be such an entity?" Quinn said.

Lynx just grinned at her. "My, my, Quinn, you're starting to ask the right questions."

"Oh really? Thanks. Do I get a cookie?" Quinn scowled momentarily and then sighed. "You guys could just tell me."

"Now, where would the fun in that be?" Lynx grinned this time.

"I'm pretty sure. I'm gonna make my guess soon, and it's gonna be right."

Lynx laughed. "Well, the odds of that are very high, because I think you already know."

Quinn laughed, because she was pretty sure she already knew. With all the hints, and with the actual name-dropping that had happened when she was synchronizing with the Core, she was moderately confident in her guess. It was exciting, and yet, considering how she'd been created, mildly terrifying to accept as fact. But she'd get through it, she always did.

She cleared her throat. "Anyway, when Eric gets back, maybe we can track the rest of these books down. You know, the bad ones."

Lynx sighed. "Well, that's the plan, you know, because . . ."

But Lynx didn't get any further.

A very faint pulse echoed under the floor again as they were speaking, stopping them both in their tracks.

"Okay," Quinn murmured. "This time I really felt that."

She closed her eyes and felt out toward the Library. She could sense the return desk, her quarters, the quarters of her assistants, the Library in general, which had about forty-five patrons in it right now and two dozen staff and golems. The book infirmary was going really well with Narilin and her cousin. In the kitchen, Cook was busy preparing a feast of some sort. Even Farrow and her bookworms were fine.

Another pulse spread beneath her feet.

It was coming from the jail.

"Where's Milaro?" Quinn asked, forgetting about the culinary books for now. Retrieving any of those books and opening other branches of the Library wasn't going to mean anything if they didn't have somewhere to come back to. "Something's wrong with the jail."

"Yeah," Lynx said, pushing himself up. "I've got that much too."

She could feel the defenses bowing, being stretched, even with three guardians buffering it with all their strength. There was a level of alarm in the presence of the golems, but they hadn't alerted Quinn or Lynx or the Library yet. They were trying to manage whatever this was themselves because that was the way of the guardians.

Quinn moved around her desk toward the door.

"We need to get Milaro. Send for him," she said as she pulled a shortsword out of her inventory and strapped it on. She couldn't afford to be ill prepared despite how rusty she was with a weapon. The foreboding about the situation crept up her spine, spreading out to engulf her.

"You can do it too, Quinn. Send out a distress call. The more he gets the better," Lynx snapped, morphing immediately into his lynx form . . . and then he was gone.

She knew where he'd gone. "Misha," she called. "Meet me in the jail with Finn and the aracnio brothers. Check on the guards!"

Quinn doubled down on the distress message that she sent out to Milaro, hoping that the power boost she herself had was enough to reach him. All the while, she was dashing out of her door with Aradie in close pursuit, heading straight towards the jail, which was only twenty feet away.

Quinn dashed into the antechamber. She wasn't sure what she was expecting, but she didn't expect to see Uno in the antechamber, straining against the glass, his hands up against it as he funneled power through to the other side. Or perhaps he was protecting what was on the other side from coming through.

Something shook against her mental barriers, against her connection to the Library. It was hot, searingly so, but empty and dangerous. She gasped for air suddenly, stumbling against the wall. Uno didn't have time or the ability to support her, and Aradie squawked, pulling her up by the leather strap that she usually sat on.

Quinn waved the owl away. There was nothing visible through the glass. Two-way or not, right now, it wasn't working. Quinn grabbed at the door and yanked it open. Finally, the pressure against her connection to the Library burst, freeing her up as she stumbled through the door, her equilibrium momentarily gone.

The pressure around her head gave way too, and even before she could regain her balance, Quinn knew what had happened.

She looked upon the interrogation room. There were no longer sections separated by barely discernible smoke walls like they had been when she'd visited with Milaro.

The dry ice effect was gone, and in front of her stood Tenejo, his eyes a fiery red. His expression was vacant, and yet, at the same time, not completely devoid of a soul. It was so loud she could practically hear it in her mind. The way his pain screamed out. It was obvious his soul was damaged.

Tenejo was no longer on his couch or in his bed or even near his part of the room. Instead, he stood within the area Narajo had occupied. It was difficult to discern the area now because it was covered in blood that had a strange greenish-red hue.

Quinn gulped and wished she hadn't because she swallowed some of the smell along with it. There was an underlying sulfur scent to it all. She glanced around, unable to see Lynx. Surely, he'd come here.

Tenejo's eyes weren't focused on anything, anything but the wall just beyond him, just beyond the dismembered corpse of his once friend. Although, from the memories she dove into, Quinn realized Narajo had always thought of Tenejo as his friend, not necessarily the reverse.

The Serpensiril stood, like he was frozen in place. In his hand he held a club, but no, on closer inspection it wasn't one. Quinn gagged at the sight. It was Narajo's arm. Hanging listlessly by Tenejo's side, flesh strands visible where it had once been attached to a body.

It was oddly disconcerting, with Tenejo's blank expression, blood caking the robe he was wearing, and Narajo's lifeless, torn-apart body strewn all throughout the room. Quinn gulped again, and Lynx was finally there. He threw something onto the ground in front of Tenejo, which woke the Serpensiril up.

Quinn didn't think that was a very good idea.

Anger flashed in Tenejo's eyes as Lynx threw a second one down and a third in quick succession. Tenejo began to move, but Lynx muttered under his breath, "Imprison."

A strange set of barriers popped up in between the three discs he'd thrown onto the ground, rendering Tenejo immediately immobile. It would have been comical if it wasn't so gory, in a way. Tenejo froze with his weapon, or Narajo's arm to be more precise, hefted like a bat. And that's when Quinn noticed that Dale was crushed up against the back wall of Narajo's cell, crushed into the rock.

"Dale?" she said. There was only a weak pulse of power from his direction. Misha appeared beside her with two golems Quinn hadn't seen before.

"These will repair him," the supervisory golem said solemnly.

"You made repair golems?" Quinn said.

"Only recently. You have been busy. You said I could," Misha said somewhat defensively.

"I know, I'm not upset." Quinn nodded. She was so relieved Misha had the foresight to create these. The naming would have to wait. "Will he be okay?"

Misha shook her head. "That is not something I can answer for you right now. I must assess the damage first. Uno, Fife, secure the perimeter. Lynx, please make sure that shield stays," Misha added.

"What about the other guard golems?" Quinn asked, knowing she'd mentioned them in her message.

"I have activated their production, but it will take a while." Misha said, her tone all businesslike.

And then Misha, Dale, and the two repair golems were gone. Quinn stared at Tenejo, still locked in his prison. She could see the way his pulse beat, and the muscles bulged at his neck. There was anger practically emanating off him, coursing through his system.

"He can hear us, can't he?" Quinn said.

Lynx nodded. "Oh, yes, he can hear every single word. He just can't move or speak right now."

"Good," Quinn said. "I think it's time we figured out what he's really doing here."

Milaro chose that moment to walk into the holding cell. He'd changed.

This time his robes were lined with golden fabric, and tied with an intricate sequence of golden ropes around the waist and draping down. His hair was slightly disheveled as if he'd been wearing a head-piece. Perhaps even a crown.

Quinn flashed him an apologetic smile. "Sorry. We've mostly taken care of it."

But Milaro simply surveyed the room, a hint of sadness on his face when he saw Narajo's corpse. "Ah," he said. "I shouldn't have been so lax."

Quinn shrugged as she watched the way Tenejo's eyes tracked Milaro's every breath. There was a new emotion in his eyes, some-thing fanatical.

Like he'd just seen all of his fantasies come to life.

Something occurred to her that she hadn't thought of before. Tenejo had ample opportunity to hurt her at all other times, and he hadn't done so. He was obviously capable of it too, considering what he'd done to Narajo.

Breaking through his restrictions and beating his own friend to death was something that would always trigger Quinn calling Milaro for help because she trusted him around mental magic. Milaro was her mentor. "Don't blame yourself. In fact, you need to leave now. Go back to the audience or whatever that you just left."

Quinn grabbed him by the hand and dragged him out of the room just as Tenejo's shield began to quake again. "Keep it locked down, Lynx!" she called out behind her, hoping that with the two remaining guardians, they'd have enough magical energy to tide them over until more could make their way.

"What do you mean? You summoned me!" Milaro sounded quite out of sorts, but Quinn dragged him to the double doors anyway before answering.

"You have to go. He's not after me, or the Library right now. Tenejo's target is—"

A massive blast echoed from the holding cells.

"Go now!" Quinn pushed him to the door, directing the Library to get him out of here. "We'll deal with this."

And even as the destination swallowed Milaro up, Quinn felt calm. She'd pushed him to safety, and now . . . now she was going to go and get to the bottom of why the Serpensiril had sent someone to harm Milaro.

As she walked back to the cells, she summoned a blizzard ball.

She was the Librarian, and there was no way she was going to let anyone hurt her Library again.

50

ALL THE SKILLS

The barrier around Tenejo practically vibrated with the force of power it took to keep the Serpensiril contained. Quinn watched as the guardians and Lynx fought to keep it under control, even as Milaro disappeared. She couldn't believe she'd been so dense. She hadn't realized who Tenejo was targeting.

As the first Librarian in hundreds of years, after obvious, explicit care was taken to get rid of every single Library affinity, she'd simply assumed, completely and utterly selfishly, that she was the target of any shenanigans that popped up. It made sense that they'd want to get rid of her, but it just wasn't the case.

Milaro had been teaching her everything. He was the one who gave her the tools to imprison that mind bomb. And he'd eventually been the one to take it out completely. There was no way they'd want him to keep teaching her.

She shook her head.

"Lynx, are you able to hold this in place?" she asked, pushing the useless anger she felt at herself for not moving the prisoners sooner aside.

"Yes." He ground out the word, but she could tell that he was pouring a lot of his own power, as well as that of the Library's, into maintaining the shield. "Not sure for how long."

She looked at Tenejo, squinting her eyes, getting that strange mana and magic sense that she had gotten once she'd synchronized with the Library again. Tenejo's life force seemed to be burning. That wasn't just an aura. It wasn't magic. It was a force tied to his very soul.

And it was angry at everyone and everything who railed against him and how he perceived the world should be.

As to why they'd been targeting Milaro, Quinn could only assume it was related to his mentoring of her, and perhaps because of this council he belonged to that she knew ridiculously little about. She knew so little about the people who engineered her existence, who had brought her into her world, into this universe. All she knew was that they were there to aid the Library, that it had been their last-ditch effort to save it, and Milaro was one of the reasons she existed.

The thing was, that council seemed largely secret. So she had to assume the mind-bomb subduing probably played a larger role.

Except she hadn't noticed that he was the target soon enough and she'd almost got him killed. By summoning him, she'd put him in such danger, and perhaps a lot of others. She didn't even know how far the elf kingdom spanned, or what his council's duties and responsibilities were, and how far they reached in the universe. She had no idea who and what could be impacted if Milaro was killed.

From the way that Tenejo's expression spread in a nasty snarl from inside the barrier, she was quite certain he knew everything there was to know about Milaro, and how much damage taking him out could potentially do.

The barrier continued to quake ever so slightly, and a crack appeared up the side. Quinn watched as Finn and Dottie all dashed into the room, lending their strength behind Uno, Fife, and Lynx to help bolster the barrier's strength. Jim and Bob, the aracnio brothers lingered just outside of the room for several seconds.

Quinn frowned and was about to say something when they finally entered, positioning themselves in the least dangerous areas, as far from Tenejo as possible. She got that—the fear. She'd have to make time to talk to them later.

Quinn, in the meantime, was trying to rack her brains to figure out what powers she had that she could use against the Serpensiril spy, or whatever he was. It wasn't like they'd ever trusted him or that he'd infiltrated. No, at most they'd just kept him at bay. Tenejo radiated power, even from behind the magic screens. There was no way it could just be *his* lifeforce fueling him, he should have begun to crumble by now.

"Lynx!" Quinn called out over the din in the room, the air thick with the power being exuded from every corner. "Where is he pulling that power from?"

"I don't know, Quinn," he replied, his voice strained. "Maybe he's being fueled by an artifact. I don't know everything. We've established the Library is not a god."

Quinn wanted to laugh, but the situation didn't warrant it. She wanted to smack him over the head for making light of it. "Do we have any more powerful containment fields, anything like that?" she asked, desperation creeping into her voice.

But Lynx shook his head. "Nothing. There is literally nothing in the storage room, your office, or anywhere else in the library that will pull off what we're currently doing. This is the last one, and I think it's about to break, so . . ."

Power leapt from Tenejo through the hairline crack in the barrier and out to Lynx. It hit the Library manifestation square in the forehead, and for a moment he just looked like he'd been stunned. But whatever Lynx was about to say next was cut off when he fell to the ground, writhing in what appeared to be pain.

He changed through so many different bodily forms, from the lynx to something that looked like a whale. Massive, so big it crushed the only desk in there, to something that looked like a ferret, back down to a tiny bird lying there on its back, before transferring yet again back into his lynx form and collapsing on the churned-up floor.

The others fueled more power into the barrier, briefly closing the gap that had been made by the crack. She could feel the strain of power from where she stood and still didn't understand how Tenejo had suddenly pulled out of the trance Milaro had kept him in.

How had Lynx been hurt? Wasn't he a manifestation? Was he broken now?

Not broken . . .

Even the Library sounded strained right then.

Quinn pushed down the surge of dread that ran through her at the sight of Tenejo practically free despite being confined in the barrier. His arm was still upraised, pointing at where Lynx had stood. The other still held his former friend's arm like a baseball bat, dangling at his side.

There was a feverish fanaticism in his eyes as he watched every move Quinn made even while it somehow never left Lynx. A strange, snarl-like grin began to spread over his nasty face.

Tenejo pointed at Lynx. "Weak Lynx," he said, cackling like a witch.

He couldn't stop, he laughed so hard he ended up falling to the ground within the barrier, which shouldn't have been possible because he shouldn't have been able to move, which meant they weren't funneling enough power through to it to keep him in a stasis.

Just where was Tenejo getting so much power from? And where had Jim and Bob run off to? She couldn't see them at all anymore.

That couldn't be her first concern, could it? Losing her cool in the midst of a crisis wasn't conducive to solving anything.

Quinn took a deep breath and recalled the magic in *Conquering Fear and Other Maladies*. This was her magic, something she could literally say was mind over matter. Compartmentalization at its finest. She took every single emotion that wasn't analytical, logical, or a fight instinct, and crammed it away, separating herself from fear and other debilitating, pesky emotions.

Immediately, every useless thought in her head stopped and she was able to view things clearly. It allowed her to view her own abilities within the slowed-down time constraints of her mind, to figure out a plan of action.

Detailed Serpensiril Anatomy allowed her to understand how to stop his mana flow, but just because she understood it didn't necessarily mean that she was going to be able to execute it.

At least not tidily.

There were points she could hit that would temporarily disable Tenejo's access to his own mana, which she could easily access with an icy blast.

Quinn pushed down the surge of dread that tried to force its way out of the compartment she'd so neatly sorted it into. She felt the sheer fanaticism in his eyes, his will to wipe out everybody. She could practically feel him trying to scream it into her head. But her newly calmed mind analyzed all the skills she'd learned, all the power she'd gained, and all the stubbornness she'd inherited.

She'd be damned before she was going to let these Serpensiril bastards take over her home.

Her mind raced through all of her different abilities. Everything. Her gravitational abilities, her combat ice, combat air magic, combat water magic, ice and liquid, freezing things until they were so brittle they burst. Everything that she had absorbed in order to become stronger and be able to stand on her own two feet and fight for the Library and for herself.

Quinn opened her eyes mere seconds after she'd initially begun concentrating, thankful for the assistance Milaro had given her in this regard. She looked directly at their prisoner, who clearly thought he wouldn't remain one for much longer. But suddenly she didn't mind so much anymore.

With a thought, she cast a dense version of her shielding over herself, one of the very first spells she'd ever learned. Then she began to summon her ice balls. She liked ice. It felt just dangerous enough and yet easier to handle than fire, in a way that meant she rarely accidentally hurt herself.

Even if it had become increasingly more difficult to manipulate ever since the synchronization.

More cracks began to appear in the barrier and Lynx remained passed out on the floor, his Library manifestation form flickering in and out from what it should be. She reinforced every single portion of her mind with the copious amounts of mental fortitude powers she'd absorbed.

There were still so many books to devour in the Library, and she needed everyone to be alive for that to happen.

She began to spin the ball in her hand, much like the vortex mind bomb had begun spinning in her head when she and Milaro discovered it.

Upon seeing the ice ball in her hand, there was a flash of hesitation in Tenejo's eyes. Just that split second was all Quinn needed to know. While he was fanatically obsessed with his cause, with the notion that chaos would only consume the weak, he still had a sense of self-preservation. While he was hell-bent on making them pay for withholding chaos from the world, there was still a massive streak of selfishness that she could rely on.

Tenejo thought himself above all others who were not the higher-ups of his species.

He was narcissism in snakeskin.

Quinn applied gravitational force to the shielding around the Serpensiril prisoner. In theory, she simply wanted to apply pressure and collapse the shield in on itself. But with the boost from her synchronization with the Library—and the fact that she'd never actually attempted to do something like this in practice, only ever contemplated it as theory—meant that she accidentally crushed the barrier so badly it exploded inwards, shards of it ripping into their prisoner.

"Oh no," Quinn said, "What have I done?"

The deadpan voice made even Dottie snicker, despite the amount of power backlash Quinn accidentally caused. It allowed, however, the other assistants and the guardians to be freed up.

She called out to Uno, "Fetch Lynx, figure out how to help him."

She focused her blizzard, separating it into six different tennis-ball-sized spheres to float above and around and follow Tenejo's every movement. The movement pattern was executed with a simple thought. Quinn was surprisingly happy with the results.

Tenejo was still picking shards of barrier out of his body, rage simmering in his eyes. Quinn backhanded him with a gust of air into the nearest wall where Dale had been crushed but a quarter of an hour before. Quinn's mind, still freed from all those pesky cares and emotions that interfered with everything, clinically examined the room. Even with the power and force of the barrier shattering, the entire Library room didn't look like it had gained a scratch.

Well, except for the wall Dale had hit.

The Library could do more than just morph rooms. It could repair itself too. Perhaps it just hadn't got to that one yet.

Blood dripped down the gashes on Tenejo's body, and he began to cast.

Quinn cocked her head to one side, assessing the blood loss. It was a fair amount, but he wasn't about to bleed out. She reached out with her hand and made a fist, activating the six ice-blast balls. Every single ball shot arrows of ice into Tenejo. On impact, they spread out, sealing him in place in an ice block, leaving only his neck and head above it. Something cracked, quite loudly, followed by a muffled scream from Tenejo.

Quinn watched him, completely detached from the fact that she was fairly certain she'd broken some vertebrae or extremities.

"I don't think you should be moving," she said in a tone devoid of any warmth. It was almost like she was outside of her own body, watching herself do this, watching a movie of someone else acting out this scene.

"I will get out of this. You will pay, Librarian. We will find our prey." He snarled at her, bloody spittle foaming at his lips.

She frowned, knowing she should probably be concerned about the fact that Tenejo was spitting blood but it just wasn't her priority. "And just what do you want from Milaro?" she asked.

"He is the downfall of everything. He has interfered in our plans for the last time." This time, there was pain in Tenejo's words, though he tried valiantly to hide them.

"No," Quinn cut him off. "I don't think Milaro's interfered for the last time in anybody's plans. You obviously don't know the man. He's rather bullheaded. You, however, you have proved sort of useless, did you know that?"

There was an odd tick to Tenejo's eye as he glared at her.

"No, really, you haven't given us one scrap of anything. I don't know that we should keep you around." She could feel the ice both covering him, and inside her. There was a cold and calculating part that was easy to cling to. The ice block he found himself in could very well become a tomb, or place him in semi-permanent hibernation.

Or else, if she just made it one whole, dense ice block, it would crush him into it. It wouldn't be too hard, and then he'd be out of their hair. Then he couldn't harm any of the people around her ever again.

"Uh, Quinn?"

Dottie's voice was very soft outside of Quinn's mental echo chamber.

"Quinn!"

Again, she recognized that voice. Wasn't that Dottie?

A split second later, Eric hovered right in front of her face. He snapped his fingers loudly, almost like a gong reverberating through her head.

Quinn snapped out of it. She blinked twice and came back from the cold, desolate, unfeeling headspace she'd found herself in and took in the wrecked holding cell. Flashes of what occurred fed back into her, from Aradie.

Quinn blanched.

All she'd wanted to do was free her headspace, and work quick enough to save people. She'd never meant to be cruel. She'd just wanted to stop him from hurting more people she cared about.

"Oh, sorry," she said, as her body started to shiver. And she wasn't talking to Tenejo. She didn't care about him. It was the rest of them. "I'm so sorry."

51

DELIBERATE CHOICES

Pulling herself back from that strange mental space took a lot more effort than Quinn expected. It also meant that people talking to her from outside of the bubble that was her current state of mind sounded distant and echoey, despite how close they might be to her.

"Quinn."

She blinked, slowly turning her head to see Eric.

He hovered very close to her, concern in his fiery eyes. "You're pulling on more power than you have before. You only need separate so much of your mind, so that the power drain doesn't overwhelm you."

She blinked at Eric. "Yes, I think," she muttered slowly, her head still quite caught up in a lack of emotion. More logic and more concentration. It was a heady feeling.

"It's okay, Quinn," Dottie said.

Quinn blinked again, still caught up in that maelstrom of focus. "I know," she said in that distant voice before turning her attention back to their prisoner.

Quinn looked at Tenejo, who was almost entombed in ice. The voices of Eric and Dottie faded into the background again and she held up a hand, hoping they'd realize she needed to concentrate fully.

Even though she knew the sound was them, something else throbbed through her link to the ice block. Perhaps it was Tenejo, with whom she had direct contact through the ice spell. The sensation running through the connection to her was pain.

And then she realized the ice block was slowly constricting, getting tighter and tighter around the Serpensiril. They couldn't have that. They needed to figure out his memories. Find where the trap was, find why he was here. For all the trouble he'd caused, there had to be something they could learn. She stopped the constriction with a thought.

So much knowledge ran through her head so fast that it was a marvel she could keep up with it. But considering all the books she'd absorbed and consumed, the information was now piling high in her head. She could sort it all in the blink of an eye. All while she felt like she was watching herself and the entire room from outside of her body.

And all the while, it drained her energy to do so.

And all the while, she felt like she was burning up from the inside.

The information on the Serpensiril and anatomy entered her mind. The way their blood flowed, the different areas of their brain, and which ones governed what actions, especially that of consciousness. Quinn accessed it all in a split second, held out her hand, utilizing several of the mind techniques that she had garnered from the books she'd absorbed at once and spoke one word.

"Slumber," she intoned. She didn't just speak it. It resonated throughout her own mind and the room, literally causing it to tremor.

Quinn smiled.

Tenejo's eyes briefly widened before closing, and his head lolled to one side. She watched as he slept. Or, probably more accurate, as his consciousness was taken away from him. That was the perfect example of all the information she'd absorbed coming together at the one specific moment where she needed it all to work out in their favor. And it had.

Except, shouldn't she have been able to do that earlier? Shouldn't this have been accessible to her in order to prevent Lynx from being hurt? Perhaps even prevent Dale from being smashed into a wall and needing emergency repairs?

Quinn frowned, slightly bothered, even in this state. If she could have just done that immediately, it would have saved so much time and so much hassle.

And that's when she heard, or maybe felt, Dottie pushing against her leg. She looked down at the bench.

"Quinn?" Dottie seemed concerned. And if she'd had the sort of face that could be read from up close, or, actually had a face, Quinn knew she would have been frowning with worry.

Finn was on the other side of her, dripping with sweat. The small Ilgonomur's brow was furrowed with worry and exertion. The aracnio twins were nowhere in sight. Quinn thought that decidedly odd.

Quinn realized all three had been fervently trying to keep the barrier up that Lynx had thrown up to house Tenejo and they were exhausted from it.

She focused on Finn's mouth, trying to discern the words.

"What did you do?" Finn asked.

"I . . ." Quinn started but blanked.

Eric took the opportunity to butt in. "Well, now you're acting like a Librarian. That was very Librarian-esque."

"Freezing him in ice and knocking him unconscious was very Librarian-esque?" Quinn asked, raising an eyebrow at him.

Eric shrugged. "Well, yes, scary Librarian-esque, but that's the stuff legends are made of."

Quinn cocked her head to one side. Librarians as legends sounded like an odd juxtaposition. She could feel herself coming back, the emotions slowly re-entering her headspace. But still, there was now a sort of divide that they weren't crossing. She knew they were there. She knew she could access them if she wanted to feel them. But right now, there was too much to do to let them flood her mind. It would have to wait.

Eric crossed his arms and stared at her. "You're not done yet, are you?" he said.

"I don't believe I am. I'm sorry, I was out of control a little before," she said, inclining her head. Recalling how she almost lost control just moments ago.

Eric shook his head. "No, you didn't hurt any of us, not even close. Tenejo posed a lot larger threat than any of us expected. You can't be sorry for protecting the Library and yourself. Without the Library, magic's likely to devour us all."

Quinn took that tidbit of information and decided she liked it. "So I'm a scary Librarian legend," she said.

Eric chuckled. "You're just starting to become a scary Librarian. Maybe not so much the legend yet."

Quinn raised an eyebrow. She still felt spacey, but oddly warm now. "Is Lynx?" She closed her eyes briefly, checking with the Library Core.

Lynx will be fine. He's less hurt than you assume.

Quinn sighed with relief. As long as Lynx was fine and he would be able to come back, Quinn could handle whatever she needed to do with Tenejo's memories right now. Taking a deep breath, she turned to the three. "I have to concentrate a bit now. Just . . . I'll be fine, I promise."

Finn frowned but nodded, and Eric flashed her a smile, while Dottie just remained close to her, as if trying to lend her strength through her presence alone.

Quinn ran through all of her abilities again, turning her back on the three who seemed quite concerned about her. Meanwhile, Finn moved and began cleaning up the mess caused by the incident. Only seconds passed before Quinn began to walk toward the ice-blocked Serpensiril with sudden clarity of mind.

All she had to do was extract the specific thoughts that they needed, right? Didn't they just need evidence about who all was involved in this huge conspiracy to sabotage the Library and drain the ever-living mana out of the universe, or whatever the plan was? Surely there had to be more to it than simply that?

They knew the Serpensiril were behind it. That wasn't news. What Quinn needed was proof that there were other species involved, and other planets, and other worlds. That's what they should have forced out of them the first time.

They'd been far too nice. They'd given so many chances. They tried to allow their prisoners some consideration, relaxation, and solitude. But all that got them was a murdered prisoner and the zealous friend who ripped him apart.

Tenejo had hurt Lynx, sought to destroy Milaro, and almost smashed Dale to pieces as well. Not to mention the amount of assassinations he'd already performed for Kajaro and his ilk for the Serpensiril agenda. He'd killed hundreds, maybe even thousands of his own species to eliminate opposition to Kajaro's plans.

This creature didn't deserve for them to treat him nicely if it could perhaps save billions, trillions, whatever the next denomination was, of people. None of that was acceptable. Maybe it was an excuse because she was sort of looking for one, but as far as excuses went, this one was at least clear.

None of his actions were acceptable. Tenejo had made a series of choices, each one as greedy as the last. He wasn't a sad, poor, brainwashed puppet. He was a vicious, ambitious, predatory creature who had consciously harmed others.

Being nice and kind had gotten them nowhere and no information. Quinn held up her hands on either side of Tenejo's temples, and she searched through his memories as if they were one of those old Rolodexes. Not like Milaro had done, simply gleaning his memories and being calm and cautious and kind in the process.

No, Quinn viewed each memory as if she was looking at panes of windows. This made it easy to disregard any non-applicable ones, any school-based ones, even assassinations. All of those didn't matter right now. She knew he'd killed so many people. What she was looking for was something that was out of place, something that he hadn't necessarily been supposed to know.

Because when it all came down to it, Tenejo was only one of Kajaro's puppets or chessboard pieces. It took a while in her mind to rifle through his thoughts, his memories. She wasn't ripping any of them out; she wasn't causing harm unnecessarily. She wasn't about to let herself become him.

But he would wake up with a splitting headache. That is, if he woke up again.

And that's when she found it. It was a different memory. It was one that was coveted and hidden with a sense of pride attached to it. She could always count on ambitious people, eavesdropping so they knew more than they were supposed to. This one reeked of opportunism. She could hear the others talking in the distance, compartmentalizing as she did, while she found the correct window to go into. Dottie was discussing with Eric and Finn what to do.

"I'm fine," Quinn said, not really focusing on the words she was saying, "but I need to concentrate and I need you all to be quiet."

Silence fell after that and Quinn dove into the memory.

Tenejo was hunkered down in a dark office with a light stick in his hand. He was leafing through papers in an office that he shouldn't be in. It wasn't Kajaro's office, because she'd already seen that in his previous memory scan that they'd done together, her and Milaro. No, this? This belonged to someone else. Not quite as high a rank as Kajaro, but very similar from the markings of opulence in it.

Quinn paused. This was a memory they were going to have to peruse and study because she didn't understand the runes on the papers. They didn't come properly into focus, and when they slipped in and out, her translation ability didn't appear to grasp anything. How could it be a language not even the Library knew?

Perhaps a code developed while the Library was temporarily out of commission?

All she could understand was the ecstatic glee that rose out of Tenejo's body, the emotion, the sheer giddiness at the fact that he had uncovered something he wasn't supposed to know. And yet, it was something he desired to know more than anything else.

Quinn had to wonder if Kajaro had placed the information here deliberately for his pawn to find, but it wasn't his office and so perhaps Kajaro didn't know that Tenejo was aware of this information. Not that Quinn was aware of it now. She still couldn't decipher this. She wondered how long it would take for them to decode it.

She was also concerned now as to why her translation ability wasn't functioning.

She plucked the memory and didn't tug it out gently. Tenejo wasn't worth being careful with. He didn't deserve her kindness. She kept it separately in her own mind, locked away in a vault of her making, to pass on to the core when she could. She wasn't taking chances with anything.

Tenejo's life had been a series of despicable, fanatically driven, deliberate choices. He could rot in hell for all she cared.

Finally free of his mind, she shook herself, allowing the segmented part full of emotions to slowly come back into alignment. Guilt nibbled on her heels, but she pushed it away. She couldn't afford that now. Plus, he didn't deserve her remorse. His mind was sticky and insidious, and spending so long in it already made her feel nauseous. She'd not been able to find even one redeemable feature.

She turned to the golems Uno and Fife, who'd returned. "You need to place him in stasis, keep him unconscious, and leave him like that. I don't care if he stays that way forever."

"As you command, Librarian," Uno said, his voice deep.

"I'm done," she said, surprised at how relieved she felt as she turned to the other three. "I've got what we need and I'm unsure what Milaro and the Library want to do with this creature now."

You can do whatever you want with him, Quinn.

"Great," she shot back at the Library. "Then I'm gonna leave that decision up to you because I've already done enough reprehensible things today. Plus, I need to figure out why my mind just went all separated and weird."

We probably need to have another talk.

"Yes, but I have a lot to do right now," Quinn said trying not to remember how long her list was. Books to retrieve, other books to locate. Then she remembered, and a genuine smile broke out on her face. "Eric! You're back! Talk to me. Tell me all about the books we were never supposed to let out of the Library."

5 2

EIGHT THOUSAND YEARS

Eric was uncharacteristically silent as he followed Quinn to her office. She could tell there was something on his mind, and her ability to read him had absolutely nothing to do with her connection to the Library. She'd always been able to read people pretty well, and wasn't completely lacking in common sense.

Her office felt cooler than normal, as if somebody had turned the air conditioning on. But that wasn't how the Library worked. It didn't have air conditioning; it just had magic. Which seemed to be much more environmentally friendly than freon.

She tossed a thought at the Library, emphasizing that she didn't like the cold, and almost immediately she could already feel the warmth starting to permeate the room. Nice. She glanced at her arm, noticing a tingle.

Those iridescent, golden-glowing blue scales briefly shimmered over her skin again. She'd not been paying enough attention while she'd attended to Kajaro to know if they'd popped up then. But . . . she was fairly certain this was her new normal. It came along with everything else since the synchronization.

Still, Quinn liked being able to do things with a thought, even if

450

that meant the occasional overlay of mana scales flared up over the skin of her arms and hands. She hadn't yet had the guts to use magic while she was naked in the bathroom, for fear that it lit up all over her body and it would freak her out ever so slightly.

But she was pretty certain the scales flared everywhere.

She flopped into her massive oversized desk chair and studied Eric for a few seconds, drumming her fingers on her desk while Aradie sat on the top of her chair and spammed Quinn with soothing and relaxing images. She sighed and waved her owl away, who indignantly went and sat on her perch, and then Quinn finally spoke.

"What?" she said to Eric. Because before anything else, he was going to need to get whatever was in his head off his chest, or they weren't going to get anywhere.

He paused, hesitant, hovering right in front of her. His wings still made that faint buzzing sound that Quinn found oddly soothing.

"You know, you can sit on the desk if you want to," she said, wondering if he ever got tired of being airborne.

He raised an eyebrow and cracked half a smile, which was much more like the Eric she knew, but it didn't take long for that brow to furrow again and the worry to leak out of him.

Quinn's patience, which wasn't the most legendary thing to begin with, was wearing thin. "Come on, Eric, just spill it."

He sighed, and then the words rushed out like he was trying not to second-guess himself. "You used compartmentalization to segment off your emotions back there, didn't you?"

"Well, yes," Quinn said, although she had no idea why he was stating the bleeding obvious. "There was no way I could have done what I needed to do while trying to feel everything I was feeling."

Eric closed his eyes a moment and fluttered down onto the desk, crossing his legs in front of her. She marveled that the two-and-a-half-foot imp could manage to seem so much larger than life. He had such a commanding presence, and she was mildly concerned that his brimstone-esque body wasn't burning a hole into her wooden desk.

Maybe she was just glad he wasn't.

"You need to be careful doing that. It can often backfire on you," he said softly. Gone was his usual joviality, in its place a seriousness he rarely exhibited.

Quinn raised an eyebrow this time. "Well, how so? I mean, I get it. It's not good to cut off emotions. I can't make myself into a sociopath. I'm not aiming to, either. I just needed to concentrate. And when I need to concentrate, I need to get rid of the distractions. And the emotions I experienced right then were a complete distraction. At least when I'm trying to access all the information I need in order to make it out the other side of a battle, I require focus. Right now, I don't know what I know well enough to simply command the information to come to the forefront. It's still a process for me, and with Tenejo as my opponent, I didn't have time to waste."

"Everything is easier and seems much more possible when you have no emotions to question or pause the actions you take, Quinn." Eric's gaze didn't leave her own. "Sometimes, it's just easier not to use them at all. And that can be very dangerous."

"You mean to say some people just don't amalgamate them again, they just keep them separate?" she asked, somewhat surprised. Why someone would want to live without emotions was a puzzle to her.

"You kept them separate, you didn't just kind of lock them away?" Eric asked.

Quinn nodded. "I didn't get rid of them, I just pushed them to the side so I could concentrate. You know, compartmentalization."

"That's more like separation, which is a very important distinction," Eric said. "Still, be cautious. It can be extremely dangerous to lock off your emotions like that. There are . . . I have horror stories I could tell you when we have time."

"Maybe one of these days, you can tell me." Quinn smiled. She liked horror stories if they weren't about things that had almost killed her and others she cared about. "But I promise, I'm not going to get rid of my emotions. That would make life so colorless and dull. Ever so bland."

"Really?" he asked, his eyebrow rising up in surprise.

"Yes, really. Half the fun of any experience I have with others is feeling. Feeling the happiness, the frustration, the sadness, the glee. Heck, even feeling pain. And then there are new tastes that come with emotions of wonder and surprise and eagerness to eat more. And then there's new magic, which is just amazing." Quinn sighed wistfully, suddenly feeling very hungry. "Without my emotions, I can't tease you. What reason would I have? I can't taste Cook's cooking to the fullest. I can't appreciate it. And I can't laugh at Lynx."

Eric chuckled at the last comment, but then sobered up and studied her before speaking. "Well, when you put it that way, just promise me that you'll be careful."

Quinn nodded. "I promise you that I'll be extremely careful when I compartmentalize my emotions."

"Well, good. About time you listened to me, you young whipper-snapper." Eric gave her a wink and a grin, reverting to his usual self for a moment.

Quinn laughed, remembering that the imp was getting close to eight thousand years old and thus had a lot of footing to call her a young whippersnapper. She wished for just a second that she could have a cup of tea. Because she was suddenly very thirsty. But she wasn't about to summon one of the golems to bring her one. Instead, she turned to her owl. "Aradie, would you please go and get me a drink from Cook?"

Aradie flew off her perch with a long hoot that pretty much told Quinn that she wasn't an errand owl and would only do it this once. Quinn grinned. She was hoping Cook would send back some snacks, too. She was famished after using so much magic back in the interrogation room. "Okay, Eric, now it's your turn. You need to talk to me about those missing books. And while you're at it, I'd like to hear all about your uncle."

Eric hesitated. "You want to know about my uncle? Why do you need to know about my uncle? He has nothing to do with the Library." The imp sounded so defensive.

"Ah." Quinn smiled at him, confident that she wanted the answers even more now. "But isn't he the one who had the list? Isn't he the one who originally donated the books we're talking about?"

"Yes, he is," Eric answered, hesitantly.

"Is he part of the council?" Quinn asked, suddenly curious. She only knew that Milaro, Harish, and Siliqua were members.

"No, not personally. Not in the way you're thinking, I think. He doesn't have the time, or else he would."

"So he likes the Library." Quinn grinned.

Eric rolled his eyes. "He wouldn't have entrusted the books to the Library if he didn't like it, although right now he's not in the best mood about it. I did tell him that it wasn't the Library's fault that the books went missing, but I'm not sure how much he believed me."

"Okay, well, who is your uncle?" Quinn asked, that minuscule amount of patience eroded already.

"He's the leader of the seven overlords of Halschius."

"Oh, does that make you a prince as well? Can we tease you about being a prince like you tease Malakai?" Quinn laughed at Eric's expression while she spoke.

"No, I'm not a prince," he answered quickly, and then continued after some hesitation. "I am technically extremely expendable."

"Oh, I thought you couldn't die," Quinn said, slightly confused. He wasn't just immortal, he was like impervious or something, from what she'd picked up when they went to the Dabilian homeworld.

"There are a lot worse things than death, Quinn," Eric said, suddenly more serious than she had ever seen him in the almost two months she'd known him. A shadow fell over his gaze and for a moment, he looked like a fiery, hellish, imp of legend.

"Oh," she said, "well, just so you know, the Library and I do not think you're expendable."

Speak for yourself, Quinn.

Shut up, she thought to the Library before continuing. "You stick with us."

Eric smiled and he actually laughed. "Well, thank you, Quinn, I appreciate that."

"Great," she said, clapping her hands. "Then how about we move on to this book list?"

"Okay, okay" Eric pulled out what looked like a notepad but

turned out to be some type of magical little screen, and it was tiny. It fit in his small hands, and he peered at it for several seconds. "Okay, so you've already retrieved *DeKarlyle's Thesis of Spatial Distortion* and *Machmüller's Theory of Dimensional Dissolution and Disintegration Through Ritual Sacrifice*."

"Yes, we have both of those in our possession, and you know that, especially since you were there for the latter. So keep it going, stop stalling." Quinn kept her voice nice and easy.

"I'm not stalling, Quinn. It's complex, and you need to just let me work through this. Now the ones you're missing that aren't on the list we have and that aren't on the list we're missing, so the ones that the Library has been somehow tricked into believing that it never had are the following. *The Crown and Fall of Pocket Dimensions Due to Spatial Interference*. That's the first one.

"Yeah." He paused for a second, frowning, like the cogs in his brain were clicking together quickly. "That's not a good thing."

"I'm gathering that. Can we just get through the rest? Because I don't like the ideas I'm starting to have," Quinn said. She really didn't. The book names were just not a happy coincidence when they were all put together.

"Okay. *Ririn's Dimensional Distortion Through Sacrificial Means* and finally the *Parsneauvian Theory of Spatial Dimension Manipulation* is the last one missing out of that series."

Quinn paused and pinched her brow. She didn't want to give voice to the thoughts running through her head, but they were loud and clamoring to get out, and the Library was sort of roiling in her mind, uneasy and brimming with concern.

"Let me spitball here," she said.

Aradie chose that moment to squawk back into the room and drop a bag on Quinn's desk before returning to her perch and giving her the evil eye.

"I'm sorry," she said, somewhat glad that the interruption gave her another moment to clarify her thoughts. "I'm just thirsty and hungry."

Quinn picked up a bottle, took a swig and went back over her thoughts. Nope, they were still pretty crap. The juice didn't make those thoughts any nicer. "Just bear with me. The Library is in a pocket dimension, right? I mean, I'm correct, right?"

"It exists within its own temporally created spatial pocket dimension. Yes," Eric answered.

"Great, and it can be anywhere at any time summoned by anyone who can use the Library, is that correct?" Quinn pinched the bridge of her nose, trying to stave off the headache she knew was coming. Next thing she absorbed was going to be a plethora of healing tomes.

"Well, yes, you've been there and you've used the doors. Time-wise, though, it doesn't manipulate time. But other than that you understand it as well as I do, Quinn." Eric sounded impatient.

"Don't lose your temper with me. I'm making sure I've understood everything correctly." But she could tell that she was right because Eric's face was a lot paler. Somehow even his charcoal skin appeared a few shades lighter, which meant Quinn was probably on the right track. "And it's not good that all of these five books that have been missing. Books we weren't entirely sure were all missing, that we didn't even realize the Library should *have* in the restricted vault, all have to do with some sort of spatial-pocket-dimension-y-ritual-sacri-fice-manipulation thing."

Eric let out a long-suffering sigh. "Yeah, I would say that's a very bad thing."

"Great," Quinn said, trying hard to stem the panic she could feel rising up within her. She knew chaos could exist in the pocket dimension, but as they filtered it out of the universe's magic, it was well controlled and contained within the filtration chamber. Her head was hurting. "This, for example, would be an absolutely opportune moment to compartmentalize my emotions. Except I also need them to help me judge how to react to this. So what do we do?"

Eric shrugged, and then squirmed uneasily. "You're the Librarian."

Quinn might have snapped a little. "Yeah, and I've known about magic and been the Librarian for like seven weeks. You've been alive for almost eight thousand years. You don't have any ideas?"

Eric burst out laughing. "You know, that's a really good point," he said. "And I think I can come up with some ideas. But all flippancy aside, I think you should call Milaro and Lynx and make sure the Library is present. Because this has officially become a shit show."

"Great," Quinn said, biting into one of the donuts Cook had sent like they knew she'd need the sugar rush. "And here I was hoping I'd overreacted."

53

NOT POSSIBLE AT THIS MOMENT

"'This is actually a lot worse than I imagined," Milaro said, as he idly twisted a long lock of his hair. Quinn had observed that habit of his several times now.

"Can we even keep the Library open at this stage?" Siliqua asked. She was fidgeting with a pen in her hands, her brow furrowed with worry. "Isn't it too dangerous?"

"Well, we can't close it up to patrons again," Lynx said. "It's the flow of magic in the universe. We almost went into full meltdown, and we barely avoided it. We're only just getting the power back that we need." Lynx stood up and started pacing, which was odd considering he currently looked translucent. Quinn watched portions of her office through his pacing body, fascinated.

No, shutting out the patrons at this juncture would put everything we've worked for in jeopardy, the Library, who had decided to take part in this meeting, added.

Quinn listened to all of them argue. Lynx, the Library, Milaro, Harish, Siliqua, and Eric. They discussed aspects of the Library she'd never really been there for. From older power levels, to heightened security through golems like they used to have.

Which reminded her that she thought Misha should have more

security golems at her beck and call now. Maybe. Had enough time passed?

She looked around her office, which had, thanks to the Library's innate abilities, managed to double in size. Now there was a conference table, literally, with doughnuts in the middle of it, courtesy of Cook. She looked at it and wondered if maybe they had pulled some information from some dramas back on Earth. How else would they know that this is what a conference room, or part of a conference room, looked like? At least it did in most of the procedurals she'd watched.

She tapped her chin, trying to figure out how they'd done it.

"Quinn?"

She looked up at Lynx, blinking. "What?"

"Are you still with us? Do you want to help us save the Library? Or was there some important daydreaming you were doing?" There was a shift in his tone, like he was irritated by her spacing out.

She resisted the urge to snap back at him and answered genuinely instead. "Of course! Considering it's literally what I'm supposed to do." Then she paused and sighed. "Sorry, I was just contemplating some things, and you were all talking about stuff I couldn't contribute to."

"Oh," Siliqua said. "We're sorry. It's just that there's so much we have to be careful not to repeat, or not to invite."

Eric nodded. "We must make sure we're prepared for what's to come. But we realize it's been a lot. For all of us."

Quinn shrugged. "Well, to be fair, it's been a lot for the entire time I've been here. This sort of just feels like normal every day. Oh wait, there's another crisis on hand. Right?" Everyone at the table looked at each other somewhat uncomfortably. Quinn shrugged again. "What? It's true. It's not like we've had many moments of peace."

"Well, really," Eric said, crossing his arms as he hovered at her side. "I mean, we've had a few days here and there of peace."

"Yes, and those were super-hectic days where we had to check in thousands of books because people decided they didn't want to be fined, after all." Quinn looked over at him, frowning.

"Well, when you put it that way . . ." Eric said, his voice trailing off.

Quinn sighed. "Look, I get it. This is unexpected and unprecedented, and so am I. So we just need to figure out how best to deal with it, because shutting the Library is obviously not an option. Won't shutting down the Library again stop our filtration? Isn't that just going to ruin everything again?"

"Well," Milaro said, leaning forward and steepling his fingers. "Yes, it likely would."

Quinn tried another approach. "Couldn't we just get a heap of people in here, close the doors, and get all of those people to pour a heap of power into the reserves?"

"Well, that's an option"—Milaro frowned—"but given how the Library's system functions, that's not a good one. It requires ingoing and outgoing mana and magic to be balanced and retrieved. It's why the fine system doesn't exclusively consist of people giving the Library some of their power."

"Oh," Quinn said, oddly let down by the logic. She was just desperately trying to see if they could prevent a potential catastrophe by removing the Library's borrowing and return functions from the picture while they powered up. Until it was safe. "Well, I guess it wasn't going to be that easy."

"We've only just started getting power levels even close to stable," Harish said. "We're still a long way off from being completely out of the woods. While this is taking us longer to delve into than I'd have liked, it's best we don't rush anything."

"I'll agree with you there," Quinn said and then she turned to the manifestation. "What about Lynx? Are you safe now?"

The Library spoke up again, intoning throughout the room. *Well, he's as safe as he can be.*

"How can we be sure this won't happen again?" Quinn asked, raising an eyebrow.

"The owls' memories appear to have been slightly image-modified." Milaro spoke up this time, shifting in his seat like the words made him uncomfortable.

"Wouldn't that require some super-strong mental magic?" Quinn asked.

Milaro scowled, and she could tell this was really eating at him. "Yes, this would require very strong mental magic. It's verging on such strength that I should probably personally know the individual responsible for inflicting such a memory wipe."

"You should know them?" Quinn had to suppress a laugh at that. "What do you mean? Aren't there, like, trillions of people in this universe?"

"Well, yes," Milaro said. "But the number of people who can utilize mind magic to such a degree of finesse that leaves the owl in question unaware of the tampering but is also practically able to convince an entire room of scholars, Library assistants, and a king that it was true, that's a high level. Well, frankly, apart from me, there might be a few dozen people who could reach it."

"Oh," Quinn said somewhat taken aback by the information. "Well, that's great. Anyway, what we need right now is to figure out how to proceed. *Ririn's Dimensional Distortion Through Sacrificial Means*, *The Parsneauvian Theory of Spatial Dimension Manipulation*, and the *Crown and Fall of Pocket Dimensions Due to Spatial Interference*. I need those three books. Can you locate them just with their name?"

Lynx hesitated. Milaro sighed and fell back into his chair.

And the Library answered. *No. Not possible at this moment.*

Quinn pinched the bridge of her nose, trying not to lose her temper. Not that anyone could do anything about the situation, but the frustration was starting to boil over a wee bit.

Just answering her question wasn't enough. It would have been nice if there was an explanation offered. However, it seemed the Library wasn't intuitive in that way, at least not today.

"Would you care to explain to me why this is not possible at this point in time?" she asked.

Lynx looked away from her, down at the ground, and didn't meet her gaze again. Milaro did the same.

Finally, the Library spoke up. *Due to the erasure of certain informa-tion in the system, in our memory, the recollection of those tomes is incom-*

plete. While the names are flagged as something we should know, there is no further information available on them, including being able to trace where they're currently located.

Quinn sighed. "So it's currently not possible to locate accurately. Great, okay. Can you do a divination spell? Is there a divination set of books I can just go absorb and voila, we can figure out where it is?"

"That is a very interesting thought," Eric said, his wings suddenly moving faster as if excitement had caught him. "Actually, give me a little bit. I will go and check the divination section. I think there's something we can use. I'm not an expert in rituals, but they can do some nifty things."

"Oh, well, that's great," Quinn said, feeling a little bit more proactive about the whole situation. "You didn't want to stay for the rest of the meeting?"

"Oh, no, you'll catch me up. Don't worry, darling, I'll be fine," Eric said, winking at her before he flitted out of the room so fast that Quinn could barely see him go. He was just a streak of red and black.

"Huh, learn something new every day," she muttered.

"Well, that's a fortuitous turn of events," Siliqua said, letting out a breath. "I just wanted to update you that Cadre is due to arrive in the next day or two. The Library will vet him. And I was wondering, Quinn, if you wanted to meet him first, before he does anything?"

Quinn raised an eyebrow, recalling that Cadre was the Serpensiril-species-related friend who would help with the sequencing. "If I'm here, then I'd like to meet him, but otherwise I don't want to hold him up. Is that a good enough answer?"

Siliqua nodded. "Yes, if you're here and not away retrieving books, I'll introduce you to him before things get started."

"Fantastic, so that's the sequencing taken care of. Do you need more from me for the sequencing?"

"No, we do not." Siliqua smiled.

"Then let's get back to where we got derailed from," Quinn said. "It's highly unlikely we'll have dumb luck again, like we did last time we went to retrieve one of the culinary books."

"That was more than just dumb luck. I have no idea how it

happened," Milaro said, drumming his fingers on the desk absently, "like the odds of that book being on that island? A hop, skip and a jump from where a quasi-cult was trying to open a dimensional portal to do whatever? That was some pretty nifty coincidence."

"You don't believe in coincidences, do you, Milaro?" Quinn thought this discussion sounded vaguely similar to a previous one.

"No, I do not. Not usually," Milaro admitted, "And this one, that was very close to being suspiciously coincidental."

"Do you think there's a possibility of us having some more of these types of coincidences?"

Milaro gave her a grave look. "I would hope not, but given your previous history, I think suspicious coincidences tend to follow you around like a bad smell."

"Oh great, now you're questioning my personal hygiene." Quinn cracked a grin.

Milaro actually laughed. "I'm not, you know that. I'm just concerned about the history of trying to find these books."

"Speaking of which, since we currently don't have a divination ritual that will allow me to locate where these books are kept, and we don't have a location tracker or you don't have a tracking device or something attached to the books, and can't locate the ones we really need to get out of circulation, I'd say our next best bet is to obtain the other culinary books, you know? So we can eventually open the culinary branch, right?" Quinn wanted to get the meeting over and done with.

"Yep, sounds like a logical next step," Milaro agreed.

"Something to while away the time, Lynx?" Quinn peered at him. "Maybe you want the Library open, maybe you don't. You've been staring at the floor for the last five minutes."

Lynx sighed. "I'm concerned about potentially allowing you to perform rituals."

Quinn raised an eyebrow, "I appreciate that you're concerned for me, perhaps even a bit about me. But I'm here. I have all the magic affinities; I may as well use them."

Lynx chuckled, "Yeah, may as well. Time to get the other culinary books then."

"I'll take Malakai and Aradie with me. I'll probably end up taking Eric with me too; he's usually really helpful." Quinn was already planning the whole trip out in her head. "I mean, once we have another branch open, isn't that just more power we can gather?"

Lynx smiled and nodded.

"What about Finn?" Milaro asked suddenly.

"Finn? The little Ilgonomur?" She'd seen them around here and there, but if she was honest with herself, they seemed to be more of the lurking type.

"Yes. How is Finn doing?" Milaro asked, oddly insistent.

"I don't know, okay, I guess?" Quinn mulled it over and then had a thought. "They did help a lot with the Tenejo debacle. Why? You sound overly curious."

"Finn's been here the longest, with Eric and Geneva, and the aracnio twins, and Danio, but I rarely see Finn. I was just curious if they had potential to supervise as well." Milaro's expression was so serene Quinn was quite sure he was using it to cover a lie.

"Probably. I think they're quietly efficient, but I'll double check with Misha next time we need someone." Quinn tucked that thought in the back of her head, there had to be a bigger reason that he was curious about Finn, and she was going to figure that out, because apparently he didn't want to tell her. "Anyway, I want to open the culinary branch, thus I need three more books, and since we have the locations for those. I think that's our best bet for now. Do what we can, don't dwell on what we don't have answers for yet."

Pragmatism at its finest.

"Sounds like an excellent idea," Harish said. "Having another of the branches open allows the mana to flow freer. It'll enable us to capitalize on the amount of power we're using and gaining."

"Excellent, but first I want more firepower and healing power on my side, so I need suggestions for some healing books." Quinn was determined to be more self-sufficient next time she ran into trouble. And she had no doubt she'd run into it.

"Oh," Milaro said, sitting up perfectly straight as if she'd just caught his interest, "then I have just the thing for you. *Mind Over Matter: As Mana Translates to Healing* and *Powerful Ice Tactics for the Bold*. Those two, definitely."

"Great!" Quinn grinned and sent the book names to Misha. "I'll absorb them as soon as I get my hands on them. Hey, Lynx, can you get us the location for the last books for the culinary branch?"

Lynx frowned as he spoke. "There are two orphaned books where the original borrower and their family are gone, but they're in pretty easy locations to find." He paused for a moment, the frown deepening. "Hm, and then there's one that seems attached to an individual who seems reluctant to return the books."

"Oh, great." Quinn rolled her eyes, trying to ignore the feeling of trepidation that tingled down her spine. She didn't want a repeat of Kajaro. That was the last thing they needed.

"I'm assuming divination rituals will take a while to set up?" Quinn directed the question to Siliqua.

"You'd assume correctly, Librarian." The wood elf inclined her head in acknowledgement. "Frankly, I need to find an expert in rituals that I can trust first."

Quinn nodded, half to herself as Tim entered the room more silently than he had any right to and placed the two tome suggestions from Milaro on the desk. "Well, I guess we should prep everything we need to go and retrieve those culinary books." She looked at the map Lynx had opened in her face.

"Those are the two locations of the orphaned tomes." He said.

"All right." Quinn stood up, determined to get ready and get to those books as soon as possible.

She eyed the ones she needed to absorb and checked her energy and mana replenishment stores. There were definitely enough energy balls to top her off.

Quinn grinned. "Just give me a bit to absorb these and replenish my energy, and then we'll head off and get the easy books out of the way."

ALL THIS FOR A DAMNED COOKBOOK!

E_VEN AS_ Q_UINN STEPPED OUT OF THE_ L_IBRARY THROUGH HER FAVORITE_ double doors, she realized she should have fully anticipated falling on her butt on the other side of the door. It had become somewhat of a running joke that she would.

Dusting herself off from the inevitable fall through yet another dimensional doorway, Quinn was starting to wonder if she should ask the Library if it was deliberately placing the door two feet above the ground so that she lost her balance in the slight shift of equilibrium that occurred when she stepped through.

By the same token, though, it was sort of nice to know the Library had a sense of humor. Even if it involved pranks.

Quinn peered around and discovered that they were in what appeared to be a very old, burnt-out city. Originally, it would have had buildings clustered throughout the whole area. There were still so many partial stone structures left that she could have sworn it was a large city. Any wooden portions of the structures however seemed to have been turned to ash long ago.

If the fire stains against the stone were anything to go by, then something very hot had burned this entire city down a good many years ago. Some of the bricks and stones were even cracked. Although that could have been a combination of fire on top of normal weather exposure over time.

This didn't sound like a peaceful "this species has gone extinct" sort of place to Quinn. In fact, it sounded a lot more like "this species got wiped out by something large and fire-breathing, oops" sort of destination. She ran a hand that was already covered in soot from touching the stone walls through her ponytail, glad that it was already dark brown anyway.

"Well," she said, looking around and wishing that sometimes when she opened her mouth, she didn't insert her foot, "this doesn't look like it is going to be easy. I'm rethinking that whole 'let's do the easy stuff' strategy."

"Oh, are you now?" said Malakai, laughing softly. He pointed off to the northwest, and Quinn shrugged before they started moving slowly and cautiously in that direction.

She could see ash from the burned-away wood caked onto the floor, onto the ground in the cobblestones, raked over the stones that were the remnants of the buildings, leaving black soot stains everywhere.

High in the sky, there were two suns. One was yellow like she was used to seeing, and the other was a vivid bright orange in a glaringly aquamarine sky, which was a stark juxtaposition to the city in ruins around them. An uneasy sensation suffused the whole area around them; it basically fed up from the ground, leaking down to her from the destroyed walls.

And there was something oddly familiar about the whole scene. She couldn't shake the ominous sensation.

"Do you get the feeling," Malakai asked, his back to Quinn's as he surveyed the area ahead of her, "that perhaps we're being watched?"

Quinn sighed deeply, and Eric laughed before speaking a little louder than necessary. "Well, of course, we're being watched. We're not the only beings here. It's not an uninhabited planet. The species that borrowed the book just died out," the imp said quite emphatically.

Just as Quinn was about to retort, there was a rumbling under her feet, very subtle, gentle, almost like something was trying to be stealthy when it was sincerely not a stealthy creature at all.

Quinn sighed again, this time resigned to whatever was about to come. "Oh, this is not what I had in mind."

"I thought you knew better," Eric said, a smug grin on his face.

"Well, I do know better, and I did know better. Also, I didn't think this would happen just because I said we should get the easier books first. I didn't say it was *going* to be easy. I didn't think I invited fate to come and smack me in the face, but apparently, I did." Quinn felt all sorts of grumbly. "I need to be more careful with my words."

"Did you, though?" Eric asked. "I mean, sometimes, Quinn, I think you like a little bit of this danger."

Quinn gave him a very flat stare. "It's not that I like the danger," she said, thinking about it seriously for a few seconds. "It's that I enjoy the fact that I now have abilities that I can use to help solve these little incidents."

"You mean get the books back for the Library, right?" Malakai said.

"Well, that too," she said with an impish grin, doing her best to imitate Eric's.

They continued making their way toward what felt like the origin of the rumbling, taking street by street and alley by alley where they came up, moving cautiously. Quinn wasn't confident in sending Aradie out when they didn't know just what they were up against, but it was starting to look inevitable.

"So," she asked as she picked her way along the cobblestone street that seemed to have no end in sight, "are we just waiting to be ambushed, or are we trying to figure out exactly where they're located?"

Malakai shrugged, never meeting her eyes as he kept his own on all the shadows cast by the multiple suns.

The streets around them were old, sort of like Quinn had imagined they would be in Europe: cobblestone, partial bases, and the initial floor of buildings stuck out as if they were waiting to be rebuilt.

The structures had probably initially been like two- and three-story Tudor houses that had a lot of rockwork in them. Gone were the beams and the beauty, all burned away, but the alleyways and the streets, they wound close together all at once, with barely a break for any ground whatsoever, let alone a park or garden. It made every single corner hold a potential threat because they couldn't see around them.

"Aradie, please go scout," Quinn asked, resigned to having to send her owl out. "Just be careful."

With a mournful hoot, Aradie took off. Quinn could sense from her reticence that everything around them wasn't safe and that Aradie didn't enjoy the sensations she was experiencing. She also felt underlying concern directed toward Quinn.

"What's something that my nightowl would be cautious about?" she asked as she interpreted some of the visions already feeding back to her.

"Aradie?" Eric asked.

Quinn nodded, focusing on whether or not she could see anything suspect in her owl's vision.

"Well, she's almost impervious, like me, so it would have to be something a lot bigger than her and us, really," Eric said.

"Bigger than us? Great," Quinn said.

"You know, Quinn," Malakai said, "I think deep down, some part of you is probably raring to try out your new skills and be all daring like."

Aradie hooted a low note of agreement and as she flew overhead.

Eric scowled. "Hey, I just said that!"

"Oh, well, now you're just all picking on me," Quinn grumbled. "Where is this damn book?" she asked as she looked at the map in her HUD again. "Why can't the Library just drop us directly where the book is?"

"Well, that's simple," Eric said. "The guidance system needs upgrading. There's only so close it can get us with limited energy expenditure. The power levels aren't there yet, but they should be soon."

Quinn stared at him. "Library of anywhere and everywhere, my ass." She sighed and continued slowly, scouring the area as they moved further into, or out of, the city. She couldn't tell yet; there were too many building remnants all around them, and not enough to go on to even know where they were headed.

And then there was a soft whoosh, a soft rumble. Quinn paused, desperately wishing it was part of her imagination.

Malakai whispered, "Did you hear that?" His tone was suddenly serious, no longer playful.

Quinn wanted to say, "No, I didn't hear anything. Everything's absolutely fine. Let's quickly grab the book and go home." But that would be a lie. She'd heard the sounds, the ones that were barely there, as if something was trying to sneak up on them and failing abysmally. She guessed, with a couple hundred years of no other residents in the area, that whatever this was, it was probably no longer used to being stealth-checked.

Quinn reached out with her senses, finely attuned to all life around them, and found several alarmingly large, ambiguous shapes that she couldn't quite define. Something about them felt like she should be able to identify them. She looked around the tatters of the city, the sheer magnitude of fire damage from another time, fire damage that didn't appear to have begun inside any of the buildings themselves. She didn't like the ideas that were coming to her.

"You realize this isn't looking good, don't you?" Quinn asked softly.

Eric shrugged. "Fire's not gonna hurt me."

"Yeah, Mr. Ancient and Impervious to Damage, thanks for that contribution," Quinn quipped at him.

"What are you bitching about? Your abilities are water and ice and other stuff. Hell, if you need to, pull a layer of chaos over yourself. It'll probably eat everything in range." He scowled at her, his short temper showing through.

"Including my allies," Quinn said.

"I was just kidding," Eric joked, faking a laugh for a second.

Quinn raised an eyebrow.

"So we're all on the same page," Malakai said. "We all know this is gonna be a fire-breathing something or other, right?"

"Do you think it'd be something like salamanders?" Quinn asked, keeping her voice soft as they continued to move through the streets. It wasn't too difficult to keep their footsteps light and soft. The ash caked into the ground helped acoustically dampen the sound.

"Well, fire-type lizards are likely," Malakai said. "This is the correct region of this solar system for them, I think. But I didn't realize they lived on this specific planet."

"Probably came over from another one. It's not infrequent that they overpopulate," Eric said matter-of-factly.

"Great," Quinn said. "Anything else?"

"Well, it could be drakes. If it were drakes, I think we'd already be burnt to a cinder and we wouldn't be having this conversation." Malakai shrugged.

"Speak for yourselves." Eric laughed again.

Quinn took a deep breath. Sometimes Eric's needling could be a little much. "If you do that once more, I'm gonna use the emergency teleport to teleport you away."

"Take away all my fun, Librarian. You're mean." Eric pouted.

"Fine, I'd prefer to be mean and alive." Quinn winked at the imp before turning her attention back to Malakai.

"City cats too," Malakai said.

"What?" Quinn asked, not thinking she heard right. "Come again?'

"City cats are another creature we could potentially encounter. They're a part of this system too." Malakai was still hyper aware as they continued to move.

"Like the catamaran ferry boat or like a cat that like traverses the city?" Quinn asked for clarification.

"Neither of those." He didn't bother to look back at her. He was too focus on scouting their surroundings. "You'll notice if you see them. It's difficult to explain."

Great. She was getting images from Aradie now. There were lizards half-hidden in the soot caked around the buildings, barely visible. "Can salamanders camouflage?"

"Depending on their species subtype? Yes," Eric said. "We have a lot of them in Halschius. Perfect temperature for them down there."

Quinn put a finger over her mouth asking them both to be quiet. Malakai rolled his eyes, as did Eric, and they all readied for combat. The next corner they rounded was less of an alleyway and more of a street. It was wider by a substantial amount, probably enough for two cars to go down side by side if they were being cautious. The cobbled stones were smoother here as if it had seen a lot of traffic in its lifetime. Even the soot wasn't as caked onto the ground as it had been in the alleyways.

"They're over there," Quinn said, pointing, knowing through Aradie's visions that's exactly where they were. Eric held up fingers two, three, four, and waved it about. Quinn counted through Aradie's eyes and held up five. Eric simply nodded and shrugged. Quinn took a few seconds to cast a new healing ability over all of them. A heal over time that would regenerate them while they fought.

"All this for a damned cookbook," Eric said.

The salamanders orchestrated attack would have been perfect had it not been for Aradie and her connection with Quinn. As it was, they were the ones taken by surprise. As sounds of fighting echoed around them, the remaining creatures headed their way started moving faster, stealth forgotten.

Quinn grinned. Having her very own nightowl scout was full of perks. "We need to work through these ones first," she said.

"I'd never have guessed," Malakai said, slashing one of them down the side with his sword. A trail of fiery brimstone leaked out of its side.

"Ah," Eric said, "I guess these ones are the same subspecies as the ones from Halschius. Maybe they're on vacation."

"Shush," Quinn said.

"You don't even let me banter while I'm fighting. Damn Librarians," Eric muttered under his breath as he punched yet another one of the salamanders in the face. He was so tiny compared to the salamanders, who looked like seventeen-foot crocodiles on a wee bit of growth hormone, that it was almost comical. How far the creatures flew with the force of the punch, however, was quite seriously amazing.

"Did we not know they were here? Like as a general rule?" Quinn asked.

"The Library's databases are currently still catching up on being five hundred years outdated," Malakai yelled out, as a high-pitched squeal escaped one of the lizards. He slashed up the underside of one of their mouths just before the instant where lava spewed from its mouth. Luckily, it ended up spewing all over its face. Somewhat out of breath, he continued. "It'll take a while to get all the information up to current parameters."

Quinn nodded, not letting herself get distracted from her routine of dousing the creatures in water and then flash-freezing them. It required relatively little mana and energy to maintain. It helped when Malakai slashed through them, breaking them into thousands of little pieces. But it wasn't a strike the elf prince could use continually, it required some sort of rest between from what Quinn had seen.

By the time they were on their third, Eric had already dispatched two of the first five by himself, with a little bit of help from Aradie's laser eyes.

And that's when the rest of them arrived.

The whole fight became a blur of lizard claws, fire breath, magma flow, ice, water, sword fighting, and screaming. The streets had the soot washed into insignificance by, mostly, salamander blood.

Quinn found the heat oddly comforting.

"These aren't so difficult, you know," Eric said, as they finally got down to their last couple.

"That's just what somebody impervious to damage would say," Quinn snapped at him as she dispatched what she hoped was the last one. She had cuts running all down her arms, but the regeneration she'd cast before they started fighting was helping keep them at "not quite grievous wound" level.

The armor she'd worn was shredded like paper now. Quinn was winded and bleeding and so exhausted. She grabbed a mana potion out of her inventory and slugged it back as she popped an energy sandwich into her mouth.

"Well," she said, quite happy with the way things had turned out.

Frowning at the corpses, she was about to ask Malakai if they looted corpses like these, when something happened that made her freeze on the spot.

The roar wasn't just loud, but it seeped into every single pore of her body, holing up to attempt and arrest her limbs. She was barely able to shake herself out of it, and her head began to pound, just as her whole body shook.

"That wasn't a salamander," Eric helpfully stated the bleeding obvious.

"No shit." Quinn sighed out the words as the drake's approach grew closer.

Casting another round of regeneration on all of them, Quinn prepared herself as best she could. Fighting a drake to retrieve the damned lost cookbook had definitely not been on today's to-do list.

55

RATHER SPECIFIC
AFTERTHOUGHT

Quinn wasn't entirely certain how she pictured drakes before. Sort of part dragon, massive, with wings attached to its little forearms, like a defenseless flying T-Rex. But whatever was coming towards them was not what she'd imagined.

It approached, screeching loudly, from a mouth that looked like a cross between a crocodile and a dinosaur. It was probably close to the size of an elephant, yet it had four limbs and another arm like a pterodactyl's that was attached to a portion of its wings, with a little claw at the end of it.

From the look she got, it seemed fiercer as it approached. It wasn't nearly as large or bad as she'd assumed, and right then appeared to be fueled by rage at having its companions killed. She relaxed momentarily, which was a huge mistake on her part.

Quinn realized this as soon as the thing opened its mouth, which she thought was to screech again, but instead, it let out a wall of flame.

The fire jettisoned toward her.

Hot. Dangerous. Lethal.

Instinctively, she shot an ice wall up in front of them at the very last moment, before diving away with the rest of her party. Or in this case Malakai because Aradie and Eric had already absconded, their flight unhampered by mana and energy limits.

The ice wall existed only for a split second before exploding apart into melting ice shards and a cloud of steam that shrouded the entire section of the street. The fire's stream barely missed her as the flame shot by, singeing part of the remnants of her outfit. She glanced down at her arm, the sleeve completely destroyed, making a mental note to learn a mending spell as soon as possible.

The blue-gold of her scale overlay faded from her skin where the fire narrowly missed her as soon as the threat disappeared.

There wasn't much time for thought as she and Malakai scrambled for purchase behind one of the sturdier and thicker stone wall remnants of the city.

"What were you doing standing there?" Malakai asked, even as he wedged himself out of their secure hiding place while the drake was wheeling around to make another run down the main street and loosed three arrows in quick succession, straight up at the creature. One of them, from what Quinn could tell with the way the thudding arrow hit its target, definitely found purchase in something soft. Hopefully a joint. The creature screeched and for a moment Quinn's ears rang.

"Just what were you thinking standing there until the flame almost hit you?" he asked again, glancing down and glaring at her.

Quinn studied him. How did she explain that her brain had caught itself once again stuck in that loading space of "magical and fantastical" and "this is now my life." That, for all intents and purposes in front of her was a living, fire-breathing dragon. And she was just a girl from magicless Earth.

"To be honest, I wasn't really thinking," Quinn finally answered, as the creature wheeled around in the sky trying to spy its prey. But Quinn and Malakai had hidden themselves fairly well, and Aradie and Eric were nowhere to be seen.

Quinn probed outside of their hiding spot, extending her senses, glad to see that Eric and her owl were doing fine. They were getting ready to ambush the massive sky creature when it least expected.

Malakai was fiddling with his bow. "I guess that's how the entire city was burnt to a crisp," he mumbled.

Quinn nodded. "Now that would be an accurate assessment. I didn't think it was the salamanders. They didn't really spit fire so much as lava. Well, maybe they just melted the rocks."

There was a silence that Quinn found extremely unnerving all around them. She peered out from her hiding spot and for a few seconds, there was no sign of the drake.

"Did it go away?" Malakai asked hopefully.

"Not bloody likely," Quinn said. "I mean, would you? It's obviously seen us. It knows we're here. It's not just going to go away. I don't think it's big enough to swallow us whole, but it could probably bite us in two if given the chance. And it's probably a lot more clever than we give it credit for."

"Because it's hiding and lying in wait for us," Malakai said.

"Exactly," Quinn said. "Of course, it could also be scouting and trying to come up with an alternate approach. Because why would retrieving a cookbook be easy?"

Malakai snorted a soft laugh. "When you put it that way . . ."

Quinn frantically searched through the arsenal of knowledge that she'd absorbed from way too many books already in the Library, trying to figure out exactly what she could pull out of her bag of many tricks.

Suddenly, the drake was there again, back at the entrance to the city, or at least where Quinn assumed the entrance to the city was. It took a long run-up to swoop over the entire street area. Probably over the entire city. Even if it was smaller than she'd originally thought, its flames had an extremely large reach.

This time, Malakai boosted himself out of their hiding place, doing that strange double jump he did. This was how he could fly. He practically hovered in the air aiming his bow while in the sky down onto the drake. Aradie and Eric flew in tandem, equal laser eyes from the owl, and what looked like brimstone from the imp, searing into the joints of the massive flying creature. Those joints were one of the only weak spots she could see, apart from the eyes. And those were protected by a pretty formidable eyebrow ridge.

Quinn, on the other hand, realized that more ice or water was only going to create steam when it clashed with fire . . . or smoke. Thus nobody would be able to see a thing. Technically she could probably pull the air away from those big wings, but she wasn't sure how that would affect Aradie and Eric. Instead, she chose to try and suffocate the fire by pulling the oxygen out of it.

She knew how to do it in theory, but wielding the ability was a lot more difficult than she'd anticipated. The first time, she had pulled fire to her hands and screamed. Luckily, she'd been wearing gloves. They weren't completely flame-repellent, but they hadn't burned her hands to a crisp at least, especially as the soft blue-gold of her magical scales faded as she removed the gloves to heal her hands. Perhaps that whole heritage thing would work to her advantage.

"Damn it," she said. "Okay."

Working with live flame wasn't the best option. She felt far too vulnerable. She tried again, and this time managed to stave off some more of the fire, but it backlashed into her hands again and went up her left arm this time, and her magical scales didn't react quite fast enough this time.

"Damn it!"

This wound required her to use healing magic on her arm, as the skin had been slightly blistered. She gritted her teeth while it healed and then applied regeneration once again to make sure that none of the burns were sticking.

But even then, it healed much faster than anticipated.

Back in the hidey-hole they'd carved out, Malakai was panting for breath. Streaks of red ran down his usually white sleeves.

"Did you get hit?"

"Yeah, kind of," he said, still gasping for air, then added, still out of breath. "What gave it away? The trail of blood?"

She ignored him.

The drake was taking its time to scan around before taking another pass at the street. It had obviously figured out where the perpetrators were who'd killed all the salamanders. Or maybe it was just hungry for live barbeque.

Quinn shook her head at Malakai. "No, you don't just get sort of hurt. How did you do that?"

"Some sparks hit me on the way down." He shrugged, like it was no big deal.

"Well, at least you can heal yourself, somewhat. Look, I've got to figure out exactly what it is I can throw at this thing," Quinn said. "They're immune to mind magic, right? Dragons are immune to mind magic?"

"Dragons aren't immune; they just have great defenses most of the time, if legend is true," Malakai said, as he exerted healing magic onto his arm. "Drakes are from the same family, though, so we've got to think they'll be at least somewhat resistant."

"Well, yes, that's a good supposition. Where are Eric and Aradie?" Quinn asked, as she wracked her brain to figure out something she could do. Playing with oxygen manipulation around so much fire didn't appeal to her sense of self-preservation.

Aradie flashed a picture from high atop a still-standing stone structure where she was watching from the shadows to see where the drake would attack from next. From what Aradie was projecting, it seemed the creature wasn't as highly intelligent as Quinn had anticipated, since its attack patterns appeared to basically be burning everything close to them until, well, it burned everything.

"Okay, so mind magic's out," Malakai said. "You've got ice?"

"Well, the ability didn't leave me, but that creates too much steam when it contacts fire." Quinn pursed her lips in thought.

"Good point," he said. "Okay, so ice and water are out. What about air?"

"I'm trying, currently, to suck the oxygen out of the fire so that maybe it doesn't, you know, flame?" She looked up at him, since he was still standing.

Malakai frowned at her. "Well, that's a great idea, but Quinn, why aren't you just using your gravity abilities?"

Quinn blinked at Malakai, remembering how she commanded

the miasma drones in the filtration chamber to drop to their deaths. Why on whatever planet they were on hadn't she thought of that herself? Why couldn't she command this massive elephant-sized one?

"The thing about the gravity stuff, the drake's a lot bigger than the miasma flies were. I'm a little nervous about, you know, trying to bring something that large down with my mind." She sounded a lot more confident than she felt.

"But it's not with your mind. It's magic," Malakai said, poking his head out to watch where the drake currently circled their little street area. "Awesome magic that should be able to force a flying creature to the ground and make it easier for us to battle it."

Quinn nodded slowly, as another roar echoed outside, this time much closer. "Oh. Good point."

This time, Quinn stepped out from their hiding place while Malakai leapt up to one of the stone walls to fire at the drake. Quinn felt open and exposed, standing in the middle of the street, as anyone would. But the only way she knew how to execute the power was to face her target and use hand gestures while she focused the power into a word. And that was something she couldn't do from behind stone walls. She just had to time it before it decided to attempt to singe to ashes.

The approaching creature screeched loudly. It was large enough that flying any lower to the ground would cause massive maneuverability issues. Which was probably why it hadn't tried to perch in close and fry them, because its wings would get caught on every bit of stone around here.

She could see it breathing in, getting ready to let out a massive stream of fire. She held out her hands and crushed them into fists while she said, "Gravitas."

At first, it looked like the drake had a massive hiccup, and it sort of bumped in the air as if it accidentally hit an invisible speed bump too fast. The fire that was supposed to be a stream seemed to engulf the drake itself. Not that that made any damage happen. One of the keys to wielding fire, was apparently being mostly impervious to its damage. It seemed to make the drake angrier if the scream was anything to go by.

Quinn aimed again. "Gravitas," she said, her voice deeper, putting more power behind it, feeding it with more of her mana and energy combined.

This time, a fiery burp escaped it. Sadly, it was pinpointed directly on Quinn, exploding about two feet from her ear. Her head rang. Her hair singed. And she was oddly irritated by the fact that she'd just lost a few really nice curls.

The drake was even closer now, attempting again to get ready to roast her. But Quinn reached out once more, made her fists and yelled this time, "Gravitas," as she punched the air beneath her with her fists.

This time, it was like the air around the creature warped, and it plummeted directly down, not angled at all, straight into the cobblestone pavement beneath it. Falling forty or so feet with gravity pulling it down meant its wings couldn't fight against the tug and bashed into the remnants of buildings on its way down, bones snapping as it did so, until it lay in a heap on the ground, feebly trying to push itself back up with a broken wing.

Quinn gasped and fell to one knee. Her shoulder hurt on the same side she'd been burned on. She glanced at it and realized the pad her owl usually sat on had been obliterated, and her whole shoulder and upper arm were a mess of gooey crimson flesh. It took all her willpower to retain her stomach contents.

Yet somehow, it didn't hurt the way she'd imagined it should. It *did* look disgusting.

Aradie swooped down onto the other shoulder, hooting gently as she did so. All of a sudden, there was a glow around Quinn as Aradie healed her.

Quinn blinked, suddenly feeling a bit groggy. "Wow, you can do that? You could have told me."

The bird's coos sounded oddly chastising.

"I know, I know, I didn't ask." Quinn sighed, focusing back on the drake.

Aradie let out a noise that sounded much like a chuckle while

Quinn watched Malakai and Eric go to town on the injured drake. Eric used his superior speed and agility to hit the drake before it could even react, and Malakai's sword attack cleaved into the thing like it was butter. She almost felt sorry for it being grounded and out of its element. It didn't take long for it to be defeated.

Quinn sighed. "That really hurt." She'd never been so glad to have learned a spell like regeneration before in her life. She was pretty sure it had saved all of them more than once today.

Finally, with the creature dead, Quinn sat herself down, all sooty, tired, and beat up. She wasn't the only one.

"Good thing we have magic," Eric said, wrinkling his nose disdainfully as he smelled them all. He activated a cleansing spell.

It was an odd sensation to have all of the soot lifted from her skin, but at the same time, it felt pretty good.

Quinn glanced around. There were a lot of dead creatures around them, and with all the burned flesh thanks to Mr. Now-Dead-Drake, there was an ugly smell lingering too. "I was going to say I'm famished after using that much magic, but my stomach just turned. Let's just eat a couple of energy balls and find that damn book."

This time, when she brought up the map, it was easier to locate the book. It appeared to be in one of the buildings in the center of the city. Quinn studied it, trying to figure out exactly how to get there from where they currently were.

Aradie hooted.

"Follow you?" Quinn shrugged. "Okay, lead on, let's go and get that damned book. This one's already taken much more time than I wanted it to."

Quinn kept her senses stretched out, wary of encountering another drake. Despite Aradie's healing, her shoulder still hurt badly. It was less the new flesh and more the aching muscles. She didn't think she'd be up for any type of potential physical combat any time soon. They worked their way through the surprisingly ordered streets toward the center.

"Looks like it might have been a town hall at some stage," Eric mused, his eyes flashing brightly.

Just like every other structure, it didn't have a roof, and only had one doorway. Quinn frowned. "We could have come through right here."

Malakai shook his head. "Pretty sure this was the drake's nest. Library won't drop you into danger if it can help it . . . or unless its sensors are being obfuscated."

"That's a rather specific afterthought," Quinn murmured, as she delicately stepped through and into the main chamber. "On the bright side, we can leave from here."

Her senses still extended, Quinn still felt uneasy, even though apart from rodents and other wildlife, there didn't appear to be anything else around them. The main hall was large, like a lobby, and her map led her right to the middle of the room.

Quinn frowned. "There's no book here." Her head was starting to throb in time with her shoulder.

"If you'd get off that stone under your feet, I think you'd be enlightened," Eric drawled as if he'd never been so bored in his life.

Quinn moved and glanced down at the big cobblestone. It was maybe two feet squared, so really more of a thick tile. Malakai nudged her aside and crouched down, drawing a dagger to clear away the soot and dirt around the edges, leaving a clear, if thin gap. He then dug his fingers in and lifted with Eric's help to leverage the brick out.

Underneath, in a small cavity, nestled alongside some brittle papers and a few jars of herbs, was the book.

Quinn reached in, dusted it off, and hugged it to her chest, thinking it odd for it to have been locked away under the floor in a town hall. But she wasn't about to argue now she'd found it.

She grinned at the others. "Two down, and two to go."

5 6

———

ANYTHING BUT

APART FROM THE SALAMANDERS AND THE DRAKE, QUINN THOUGHT retrieving the book had been almost too easy. They didn't linger in the Library after they brought the book back. Quinn slammed the book onto the counter and stared at Lynx.

"I am returning *Emergency Supplements and the Taste Palette*," she said, flashing him a big grin.

Lynx sighed. "You could just come in and scan it in yourself."

"Nope, I'm technically still on a mission." Quinn grinned. "No Librarian stuff for me!"

Lynx at least had the grace to laugh and then he wrinkled up his nose. "You guys kind of smell," he said.

Quinn blinked and sniffed herself. "Oh, that's us," she said, glancing over at where the aracnio brothers had been serving some patrons who'd come into the Library.

Their many multifaced eyes stared at her for a few very awkward seconds before they half-smiled and waved at her. Quinn felt slightly guilty for having thought the odor might have come from them or a patron. But also thought that stare had been quite unsettling. They'd never practically looked through her before. She knew they hadn't read her mind; her protections were too strong for that.

What an odd interaction.

"We're just gonna renew some supplies, have a quick shower, and head straight back out," she said to Lynx, pulling herself back to task.

"What did you do?" Lynx looked over their half ruined, if magic-cleaned attire. "Wrangle an entire herd of salamanders?"

Quinn narrowed her eyes at him. "Yes, this sounds like you knew something and didn't tell us again, Lynx?"

"No," he said hurriedly, "they're just native to that world, that's all. I didn't think you'd encounter an entire flock of them."

"Is it a flock or a herd?" Quinn paused, curious. "Or a congress or parliament or something even cooler?"

"I don't know." Exasperation leaked into Lynx's tone. "They're salamanders."

A short while later the small expedition group congregated back in front of the check-in desk and Lynx looked them over. "You have the location of the next one. The door should open to allow you into the world.

"Which one are we after this time?" Malakai asked, and proceeded to swallow a large yawn.

"*Making the Most on the Road: A Field Cook's Guide to Culinary Rein-forcement*," Lynx said, as if it was a lot of effort to tell them the name of the book. "Thank you so much. When you get back, I'll have the approximate location of the other one for you."

"Consider it done." Quinn winked at him, feeling oddly in a great mood thanks to the shower, even if her shoulder still felt sore.

"Just remember," he called after them as they approached the double doors, "there's a reason the books haven't made it closer on their own."

"Yeah, yeah, I get it," Quinn said. "They don't have arms."

"Or legs!" Eric cackled in response.

Lynx side eyed the imp before continuing. "Well, yes, and some-times they've been put in a spot for safekeeping,"

Quinn cringed. "Oh, to keep it so safe that you actually forget where you put it."

"Exactly," Lynx said.

This time Quinn activated her hover defense before she stepped through the Library door and successfully avoided falling flat on her backside.

"You're getting better at that," Malakai said, grinning. "I see you didn't land on your face this time."

"Well, I figured maybe I should use my brain instead of completely forgetting that I have magical powers and just plowing through the door and falling flat on my face because the Library, it seems, has some weird sense of humor that wants to see me fall . . ." She trailed off. The Library door had closed behind them, shrouding them in darkness. "Why is it so dark here?"

"Are you scared of the dark?" Eric asked, and suddenly there was light before Quinn could call up on her own light spell.

Quinn frowned. "Is your tail on fire?" she said to Eric.

"Don't even. Not a word, nothing, no comments or I'll let you walk around in the darkness." His scowl appeared more sinister in the dim light.

Quinn didn't comment on anything else. She frowned but she understood that she shouldn't pick on him right now because he was slightly sensitive about using his tail as a torch. Even if it was sort of cute. She wasn't about to tell him that.

She studied their surroundings. They appeared to be in a large basement-type area if the brick walls and lack of windows were anything to go by. The room had columns all throughout it, just brick columns that supported the ceiling that had to be maybe ten to twelve feet above them. She couldn't quite get a grasp on the scope of the space due to the lighting.

It was quite tall for a basement, but since coming to the Library, Quinn had realized that architecture, the worlds over in the universe, was very often different than she expected. Plus dependent on the creatures or species who lived there; they required the buildings fit their bodies.

As her eyes became accustomed to the darkness and the flickering shadows, she noticed a very strange sound.

The noise sounded like something scraping, or being scraped, across the stone floor. Given the stone walls, Quinn had half-expected tiled floors, but these were smooth, more like concrete. She looked around, peered in all the corners, walked around all the pillars, and then heard a sort of dragging thud but it wasn't as if it was something heavy. It was almost as if it was something light. Like perhaps a book.

Quinn still couldn't see. "You hear that, right?" she said to Malakai.

"Yes and I'm trying to find it." He sounded irritated.

Aradie hooted and held up a wing while she sat on Quinn's shoulder. She'd taken up residence on the right-hand side while Quinn's left shoulder was still somewhat tender.

"What? Where?" Quinn followed the wing and looked at the stairs that she hadn't seen before because the stairs were in darkness too and that's when she realized there was literally a book dragging itself down the stairs toward them and where the Library door had initially opened.

"Well," Quinn said, "there's something you don't see every day."

Malakai and Eric actually laughed.

"I wasn't trying to be funny," she said.

"No, but you succeeded anyway," Eric said. "You know we like our entertainment, Quinn."

She glared at the imp.

"Well," Quinn said as the book continued to drag itself toward them. It didn't have far to go now. She felt like giving it a sense of accomplishment. "Lynx did say they usually find their own way mostly home?"

"Yeah," Malakai said. "Somehow I pictured them growing little legs or something, not this strange, torturous dragging."

"Sort of like a shambling zombie," Quinn muttered. It didn't appear as if Malakai or Eric heard her.

As they watched, the book inched along by using its covers as legs. It moved the front half and then dragged the back half. Moved the front half. Very much like an inchworm.

Quinn shook her head, partially hypnotized by the movement. She reached down and picked it up once it got close enough. Sure enough,

Making the Most on the Road: A Field Cook's Guide to Culinary Reinforcement had found the Librarian.

There was a release of power of some sort, like a whoosh of relief and wind that happened when she held it firmly in her grasp. She looked around. There was nothing else in the basement. There were no sounds, no ominous feelings, no sensations of cultists sacrificing others to open dimensional portals above them.

"I guess we head back to the Library," she said.

"Yeah." Eric sounded just as confused.

Malakai shrugged. "Don't look a gift book in the mouth," he said, and Quinn summoned the door.

Back in the Library, Quinn realized they'd only been gone for about an hour. It was late afternoon now, and she didn't want to retrieve another book that night. She plopped the book she'd been clutching on the return desk. Lynx raised an eyebrow in her direction.

"What's up with you?" he asked.

"Well, that one was anticlimactic," she said. "I mean, the first one we had to kill like eighteen, twenty salamanders, not to mention the damned drake, which really hurt. My shoulder is still tender. But this one was sort of boring. We just walked in and the book was already making its way to us, slowly, kind of creepily, almost like a corpse dragging itself along the floor, but it was genuinely trying to get to the Library."

Lynx smiled and scooped the book up. "What a good book." He beamed a smile at her.

Quinn cleared her throat and continued. "I just sort of . . ." She shrugged

"Expected more fighting," Lynx finished for her.

"Yes, exactly!"

"Quinn, do you secretly like having powers that can kick the crap out of things?" Lynx grinned.

"Yes, I think I do. I'm not ashamed to admit it," she said.

"Good, because everybody else can tell. But the good news, Quinn," Lynx continued, "is that because the book was legitimately trying to get to the door or as close to it as it possibly could, that means the Library signal is getting stronger. It's reaching its destinations with more efficiency. We should be able to pinpoint with more accuracy pretty soon, and there's actually hope it won't take forever to get all the books back."

"Well, I guess that's a good thing," she said, feeling less grumbly.

Malakai had already headed to the kitchen. She was pretty sure he hadn't eaten much when they picked up food to take with them before leaving the last time. Aradie had immediately flown off, briefly flashing Quinn a vision of the nightowl roosting tree.

Quinn rubbed her left shoulder again. Eric was nowhere to be seen. "I might . . . who could help me heal my shoulder?"

"Quinn, it's healed." Lynx sounded like he was trying to be gentle. "Aradie healed it, right?"

"Yes," Quinn said, "which reminds me. I had no idea she could do that."

Lynx sighed. "Aradie can do a lot. It's her choice to be here, just like all the nightowls. Your shoulder is going to be a bit tender. Frankly, even with her healing you, it appears to have recovered remarkably well. Take it easy."

"Fine, I'll sleep or shower or something," Quinn said, still a little disgruntled.

"You came back to the Library to return the book, and I get the feeling you're not heading back out tonight, so go have some food, go relax, and honestly, you should probably talk to Cadre." Lynx smiled softly as he spoke.

"Cadre's here to help with the process of sequence replacing?" Quinn's eyes widened and all thoughts of fatigue fled her mind. "Already?"

"Yes, because you and Milaro agreed he could be here." From Lynx's tone, Quinn could tell he didn't exactly feel the same way.

"I know we agreed. I'm not arguing that point," Quinn pursed her lips in thought. "So is he already here? I thought he was going to be a few days."

"Well, it's been almost two days, Quinn, so it's pretty close to a few. No need to be pedantic." Lynx raised an eyebrow.

Quinn frowned. "So how goes the restrictive tome location?"

"That's why you need to meet and talk to Cadre. The process, as you suggested it, is obviously not going to be quite that simple."

Quinn gave him a scowl. "Fine. Maybe we could all have dinner together."

Lynx hesitated. "I wouldn't recommend eating with one of the Migalexutal. That's Cadre's species. But the good news is that they only really eat every couple of days, so you could probably just talk to him after you have a nice sit-down dinner yourself."

Quinn raised an eyebrow this time. Then she shrugged. "We're not leaving until tomorrow anyway, so I'm going to get a few more books to absorb, eat some food, shower, and meet Cadre."

Just about to leave the area, she paused as an afterthought. "Didn't you say the last book that we have to retrieve is *Honor Among Pies: Regeneration at Its Finest*. Didn't you say the person who borrowed those books will probably also be reluctant to give it to us?"

"Something like that," Lynx said, "Savinth is—hmm, how can I put this?—can be very stubborn." He paused, and Quinn's mind was already moving on. "I'll see you when you're ready to talk to Cadre," Lynx said as she turned to leave.

Jim and Bob nodded their heads in her direction, but wouldn't meet her eyes as she walked past, and Quinn returned the gesture and paused for a moment in front of them.

"Hello," said Jim.

"There," continued Bob.

"Hi, Jim and Bob. Are you enjoying your time in the Library?" she asked, trying to be polite, which was difficult especially since their behavior over the past several days had changed.

"The Library is a wealth of information," they said in unison. They almost sounded robotic sometimes.

Quinn nodded. "That it is. That it is. Thank you for everything you do." She headed to grab some food, wishing she knew why things felt off with the twins.

Later, after a scrumptious meal that tasted suspiciously like shepherd's pie, Quinn sat in her office. She didn't like the sound of this

Savinth person, and she was really hoping that they weren't anything like Kajaro. She didn't need another alien object in her head trying to blow her up.

Although her mental defenses were quite formidable now, if she did say so herself.

Done with dinner, she sipped on a cup of tea, one which she'd never heard of before in her life and wasn't even going to risk pronouncing incorrectly.

Siliqua and Harish walked into her office, trailed by somebody she assumed was Cadre, only from the vague references to his species, she had to admit to being a little shocked at his appearance.

"Well, Librarian," Siliqua said, "please meet Cadre."

Quinn stood and tried her best not to ogle their guest. Cadre looked sort of like a gecko. Except much, much larger. He stood about four feet tall, was extremely slender, but had beige and red skin tones instead of being green or brown. He was actually quite beautiful, and his double-lidded eyes flickered constantly through different hazes of red. He was delicate in appearance, thin arms, thin legs, slender body, and a robe that covered him from head to foot with a cowl hanging down his back.

"Good evening, Librarian," he said with a lilt to his voice. She secretly thought he looked like a TV celebrity animation that she'd seen on television, just a lot larger than that one had been.

"Good to meet you too, Cadre. Do you think it'll be possible to do what we want to?" She was suddenly too tired to beat around the bush. She was about to get post-food sleepiness.

He cocked his head to one side and said, "Yes and no."

"Elaborate, please?" Quinn asked.

"From what I've studied of both your and the Library's specific genetics. The solution should be possible, yet it's not going to be simple. It will take time to engineer the solution, and in that time I'd suggest the Librarian and its allies seek ways of becoming stronger." His voice was soothing, soft enough that Quinn would have expected to strain to hear it, but didn't have to.

"Is that advice," Quinn asked, "or are you prescient?"

He shook his head, "No, I am not. It's simple advice. But there are likely reasons the sabotage was performed in this intricate way. Once we reverse this problem, and we *will* be able to reverse it in time, then nothing will protect you from the knowledge of those who are involved."

Quinn could feel the ominous overtones in his words. It wasn't a warning, just facts. "Do you think it's a trap?"

Cadre shook his head. "No. I don't believe they thought this far ahead to such a unique solution for this puzzle. What they set in motion has taken thousands of years. If we undo it, they'll know, and I doubt they'll be so subtle next time."

Quinn nodded and could feel the color drain from her face at the thought. "Thank you. Do you need anything from me?" she asked.

Cadre smiled. "Not right now. I realize the Librarian is busy. But in a few days, I'll need of your assistance. If it's okay with you, might I borrow Harish again? We were figuring out several different approaches. And I must say, this is a welcome conundrum. I was finding new stimuli difficult to obtain. You have my thanks."

"Sure. Go and figure stuff out." Quinn watched the men walk out, Harish paying rapt attention as Cadre spoke. Then she turned to Siliqua. "Like peas in a pod?"

Siliqua laughed. "A very apt description."

"How are we looking on the restricted vault books' location recovery?" Quinn asked.

Siliqua hesitated a second and sighed. "We're gleaning some information, but . . . it's difficult. However, Cadre did have a few ideas I'm about to implement. Still, I'm thinking it'll take at least a week until we can pinpoint any of them with accuracy."

"And failing visiting every world and seeing if I can feel out if there's a magical book trying to usurp the dimension through sacrifice—we basically have to wait?" Quinn asked, already resigned to the answer.

"Accurate." Siliqua was quiet for a second. "I'm sorry, Librarian. But at least you can get the branch opened while you wait."

And get stronger. Quinn thought, but didn't say. A whole week to just work on her abilities and grow? That would be ideal.

"Yes," she answered, instead of spilling all the ideas in her mind. "Tomorrow we'll get the last book for the culinary branch, and get it opened."

"Then I'll take my leave and assist Cadre with my husband." Siliqua smiled. "I'm glad you were found, Librarian. Thank you for everything."

Quinn watched the wood elf walk away, a thoughtful smile on her face. This was good. Just one more cookbook to go and the Library would gain another link of power.

All they had to do was get one more book.

It sounded so simple. And yet Quinn couldn't shake the feeling that it was anything but.

SINKING SENSATION

Quinn was surprised at how well she had slept. They hadn't done much the day before, really.

Okay, so maybe fighting salamanders and a Drake did amount to much and she had reason to have fallen into an exhausted, dreamless sleep.

She sighed as she waited for her teammates to arrive and glanced at Lynx, who was fiddling with something in the console. He frowned, and the runes in his hair swirled in an almost languid fashion.

"Do we know much about who has this *Honor Among Pies* book? Do we know?" Quinn asked him, partially enthralled by the runes.

"Yes," Lynx said, refusing to make eye contact as he delved further into whatever had caught his attention in the console. It felt like deliberate avoidance.

Quinn moved closer. "Are you going to tell?"

Lynx sighed and finally turned to look at Quinn. "Her name is Savinth."

Quinn raised an eyebrow. "Elaborate."

"Well," Lynx said, breaking the eye contact again, "Savinth is a human species . . . variant."

"Explain," Quinn encouraged him.

"Well, they're old. Not because of heritage like you, though, and not like me. Their human trait is basically that the entire species is kind of cursed, so they have very long lifespans."

"Cursed but only kind of?" Quinn said, her interest piqued. "Is there nothing that can break that curse?"

Lynx shrugged. "I don't know. I'm not one of them."

Quinn pinched the bridge of her nose and counted to three internally. "Okay. Got anything else?"

"Well, Savinth is a very . . . a very acquired sort of taste. She's very opinionated and sometimes can be downright nasty." Lynx's mouth twisted as if the words were distasteful for him.

Quinn blinked. "Like, 'try to kill me so they don't have to give me back the book' nasty?"

Lynx shook his head. "No, not like Kajaro nasty. Just sort of . . . their sense of humor might not be everybody's cup of tea, and sometimes they can just be a little bit too blunt."

"I can deal with blunt," Quinn said.

Lynx seemed to hesitate but then barreled straight on ahead. "Also, they kind of have reasons and persuasions about a lot of topics, and they're extremely good at manipulating you into a corner so that you loan them the exact book they want, even if maybe they should have returned other things first."

"Oh," Quinn said. "You mean like just a regular person who really wants something?"

"No, in a way that you won't probably notice until you're already doing what they wanted." Now he sounded positively grumpy.

"Oh, so like in a magical mind magic way?"

"Vaguely more in a . . . no, that would probably be right," Lynx said after a moment's pause.

"Well my walls are pretty bloody solid now. But I'll reinforce them a bit more. Anyway, talk to me . . ." Her voice trailed off as Malakai, Eric, and Aradie joined them. The owl swooped onto her shoulder, which felt much better today. It was no longer tender like it had been after being nearly burnt to a crisp and healed yesterday. "Great to see you guys. Nice and not on time."

Malakai shrugged. "If you give me hazard pay, I'll start thinking about actually making it exactly on time. I might even be early."

"What sort of prince are you that you need hazard pay?" Quinn heckled him with a grin.

He wasn't put off in the slightest. "Pay just tells me how much you appreciate me."

"You'll have my respect forever?" Quinn offered.

Malakai laughed. "I think I've already got that."

"Dream on. No," Quinn said. "That was mean. You're right, you kind of sort of already do."

"See, I knew I was right," Malakai said. "Anyway, you said Savinth is human."

Lynx nodded. "A human genome type E-31,785."

"Wait, did you just say there are at least 31,785 different genome archetypes of humanity?" Quinn said.

"You're overcomplicating it." Lynx paused and continued. "But essentially you're correct."

"Okay, that's something for future me to bug you about," Quinn said. "So a human genome species that has magic?"

"Yes, not from Earth," Lynx clarified.

"Do a lot of non-Earth humans have magic?" Quinn asked, overcome with curiosity.

Lynx shrugged his shoulders. "It's not quite like that. It's the atmosphere they're born into and raised in. There are a whole lot of contributing factors."

"I can work with that," Quinn said, and then a thought struck her. "Did I have a designation like that, a number?"

"No, you didn't. When you arrived," Lynx said, "A: We didn't have enough power to tap in and assign you anything and create an addition to the database. And B: now that we know your origins and that the Library is aware of them, you're not technically classified as human anymore."

Quinn knew that, and yet it felt oddly strange to realize she wasn't considered a human being. It was a strange sort of sensation that shivered down her spine at the thought. One of these days, she was going to sit down and explore that when she didn't have a to-do list three miles long.

"Do I have a species designation?" Quinn said, mildly curious.

Lynx hesitated again and the Library interjected, *Your . . . species is currently still undergoing examination and evaluation.*

"Oh, that's a great way to totally avoid the question," Quinn said, "but I guess it's also accurate."

The Library continued. *Just pay attention to this next retrieval for now. Please.*

"Do I need to worry about time dilation where we're going? Will there be flying, fire-breathing creatures waiting to barbeque us? Is there anything we should know about that you haven't told us yet? Because you tend to do that." Quinn crossed her arms and glared at Lynx, taking out her frustration at the Library on him just a little.

"Nope," Lynx said, shaking his head. "The Library has a solid level of power now, so when I push you through this portal, you should come out pretty close to where Savinth's last recorded location was. Now this could be a bit off because it has been, you know, a few hundred years, but we should be pretty good."

And then Lynx turned to Eric and frowned. "It's probably a good idea for you to stay here, Eric."

Eric raised an eyebrow, and if possible, his wings seemed to flicker faster with irritation. "What's that supposed to mean?"

"Well," Lynx said, "Savinth isn't partial to imps for a multitude of reasons that are very personal and mostly extremely violent in her history."

Quinn raised an eyebrow. "Are you okay with that, Eric?"

He shrugged. "Not all of my brethren are as dashing and charming as I am. Can't help it if you've been lucky enough to experience the best."

Quinn's eyebrow raised so high it almost jumped off her face.

He winked at her. "But, you know, I'm going to leave you to it. Time to get some food from Cook." And he was gone so fast Quinn didn't even have time to use her senses to see if he was lying.

Aradie hooted next to her. "Yeah, I thought that was a bit of bravado too," Quinn said.

"But you should be fine with Malakai and Aradie," Lynx said. "Savinth shouldn't be hostile."

"Shouldn't?" Quinn asked.

"Yes, and we're leaving it at that. Okay, off you go. This is where you need to head." And he pushed an image toward Quinn's mind.

When Quinn, Malakai, and Aradie stepped through the Library doors, the world beyond it changed drastically from where they'd been.

First of all, the door was flush with the ground, and Quinn didn't even need her hovering ability to save her from falling flat on her butt. Beyond the door were beautifully manicured little cobblestone paths set inside of lush green grass with wooden borders separating the paths and streets from parks and sidewalk decorations. They weren't in a forest, but there were trees scattered everywhere. Huge trees, many with fresh blooms on them making it feel like a perpetual spring.

It was a beautiful sight to behold. In fact, it sort of looked like what you'd imagine a cozy European village looked like several hundred years ago. Well, almost, if she disregarded the fact that this place had a fresh and not pre-plumbing scent to it. That, and the purple hue to the sky didn't exactly scream Earth. Not to mention the visibly rotating, color-shifting sun in the sky.

But other than that, definitely European village vibes.

Suddenly, somebody cleared their throat to the rear right of her. Quinn whirled around to the side to see who made the sound.

Leaning against the wall that held the door they'd just stepped out of, was a human woman. Except her eyes were flecked with gold, all through the whites of the sclera, all through the color of the iris, and the darkness of the pupil. They were just mesmerizing eyes.

"Yeah, thought you lot might show up," she said. "Send me a bloody Darigháhnish."

She was about four inches taller than Quinn, and stood there, tapping her foot on the ground, waiting, with her arms crossed as she leaned against the building.

"Um, hi," Quinn said, unsure of exactly how to greet this individual. She couldn't understand how she knew, because she didn't inspect her. It's not like she was wearing a name badge, but Quinn was pretty sure this was Savinth in front of them. "I'm Quinn, I'm the current Librarian."

"Are you now?" Savinth said, looking her up and down. "You'll do, I guess. All right, come on up the back."

They moved and began walking around the building, to where there was an outside set of stairs. Quinn turned and glanced at Malakai. Aradie, still affixed to her shoulder, simply ruffled her feathers and made herself more comfortable. Savinth was still grumbling as they walked up the stairs, and ushered them into what was probably a loft apartment. It was quite spacious, considering the size of the adorable little Tudor building.

"Surprised they didn't send an imp at this rate," Savinth muttered as she closed the door.

Once inside the second story of the lovely little Tudor cottage, Savinth turned to Quinn. "And, just what are you? You're not human."

Quinn shrugged, because it was true, but she wasn't exactly sure how much she should be telling people, nor did she have any clue as to what, exactly, she was. "I'm the Librarian."

"Nah," Savinth said, "You look human enough. For now, at least, I think."

Quinn desperately wanted to ask what abilities Savinth had that made her so certain Quinn wasn't human. But she thought that might be the height of rudeness among magic users in the universe.

"Anyway," Savinth said, "do you guys want a drink? Something, anything?"

"A water would be great," Quinn said.

Savinth raised an eyebrow, "Yeah, water would be good anywhere, wouldn't it?"

"Yes?" Quinn said, not really understanding how she'd offended this other fellow human-esque person.

Once Savinth had placed a bowl of food in front of Aradie, and two glasses of water on the table, Savinth cleared her throat, "Okay. I want you to tell me why I should give my book back to you."

"Because we're trying to open the culinary branch, and it's literally the only book left missing that's preventing us from being able to," Quinn said, hoping she sounded more confident than she felt.

Savinth's eyebrows shot up, "Really, the branch is closed?"

"Yeah, the whole Library was closed for almost five hundred years," Quinn said. "We only just reopened."

"Wait." Savinth held up a hand, frowning. "I knew the Library wasn't letting me in to return the book, and I got pretty pissed off, I can tell you that. I thought my last conversation with—what's her bloody name, Kor, Korradine?—whatever, whoever she was, I thought she'd banned me. I wasn't going to give you the book back when I kept getting pinged for it. I'd already tried to return it so many times before now."

"That seems to have been the case for a lot of people. They didn't believe the Library when it came back online. They thought it was gone." Quinn still felt waves of sadness at that thought.

"Oh, no, no, I believed you were wanting your book back, I just . . ." Savinth trailed off, a thoughtful look in her eyes.

Malakai brushed his hand across Quinn's forearm to stop her from saying anything, and spoke. "I don't suppose you'd tell us what the conversation was that you had with Kor?"

"I mean, it's no secret, you probably have it in your security logs. I wanted this book and one of the restricted books. She refused to give me the restricted vault book, even though I'm in great standing, and have been for hundreds of years." There was a trace of deep frustration in Savinth's words.

"A restricted cooking book?" Quinn asked, suddenly feeling a strange stirring inside her. It was as if her Library attuned senses were waking up, trying to recall something.

"Yeah, right. She said it was only for specific people to take out and that I didn't qualify to have free run of all the culinary books." Now Savinth sounded angry.

Quinn tried to figure out the best approach. "Could you tell me which book it was? What sort of food it cooked?"

Savinth laughed, "Oh, I guess you probably already have it in the vault so you wouldn't have needed to retrieve it. *Everlosst's Mind-Altering Treats.*"

"Oh, that's not on our list." Quinn smiled, hoping it looked genuine, while her mind went into overdrive. That book wasn't in the vault. It had to be another one of the missing ones. "It's good to know I didn't miss one in the branch reopening list."

Savinth nodded, hesitated for a second, and then spoke. "Okay, wait a second, the Library was shut for five hundred years? I wasn't banned?"

"No, you weren't banned." Quinn laughed, but secretly wanted to check that banning. "Why in the universe would you think you'd be banned?"

"Damn that Korradine, that pesky interfering . . ." Savinth ranted, her cheeks flushing with anger.

"Did she do something else?" Quinn wished she could just automatically know everything the previous Librarian had done. There seemed to be layers to her machinations.

"She led me to believe I wasn't welcome back in the Library. I already had *Honor Among Pies* when I went to try and get *Everlosst's.* She told me the likes of me shouldn't bother returning. She'd just take the time and power to recreate the book and write the copy I had off."

"Oh," Quinn said, feeling bad for the other human. "I guess that's why you wanted to know why you should give it back."

"Yeah. That right there." Savinth sighed. "So you see, I haven't exactly been in a welcoming mood, what with all the pings for the book."

"Speaking of which, Quinn said. "I don't suppose you'd be willing to let us bring it back so we can open the culinary branch?"

"Sure. I mean, now we've cleared that misunderstanding stuff all up." Savinth hesitated. "Except. Well, you see . . ." She paused.

Quinn felt like her stomach was filled with lead.

Finally Savinth stood straight and looked Quinn square in the eyes. "I hate to tell you this but *Honor Among Pies*, if you want that book back, you're going to have to help me go get it."

Malakai's smile froze, and Quinn could feel his frustration. Aradie huffed in her ear. And Quinn plastered on a smile, despite the sinking sensation in her gut. "Of course we'll help. Do you remember where it is?"

"Of course I do." Savinth scoffed. "I didn't leave it somewhere accidentally. I just got annoyed, and I'd got my goodie out of it, and now the Desilish clan have been using it for a while, and we might have had a falling out shortly after I loaned it to them."

Malakai groaned. "The Desilish clan? Seriously? Why didn't you just give it to a pack of wild salamanders? We'd have a better chance of retrieving it."

Quinn glanced around. "I take it this is bad."

Savinth shrugged. "In my defense, I thought you'd banned me for asking about a book, and on the bright side, at least it'll be full of magic energy when you get it back."

5 8

SOMEWHERE IN BETWEEN

Quinn blinked at Savinth, a whole range of questions on the tip of her tongue. All she really wanted though was to retrieve the overdue books they needed, replenish the Library's power, open some branches, and get some time to herself for another training montage.

Why did it seem so much to get some time to herself to train? It was like every other isekai protagonist in a story or comic managed to find training montage time, but not Quinn.

Oh no, *she* had work to do.

Although, she guessed this was just her life now, not actually a comic, a movie, or a story.

She sighed and still couldn't quite formulate what she wanted to say to the other human because a part of her was angry. "So, basically you're telling us that you borrowed the book from the Library, got pissed off about a conversation you had with Kor, and couldn't get back into the Library to return it. So you assumed you'd been banned, gave the book—that didn't belong to you in the first place—to these other people—"

"The Desilish," Malakai interjected, extremely unhelpfully.

"Thanks. Thanks for that, Mal." Quinn scowled at him. "You gave this book to the Desilish and then you had an argument with them as well. And now you need our help to get your responsibility back which you'd probably never have attempted to retrieve if we hadn't come looking for it."

Savinth nodded. "Yeah, that's about it. That's a really good summary."

Quinn stood gaping at the other woman, who just had taken the whole admonishment in her stride. Savinth was busy outfitting each one of them with hooded cloaks and boot protectors, which were sort of odd little boots that you pulled over your shoes and cinched up just under the knee. A very strange little set-up of protective gear.

But Quinn was curious. "Why do we need these again?"

Malakai sighed. "The Desilish make their homes, their bases, in swamps."

Well, this made sense. Given they were headed into a swamp, it was probably the best type of boot protection they could get on short notice. The cloaks would hopefully keep bugs off them too.

Mostly.

A thought struck her, and Quinn gave Malakai a curious look. "What? We're going to get the book back from swamp creatures?"

"No. Why would they . . ." Malakai paused. "It's the plants, the atmosphere. They're not a species. They're like a clan of like-minded individuals who've come together. Basically a witches coven."

Static surrounded the word *witches* when he spoke it, obfuscating it ever so slightly. She could tell the translation capabilities were struggling with finding an exact term for what the Desilish were.

It was a close translation, but not quite a precise one. And it didn't get down into the nitty-gritty of the word's definition, but it was the closest thing that it had. So the translation spell or whatever it was had picked the most comparable term for it. She was doubly curious to see exactly how these Desilish were similar to witches.

"Well," Quinn said, "I guess we're going to clean up Savinth's mess."

"You don't have to put it that way, love," Savinth said, and then chuckled. "Actually, that's probably a highly accurate way to put it. I do leave a lot of mess."

"You know I'm going to fine you for this, don't you?" Quinn asked.

"Yeah. Yeah. I get it," Savinth said. "I know I should've gone and retrieved the book myself, but this clan's grown over the last century. It's not as small as it was when I had my initial falling out with them."

"Great," Quinn said, not meaning it in the slightest.

They set out from the lovely little cottage and walked along the beautifully manicured path. There were other gorgeous little Tudor cottages scattered all around. And if she looked out over the very gently sloping valley, there had to have been at least, well, maybe three or four hundred houses. They dotted the hills and the lanes, the fields and the parks.

It wasn't a small area.

She suppressed a sigh, wishing she had more time to examine the area. It reminded her of images of Earth, and she wanted to explore.

As the group reached the end of the path, there was a something-pulled carriage. Quinn had never seen the creatures before. They didn't really resemble horses. They were sort of more like a rhinoceros crossed with a zebra. A thin layer of dark red and white striped fur covered their bodies, but they were stout like the rhino with two horns at the end of their snouts. Quinn nodded toward them.

Malakai grinned, "Never seen a jackalaka, hey? Yeah, you'll be happy. They fart like crazy. This is going to be a very smelly ride."

Quinn looked from Malakai to the jackalakas and laughed. "Great. So we're going on a flatulent ride to a fetid swamp."

"Pretty much," Savinth agreed.

Aradie pulled some of Quinn's hair across her beak. "That's not going to filter anything," she said to her owl. A low hoot, slightly offended, was all she got in response.

Slowly, all of them piled into the cart. It began to move along the path at a very brisk pace. Aradie launched herself off Quinn's shoulder, maybe to scout, but also partially to avoid the stench that drifted back to them in the cart after every ten steps or so.

Finally, they left the idyllic setting behind them. Quinn looked around. It was dusty, musty, and severely lacking in any type of vegetation. In fact, it looked like all of the land around them had died. She twisted, turning to look back at the beautiful village they'd just left and realized that a magical dome encased it.

"Oh," she said. "Is that to preserve the setting or just to preserve the weather?"

"A bit of both," Savinth said. "We find it allows us to control our harvests and our supplies. We're not only self-sufficient, we also provide a good amount of produce to surrounding domes."

Quinn glanced back again. "Are there a lot of domes? Is the swamp in a dome?"

"Oh, no. The swamp is definitively a swamp."

And as they moved through the barren waste, the deadened trees, the blackened soil, the cracked ground, slowly, it began to change. The foliage and trees regained leaves and a semblance of life, but it was on the darker side.

As if death had come to visit this area and only relented slightly. An ominous breeze passed over them as they approached the swamp and the hairs on the back of Quinn's neck stood on end.

The path toward their destination gave way to new vegetation and smells. The trees grew more plentiful, yet somehow more twisted, and a strange, musty, rotting scent suffused everything. They reached the edge of what Quinn would have called the start of the swamp, where the ground became marshy, and the smell was even worse. She didn't like having a super sniffer in this type of environment. The breeze had stopped once they entered the area, and the stagnancy only exacerbated the scent.

Leaves rustled, both on the ground and in the trees, but when she looked, there was no glimpse of anything to be had. The only hint that there had been anything at all to start with was the way the leaves moved, without even a hint of a breeze in the air.

"We'll have to leave the jackalakas here with the cart," Savinth said. "That's why you got the boot protectors."

Quinn glanced down at her feet, which sank about an inch into the ground. It wasn't mud-pit muddy, but it was definitely not as firm as dirt underneath her feet.

"Yeah, I get that now," Quinn said. She looked around, trying to gain her bearings in unfamiliar surroundings. She much preferred the rainforest they'd been through last time. That was something she'd witnessed before herself.

Swamps, however—she glanced at the shallow waters, expecting to see crocodiles and other strange slithering creatures. And yet there was nothing in there. Not even over the past couple of minutes. There were no air bubbles breaking the surface, even though her senses told her there was something lurking beneath. The place was likely teeming with wildlife.

"So, Savinth," Quinn said as the other woman returned from leaving the cart at the entrance to the swamp. "Tell me, this fight, is it 'I borrowed your leaf blower and forgot to give it back' or is it more of a 'You stole my husband and I'm going to kill you' sort of falling out?"

Savinth chuckled, and began to lead the way along the delicate path in the swamp. "Yeah, I'd put it in the middle of those two. It's more of a 'I won the baking contest because I knocked their pie to the ground and accidentally stepped on it' sort of falling out. So . . . somewhere in between."

Quinn groaned, and Malakai cleared his throat. "It should be pointed out," he said, "that the Desilish have been on very strained terms with the Library for about a millennium now."

Savinth looked away, and her cheeks colored.

"Seriously?" Quinn liked this woman less and less. "You knew they were on bad terms with the Library? And you gave my cookbook to somebody who hates my guts?"

"Well, they haven't met *you* yet, Quinn," Savinth said. "I'm quite sure they'll find you lovely."

"That's not the grand gesture you think it is." Quinn paused. She knew she needed to keep her temper, keep herself under control, and just kind of mediate things out. But she was a bit pissed at Savinth. This was all so juvenile.

"How old are you?" she asked Savinth, who looked at her in shock.

"You're asking my age?"

"Yes, I'm asking your age."

"I'm 823. But that's not a question you ask people!" Savinth's eyes flashed with annoyance. The gold flecks in them expanded momentarily before returning back to normal.

Quinn sighed. After eight hundred years, she hoped she'd gain a little bit more wisdom. But she did understand reacting to situations.

"And how old are you?" Savinth inquired.

Quinn paused for a moment and answered, realizing she'd missed her damn birthday. "Twenty."

"You're young." Savinth sighed. "Okay, I loaned the book out because after my altercation with Kor and my inability to access the Library, I wanted a little payback."

"And then you had your falling out." Quinn didn't ask the question. The facts were the facts after all.

"That I didn't plan." For the first time, Savinth actually sounded regretful.

Malakai piped up smoothly in the middle of the argument. "Didn't you speak to anyone else in your dome about the Library?"

Savinth shook her head. "Most of the people in my dome aren't exactly fond of reading, or magic."

Quinn raised an eyebrow. "But they live in a magical dome."

Savinth shrugged. "I didn't say they were smart."

Suppressing a chuckle, Quinn cleared her throat. "Just what was your falling out about?"

"Well, you know, I just got really ticked off. Originally, I gave them a book in exchange for three of their recipes."

"You got recipes off a Desilish?" Mal said, clear surprise in his voice that gave Quinn pause.

"Well, that was the deal," Savinth grumbled. "I did not, in fact, end up getting the recipes from the Desilish."

"Oh no," Quinn said. "What did you do in retaliation?"

As they picked their way very carefully along the narrow, muddy path, Savinth sighed. "You see, they have this little herb garden. It's not so little. It's pretty bloody big. Probably more like an herb field. And since they went back on their word and didn't give me the recipes, I may or may not have taken their entire crop of starweed."

She said the last word so quickly, Quinn didn't quite hear it. It was obvious, however, that Malakai had.

"Are you stupid?" he said, stopping abruptly. "You took their starweed?"

"Okay, so pretend like I'm new here and tell me what starweed is?" Quinn asked.

"That is an excellent question, foreigner."

Quinn paused. Her senses hadn't picked up anything other than the lingering sense of life in the swamp, and that voice didn't belong to any of their group.

"I am a foreigner, and I'm glad I ask great questions," Quinn said, turning very slowly, trying to use her senses to find whoever it was who had spoken.

"You won't find us." There was a smugness to that tone.

But they were wrong, because Quinn could sense beings, and she'd missed it because she'd assumed they were simply animals lurking in the swamp.

"Well, you're behind that tree, and there are about three of you in the swamp," Quinn said, "for a start."

"Very good nose."

"Nose, senses, very similar," Quinn said with a shrug. "Enlighten me. What is starweed?"

"I think it would be best if Savinth explains that to you. We might like to listen to her definition too."

The woman who spoke stepped out from the trees. She was about six feet tall, willowy, but not like Narilin. Instead, she was just simply tall, and she had long, beautiful arms, with about eight fingers on each hand, from what she could see. Her face was humanoid, but instead of a nose, there was a flat surface with a tiny slit, and her eyes were almost anime large.

"Well," Savinth said, her voice clipped with anger. "So nice to see you Jasper."

The woman practically growled in her throat. "You owe us."

"And you owe me!" There was a slight pause before Savinth continued. "But I might have overreacted."

"No buts, Savinth. You took a precious commodity from us, and you knew it." Jasper's voice was silky smooth, but danger lurked behind every word, setting the air on edge.

"Perhaps I overreacted," Savinth spat out, "but you reneged on a deal. I still don't have what you owe me for giving you the damn book."

"That book should always have been ours," Jasper began, her focus entirely on Savinth.

"I would just like to say," Quinn interjected, "that this book doesn't belong to either of you. And it's important in a whole different way you're not considering."

"And how would it be important to you?" Jasper sneered at Quinn.

The amount of vitriol in her tone snapped something inside of Quinn. "Because I'm the Librarian, and I want my fucking book back."

59

SECOND SKIN

Jasper's expression cycled through myriad emotions before finally settling on angry annoyance.

In hindsight, perhaps telling them they needed to give Quinn the damn book back, while surrounded by at least four magic users Quinn could specifically sense, and probably another four to six others that were attempting to conceal themselves, had been a highly foolish idea.

Jasper was practically spluttering. "The Library has no authority here," she said, but some of the confidence was gone from her tone.

And yet Quinn couldn't help but push the goading a little further. It was almost like she had no other option. "Maybe, but you've got my book, and I want it back."

"You're the Librarian?" Jasper asked, disbelief coloring her tone.

"Last I checked." Quinn felt a prickly sensation all over her skin, like every single hair was standing on edge, as if she was being scanned, sized up, dissected in a magical way. Almost automatically, Quinn pulled her shielding around herself like a thick outer layer of skin, and extended it around Malakai, Aradie, and reluctantly also Savinth.

She only just managed it in the nick of time, before a surge of power came from all around them, from those beings that she'd pinpointed as a hundred percent being the Desilish, and the ones she'd still been on the fence about perhaps being swamp crocodiles.

It ranged in toward them, rushing into the middle, and converged on their group. It shook the shielding she felt around her against her skin, making her slightly nauseated for a few seconds, while Savinth fell to one knee, and Aradie had to settle in a tree to steady herself. Malakai was the only one who seemed unfazed.

"Oh," Quinn said, "that wasn't a nice greeting. If you've harmed that book, I hope you know I'm going to have to fine you."

"I didn't borrow it," Jasper said. "We haven't borrowed anything from the Library in over a thousand years."

"Really? So why did you take the Library book?" Quinn asked, trying to keep her tone amicable while she surveyed the surroundings. Being outnumbered was never favorable, but Malakai was pretty handy with his weapons.

"We didn't know it was a Library book." Jasper spat out the lie too fast to make it believable.

"I'm taking it you didn't check the spine or the interior of the book? You know those stamps allow us to trace the book when we need to get it back, right?" Quinn almost had the layout of the other potential attackers now, and she could tell Malakai was doing the same. From the images Aradie shared with her, she knew her little team were all on the same page.

"That's beside the point. We didn't realize Savinth would swap us a Library book for the deal that she made with us." Jasper's eyes darted from side to side. She wasn't very subtle about having set up an ambush.

"A deal, may I remind you, that you reneged on." Savinth spoke, having regained her footing after the pulse knocked her to one knee. "Give me the book back."

"So you can give it to the Librarian? We don't want to help their kind," Jasper scoffed.

In the corner of her vision, Malakai pulled something Quinn had only seen him do while training with her occasionally. Shadows engulfed him until he was practically invisible, melding into them. She knew he was technically an assassin type of class, and yet she'd never really witnessed him fight that way. He usually used his bow or his sword.

Now, she could feel him only because her shielding still covered his skin like a spare epidermal layer. It was the only way she could trace him. If she hadn't cast her protection on him, she'd not have been able to feel his presence at all, despite her extended senses. And that was quite formidable.

"Where did he go?" Jasper said, her tone revealing some concern.

"He does that sometimes." Quinn shrugged and smiled and conjured about a dozen tiny ice balls, swirling them around in her hand. While Malakai moved toward some of the other hiding figured, Quinn kept her focus on Jasper, thereby hopefully keeping Jasper's focus on her.

"Are you going to explain to me why you didn't know the books belonged to the Library, or am I just going to have to assume that you're that dense?"

Jasper sneered at her. "You are young."

A rush of power smashed into Quinn, and she was thankful for all the training Malakai had pummeled into her to make sure she could maintain her shielding under any circumstances.

"You—you're not human," Jasper said, her eyebrow ridges rising in surprise.

Quinn shrugged. "So people have been telling me lately."

"What are you?"

"I'm the Librarian," Quinn answered, cocking her head to one side and grinning. "I thought we'd already established this."

The ice balls, in the meantime, had shot up into the sky so fast they were practically invisible. They started circling quite a ways above Quinn, out of sight, out of mind, as long as she could keep the attention of the other people on herself and not on them. Quinn attempted to send out telepathy for the first time to somebody not directly attached to the Library.

Don't kill them, she warned Malakai.

That's the plan. His voice came back to her, a fuzzy echo inside her head. She tried not to let herself heave a sigh of relief. She could feel that the book wasn't present with the group of people surrounding them. It was farther off to the southeast, maybe. If she wasn't getting her directions wrong, she'd never been very good at those.

"What's your offer?" she asked.

"There is no offer, Librarian. Your kind have ruined magic knowledge for everyone. You can't just gatekeep a species or a clan of people out of the Library just because you don't like them." This time Jasper did spit on the ground, defiance and anger flashing through her eyes.

Quinn raised an eyebrow at the information though, wanting to know more.

"What do you mean?" she said, sensing Malakai was almost done with whatever preparations he'd been making to finally unleash his attack. Meanwhile, Aradie shot her several images to let her know exactly where a few of them were located. Two of them she'd be able to easily put out of commission with a couple of well-timed ice bullet shots, as long as she aimed them fast enough. It was a good thing she'd picked up some healing spells.

"We didn't come here to talk. We came here to kick out unwanted intruders from our domain," Jasper said finally and launched a volley of fireballs at Quinn. At the same time, Malakai unleashed his attack, and Quinn instructed her ice balls to rain down on the two targets within the range Aradie had given her.

Savinth, on the other hand, dashed to the side, grabbing one of the watchers out from behind a tree and bringing her to the ground, grabbed the back of her hair, and held a knife to her throat.

"Well, that was a little bit anticlimactic," Quinn muttered.

"You haven't seen anything yet," Jasper growled.

And that's when everything happened at once. The individual Savinth caught twisted unnaturally, partially dissolving around the knife and reappearing on the other side. She grabbed Savinth by the back of the head and smashed her face into the almost-mud of the ground.

Quinn shoved power into her shielding as Jasper leveraged a fire spear directly at her. The Librarian brought up her arms in an X in front of her body, reflecting it with a mind blast shield to turn the spear straight back where it had been cast from, but the heat left her skin reddened and tingling from the close call.

In the meantime, Aradie dive-bombed one of the covert Desilish who was hiding some ways away, flashing with laser eyes and her beak. Quinn could sense, vaguely, Malakai locked in a dagger-to-dagger fight behind one of the other trees. She could only catch glimpses of the elf and she wasn't entirely sure if that meant he was flickering in and out of the shadows he'd concealed himself in, or if the underbrush was just in the way.

Quinn twisted out of the way and rolled to the side shoving herself behind one of the trees as Jasper yelped. Quinn had already sent several more of her ice balls floating up above her head and shot them down, aiming for Jasper's limbs as well as the individual who was currently fighting to keep Savinth under control.

One of the ice balls hit Savinth's opponent's foot. The attacker hadn't realized it was aimed at her, yelped, and released her hold on Savinth's neck long enough to give the other human the chance she needed to break free and fend for herself, allowing Quinn to focus fully on Jasper.

Not a moment too soon. Quinn dove to the side again as a fiery lance cut into the mud right next to her. It left a seared gash up her thigh and a hole in her jeans which she didn't appreciate. She barely had time to register that it didn't really hurt. She hadn't had enough wits about her after assisting Savinth to recognize the attack in the split second, but now she had all her attention on Jasper.

Quinn sent a trickle of healing to the spot to take away the sting and ward off the swamp dirt from getting into her wound. She didn't really know enough about fire magic to delve right into it or understand exactly what it was Jasper was doing, and ice was a very bad opponent to fire.

However, as she learned with the drake fight, air—or the ability to extract it from fire—was a pretty formidable tool. It just required a lot of focus.

Even though she could still sense Aradie and Malakai's fights going on in the back of her mind, she realized that they had a lot more combat experience than the Desilish did and thus they were gaining the upper hand. As was Savinth, especially since it appeared her opponent didn't have any innate healing abilities and thus couldn't heal the damage Quinn had done to her foot. The pain appeared to be preventing her from vapor shifting or whatever that had been.

Jasper, on the other hand, was like a bomb ready to go off. She was pissed and the emotion tried to envelop Quinn in waves. She readied air in her mind, knowing exactly what she wanted to do while she controlled a few more little ice balls hovering around the areas Malakai, Aradie, and Savinth were fighting in, just in case they needed help and she could separate her consciousness enough to aid them.

Seconds later Jasper hefted a fire javelin in her hand, Quinn activated her ability to think fast. She focused on the flame immediately, aiming her oxygen depletion ability at it. The look on Jasper's face was priceless. As the spear wicked out of existence, she tried it again and Quinn sucked the oxygen away, taking several more steps toward her.

"What the hell?" Jasper yelled, and this time a wall of flame rose up directly in front of Quinn. The only thing that saved her from being engulfed by flames was the fact that she maintained her shielding like a second skin around her body all the time.

She rolled to the ground, to put out the flames that sprang up because of her clothing. The shielding really only protected her body. She stood as fluidly as she could, aiming a gust of wind and an ice blast directly in Jasper's face. It hit her head-on in the chest, leveraging her back against the tree she'd originally been hiding behind. Then Quinn blasted more for good measure and froze her opponent directly to the trunk.

In the meantime, Aradie finished her own fight and Quinn could sense the unconscious forms of about nine other Desilish all around them. Savinth's opponent was groggily restrained by a glowing rope Quinn had a lot of questions about. She approached Jasper, who couldn't free her hands and seemed to be having a little bit of trouble talking.

"I was thinking," Quinn said, "now we've got all that out of our systems, that we could maybe have a civilized conversation."

Jasper spat, some of it catching on the ice to freeze immediately. "Damn Librarians, you always play judge."

"No," Quinn said, "Not that I've ever had the chance to meet another Librarian. I've been one for almost two months now. I've lost a bit of track of time here, but I am not judging you. Well, I wasn't at first, but I might be a little judgy now. You stole my book, you won't give it back, and you're being a bit rude. So what do you mean I'm *always* being a judge?"

"Korradine ruled with a scalding, corrupt fist, and the Library let her."

"Excuse me?" Quinn blinked at her and said, "What did you say?"

"The Library is corrupt."

Quinn waved the statement away. "We all know that's a lie, but what did you say about Korradine?"

"She ruled the Library with a corrupt fist, thereby making the Library a corrupt accomplice." Jasper's voice sounded hoarse, and Quinn relinquished some of the cold in the ice, bringing it closer to melting.

"I think you need to tell me exactly what you're talking about, because the Library was shut for almost five hundred years because Korradine retired before any other Librarians could be found. It's only been open again for like six weeks." Quinn was really curious now.

Jasper's expression changed from one of seething anger to surprise and skepticism. "You're bullshitting."

"No," Quinn said, "I am, in fact, not shitting you at all, and I think it's about time we had a proper talk."

6 0

SHADOW OF A DOUBT

Quinn wasn't entirely sure what she'd been expecting when Jasper finally agreed to speak, but quaint cottages surrounding a thriving series of herb gardens had not been it.

The swamp was still undoubtedly there, but this clearing in the center was abundant with bright greenery, growth, and beauty. She could even hear little birds in the trees and insects chirping. Occasionally, she even caught a glimpse of them. Bright feathers flashed across her vision, and butterflies with vibrant wings fluttered through the herb gardens. It was teeming with life that she hadn't attributed to being in the middle of a swamp.

Sort of like an oasis.

Several chairs were placed around a large round table outside one of the little cottages. The seating wasn't uncomfortable, but the silence was.

It was getting very, very awkward. Like all of Quinn's high school cafeteria nightmares had come together and mashed themselves into one place. She steeled herself to speak, only to have Jasper beat her to it.

"I truly appreciate your not killing my clan members," Jasper said, as if she was struggling to get the thanks out.

Quinn raised an eyebrow, because she didn't want to kill people. She just wanted her book back, and didn't appreciate being attacked. "Whyever would I kill someone who wasn't attacking me, or us, with a deadly force?" she asked.

"Okay," Jasper said, pausing while she gathered herself, "but nevertheless, I would like to express my thanks."

"Then you're welcome," Quinn said, slightly perturbed by the fact that she'd just been thanked for not killing people. Wasn't that just a sort of given? *How will you be a decent person? Oh, I don't know, I won't kill anyone?*

The silence settled again, becoming even more awkward than it had been earlier. Quinn looked at the drink in front of her. It was a clear liquid, didn't smell like anything. It was probably water. She took a very tentative sip. It was refreshing water, sort of like the stuff that had electrolytes and maybe a little spritz of lemon in it back on Earth.

"So," Quinn said, trying to gather her thoughts together, "explain to me why you didn't honor the deal that you struck with Savinth."

She was trying not to show her unease, as idyllic as the setting around them was. The people here had tried to ambush them, and Quinn was pretty sure they just weren't used to fighting enough, and thus their attacks hadn't been as effective as they could have been. She didn't think they were trying to kill them or scare them off, but that didn't belay the fact that they had, in fact, been attacked by these people.

They seemed to hate the Library, too, or at least despised the previous Librarian. Quinn needed this information from them. She needed to understand why they hadn't been privy to the Library's lack of functioning over the last several hundred years. Although, she guessed if they no longer frequented the Library's facilities, and didn't have any books out, they wouldn't have had a reason to find out.

Not only that, but why would they say Korradine corrupted the Library? *That* was what she needed to get to the bottom of.

Jasper's expression was schooled. But Quinn could tell there were emotions flickering just under the surface as the Desilish member attempted to find the best words to answer the question.

Quinn took another sip of her water and turned around to observe the area again. There were a mixed bunch of amazing creatures and people. It made her feel like she was in a fantasy novel. She spied a similar species to Finn, like an Ilgonomur it was short in stature with big eyes, but it was slightly taller than Finn, coming in at just over four feet tall, and it had webs between its fingers. Then she spied a few variants on the aracnio twins. The only difference in any of them appeared to be how their legs moved.

There were three different types of fae that she could see out there tending the gardens. They fluttered to and from the plants, light emanating from their hands on occasion. It was fascinating to watch. There were so many more people bustling around the massive area that she couldn't even identify.

Finally, everybody else surrounding the table who belonged in Jasper's delegation had given her what they probably thought were very surreptitious nods, allowing Jasper to give Quinn a reply. "We don't give out our recipes. They are a matter of clan pride."

Quinn resisted the urge to scowl, and kept her face as neutral as she possibly could. "So you deliberately and falsely made a deal that you knew you wouldn't uphold."

Jasper opened her mouth, closed it again, then opened it again, looked away, and refused to meet Quinn's eyes.

"I'll tell you why she did it," Savinth interjected. "Because she knew it was a Library book, and didn't know that Kor wasn't in the Library anymore; none of us did. She thought she'd never get access to any more cookbooks from the Library, and so this was her only way to get one, right?"

Jasper let out a very long sigh. "If you hadn't taken our starweed, we'd have returned it to you."

Savinth threw her hands up in the air. "But I still wouldn't have had the recipes you promised me. And where's the deal in that? That's not even a deal, that's thievery."

"Enough," Quinn said, raising her voice ever so slightly. Her head was starting to pound. If she let them, these two would go at this for hours; she could tell. "At this rate, I'm going to fine you both. I'm not exactly sure how I can go about that, but I'll figure out a way. I'm sure the system will let me. Now, you really need to tell me about this feud."

"What are you going to do about my starweed?" Jasper said, her voice sullen, like a sulking toddler.

Quinn blinked. "You still don't have starweed?"

"No. She took the whole lot of it, roots and all. There is no way to grow more of it back. It's very difficult to come by."

Quinn blinked and glanced at Malakai, who shrugged like, 'I don't know.'

Aradie sent messages to her mind. *I do believe that Farrow may have some starweed in one of our terrariums back at the library. You could offer this.*

Quinn sighed, reaching out with her thoughts to thank her familiar. "Okay, hypothetically, if I could come up with some starweed for you, would you give me back my bloody book without having to come to blows again?"

"Well." Jasper sighed, refusing to meet Quinn's eyes again. "We should probably give it back anyway."

"Yeah, it doesn't belong to you," Savinth said.

"It doesn't belong to you either," Jasper threw back.

Quinn realized there was probably a lot more to the disagreement between these two, but right now, she didn't have the time nor the inclination to figure out what it was. That could be future Quinn's problem, or hell, she'd just leave them to duke it out themselves.

Once she got her property back.

"Fine. I know where to get starweed," Quinn said, "Will you just tell me about the Library feud?"

Jasper fell back in her seat, the slit of her nose flaring, her eyes focusing on anything that wasn't Quinn. Finally, she let out a huge sigh. "You can really get us starweed?"

Quinn glanced at Aradie, who let out a low hoot and nuzzled her. "Yep."

"Fine, I guess I owe you that much." Jasper's tone was still abrasive, but her scowl disappeared.

Quinn used all her self-control not to make a snappy comeback and simply waited for the woman to start speaking.

"Well, I was still very young when this happened, you have to understand. I went to the Library with my grandmother quite frequently. She loved to do new spins on some of the recipes in the books. You know, making an energizing cocktail with a different flair or a revitalizing stew with different ingredients to give it better flavor. She was just very adventurous when it came to cooking." There was a sad smile on Jasper's face, and Quinn tried to leave her enough time to collect herself.

In the meantime, she also tried to get her head around the fact that this person was telling her she went to the Library and witnessed all of this when she was very young and had now been feuding with the Library for over a thousand years. This meant that the individual in front of her was over a thousand years older than Quinn, and Quinn had just threatened to fine her.

How was Quinn, in all her twenty years of life, supposed to be able to enforce any of this? These beings, these creatures, they had so much more life experience than she did. So much more overwhelming power than she did.

She didn't quite understand how she could navigate that and maintain the role of Librarian that was technically supposed to demand things of people who had lived for more than millennia. It was a huge conundrum for her mind. Very difficult to grasp the concept of beings that were thousands of years old when humans were lucky to live to be eighty.

"Quinn," Malakai said, his fingertips grazing the top of her shoulder in a light tap, "you spaced there a little."

She blinked at him, all of her heavy thoughts melting away. "I'm terribly sorry." She turned to Jasper. "I was just . . . I didn't get to do much with my grandmother."

"Oh," Jasper said, "that's sad."

"Yeah, it is a little, isn't it?" Quinn gave a half smile.

"Still, I was just reminiscing on my grandmother and how much she loved the Library and everything it stood for and the books and how much fun I always had going to visit until that one day." Jasper's expression had softened.

"It seems tragic to lose access to things she loved from one interaction." Quinn encouraged Jasper to continue.

"Well, we were waiting in line and one of the assistants was assisting us, and we returned a book. Everything was fine. Just the same as it always was when we went there. We'd never once had an overdue book back in the day. Grandma really drilled that into my head. She was inordinately proud of that fact." Again, Jasper's smile took on a wistful quality.

"About how old were you?" Quinn asked.

"Oh, I was very young when this occurred." Jasper paused for a moment before continuing brightly. "Yes. I believe I was twenty-seven."

"Yes, very young," Quinn said, trying not to show her reaction on her face. Twenty-seven wasn't old, but in the grand scheme of the universe, she guessed it was almost infantile. The elves did consider Malakai barely more than a teenager, and he was thirty.

"Well, she was looking for a very specific book that day, and in order to save time, we asked the assistant if it was in the Library because we'd been the last ones in line and it wasn't busy. I think it was Tirello was the name of the Librarian assistant who was helping us, and he frowned when he saw something in the system. So he called the Librarian over and Kor came. She always seemed so domineering and imposing to somebody of my age. Tall, and her eye would just bore into me." Jasper frowned at the memory for a second before continuing.

"She came over, glanced at the system, looked at my grandmother with a sneer and told her, 'You cannot borrow that book. Pick another one. Find something else.' And she was about to walk away when my grandmother said, 'Oh, is it already out of the system? Is it borrowed?' And Kor looked at her and said, 'That's none of your business.' 'Well, if it's borrowed, I would simply like to get on the wait list,' my grandmother had asked. And Kor snapped at her. 'We will not be lending that book to your kind.'

"My grandmother was always very sweet, but you just don't speak to her like that. She asked very specifically to speak to the manifestation of the Library. Sometimes he could override Kor, or anyone else for that matter of fact. He was an integral part of the Library. She said he was not willing to come and help her, to which my grandmother replied, 'Lynx is always willing to help. Please bring him here now.'

"Kor told us that this was a trivial matter, and Kor had the right to make the decision. And that my grandmother was now not welcome at all in the Library, nor was she ever permitted to borrow books again and she banned us. She had the security golems literally throw us out."

Quinn sat, her mouth agape. "So you didn't see Lynx?"

"No, we didn't see the manifestation. He wouldn't come out." Jasper's answer was very confident.

"I have to ask very specifically—you were sure her phrasing was that he *wouldn't* come out? That he didn't need to be bothered with something this trivial? Did you see him at all through your whole stay there?" Quinn was starting to get a sinking feeling in her stomach.

"No."

"Was that unusual?"

"We were only there for about fifteen minutes in total, though I have to say it seemed much longer at the time." Jasper paused and then frowned. "Usually he was around when we went and visited. I don't recall another time that he wasn't present somewhere near the front of the Library."

"Okay. I don't suppose you remember the name of the book she was looking for?"

"Oh, yes, I remember it clear as day, it's like burned into my mind: *Dire Consequences of Misusing Monster Parts: How to Avoid Pitfalls.*"

Quinn blinked. The book that had been close to *Machmüller's Theory of Dimensional Dissolution and Disintegration Through Ritual Sacrifice.* There had to be a link there. She attempted to keep her calm, but did notice Malakai's eyebrows practically shoot off his face. "Do you perhaps know why she was after that book?"

Jasper actually laughed. "Surely you've looked around this place. There are so many monsters in the swamp; we use what we can to supplement what we grow. Plus, Grandma always wanted to see how far she could push the lessons in the books. It was part of her charm."

"I'm sure it was," Quinn said, hoping her smile seemed genuine even though worry was trying to gnaw a hole in her gut. "Well, let's get you some starweed and a Library unbanning, if you'll accept my apology for my predecessor's behavior."

Jasper studied Quinn for several seconds. "I think . . . that would be acceptable. I'll go and get you the book."

While she waited, Quinn kept going over the odd occurrence as had been described by Jasper. They needed to check that cookbook in more detail. Because she knew, without a shadow of a doubt, that she was missing something important.

A FAINT HINT OF BELLS

QUINN CLUTCHED THE COPY OF *HONOR AMONG PIES: REGENERATION AT Its Finest* in one hand, while she opened the door to the Library with the other.

"Library, I need you," she said softly, placing her free hand against the door of one of the Desilish cottages. She wasn't entirely certain if that was how other people accessed the Library, but it was the way she felt came easiest to her to access the power she needed to open the gateways.

Like a strange synergy had been reached.

She brought Jasper and Savinth with them, so they might rectify standings, and stepped through the door and into the great hall.

It was busier than Quinn expected. There was a line of about a dozen people waiting to return books. Jim and Bob, the aracnio twins, stood to the side as they supervised some of the newer assistants whose names were completely escaping her right then. Their heads were bent together, likely chatting, but they paid very little attention to their charges.

Quinn frowned. They should be more alert; the Library was busy. She could sense more than feel that there were other doorways opening, even now, allowing even more patrons to enter the Library.

Energy pulsed around her instead of draining from her. It was a refreshing change.

Quinn walked up to the desk, book still tightly tucked under her arm.

"It's about time you got back," Lynx said without even looking up from his work. "Why are you so late? She didn't try to . . ."

But his voice trailed off as soon as he noticed that Savinth was standing directly next to her.

Quinn took that time to inspect the two people she'd brought with her.

Name: Jasper Agen

Species: Alyenarvor

Affiliation: Desilish

Current Relation to the Library: Strained.

Quinn raised an eyebrow and muttered under her breath. "Well, no shit, Sherlock." Then she moved on to:

Name: Savinth

Species: Human Genome Type

Affiliation: None

Relationship with the Library: Book Status—Overdue, fine to be levied.

Quinn had to suppress a grin at the latter. She *had* promised she'd fine them both, after all.

"Good to see you, Savinth," Lynx said, very obviously not meaning a word of it.

Savinth shrugged. "Good to see you too, Lynx. Maybe next time, just let me keep the book."

"No," the manifestation said, and turned to Jasper. "I remember you," he said. "Didn't you used to come with your grandmother?"

Jasper scowled, but it softened. "I remember you too."

Lynx's eyes narrowed as if he was reading the situation. "How did you come to have the book?"

"Long story, Lynx," Quinn cut in. "Don't have time for that now. I'm going to reactivate Jasper's ability to enter the Library of her own accord."

"What do you mean?" He paused. His eyes flickered. In fact, his whole body flickered for just a split second, and he looked at Jasper, and he said, "How did that happen?"

"I always thought you knew," she said, and shook her head. "Can it be rectified?"

"Of course," Quinn said, and instructed the console simply to reverse the banning and give Jasper the access of regular patrons again.

"As simple as that?" Jasper asked, her eyes widening in surprise.

"We don't want to bar people from knowledge. Not ever, but there are some people who . . ." Lynx paused. "I believe the right phrase would be 'are dicks'. People who just want to ruin everything for everyone else."

Jasper laughed, and it was actually a very festive sound.

Quinn couldn't help but smile. "Okay, give me a minute, and we'll go and get that starweed for you.

"Thank you." Jasper was glancing around, her eyes practically as big as saucers as she took it all in. Like memories were coming alive.

Jim and Bob scuttled over momentarily. "Oh, what's all this," Jim said.

"Why are you going to get starweed?" Bob continued.

"We use it in a lot of our recipes," Jasper offered. "It's always been one of our staple herbs. Potent and magical for a variety of uses."

Jim and Bob studied Jasper for a second. "You're one of the Desilish," Bob said.

"We haven't seen your kind for hundreds of years," Jim finished.

Jasper raised an eyebrow, and Quinn had to cut in yet again. "So glad we could all have this little chat, but I have things to do, and I think one of the assistants needs your help."

The aracnio brothers inclined their heads and moved over but not toward the other side of the desk. No, instead, they made their way to one of the exits.

Quinn raised an eyebrow in Lynx's direction, but he shrugged. There was something off about the twins lately.

"Sorry about that," Quinn said brusquely. "Now, I'm sure I said I have a fine to levy. You both have to donate energy, and I'm going to make you stay after I give you the starweed, get you settled, and get you donating straight into the system, okay?"

Savinth laughed and said, "Fine, I've got energy to spare."

"That's it, that's the fine?" Jasper asked.

"I can give you a worse one if you want it," Quinn said.

"No, I'm perfectly happy with giving you energy for whatever reason you need it," Jasper added hurriedly.

"Very well, follow me so we can get the starweed sorted." Aradie hooted in Quinn's ear and flew off, probably headed to visit her owl friends or check in on the little one who'd had his memory adjusted. She really preferred to have Aradie's company. It always made her feel that little bit safer.

Especially now she knew about the laser eyes and healing.

"Come along in here." She walked past the kitchen, even though she really wanted to see Cook, and ended up in Farrow's area. "Farrow, I'd like you to meet Jasper."

"Ah," Farrow said, "you are an alyenarvor. You have an amazing affinity for wildlife and plants. It is my honor to meet you."

"Thank you," Jasper said, her cheeks actually coloring. Savinth crossed her arms and leaned against the wall, scowling slightly.

"You could be nicer," Quinn muttered under her breath. "You're the whole reason we had to come and do this."

"If they'd have just given me the recipes they promised, I wouldn't have taken their starweed," Savinth grumbled.

"What I want to know is what you did with it. Did you waste it?" Quinn asked, still overall very confused.

Savinth didn't answer but at least had the good grace to look extremely guilty.

"Farrow, this lovely lady, needs a seedling plant of starweed so that they can restart their crop as the previous one was—she gave Savinth a very curt sideways glance—"unfortunately, destroyed."

Farrow let in a little gasp of air. "Destroyed? Oh, that is a shame. I do have starweed. I can probably spare you about three bunches, but no more. Including roots, will that be sufficient?"

"That would be amazing," Jasper said, the relief in her voice was practically palpable.

"Fantastic. You can leave these two here with me, Librarian. It will take some time to extract the starweed so that we might avoid damaging the root system."

"Great. I have way too much to do as it is." Quinn flashed a smile at Farrow and turned to her guests. "Please, feel free to make yourself at home, Jasper. The Library welcomes you back."

"Um, Librarian," Jasper said, walking up to her just as Quinn was about to leave. "Thank you."

"Oh, you're welcome." Quinn wasn't entirely sure how she should feel about being thanked for helping. But she definitely liked that nice warm, fuzzy feeling. Still clutching the book she'd retrieved under her arm, Quinn hurried away from the terrariums and magical hydroponics area and headed toward the kitchen.

She popped her head around the doorway to the cooking prep area. "Cook!"

Cook looked up at her and a smile broke out across their face. Well, as much a smile as they usually managed, anyway. "Librarian, it is good to see you."

"Thanks, look what I've got." Quinn held up the book, visible even from the satchel she'd placed it in to make sure it didn't contain lingering chaos energy. If possible, Cook looked even happier. "I'm about to go and see how I activate the new branch."

"Excellent. I will finish preparations for the next meal, and if it is permitted, I will come and join you."

"I'd really like it if you'd do that," she said, meaning every word.

"Thank you, Librarian," he said. "Are you hungry?"

"You know, I am a bit peckish," Quinn said.

"Then I will prepare something and bring it with me when I come."

"Appreciated, Cook. Thank you." Quinn dashed out toward the check-in desk and clambered up into the side that people weren't lined up in front of.

"I'm really glad you retrieved it without too much trouble," Lynx said as she approached.

Quinn slammed it down on the desk and struck a victory pose.

Malakai raised an eyebrow. "Are you trying to pummel it through the desk?"

"No, I'm not. I'm just, I'm excited. We did it, we have all the books and if the system is correct, we have all the plants." Quinn could feel that excitement bubbling up inside. She turned to Lynx. "That means we can open it, right?"

"Well, yes, yes it does. Just let me look at it." Lynx pulled it out of the satchel. The book had no telltale sheen advising them of a chaotic presence infesting the book, which made Quinn heave a slight sigh of relief.

She looked over it with Lynx. "Well, what do you think?"

"I think it's a book, Quinn." He rolled his eyes.

"You can be so damn literal sometimes," she complained. "I mean, can we do this?"

"Yes, but it's not just us standing here going, 'Oh, please, Library, open the branch.'"

"Then what do we need to do?"

Lynx smiled. "Well, we're going to need the supervisory golem. I've already sent for Milaro. We should probably have Narilin on hand just in case some of the books are damaged inside." He frowned as if he was trying to remember how exactly to go about all of this since he'd not done it in so long.

"How long has it been since you've opened a branch?" she asked gently.

Lynx hesitated. "Oh. Maybe just short of an eon? I can't even remember. I think I opened the academy last . . . which doesn't quite count as a branch, but is close enough."

She nodded and waited, but he seemed lost in thought. Trying to be helpful, Quinn prodded him. "How does a branch separate itself? Is it sealed off into a little bubble and we have to bring it back from it?"

He blinked at her, like he wasn't expecting the question. "It's inside the Library's pocket dimension if you will."

"That's not entirely accurate—" Malakai began but was silenced by a glare from Lynx.

"Have you been here for most of existence? No, you haven't. Let me do this."

Malakai held up his hands in surrender.

Lynx continued. "There are prerequisites and power requirements, energy requirements, book and plant requirements, which we've all met now, yes, but we need all of those in order to reopen what we pretty much decommissioned. It was shut down in great haste and will likely be in a similar way as the main branch was when you first arrived."

"Great," Quinn said, not really meaning it. Still, at least now it wasn't just Quinn and Lynx. They had a whole staff to help them begin to deal with the next branch. *Misha.* She summoned the supervisory golem a split second later.

Misha appeared almost immediately.

Quinn turned to Lynx. "I'll let you worry about fetching Narilin and Milaro. Cook will be on their way very shortly with some food for us, which I'm sure we'll all love."

"Just one thing," Lynx said, frowning as he looked at something on the console in front of him. "Why was Jasper banned, Quinn? When did you do that?"

"It wasn't me. Kor banned Jasper a thousand years ago." Quinn sighed, and hoped she could avoid going over the whole story, at least right now.

"What?" Lynx said, "that doesn't even make—"

But Quinn cut him off. "Let's get this branch open first, shall we? We can talk about that later, like everything else."

Lynx grinned. "Fine, I'll make sure to fetch the others."

She knew it would take him approximately three minutes to blink in and out of the areas and have the conversations he needed to have. She turned her attention to Misha. "How is Dale?"

"He's recovered all of his functions and will be operating at maximum capacity very shortly. I have, however, finished activating the remaining five security golems. One has been recommissioned every half day so as not to stress the energy reserves too much."

"Thank you, Misha." Quinn smiled tightly. Even if she'd wished the security golems had been instantaneous, at least they had them now. She knew Misha did a lot around the Library and wasn't sure where she'd be without the supervisory golem. "What did we end up doing with Tenejo?"

"He has been placed in stasis and is currently confined while we figure out the best way to formulate the prison dungeon, as you will."

"Dungeon?" Quinn wasn't sure how she felt about that. Heck, she wasn't sure how she felt about him still being alive. His only redeeming information was that she was convinced he held some knowledge that might help them. "He's in stasis?"

"Yes, and I currently have six security golems maintaining said stasis around him, allowing for two of them to still function with other parameters."

"Isn't that overkill?" Quinn asked.

"Not necessarily. If you wish to keep our Serpensiril guest alive, then it is the only way to confine him," Misha answered and then hesitated.

Quinn nudged them. "What is it?"

"I do believe the five newly revived security golems would greatly appreciate being named by you, Librarian. They deserve it."

Quinn grinned, glad that the names-versus-designation thing was now a given. "I'll get to that as soon as we've opened the branch, okay?"

Misha flashed her a smile. There was always a faint hint of bells ringing somewhere when Misha smiled. It lit up the room, which was strange for a golem, and yet for Misha, somehow completely natural.

"It's good to see you have things under control, Quinn."

She whirled around to find Milaro standing there. An air of relief rushed out of Quinn when she realized how worried she'd been about him. "You know," she said, "I'm sorry I almost dropped you into danger."

Milaro chuckled. "No more danger than I'm usually in. I'm quite certain I could have handled it myself, although there may have been some hefty damage done to the Library in the process."

Quinn raised an eyebrow, realizing she had no clue just how powerful Milaro was. He was old, after all, and with age and access to copious amounts of magical training—well, she assumed there also went power. She didn't have the ability yet to gauge somebody else's power levels, but she was sure there was a book on that. It was yet another thing to rectify.

As Narilin approached, Lynx was already back behind the desk, leafing through *Honor Among Pies*.

"You know, Cook," Lynx said as the last member they needed arrived, "I think a few of these recipes in here would greatly assist Quinn."

"Definitely, Lynx." Cook handed what looked like a delicious sub sandwich to Quinn. She bit into it, and it practically melted in her mouth. All sorts of salamis and spicy sauce. Oh, it was like they lived in her head and knew all of her food fantasies.

"All righty," Quinn said, clapping her hands. "Let's return the book, shall we?"

Quinn scanned the ultraviolet light over it just to double-check and, when nothing was flagged, put it into the Library's system.

Culinary Branch Requirements: Met

282/282 Books Retrieved

287/287 Herbs, Plants, and Other Ingredients

Energy Level Required: Low

Mana Requirement: 3,827

Energy Fuel Required: 3,921

The Culinary Branch has met all requirements to be opened.

Do you wish to proceed?

Yes or No

"Yes," Quinn said.

And the Library shuddered in anticipation.

62

LEVERAGE YOUR STRENGTHS

THE RUMBLING BENEATH THEIR FEET CONTINUED. IT WASN'T ENOUGH TO unseat them, nothing like the shaking of a wet dog as it had been when the Library at her university sucked her into this pocket dimension in the first place.

Instead, it was almost like a jolly laugh. Sort of like she'd imagined Santa might laugh when he was doing that whole bowl-full-of-jelly thing. The sound was encompassing. It felt warm, not foreign, not invasive, not dangerous, but something fresh and safe.

"What is that?" Quinn asked.

Lynx, whose eyes had been flickering in the way they did when he switched off and into another portion of the system, was aware enough to answer her question. "Well, it's shifting out of the dimensional storage and into this dimensional pocket."

"What now?" Quinn asked, her tone flat. She hadn't understood much of that.

"Well." Lynx paused and finally focused on her. "You realize we're in our own dimensional pocket dimension, right? So to speak, anyway. The reality of it is actually far more complex than that and there are only a few beings in the universe who'd completely understand the theory behind."

"Lynx, you're tangenting," Quinn chided gently.

"Ah, yes. Sorry." He smiled somewhat sheepishly. "Anyway, in a roundabout way, it means the main branch of the Library is currently encompassing a specific amount of space in our individual little dimension. We can fold space down so that it takes up less energy, and put things into a sort of storage. Think of it like a storage locker with everything having its perfect place."

Quinn chuckled, although she felt a sudden need to know how the hell he knew about Earth television. "When everything hit the fan, you shifted all the branches back inside the pocket dimension and that gave the main branch more power so it could continue to operate for longer. Is that correct?"

"Yes, like an emergency power base, if you will." He seemed relieved that she'd understood what he was trying to say.

The rumbling continued and Quinn raised an eyebrow at him. "So what's the noise?"

"Oh! Well, it's shifting back now." He cleared his throat and continued. "The power, that is. We're pulling energy from the core, from the filtration chamber, and you're probably donating a little bit yourself right now, not to mention the sheer amount of mana it's taking to manifest it. It should be done soon. It's usually just that initial shove."

As if he had triggered it, the Library finally settled.

"Wow," Quinn said. "Now it feels too quiet."

Even the people who were lined up in the return lane had gone still, their faces filled with apprehension at the strange rumbling throughout the Library. But since it didn't feel dangerous, nobody was panicking. And now the vibrations were gone, they seemed eager to get the rest of their business out of the way.

"So where is this branch located?" Quinn asked, suddenly feeling very excited.

Lynx's eyes stopped flickering and he turned to face Quinn full-on as the Library patrons and assistants resumed their normal activities. "It's the culinary branch. By definition wouldn't you think the Library would place it close to the dining hall?"

"Oh," Quinn said, narrowing her eyes at his sarcasm. She was about to say more when she noticed Cook standing next to her with an odd golden glow suffusing them. It was almost like a full-body halo.

"Wow, Cook looks like they're leveling up," said Quinn, forgetting her irritation at the manifestation.

Lynx smiled. "In a way, they are."

Cook turned. Their face was more defined now, the mouth less slit-like. Softer. "I should like to see the culinary branch. Will you accompany me, Librarian?"

"Gladly," Quinn said, a shot of adrenaline rushing through her. She felt like she could walk on air. Which, technically she could.

The procession headed toward the kitchens.

"The new branch is definitely located through the dining hall," Cook said, smiling.

Quinn could tell they were excited about having the culinary branch open, about what they might find within its walls.

"Do you have memories of the time before?" Quinn asked Cook.

Cook shrugged. "Not precisely, though I do know what to expect. It does not necessarily work that way. While I am aware of the knowledge gained before I came into being, the me I am now, is not the me I was then."

Quinn nodded, feeling slightly melancholy at the thought that the previous incarnation of each position in the Library had lost a part of themselves when they were returned for energy. Or however that worked. "Do we know what to expect?"

Cook pondered that for several steps. "I am unsure if there has been damage, considering the haste with which the branch was shut down. If so, there might be much more to do than anticipated."

Narilin, who walked next to them, *tsked* under her breath. "Exactly. I bet even more books have been damaged. I have yet to finish repairing the ones I initially received. It takes a lot more time than you think."

Even though Narilin sounded quite exasperated, Quinn could feel a sensation of excitement under all of it. For all of them, this was the next step to getting the Library fully back on its feet.

Finally, they came upon the dining hall. It had expanded over the several weeks that the Library had been open. There were now about twenty tables that could seat ten people each. Not that they regularly had two hundred visitors to the Library who decided to sit down and eat, however. Just in case. Cook liked to be prepared.

Now there were ten rows on either side of a walkway that led through to a massive set of arches with columns just on the inside of them, reaching up as if to support the arch. Each pillar held intricate carvings that were a sight to behold. Quinn had no idea how the stone got carved so well because it wasn't marble. But, then again, magic.

The stone pillars rose up and each scene was a depiction of a culinary feat. Shopping and selecting different ingredients from a market, food preparation with cutting boards and the portioning of meats, food simmering over open flame and on stoves, pastries being kneaded before they were shoved into the oven, and people savoring all of those meals.

Every single image held a feeling of joy.

And they all moved like a stop motion film.

Fascinating.

Quinn was suddenly extremely hungry, even though she'd finished her sub while the ground had been heaving.

She couldn't spy beyond the arch yet. There was what looked like a sheet of bright light concealing the entrance. Everyone else paused at the threshold, but her own curiosity took a hold of her, and she stepped through the veil of white light and gasped at what she saw.

Quinn wasn't entirely sure what she was expecting from a culinary branch, except for, well, cookbooks. Magical cookbooks that didn't just have normal recipes. She guessed you could probably leave the magical ingredients out, substituting them with regular ones, and thus you would have regular meals. She hadn't really given that a thought before.

Upon stepping through she was faced with what looked like a high-end commercial kitchen right down the center area. Massive stoves with prep areas attached to them. They looked commercial grade, as seen in hotels, gas stoves.

Rows and rows of them

Except they were larger. A few of them even strong enough to hold what appeared to be large cast-iron cauldrons.

Above them, supported by literally nothing, were what appeared to be ventilation hoods. Magic probably whisked away any steam, smoke, or stench. Furthermore, it all looked like stainless steel. She doubted it *was* stainless steel, but it was probably something very close to it.

On one side, there were sinks with shelving units above them. They held cooking appliances and implements, cutlery and crockery, and a whole range of things Quinn couldn't identify.

There were knives, assortments of them, arrayed everywhere. Anything and everything a person could dream of in a kitchen was here, including something that looked oddly like stand mixers to her. Along the opposite side from the shelves was a plethora of terrariums with herbs and amazing spices growing in them, if their scent was anything to go by. There was even mint in there somewhere. She bet a cup of that mint tea would hit the spot. Quinn also assumed, hopefully correctly, that these terrariums had essentially been reconstituted by the herbs Farrow had given them to open the branch.

She thought people on those cooking reality shows would have had a fit over this array of supplies.

And then there were the bookshelves.

They rose up all around the perimeter of the room. And then again up on a second level, just like in the main branch. All she wanted to do was grab a book and cook something delicious. Only she had no idea where to start.

Although, if she was being realistic, she'd probably have to give the book to Cook and get *them* to prepare the meal. Quinn's cooking abilities weren't one of her strong suits.

After her initial glance around and the shock of this brand new and massive space, Quinn noticed a few things.

"Oh," she said.

Books were scattered all over the floor. Sure, the majority of them were in the bookshelves, but a large number of books seemed to have been shaken loose. They lay on their sides, some ripped open, dozens of pages skimmed across the floor when a draft caught them.

Milaro gave her a pat on the shoulder. "It's okay. It's not as bad as the Library was. This branch, it needs a little bit of, what do you call it? TLC or something? Tender liking care?"

"Tender loving care," Quinn corrected absently.

Somehow, Milaro always knew just what to say to pick her mood up that little bit. Malakai also seemed to have got that habit from his grandfather. And right now, Quinn was very grateful for them both. They'd get the Library back to its heyday and cut down the bastards who tried to destroy it. "Yeah, we'll get it back."

Narilin, on the other hand, was a little bit perturbed. "This is horrible," she said. "Look at the books."

Quinn sighed. The Salosier was correct.

There were so many books strewn about, many had tumbled down from the bookcases, some were near the cooking stations, others away from the cooking stations, in places she didn't even think books should have been able to get all by themselves. Even at this close distance, she could tell some were torn and some were hurt.

"I'm sorry, Narilin," she whispered, suddenly feeling inordinately sad.

The Salosier shrugged. "I have yet to finish repairing everything from the main Library. But I'll make time for these, too."

"Well," Quinn said, "that's why you're the book doctor. You take care of our books for us."

Narilin blinked at her. "Thank you, Librarian. I guess I am a book doctor." A small smile tugged at her otherwise serious expression.

"You didn't know?" Quinn raised an eyebrow.

"Well, I applied to be one of the Librarian's assistants." Narilin still smiled faintly as she spoke.

"You are an assistant. But you're also the book doctor, and I'll help where I can. Be sure to send me the easy ones so you have time for the ones that need you most."

This time, Narilin chuckled. "I'll send for the carts."

Just then, Carty trundled into view. "I'm here, Miss Narilin," he said, in that impossible-to-place accent that Quinn still loved. "I'll get right on this."

They watched as the little cart trundled away, lifting the damaged books onto him carefully with magic. Quinn took another look around as the fallen books were taken care of. Dust was everywhere, signs of neglect, of almost five hundred years of absence of any actual being doing anything within it.

The whole section definitely needed some tender loving care.

And then, she glanced at Cook, whose face was positively beaming. "You're overjoyed by this, aren't you?" Quinn asked.

"Yes, I actually am. This is wonderful, Librarian. I am so glad this was the first branch you opened."

Quinn grinned. But even as everybody else set out to explore the newly opened branch, a beep sounded through her head, like she'd forgotten about something. Acknowledging that something was missing, like an alarm and yet not an intermittent one. The sound cut off, and a sheet of information appeared in front of her vision.

Quinn groaned.

Culinary branch officially opened.

Beginner books verified, relegated to main branch Library.

Scanning present books for signs of infection.

Infection: Not Detected

Books deemed safe.

Analyzing intermediate, advanced, master, legendary culinary books.

Processing,

processing.

Error

Missing the following number of books.

And then a list scrolled in front of her eyes so fast she barely even had time to register that it was writing.

Quinn groaned. It appeared that Lynx had been correct when he said that there'd be more books to get once they'd opened branches. Right now, Quinn had a lot to do.

Culinary Branch Books Missing: 3,795

Lynx nudged her with his elbow, a huge Cheshire cat grin on his face. It looked out of place when he was humanoid. "You know what's really funny?"

Quinn raised an eyebrow. "Do I want to?"

"This branch has the fewest books, and thus the least amount missing." He practically cackled at the expression on her face.

She sighed. "Then I guess we just have to get some more back, right?"

"You're going to need more assistants." Milaro piped up on the other side of her.

"And more golems," Misha said, preening ever so slightly.

"And more power," Malakai added in, leaning against one of the massive stoves.

"Speaking of which . . ." Milaro grinned, and the expression looked positively evil. "I had some books you should concentrate on delivered to your room."

"Not to mention you still have to figure out why I have no memory, what the Serpensiril are up to and who their allies are, and what's wrong with the filtration pillar Ashiron." Lynx tagged onto the end, making Quinn groan again.

Aradie chose that moment to sweep through the entrance and land on her shoulder with a low hoot of greeting. At least she didn't have anything else to add.

"Well," Quinn said, "I guess we still have our work cut out for us."

LATER, up in her chambers, Quinn went through the list of the number of books still missing. The ones they knew about, the ones that were recorded, and the new ones the culinary branch was missing. So many names, so many variances of magical everything.

And then she made a list for herself about the things that she still needed to accomplish. And at the top of it, she wrote, "Why did Korradine's behavior change?"

Even Lynx had seemed flabbergasted when she'd explained what transpired to get Jasper and her grandmother banned.

Surely there had to be a reason for it, other than she just got bored, or she suddenly sympathized with chaotic magic. Because that didn't seem likely. Not when she'd never been interested before, from all accounts. Maybe if she'd only been a Librarian for a few thousand years. But by all accounts, it had been much longer than that. How could she have hidden such a double life for so long? Logic dictated that it was far more likely that an incident had occurred, a trigger, perhaps.

Quinn still had to deal with Tenejo. She had to figure out the Korradine mystery. She had to get all the other branches open. She had to retrieve those pesky books Eric and his uncle were panicking about. Not to mention, figure out the rest of the books that were missing from the restricted vault.

But first, while they still figured out the details of so much on their list, Quinn was determined to get stronger.

She pulled the first book in the pile onto her lap.

The Seveshall Guide to Mastering Compartmentalization: How to Leverage Your Strengths

Yes.

Quinn would get strong enough so they'd never hurt her friends again.

———

LIBRARY SYSTEM RESET:
REBOUND - PREVIEW

Chapter 1

Still Marked

Books lay strewn all over Quinn's bedroom. Half were open for her to refer to texts she'd already absorbed so she could get the best of the information. Things like ice could be manifested anywhere there was a hint of water for example.

Which included inside living, breathing things.

For medicinal purposes it required a very steady mind and will to maneuver something she couldn't see. Diagrams were easier for her to understand when they were drawn on paper, rather than simply rotating in her mind.

Right now, she felt like an over absorbed sponge, practically bloated to the point of spilling.

Two weeks wasn't even remotely enough time for Quinn to power up and become invincible, but it was all the time she'd got. So she'd made the best of it.

Quinn pulled her hair into a high ponytail as she stood at the top of the staircase looking out over the Library, ready for another new day. She glanced down to see Lynx standing at the bottom of the stairs. Instead of taking them two at a time and risking breaking her neck, she simply leapt over the railing and floated gently down to stand right in front of him. She grinned at him.

"Well, now you're just showing off," he said, but there was definitely a twinkle in his eyes.

"I've got magic. Why shouldn't I show off?" Over the last couple of weeks, she'd found a new appreciation for all things magic related.

Lynx disappeared for a moment and then tapped on her shoulder from behind her.

Quinn laughed. "Fine. You can show off too. Anyway, what's up? Why'd you call me?"

"I need you to go over a few of the new timetables so we can allocate all the newly trained assistants into the roster." He moved to stand in front of her again.

"Can't you do that?" she said.

"Yes, I can do that and have done that, but I need you to look at it and tell me if you're okay with it." He paused and continued when she raised an eyebrow. "To finalize it."

"Wow, Lynx, copping some attitude there."

He raised an eyebrow. "You've been very busy, which is fine, but you can't always fob all of your responsibilities onto me. I *do* have a few of my own."

"I'm aware of that," Quinn said, and she really meant it. But she'd been trying to play catch up on her magical affinities as well as on digesting all the information she'd absorbed since arriving. "Thank you for all your help while I've been training."

"How are your powers feeling?" he asked. "Are you still feeling some of the affinities more than others? Do you feel better equipped to defend yourself and the Library now?"

"Some of the affinities are definitely more viable than others. Not sure why. Library and I will have to figure that out. But I definitely feel ready to defend everything." She said the latter smugly and flexed her hand once. A sheet of very hard, very cold ice appeared around it that she managed to render flexible. Underneath it was a tiny air pocket between her skin and the ice that protected her skin from ice burn.

She'd learned so much in the last two weeks from compartmentalization theory, to finding strength in dodging, parrying with mind magic, forceful mind segregation, telekinesis, and even advanced telepathic techniques.

Her favorite so far was the speed enhancement and control that she'd learned. Especially the speed as applied to elements that could allow her to instantaneously cause the blizzard she'd been using with the ice balls. The blizzard balls had been her own manifestation of that type of ability. And now she'd devoured three books with specific focus on blizzards.

And then there was the ice, water, and air intermediate teachings. Not to mention the fact that Milaro had drilled her every single day for the last two weeks on her mental protections, her mental retaliation, and her ability to mentally access the compartmentalization without turning into a cold sociopathic killer.

Hopefully anyway.

Sadly she'd only just gotten into some aspects of chaotic magic theory in the last couple of days. Chaos affinities were largely found innate in creatures like imps that stemmed directly from chaos. She still had a lot to learn in that regard. Overall though, her progress had been fantastic. Now she just needed to keep practicing the practical applications.

"Yeah," Quinn said again. "I think the training has been going really well."

"Great. There's a lot to do. Let's go down the list. We have a very slight problem. The culinary branch is in full operation now and we've been able to alert all of the people who have overdue books from that specific branch."

"But that sounds like a great thing," Quinn interrupted, not understanding.

"And if you'll let me finish..." he continued, ignoring her interjection. "Word of mouth is finally starting to work. Before, it seems, many thought the books were malfunctioning and the Library wasn't actually back. Now, however, we're starting to get people coming in and bringing books back that are very obviously ours and that the

Library recognizes, but those tomes are from the other, as of yet still closed, branches. Thus we are starting to build up a stockpile of books that require the branches to be opened in order to be returned in the first place."

"Oh," Quinn said. Given how many books were still missing from just the Main Branch and now the Culinary Branch... "Do we have a lot of them yet?"

"Well, not so many, yet. It's only started over the last few days. We have..." he paused and checked something, "ninety-eight books so far, in four days. I can only assume it'll start compounding as time goes on. While it's a good thing that people no longer think the return of the Library is just a rumor, right now those books must be placed in holding until we can reopen those branches."

"But when those branches open, we'll already have a head start, right?" Quinn asked, clinging to that silver lining.

"True." Lynx frowned in thought. "Anyway, people who know they have a book or that their family has a book have started returning them."

"We should provide a specific storage room for those. Maybe off of Narilin's infirmary?" Quinn asked, directing the question to the Library.

Done. You also have yet to make time for me.

"Sorry. Been busy." Quinn cringed.

I'm aware.

Quinn sighed and spoke to Lynx again. "Doesn't that mean we're getting some of the original books back much quicker now?"

"Yes, you'd think so, wouldn't you? You'd be right too. It's just that I never foresaw the branches being closed at all, so this problem is yet another thing I overlooked." Lynx sounded positively dejected.

"Hey." Quinn reached over and patted his currently solidified shoulder. "Your overlooking things had nothing to do with you. We're going to get to the bottom of this and you'll be back to normal in no time."

Lynx laughed softly. "Thanks. I know it'll work out, it has to. It's just that I'm frustrated.

"And I get that. I'm upset for you. I know Harish and Siliqua will find a way to rectify this. In the meantime," Quinn raised an eyebrow. "Well, I guess I should take care of the Library today and not necessarily jump head first into..."

"Jump head first into what?" Milaro said, appearing suddenly the way he seemed to sometimes. "You know, I've talked to you about all this head nonsense."

Quinn rolled her eyes. "You know that's not what I'm talking about."

"I know, but I couldn't resist."

Quinn smiled despite herself. Milaro and her were back exactly where they used to be. She was used to things now. Used to this ridiculous propensity she had for absolutely every single affinity out there. And used to the fact that she was the Librarian, and that it was a good feeling. Quinn decided she very much liked being part mystical creature.

"Before you get started on Library stuff, though," Milaro said, "Cadre, Siliqua, Harish and I need to speak to you."

Quinn raised an eyebrow. "And just what do you need to speak to me about?" She wasn't trying to be facetious, there were many things they could talk to her about. From Library protections, to sequencing, Librarian mind protections to filtration chamber problems...

"The Serpensiril we have in stasis." He grinned at her. "It's still being maintained by six of your security golems."

"Oh," Quinn said. "Yes. Progress on that front?"

Milaro sighed. "I, unfortunately, am not able to, shall we say, dive into his mind anymore. There has been some alert aimed at my specific magical signature. Any time I get close to his mental space, shall we say, it's like he begins to react whether or not he is in stasis. We cannot afford for him to break out of that stasis given what happened last time."

"Can't you just kill the bastard?" Eric butted in, his wings making more of a hissing noise than their usual humming. It made Quinn wonder if the sound reflected his moods.

Quinn laughed. "We're not prone to killing people."

"He ripped his friend apart," Eric said flatly. "I would think he's classified less as people and more like a monster."

"First you love fining people. Now you don't mind killing them? Where does that end?" she asked.

But the imp didn't answer the question. He just barrelled on ahead. "Quinn, he's taking up too many of the Library's resources. Keeping him in stasis, if we can't get anything good out of him, is only going to make things worse in the long run."

Quinn blanched. Some of that was due to the fact that they'd had this conversation about half a dozen times over the last two weeks and Quinn refused to kill him outright. Maybe it was because part of her remembered how close she'd come to doing it herself. There was a part of her that was terrified of killing other beings. If she started condoning it, how much would the line blur? How much would she change if life became inconsequential as a means to an end.

Self-defense was one thing, and she could twist Tenejo's previous action to mean his death would protect the Library and more... and yet that was a type of trauma she wasn't ready to deal with.

Yet.

"I know, I know," Eric said when her pause went on too long, "Stop being such a bloodthirsty Eric."

Quinn sighed and tried very hard not to laugh. She almost failed. "Anyway, we do need to go over what we're doing with Tenejo."

Lynx piped up. "That's going to have to wait, Milaro. She has to check on the assistants and code them into the system."

"Fine. I'll see you this afternoon. We'll meet in your office to start with, and then we'll venture to the dungeon as it has been prepared by the Library."

Quinn shuddered ever so slightly. "You know I hate that word."

"Well, you can hate it all you want, but that's the reality of it, Quinn. The Library has enemies and we need to figure out who they are." Milaro's tone was grave, heavy even.

"I know..." Quinn sighed.

"Sometimes I forget how young you are," he said kindly.

"Thank you, oh millennia-old grandfather figure of mine," Quinn said, and turned her attention back to Lynx, her back pointedly in Milaro's face.

Eric chuckled. "I still think we should be fining people more. I can't believe you gave the Culinary Branch a 30-day grace period."

"Eric, there's only like 20 days of it left. Start thinking up awesome, scrumptious fines, will you? And I'll even let you hand out the first one." Quinn waved him away, trying to focus on the rest of her conversations.

That appeared to mollify the imp somewhat. "Thank you," he said. "Also, my uncle will be delivering an information packet, I guess you could say, in person in the next couple of days."

"What?" Quinn said, already hating the day. It had gone from 'planned more training like the past two weeks', to a 'nope-you're-done-with-rest-here's-everything' day. "Information packet? Can't he just send it?"

"No, my uncle... Anyway, you're going to get to meet him and you'll understand why I think he's just the best person ever." The sarcasm practically dripped off Eric's words as he darted away before Quinn could say anything else.

Quinn pinched the bridge of her nose and let out a long-suffering sigh.

"Hey," Lynx said, nudging her again. It was like he'd picked up Malakai's bad habit. "It's okay, let's just go and give all of these assistants the access they need and bump the other three supervisors you were going to bump up."

"How many new assistants did we end up with?" she asked, grateful to have Lynx request something specific.

"Oh, there's like a dozen of them."

"A dozen? I guess we have expanded a bit, right?"

"A lot," he said.

"Oh." She smiled. "You had to get people for the culinary branch and some to help Cook in the kitchen, right?"

"Yes. We are very close to filling those 200 seats in the dining hall on a semi-frequent basis now." By this time, they'd slowly walked to the reception area where the grand welcoming check-in desk stood. There were three lines leading away from the right-hand side of it.

Quinn blinked. "Okay, is it just me or is the check-in desk bigger now?"

"Oh, it's not just you. Of course, it's bigger now. The Library accommodates what it needs to function." Lynx grinned, and pride in the Library practically oozed from his... manifested form.

"Oh," Quinn said. "That's kind of awesome."

"Yeah, it leaves us room to do all of the admin and be on hand if we're needed by the assistants and supervisors on the left-hand side, and it allows all the books to be checked in..." But he stopped short when Quinn gasped ever so softly.

"Wait," she said, "Is that... is that a line going back into the Library?"

"Oh yeah, those are inquiries. So the other side is now... Look, just come up."

They walked into the check-in desk and Quinn realized it was more spacious inside too. There was a double-sidedness to it now. One where people could make inquiries and the other where people would check in their books.

"Oh," Quinn said, "I think I could get used to this." As they went over all the information of each assistant and transferred the information fully into the system, Quinn noticed several species listed that she'd not seen before.

"Wow," she said, "we reached a lot farther with the applications this time, right?" The names meant practically nothing to her without visuals though. She'd have to inspect all the new assistants in short order so she could understand them better.

"Yes and no. Three of these only have five of the prerequisite affinities that we require. They will basically just be taking returns, they're not going to be doing anything serious."

Quinn hesitated and then asked the question on her tongue. "I don't suppose you've found anyone who has the Library affinities?"

"Nope, not another one yet. Not even one," he said. There was a strange flicker over him.

"How are your memories going?" she asked on impulse.

"Well, I have sat down with Cadre several times now. I've been back to the Core a few times and I think, you know, I think eventually it's gonna be all okay."

She watched him for a second and wondered if he realized how transparent he was being. She shook her head. "You don't need to make me feel better, Lynx, but I'm sure it will be okay. In the end..."

"Of course, I've got the amazing Quinn looking out for me, right?" His dark violet eyes sparkled again.

"Yeah, we'll get your memories back. Yours and the Library's." Quinn meant every word. "So, has there been any news on ways to get those missing books back sooner?"

"Look, you're probably going to have to talk to Siliqua and Harish. The Core is trying its best to figure out ways to trace the books that were once the Library's."

"They're still marked as the Library's, so there's got to be ways to trace it using the name." Quinn frowned. "I mean we have tracking systems back home. There had to be a tracking system here too. Just magical."

"You would think so," Lynx said. "No, there... there is, and that's what we'll talk to Eric's uncle about when he gets here."

"Oh," Quinn said, "well that makes sense. So we're doing pretty good here."

"Yeah, if you can just allocate Deflin, Malice, and Argo to the supervisor role. That's all I really need from you right now. You can go and do whatever you need to."

"Lynx, are you okay?"

"I'm as well as can be expected right now, Quinn. Thanks for asking." He went back to work and Quinn felt, for just a moment, ever so slightly out of her depth.

It had been two weeks since they opened the new branch. And while they'd made some progress, they still had so much to do. They'd even had to resort to Eric's uncle in order to figure out the intricacies of the missing books and how to locate them. They also still had to figure out the Acheron pillar. There were also a couple of things she needed to talk to Misha about in that regard.

Finding the Serpensiril's allies was coming up a dead end. Everybody knew there was no way the Serpensiril had orchestrated this whole thing all by themselves.

She was going to have to take Jasper up on her offer of seeing if she could divine for them. After giving Jasper back access to the Library, the woman had promised Quinn to come to their aid at any time should they need her.

The Librarian sighed and looked around her home. Books had always been such an integral part of her life. Now they had the perk of being magical. She made a small ice sculpture of Kajaro in the palm of her hand, and crushed it with her fist.

Despite all Quinn's best efforts, it was looking more and more like the Library needed all the allies it could get.

Preorder Book 3 Now!

CHARACTER & SPECIES
GLOSSARY

Characters (who appear frequently)

<u>Quinn</u>
>   **Age**: 19
>   **Species**: Human? Librarian
>   Lynx (Links)
>   **Age**: Infinite
>   **Species**: Library Manifestation

<u>Dottie</u>
>   **Age**: unknown
>   **Species**: superellex futora
>   **Physical Description**: A moving, talking, bench

<u>Milaro Seveshall</u>
>   **Age**: 3500
>   **Background**: King of Elves
>   **Species**: Areiltháhnish/High Elf
>   Korradine (Korradine? Spelled both ways)

Age: Several Millennia (Deceased)
Background: Previous Librarian

Malakai Seveshall

Age: 30 (in elf years)
Background: Milaro's Grandson. Weapons master.
Species: Part darigháhnish (Dark Elf)
Fun fact: Able to wiggle eyebrows independently of each other

Kajaro (KaajAriuusucjo)

Age: Unknown (Immortal) Sort of died one time
Background: Known for keeping overdue books.
Species: Serpensiril

Misha (G-Alpha-724):

Age: Newly Created from base files
Parents: Quinn and the Library (technically)
Background: Supervisory Golem
Species: Golem

Tim (Shelving One)

Background: Cleaning and Shelving
Species: Golem
Physical Description: Clay type of golems. Orange-brownish and stood about seven feet tall. After naming Tim remained at seven feet tall, but his head became smoother, almost as if he were bald.

Tom (Shelving Two)

Background: Cleaning and Shelving
Species: Golem
Physical Description: After naming Tom, on the other hand, grew several inches, almost a foot maybe, and his head, while still clay, looked like it had hair carved into it.

<u>Cook (Cook)</u>

Background: Cook

Species: Golem

Physical Description: Stocky, shorter and more powerful in appearance, about maybe five foot eight. He can grow and maintain rudimentary ingredients and cook them all to a very palatable level of taste. After naming Cook grew perhaps an inch, and the muscles refined. The top of their head turned into a chef's cap, and their face took on slight human definition.

<u>Farrow (Caretaker)</u>

Background: Caretaker

Species: Golem

Physical Description: Willowy and around the same height as the cook, but not made out of clay or metal. It almost appeared to be wooden-esque, like a carved doll that moved. Will take care of the bookworms and the night owls and maybe the silverfish, depending on how recovery goes. They resemble a living tree. After naming their limbs became more defined and their appearance altered to look like they were wearing a long wispy dress.

<u>Carty</u>

Background: Book Trolly??

Species: superellex futora

Physical Description: A talking, self propelling cart.

<u>Narilin Jenishu'Salosier</u>

Age: 297

Background: First Applicant for Assistant, top of her graduating class, had all 16 requirements for assistant

Species: Salosier

Physical Description: Their first applicant was about six feet tall. Their form was willowy, similar to Farrow, but actually supple like a tree. Their hair was dark green but upon closer inspection made of leaves that cascaded on thin vines down their back all the way to the floor. Their skin was green, with obvious yet faint bark lines, and their eyes glowed silver like a lake of mercury.

Aradie

    Age: unknown
    Parents: Unknown
    Background: Night Owl
    Species: Night Owl

Hirish

    Age: 500+
    Background: Milaro's childhood friends
    Species: Areiltháhnish/High Elf
    Physical Description: The tallest one stood about seven feet tall, as dark as Milaro was pale. He had bright white hair and fangs that just peeked over his lower lip. His ears were so spiky she was sure they would draw blood if touched.His eyes were completely white.

Siliqua

    Age: 500+
    Background:Milaro's childhood friends. They have "sons"
    Species: Waldientháhnish/Wood elf?
    Physical Description: She was slightly taller than Quinn, maybe five foot five, with a deep tan and long, delicate ears adorned with many piercings and chains linked together in an intricate filigree that ran the length of her ears.

Geneva

    Age: 321
    Parents:
    Species: Fae Firionas
    Physical Description: She was maybe two and a half feet tall and hovered in the air like a hummingbird. Her coloring was beautiful. She had long, literally golden hair and skin that was faintly golden-

tinged as well. Her tiny feet ended in points with little shoes on and her wings had iridescent rainbow colors running through them. She wore a striking deep red dress that offset the whole thing. Her voice sounded soprano.

Eric (Ekirusca) Marabiza
>   **Age**: 7682
>   **Species**: Imp
>   **Physical Description**: The imp was, quite simply put, fascinating. With blackened skin and what looked like fiery embers at the end of the fingertips and toes. The imp had sharp teeth and fiery eyes. Even the long black hair was tinged with what looked like a never-ending flame-fall.
>   **Fun fact:** Really likes imposing fines
>   Finn (Findalay)
>   **Age**: 200+
>   **Species**: Ilgonomur
>   **Physical Description**: Small, petite, and with huge eyes that just seemed to see everything.

Danio
>   **Species**: Centaur
>   **Physical Description**: His hind quarters were a bay color, beautiful chestnut-y coat with a gorgeous black tail. His hooves were especially polished and his dark red hair cascaded all the way down his back, only tied together by a hair tie at the very end. He stood easily seven feet tall making him about half a foot taller than Malakai.

Jim
>   **Background**: Bob's twin brother
>   **Species**: Aracnios
>   **Physical Description**: spider species

Bob
>   **Background**: Jim's twin brother

Species: Aracnios
Physical Description: spider species

Arilin

Background: Narilin's sister
Species: Salosier
Physical Description: "Oak" sister, Their skin some form of oak, more orange than red or brown. 12 of the 16 affinities. Horticulture specialty.

Marilin

Background: Narilin's sister
Species: Salosier
Physical Description: "Oak" sister #2, Their skin some form of oak, more orange than red or brown. 12 of the 16 affinities. Horticulture specialty.

Jane

Background: Narilin's sister
Species: Salosier
Physical Description: One of them had white blossoms cascading down her hair and extremely dark wooden skin. Jane possessed 14 of the 16 affinities. Book infirmary.

Tenejo (Tenejorissimo)

Background: Contingent leader of Ebolibia, power level intermediate
Species: Serpensiril

Narajo

Background: Part of the Ebolibia
Species: Serpensiril
Physical Description: had a lime green coloring with the scales mottled with black in what seemed like almost even stripes.yellow eyes, forked tongues, and the same snaky nose holes.

<u>Dijaro</u>
Age: Deceased (self inflicted)
Background: Part of the Ebolibia
Species: Serpensiril
Physical Description: whose scales were a forest green type of color, but matt and not shiny, yellow eyes, forked tongues, and the same snaky nose holes.

<u>Larry</u>
Background: New library assistant
Species: Sedimentite
Physical Description: Rock Person

<u>Fife (Guardian 3)</u>
Background: Library Guard
Species: Golem
Physical Description: Highly polished suit of living armor. The armor became more condensed, their build slightly thicker.

<u>Uno (Guardian 1)</u>
Background: Library Guard
Species: Golem
Physical Description: Highly polished suit of living armor. Uno remained exactly as he had been.

<u>Dale (Guardian 2)</u>
Background: Library Guard
Species: Golem
Physical Description: Highly polished suit of living armor. He became slightly more slender and perhaps two or three inches taller, with masculine tinges to the armor he wore.

<u>Cadre</u>
Physical Description: Cadre looked sort of like a gecko. Except much, much larger. He stood about four feet tall, was extremely slen-

der, but had beige and red skin tones instead of being green or brown. He was actually quite beautiful, and his double-lidded eyes flickered constantly through different hazes of red. He was delicate almost in appearance, thin arms, thin legs, slender body, and a robe that covered him from head to foot

Savinth
>   **Background**:
>   **Species**: Human Genome Type E-31,785
>   **Book Status:** Overdue, fine to be levied.

Jasper Agen
>   **Affiliation**:Desilish
>   **Species**: Alyenarvor
>   **Current Relation to the Library:** Strained

Species

Serpensiril: A snake-like race that Kajaro was part of. Immortal - unless shot through both eyes. They also hate the Library and want chaotic magic to return to the universe.

Superellex Futora
>   Dottie's species. Living Furniture. Also Carty.

Darígháhnish
>   Dark Elf

Areiltháhnish
>   High Elf

Waldeintháhnish
>   Wood Elf

Salosier
>   The Salosier are very influential. I wouldn't call it manipulation,

but their very presence soothes and gives you sort of a new lease on life. Have a connection to the tomes in the library. Cousins to the Tecopsis.

<u>Aracnios</u>

Arachnid-based species. They appeared to have the body of a spider and four legs that touched the ground. Their torsos, however, had four arms. Their upper bodies were segmented slightly like ants, and their heads appeared to be a mixture of ant and human. Located in the Illukai Region. Allies to the Library for 24,382 years

<u>Centaur</u>

Equine based species. They had horse bottoms and a human-appearing top. They looked a lot more built and stocky in their human portion. Very powerful. Their hooves don't make a sound. From the Malino Sector, Allies since Library Creation.

<u>Ilgonomur</u>

Humanoid species. Standing about three to four feet high. They looked like mini humans. Located in the Dalyid Region, Allies to the Library for 235,001 years. Like the gnomes in computer games. Small, petite, and with huge eyes that just seemed to see everything.

<u>Imp</u>

Imps were also tiny, a bit shorter than the Ilgonomur, but they had wings, fiery red eyes, and skin that was tinted red and black. Like a mixture of embers and ash. They had little horns that grew out of their head and sharp, pointy ears. Their fangs resembled vampires. They were created as a direct result of chaotic magic gone wrong, and the Library helped them become a viable species. From the Gates of Halschius.The species has a High Lord. Survivability: Eternal. Will not die. Even when you wish they would.

<u>Firionas</u>

Fae elf species. Colorful and simply breathtaking. Their little wings fluttered so fast they almost appeared to stand still. Allies from 2,483,000 years.

Esposian

Fae species – distantly related to the Firionas Fae. From Dimensional Portal L24. Ally status: 471,000 years

ABOUT THE AUTHOR

Born in Australia, K.T. Hanna met her husband in a computer game, moved to the U.S.A. and went into culture shock. Bonus? Not as many creatures specifically designed to kill you.
KT creates science-fiction, fantasy, and LitRPG, with a dash of horror for fun! She is a member of the SFWA and NINC. Her hobbies include gaming, reading, and lake time!
No, she doesn't sleep. She is entirely powered by caffeine, Chipotle, and sarcasm.

Join her in all the places, including Discord!

ACKNOWLEDGMENTS

I have a lot of people to thank. Even those who don't contribute directly through the writing craft keep me going and help me write my best stories.

Love of my life, Trevor, and my little Bria. It's his fault I found the genre, and her fault I never give up on writing.

I wouldn't be here without the following friends (and I know I've probably forgotten to mention someone:

SSODA
Crown
Eric Ugland
Quinton Shyn
Andrea Parseneau
M Evan MacGregor
Daniel Schinhofen
Michael Chatfield
Luke Chmilenko
Tao
Jami
Geneva
Jez
Ririn
DE Sherman
Ino
Jess
<u>And of course my family:</u>
Mumskin & Papilie, Tracey, Jett, & Robbie.

<u>The entire Coteh server</u>
<u>My Legion Family</u>

<u>And every one of my Patrons.</u>
Quinton
Warren
Joshua
Corwin
ChaosOmega
Michael
Troy
Erwin
Martinalfa
Ty
Bryan
Joe
Kagami
James
Onean
Andrew
Abacus
Daavko
TableTop
Plasma Donut
Kevin
Pyro4224
PfannkuchenWolf
Smoze
Celestikitten
Jorden
SilverFox
Vantar
Supernoshus
Lisa Black
Josh Dane

Skye Chaptman
JSC
Alek M
Jerry
Not to mention my FB Group/Page, and people in my discord.
Thank you
You all help me maintain a level of sanity.

ALSO BY KATIE HANNA

Somnia Online

System Apocalypse Australia

The Domino Project

Last Chance Trilogy

KT Hanna's Author Page

LITRPG

Do you love LitRPG?
Do you want to find more of it?

These are amazing places to do just that!
FaceBook:
LitRPG Books
LitRPG Legion
Gamelit Society

Reddit:
LitRPG

Adjacent genres like Progression Fantasy/Cultivation:
Reddit: Progression Fantasy
Facebook: Cultivation Novels

MORE LITRPG

Love LitRPG?

To learn more about LitRPG, talk to authors including myself, and just have an awesome time, please join the LitRPG Group!